THE LAST PRESIDENT

ACE BOOKS BY JOHN BARNES

Directive 51
Daybreak Zero
The Last President

THE LAST PRESIDENT

JOHN BARNES

ACE BOOKS, NEW YORK

THE BERKLEY PUBLISHING GROUP
Published by the Penguin Group
Penguin Group (USA)
375 Hudson Street, New York, New York 10014, USA

USA I Canada I UK I Ireland I Australia I New Zealand I India I South Africa I China

Penguin Books Ltd., Registered Offices: 80 Strand, London WC2R 0RL, England
For more information about the Penguin Group, visit penguin.com.

This book is an original publication of The Berkley Publishing Group.

Ace Books are published by The Berkley Publishing Group.
ACE and the "A" design are trademarks of Penguin Group (USA).

Library of Congress Cataloging-in-Publication Data

Barnes, John, 1957–
The Last President / John Barnes. — First Edition.
pages cm
ISBN 978-1-937007-15-7 (hardcover)
1. United States. President—Fiction.   2. Political fiction.   I. Title.
PS3552.A677L37 2013
813'.54—dc23
2013010547

FIRST EDITION: September 2013

PRINTED IN THE UNITED STATES OF AMERICA

10 9 8 7 6 5 4 3 2 1

Cover illustration © Craig White.
Cover design by Judith Lagerman.
Interior text design by Laura K. Corless.

For Ashley and Carolyn Grayson,
friends and agents for 30 years, who didn't give up,
and got me the deal

THE LAST PRESIDENT

PROLOGUE

For the second time since "back before," Christmas crept under the world's grimy, icy blanket of soot, found the world shivering, hungry, and afraid, and brought the world nothing.

"Back before" was shorthand to avoid saying "back before Daybreak," because the word "Daybreak" called up memories that made the bad dreams worse:

Back before, when we had fresh orange juice in the fridge, and a fridge, and a kitchen, and a house.

Back before, when we had Internet, and gasoline, and emergency rooms.

Back before, when I could pick up the phone and talk to Mom, or the kids.

When I knew where they were.

When they were alive.

In the broken pieces of the old civilization, other dreams slipped in, and the cold slumber of misery was disturbed by conflicting tiny relentless hopes.

ONE:
A COLD CHRISTMAS

FBI HEADQUARTERS, WEST COAST (FORMERLY AN OFFICE
BUILDING IN CHULA VISTA, CALIFORNIA, JUST SOUTH OF
SAN DIEGO). 5:45 AM PACIFIC TIME. THURSDAY,
DECEMBER 25, 2025.

Dave Carlucci checked both black-powder four-shot Newberry revolvers and holstered them. His heavy fighting knife slid easily in its scabbard. His broom-handle-and-chain flail had tight eyebolts and no cracks. He turned to Arlene, his wife—

Outside the office door, Bolton said, "Horses are saddled."

"Yeah. In a sec." Carlucci kissed Arlene; they held each other a little longer as they always did when rough stuff was impending. "Back before sunset, I think. They'll feed us at the Castle."

"You be careful and come back. And we've got a couple Christmas treats for this evening, so take it easy on the desserts up there." She kissed him again, retying the laces that ran through the upper two buttonholes of his coat. The ruddy light from the lantern on the desk, throttled back to conserve precious vegetable oil, touched her face with gold between pitch-black shadows.

One more hug. *I'm getting too old to look forward to action;* damn, *it's* nice *to be held.* "You take care too," he whispered. Carlucci turned toward the door, speaking too loudly to Bolton. "Okay, Terry, let's do this."

Their four deputies were already mounted, vapor rising from the shuddering horses. Carlucci swung up into his saddle, and they set off at a comfortable walk, with Bichsler, riding point, holding the lantern up to reveal frozen puddles and slick spots.

"This is one long ride for something they're better equipped to do themselves," Bolton said, as they turned the horses north. "And having to keep a lantern out—"

"And I'd rather be at home on Christmas morning, too, Terry, but we're the Feds, and it's a Federal bust." Carlucci shrugged. "Besides, the lantern isn't giving anything away to the tribals; FBI riders are out all the time, anyway, dark and ice be damned."

"No shit," Bichsler muttered from the point.

Bolton sighed. "It's a dark, cold Christmas morning away from my kids. And I'll never again swing through the McDonald's drive-up and get a great big hot cup of coffee on the way."

Carlucci thought, *That sigh was too sincere. Every little thing Terry Bolton notices that isn't here anymore, Tupperware to movies to McDonald's, all those little things are just wearing him down.* His added thought, *Nothing I can do about it,* made him sad, so he was too bluff and hearty when he finally spoke. "One short nasty job, Terry, and then you can go back to being your usual sunny, jolly self."

Montez, riding drag, snorted.

They clopped along at a steady walk; except for their lantern, the only light was the stars and the distant beacon on Castle Castro.

It had been too damp to desiccate bodies and not cold enough to freeze them; Chula Vista and National City smelled like spoiled hamburger. *Maybe now that Bambi's the freeholder at Castle Castro, we'll be able to do something about all the unburied bodies. She'll be more cooperative than her father was, anyway.*

Pre-dawn glowed bruise-purple. Bichsler doused the lantern. A light sea breeze chilled them but dragged away the smell. The horses moved more confidently.

Bolton shivered. "I didn't even *own* a coat before Daybreak."

"Well, the scientists in Pueblo say there's more carbon dioxide in the air than any time recorded, so once the soot settles, you'll forget frozen-dead palm trees and complain about San Diego being like Baja used to be."

"Lying in a lawn chair on the beach with a chilled beer?" Bolton said. "Let's skip to that part right now."

They rode on through the dark, wet cold. At least there was no sleet. *This Christmas sucks ass, but giving birth in a stable in the winter probably really sucked too.*

Bad analogy. If we were in that *story, we'd be working for Herod.*

Half an hour later, dawn greased the tops of the old office buildings and hotels, the abandoned Navy ships across the bay, and the few remaining power poles. This close to the Castle, the streets were cleared of rubble and cars, and every standing storefront was walled up.

Four men in Castle Castro uniforms appeared around a corner. The leader waved. "Mister Carlucci!"

"Hey, Donald."

"Miss Castro said to come out and meet you. She didn't say what it'd be about, so I figure I'm not supposed to ask."

They swung north to follow the line of sealed buildings linked by the Castle's outer wall.

Bolton said, "This wall must've been some work."

"Yeah, 'specially without no power tools, but I'm real glad it's there. Last summer when the Awakening Dolphins attacked, we had to crowd up in the keep for three weeks, and we lost lots of garden beds we could be eating from now. I like having some room inside the walls if we need it, 'specially since we're up to eight thousand people now."

The guards on the towers at the big gate waved them through z-form barriers wide enough for a pre-Daybreak semi.

Fishing boats were pulled up for the holiday on the beaches of the old luxury hotels, which had been mostly torn down for materials to build the walls. Just for today, no one tended the vegetable beds on the old lawns. Picks and shovels were stacked by the parking lots; tomorrow would be soon enough to resume breaking them up.

Across the hills just north of the harbor, behind what remained of the chain-link fence that had marked Harrison Castro's estate, back before, the inner wall reared up yards higher than the outer wall. Wheelbarrows, piles of blocks, and stacked tools waited beside its remaining gaps.

"You built the outer wall first?"

"Mister Castro said the outer wall was what would really matter 'cause if it held we could stand a siege. This wall's just a backup. Miss Castro says she can't plan nothing better than her dad could so we're staying on his plan."

Carlucci said, "'Miss Castro'? not 'Countess Castro' or 'Mrs. Larsen'?"

"Just habit. I drove the limo that brought her here the day she was born. Most people in the Castle call her 'the Countess' now."

Bambi Castro did not look very Countess-like in thick-soled moccasins, a black baggy sweater, and jeans, with her long black hair pinned up close. She looked more like what she had been fourteen months before, a young Fed, the liaison from an obscure agency, when Carlucci had welcomed her to his office. Now *she* was welcoming *him* to her fief, which was about a third of pre-Daybreak California.

They shook hands with Quattro; Bambi greeted them with quick, hard hugs. "This will not get any easier with delay," she said. "Donald, you and your party stay here. If we come this way running, cover us."

"In your own house?" Donald muttered.

"Maybe. It's bad."

"Is this about Mister Castro's murder?"

"It is."

"Then go get'em, Miss Castro."

She nodded her thanks. To Carlucci, she said, "Officially it's *your* murder bust."

Carlucci said, "I have warrants from Judge Thanh. We're as legal as we're going to get."

Nathan Signor's apartment was in the senior department heads wing. Terry Bolton, Montez, and two of Bambi's men took a ram and went around to the back entrance; with no radio or phone to coordinate, they had to rely on synchronized watches.

After they had gone, Carlucci said, "It's good that they'll have to be silent, so Bolton can't crack the same bad joke over and over just before going into action, like he usually does. Four minutes. Let's go."

At the main door to Signor's apartment, Carlucci took the knob side, and raised his arm over his head, eyes fixed on his watch. Quattro tried to take the hinge side, but Bambi shoved him aside and took it herself. The second hand swept up to the twelve; Carlucci dropped his arm, and drew his pistol. The ram smashed against the lock.

Frightened shrieks—besides Nathan, his wife Ingrid and daughters Molly and Nellie were inside. The ram hit again and the door swung wide. Carlucci shoved through, Bambi just behind him. Bolton's ram was booming on the back door.

Nathan Signor was standing just inside. Carlucci backhanded him with the flail, knocking Signor to his hands and knees, brought it around to scissor the man's neck, and pressed Signor's face to the floor, making him lie flat. "Nathan Signor, you are under—"

Signor shrieked and curled into a ball, even against the force of the flail on his neck. Carlucci held against it with a foot planted on Signor's back, until Bichsler could wrap the man's neck in a choke collar. Bambi reached under, felt around and pulled out a knife. "This doesn't look like a real Daybreak seizure to me."

They cuffed Signor's hands behind him and rolled him onto his belly. He kicked, sending some still-wrapped packages flying and threatening to knock over a candleholder; they bound his feet to his wrists.

Other deputies had been hog-tying Ingrid and the two girls; they lay along the wall.

"Friendly coming in," Terry Bolton said.

"We hear you," Carlucci responded.

Bolton emerged from the back. "Books and papers behind the headboard. We'll search the kids' room next—"

Quattro raised Ingrid's head to try to look her in the face. "If you can assure us that the kids didn't know—hunh." She had bucked hard against him, and he pushed her back down. "Daybreak seizure, this one's real."

Bambi rolled Molly over; the girl was kicking like a poisoned grasshopper, indifferent to the agony it must be causing in her wrists and shoulders. "The kids are having them too. Catellano, get the doc."

A few minutes later, the girls had been drugged and carried out. "I suppose they won't get to say goodbye, then," Bolton said, sadly.

Carlucci said, "Yeah, I don't see any way we can let them. Terry, you don't have to see what—"

"I can deal with it."

"I *know* you can. If I needed you to, I'd order you to. But I *don't* need you to. And somebody has to go through those papers you found behind the headboard." When Bolton had gone into the back bedroom, Carlucci said, very softly, "All right, let's get this over with."

The doctor said Nathan Signor had a broken collarbone and cracked teeth. "Also, even though he was faking it before, this is one of the worst cases of Daybreak seizure I've ever—"

"Sorry," Ingrid gasped.

Carlucci squatted beside her. "Talk to us. You had a Daybreak seizure. You'll be free to talk, freer anyway, for a few minutes now."

"Sorry. Sorry. Nate was . . . Nate was . . ."

"It's okay, just let it out," Carlucci said, wiping the tears and mucus from her raw red face.

"I'm not even his wife, never met him till the mission. Mollie and Nellie are not our kids, 'ot 'r kids. Don't pun pun pun—" Her neck spasmed, yanking her head far back, in a fresh seizure.

"Dad hired Signor the January before Daybreak," Bambi said. "As an HVAC engineer. So he had go-anywhere keys and people looked right at him without seeing him, the way they do anyone in a service uniform. That's how Daybreak could slip someone in to attack Daddy twice, even with the whole Castle on alert." She stared at something far beyond the walls of the room. "Crap. Ingrid did preschool supervision. I guess we'll have to review the Jamesgram about blocking Daybreak in young children. And their girls—"

"*Not ours.* Mollie and Nellie were fosters," Ingrid said. She gasped. "Real parents are named Green, they . . . were . . . in . . . Reno. Violent abuse don't . . . send. The. Girls. Back." She drew a deep breath, and her face cleared for a moment. "It it it wants to give me another seizure, but it can't quite yet-et. Those girls *liked* me, they thought I'd be their *mom*, and Nate made me fee, feed, feed, fee fi fo fum, feed them to Daybreak ache ache. Our whole affinity group's records are behind that bed and we're all there were were were—"

Her back arched in a savage, almost audible jerk; then she went limp.

"All right," Bambi said. "Officially she's a POW, since she was trying to resist Daybreak. Sedate her, doctor, and let's get her out of here."

"I'll go arrange getting her and the kids into the Gooney Express," Quattro said. He would fly them to their main holding and interrogation area at Castle Larsen, his home base far to the north. "Tell Terry maybe they can be a family if the doctors can get them all cured."

"I heard." Bolton was in the doorway with a couple of rag dolls and a teddy bear. "The kids might want these."

"Thanks, Terry!" Quattro sounded too appreciative, but he bundled up the toys and hurried off, obviously intent on getting into the air and away from this.

When he had gone, Carlucci asked Bolton, "How many were in the affinity group?"

"Just five—the Signors, a guard that was killed in the fighting last June, and another married couple—a kitchen helper and a gardener. Round 'em up?"

"Do that."

Bolton dashed out, at least as fast as Quattro had.

Now it was just Carlucci, Bambi, and the doctor. Carlucci said, "All right. We need to start," and silently prayed *If we're doing the wrong thing, please remember You didn't make me smart enough to think of the right thing.*

The doctor said, "We have to do this?"

"That's what the orders are from RRC," Carlucci said.

Bambi added, "Which we all follow."

"And me a Catholic," the doctor muttered. "All right, just hold him down while I do this." He injected something into Signor's neck.

"What's that?" Bambi asked.

"Wood alcohol, angel dust, and some meth, he probably won't wake up but the facial contractions'll make him look like he died crazy and terrified, and the convulsions will add some bruises and broken bones for anyone who looks at the body." He pulled an old-style straight razor from his bag, lifted Signor's head by the hair, and slashed across the man's face. "Roll him over. Don't lose your grip."

As Carlucci held Signor's kicking legs and Bambi braced his shoulders, the doctor slashed, over and over, forehand and backhand across the torso, letting blood fly wherever it did, before cutting deeply across the femoral artery on each side. He finished by removing Signor's right thumb. "You'll want to get your clothes into cold water quick, you can probably get most of that off if you do."

Bambi shrugged. "The laundry staff and the maids are the only ones I feel sorry for."

Carlucci looked around; blood had splashed up to the ceiling on all the walls, dripped from limbs of the Christmas tree, pooled on the still-wrapped presents. He avoided looking down at his clothes.

"We'll have your clothes clean and dry in a couple hours," Bambi said. "We've got wood-fired dryers now. And meanwhile we can loan you something. But before you clean up"—she handed him a steel tenderizing mallet—"please pound on that thumb with this, and leave both on the floor beside him."

She pulled an artist's brush from her back pocket, dipped it in the still-warm puddle of blood around Signor's thighs, and wrote *ECCO* on the wall. "That should explain the thumb so the maids will remember it."

ABOUT THE SAME TIME. FACILITY 1 (HIGH SECURITY PERMANENT PRISON). PUEBLO, COLORADO. 8:45 AM MOUNTAIN TIME. THURSDAY, DECEMBER 25, 2025.

James Hendrix would have been happy to leave Interrogation Subject 162 alone on Christmas morning; in fact he had planned to. But yesterday, his line of questioning had sent 162 into the severe convulsions that characterized a struggle between Daybreak and its host, and often, a subject who slept it off awoke amenable.

But since Hendrix had a busy social and professional life, rather than wait around for 162 to wake up, he had simply scheduled this wakeup call for him. Hendrix's assistant, Izzy Underhill, had no family or friends to be with, so she had come over to have "orphan breakfast" with James, plus Patrick and Ntale, the brother and sister messengers he had befriended.

Either all my friends are co-workers or all my co-workers end up as my friends, James thought. *Well, probably there will be nothing new here, and it's painful for 162, and it's Christmas, so let's get it over with.*

When he opened the door slot to check, the man was curled in a fetal position, with a woven straw pad and a blanket under him, and two blankets thrown over the concrete bench that was the only furniture in the cell. It was less uncomfortable than it looked, perhaps, but it seemed like the very image of misery. James set the lantern onto a shelf, crouched next to the huddled figure, and spoke loudly. "Tell us how Daybreak will react to an attack on the camps along the Ohio."

The man shot to a sitting position, wiping saliva from his face, and yelled incoherently.

"Bad dream?" James said, almost sympathetically. "Tell us how Daybreak will react to an attack on the camps on the Ohio River, and we will see about getting you a pillow."

"A pillow would be nice," 162 agreed. "I don't know what it will let me tell. The situation is that Daybreak is on a cusp, a balance, a tipping point to use that old inaccurate term. Daybreak is pushing the tribes it controls very hard and they are starving and dying of overwork, and it is driving them down into those camps. As soon as they can cross over, they will be after your surviving towns and cities in Kentucky like a hungry Rottweiler on a litter of kittens, and they won't stop until they are stopped; left to themselves, the tribal hordes will go all the way to the Gulf. If all you do is stop them from moving, they will wander away from the river to forage, and Daybreak will just gather the survivors back up over the winter, to try again next year. But if they are actually defeated and beaten, Daybreak does not have the people or resources to create more. Remember it is not even a parasite, it is a carrion eater, and the Lost Quarter is a corpse that it has already fed on more than once once once—" 162 finished in a long scream, flailing and thrashing on the bench, and James and Izzy had all they could do to restrain him.

On their way out, Izzy said, "We didn't learn anything new, did we? That's the same thing he said last time."

"We have to keep asking because we never know when Daybreak might fail for a few seconds and let him tell the truth. Or remember, he was one of our best minds, and he's still in there trying to get out, and he might find a way to suggest something to us. Thanks for working on Christmas morning. Do you have anywhere to be for the rest of the day?"

"Jason and Beth are having me over for lunch. We all tend to get pretty quiet around holidays, you know, because Daybreak took us away from our families back before, sometimes way back before, and we missed our last few chances to talk to our parents or our siblings or whatever. It makes holidays really sad." She brushed her flyaway brown hair away from her face. "Also makes me sad that I have two fresh bruises from his thrashing. I never hurt anybody when I was having Daybreak seizures, at least as I recall, but then I'm a little bitty girl and he's a good-sized man. I hate to be a wimp, but if you think you're going to cause a seizure, maybe you should have Jason as your assistant?"

"Yeah, you're probably right. Well, I just wanted to make sure you had somewhere to be."

"That's nice of you, and I do. Merry Christmas, James."

"Merry Christmas, Izzy." He hurried on to his next stop; Incoming Crypto at the Main Post Office, where he was expecting some good news.

ABOUT THE SAME TIME. RECONSTRUCTION RESEARCH CENTER (IN THE FORMER PUEBLO COUNTY COURTHOUSE), PUEBLO, COLORADO. 9:15 AM MOUNTAIN TIME. THURSDAY, DECEMBER 25, 2025.

General Lyndon Phat stood and reached for the stack of wood by the fireplace. "I can't tell if it's really cold or I'm just old."

"It's really cold," Heather O'Grainne said. "And as president, you will only be allowed to be old enough to seem strong, reassuring, and paternal."

Phat gazed at her over his reading glasses, which perched on his nose like a last pathetic fence against the avalanche of his gray unibrow. He was short and square-built, with gray hair surrounding a monk's spot, and his deeply creased face recorded a lifetime of worry. He wore a blanket draped around his shoulders; a thick sweater; baggy sweatpants; and multiple pairs of wool socks that wilted into bundles of color around his ankles. He had been leafing through a hundred-year-old *Atlas of North American Resources*.

A guard knocked at the door. "It's James Hendrix, Ms. O'Grainne. He's waiting at the ground floor door."

"Send him up," Heather said. "And for the third time, put him on the list of people who are allowed immediate entrance, and tell your sergeant that if they ever make James stand in the snow waiting again, I will have the sergeant's guts on a stick."

"I'll tell him *exactly* that, ma'am. I'll get Mister Hendrix right now."

From his crib, Leo whimpered, testing what wasn't right with the world. Heather strode to the crib, leaned down, and put on the joyful excited tone she usually reserved for creamed spinach. "Guess what? We're going to have a visit from Uncle James! And he's going to tell us that our friends killed some bad guys!"

"Your confidence warms my heart," James said, coming in and shucking off his tent-like coat. He still looked every pudgy inch the government documents librarian he had been back before. "And we did kill some bad guys. Good morning, Leo."

Leo emitted the short "ah!" noise that he reserved for people he especially liked, and waved his hands until James leaned down and extended a finger to grasp. "You been keeping them in line, fella?"

"Ah!"

"Good. I'll take it from here."

Leo gurgled and settled; he'd be deep asleep in a minute. Heather wasn't sure what was so reassuring about James, but Leo wasn't the only one who felt it.

James drew up another armchair and pulled off sweaters, draping them over the back. "Nice and warm in here. Leo's getting big."

"They do that, or so MaryBeth Abrams tells me, along with reminding me that I'm not the first woman ever to have one. You have a charming knack for liking the boss's baby, James."

"I wouldn't have lasted twenty-three years in the Civil Service if I didn't." He sat, crossing his legs, hands wrapped around one knee. "Operation Monkey Flush turned one, killed three, and recovered two kids who were being used as cover props. The cell is shut down and there's no evidence that there were any more.

"Bambi reports they took the thumb off one of the ones they killed, as a memorial for Steve Ecco, and bagged Harrison Castro's assassin in boiling feathers, same way Castro died."

Phat folded his arms. "This is terrorism."

"It is. Terrorism exists to scare the shit out of people. And since people can't be scared of things they don't know about, Bambi and Carlucci made sure they left abundant evidence for the cleanup staff to gossip about. Chris Manckiewicz will run the story as the main headline in the next issue of the *Post-Times*, piously deploring out-of-control Feds going too far and Castle freeholders wreaking private vengeance with Federal help, and so on."

"But," Phat pointed out, "everyone knows Daybreak doesn't care about individual agents, and anyway we're much more afraid of Daybreak than it is of us, if it's even able to feel fear."

James nodded impatiently. "Sure, sure. Daybreak destroyed the modern world and killed more than seven billion people, this is—"

"That was back before, when it controlled less than one in two thousand people worldwide. In less than two years it's thrown us a century or more back in tech, it controls at least 5 percent of the surviving global population, probably more like 10 percent in this country—*of course* we're afraid of it. We're losing and it means to put an end to us forever."

"Which is why it's so important not to say that in public."

"There's something wrong with democracy?" Phat's voice was louder and harsher than Heather would have expected.

In the suspended instant of complete silence, Heather realized this was more than just another little clash; since Phat had arrived three weeks ago, he and Hendrix had bickered at least daily, but this felt different. *Say something,* she thought. The silence stretched another second before she ventured, "General, I wonder if the problem isn't that it's been a long time since any American general had to think about losing big, and it doesn't come natural to you. James pointed out the other day that if people get the idea that Daybreak is winning—and it is—they'll want to do what losers do: cut a deal. But Daybreak isn't a devil we can let anyone deal with, and there are only three ways to prevent deals with the devil. One is to make sure people know it's the devil; one is to make the devil too angry to deal."

Phat waited. "That's two."

Hendrix said, softly, "Heather's favorite has always been to make sure there's no devil."

"So this restored Constitutional government you're talking about is going to kill or forcibly convert a few million people for what they believe. *That's* bringing back American democracy?" Phat looked from one to the other. "I had the impression you were liberals, back before."

Heather shrugged. "I was a Fed with a liberal mentor. I hardly ever even voted."

James nodded. "On the other hand, I was pretty much a socialist. If you haven't noticed, Pueblo is a socialist society; almost everyone eats most meals in a common mess hall that you get into with a ration coupon. Going to Doctor MaryBeth is free, but if she says you're not sick, you're SOL. Hardly anyone has paid a dime of rent or mortgage since Daybreak day. I teach, and I get paid in firewood and food by the town government, and nobody charges my students anything. Frankly I don't *want* private business to come back too much or too far."

"But government terrorism—"

"Dead Daybreakers are a public good like clean water, education, health care, or good roads, and should be publicly provided," James said. "Wiping Daybreak out of the minds of everyone everywhere would be the best thing humanity did since we got rid of smallpox. I'm just more willing than some other people to face the fact that when you're trying to fight an idea to the death, you have to fight it with what's known to work: a cycle of public atrocity leading to reprisal atrocity till there are no neutrals left, and then be better at atrocity than the other side is."

"Peace through genocide."

"It's been known to work. Most nicer ways have not. You're a pretty good amateur historian, General. We're back a century, going on two centuries, in technology, and back a lot further in our basic situation. It wasn't us, but Daybreak, that put us back on humanity's ancient rhythm."

"The ancient rhythm," Phat repeated, and then, as if it had illuminated everything, "*the ancient rhythm.* Yeah. I see your point, James." He stared into the fire as if hoping some god would speak to him.

"I have a feeling that *ancient rhythm* is some kind of war-history-geek, boy-code expression," Heather said. "And to spill the secret to you old poops, I'm not actually a boy. Maybe someone could explain it?"

James started to speak but Phat answered first. "James means this is war the way the Romans, Mongols, or Goths knew it. Here we are, sitting out the winter like Caesar or Alaric, because in the ancient rhythm, wars start in the spring, when there's time to fight—after crops are planted, roads are dry, and ships can sail."

James nodded. "Around the time my father was born, a presidential candidate said, 'People always cite George Washington's wisdom and forget that his light was a candle and his transportation was a horse.' The man who said that is much less relevant to us today, but as for George—"

"Our light is a candle and our transportation is a horse," Heather said.

Phat nodded. "History is real information again, instead of a strange set of stories to fascinate old poops."

James rose. "That reminds me, I must go where I can be called an old poop repeatedly for a couple of hours. Leslie's due at my place in an hour." He stood and began laboriously climbing back into his sweaters, explaining from far inside one, "I'm afraid I have more Christmases to get to than I have Christmas to get to them in."

As Phat and Heather watched from her window, James scuffed homeward through the snow. "The ancient rhythm," Phat said. "You know, that's the whole story right there. The twentieth century freed one big chunk of the human race from the natural world. We could have fresh fruit in January, start wars in October, cross the ocean in February; we could let the authorities handle crimes instead of having blood feuds, and govern by popularity instead of ruling by bloodline, and make our wars about diplomacy and economics. We got detached. It was great while it lasted, but now we're back in the ancient rhythm up to our necks."

"*Temporarily,*" Heather said. "I want Leo to grow up to complain about taxes, the electric bill, and his student loans. I want him worrying about who will go to the prom with him, not how he can earn another scar on his triceps. But James is right, too, that it's an ancient war and we have to win the ancient way."

Phat grimaced. "But how do we escape the ancient rhythm once we've won?" He peered out the window again. "For a guy that old and heavy, James sure moves like a happy kid."

"He always does whenever he's going to see Leslie."

"Now there's an ancient rhythm. Old man with young girlfriend."

Heather snorted. "We can all tell that's what *he* wishes it was. But although Leslie likes sex, loves her dog, and in her own weird way, is devoted to James, as for combining them, the dog has a better chance than James."

ABOUT THE SAME TIME. ATHENS, TEMPORARY NATIONAL GOVERNMENT DISTRICT (FORMERLY ATHENS, GEORGIA). 11:45 AM EASTERN TIME. THURSDAY, DECEMBER 25, 2025.

Jenny Whilmire Grayson placed the tray of broiled venison steak, brown gravy, and fresh biscuits on the end of the long table that was not occupied by maps and toy soldiers. "Oh, my little boy is playing army on Christmas morning."

"Well, since someone was busy using up all the hot water—"

"It's Christmas, baby, for once you're getting a girl that's all the way clean. Think about this." She gave him That Smile, waited to see him react, then shucked the robe and pulled the towel from her head in one grand swoop, tousling her blonde mane. "If you're quick, dinner won't get cold."

"If I'm quick I might hurt you—"

"I *know*." She smiled in anticipation.

He dropped his own robe and yanked his sweaters off. "Nobody home but us," she whispered. As he shoved her hard against the wall, she was already screaming.

When they were done, for now, she was sore, her face was streaked with tears, and she ran her hands over her body, looking for bruised places; his chest was heaving, and his face was red as much from shame as exertion.

She lifted his chin, looked into his eyes, and said, "I invited you, baby. I invited you."

He drew a deep breath, and found another subject. "If nobody's home, who got the dinner?"

"I had Luther set it by the fire and go catch the cable car, so he could spend the rest of the day with his family."

Grayson nodded. "You're probably the main reason we haven't been poisoned yet."

"*Luther's* patient. Long before he poisons you, Maelene'll've dumped you out an upstairs window. You've got to learn she's not a private and the house does not need to pass inspection. Let's eat this while it's still hot." She pulled her robe back on, wincing more than it really hurt, and ate standing up though she didn't have to, because she knew he liked to see that.

As always, Luther had done brilliantly. They ate quickly, enjoying the rare combination of hot, fresh, and plenty. *Even the most likely next president and first lady can't count on a good Christmas dinner,* Jenny thought. *Not this year. Not since back before. Did I ever enjoy any food this much, back before?*

Grayson laughed suddenly. "You realize that neither of us took off any of all the socks we're wearing?"

"Baby, brutality can be fun, in the right mood, but bare toes on *this* floor is *too* brutal. If you find some nice girl with a cold feet fetish, you go right ahead." Before loading seconds onto her plate, she paused to bind up her hair, and noticed she had captured his gaze. "Caught you staring, baby. Now that I've taken care of your needs, how about some respect for your little Barbie doll's *mind*?"

"I wish you wouldn't call yourself that."

She shrugged. "*I* know I'm not, and so does anybody that counts— here, or in Olympia or Pueblo or anywhere else. That act is over."

"I *never* liked that act, and good riddance to it. If I'm going to be a monster I'd rather be a real monster and attack a real woman." Something on the map caught his attention and he leaned across the table to look at it from another angle. He needed information about that state forest south of Bloomington—hadn't the RRC sent some scouts through there last summer? Maybe—

Jenny said, "Jeff, why are you putting so much thought into beating up some starving, sickly hippies?"

He glanced up, smiling. "There's never enough time before to think and plan, and no time at all once it starts. Sorry I got distracted."

"Baby, I don't believe for one second that bush hippies on a map could pull your attention away from these." She sat up straight and pulled her shoulders back. Her pouty spoiled-bimbo routine, just because it was so fake, almost always made him smile and often seemed to get him talking, but today he just looked sad, and she was instantly sorry she'd tried it. "Come on, Jeff. You've been pesty for rough sex for several days, and staring out the window, and quiet for hours at a time. That means you're worried; I've had ten months to learn to read your tells. Now *what* is eating at you so bad?"

He gestured to the map. "Now that RRC agents are penetrating north of the Ohio and east of the Wabash, they're finding things worse than we thought. The tribal 'armies' aren't really armies—more like mass foot-powered kamikazes. Designed to smash their way through civilization, destroy everything they can't use right away, and die. It's amazing how big and fast a force can be if you're not planning to supply it, or get any of it back.

"They've got it timed so that they'll hit peak strength just as the ground is dry enough to move, and in each camp if they don't start to move on schedule, they'll start to starve within days. So they will move on schedule. And once they're moving . . . well, an enemy whose purpose is only to kill as many of you as they can before they die—"

"You spent your career in the Middle East, Jeff—"

"And back then I had the greatest military power in history on instant call. It looks *different* from General Braddock's position."

"Have I met him?"

"Not likely. George Washington's CO in the French and Indian War. Talented, bright, brave, and *unlucky*. The Indians trapped his force on a road in the forest. Outgunned, outnumbered, no reinforcements, cut off, four horses killed under him, and he held his force together in a fighting retreat before a sniper nailed him. Terrible reputation, though, thanks to historians who never walked that ground. If you remember the Yough—"

"I remember, baby—I wrote your memoirs. And we won."

"We got the Amish farmers out. That was our objective, so technically we won, but a few more victories like that and we won't have an army. Exact same kind of country, and very close to, where Braddock went on that expedition. That's why I was thinking of it." He gestured at the toy soldiers who pinned down the map. "On this campaign down the Ohio and up the Wabash we have to win eleven times in a row—and win bigger at less cost than we ever did in the Yough. And conditions aren't any better than they were for Braddock, and I'm not the combat commander he was. Which means I have to be a lot luckier."

"Eleven times?"

Grayson shrugged. "There are eleven of those—I don't like to call them armies. 'Hordes'—I guess that's the word—waiting for spring and dry ground to cross the Ohio and the Wabash. If even one of them gets past us and penetrates any distance into civilization, they'll move faster than we do; living on looting, they have no supply train, and they'll be killing refugees, not rescuing them. So our slow, overburdened army will have to chase after the invading horde, and meanwhile other hordes will be breaking out at other points. Everything depends on stopping them before they can start." He looked down at the toy soldiers on the map. "Isn't it strange how toy soldiers haven't gotten new equipment since World War Two, more than 80 years ago?"

One of Jenny's friends had found a bag of plastic soldiers, unspoiled by biotes, under a pile of cotton fabric in a wrecked Hobby Lobby, and knowing that now that they were uncovered they would rot within a week or so, had buried them upside down in wet sand and poured molten solder into them, creating lumpy, ungainly "solder soldiers." They had made Grayson laugh when he'd unwrapped them.

"You've been shoving them around on that map all morning."

"It's a way to think. The guys standing at attention represent my reserves; firing from one knee, front line infantry. Bazookas stand for artillery, bayoneters for cavalry. Daybreakers are grenade throwers."

Now that she could read it, she saw how grim the layout on the map was. "And if it all depends on stopping eleven attacks all at once, with only one army—"

"That's our biggest advantage, that it won't be all at once—the only good news that Heather O'Grainne's intel operation had for us. The tribals're planning to hit first along the upper Ohio, where it's a shorter distance to better looting, and then unroll the attacks down the Ohio and up the Wabash—the Wabash hordes are farthest away from their own supplies, and will have to travel a long way through country that's already been looted and burned over, so they'll start last."

"Why don't they go in random order? You'd never be able to catch them—"

"If it were me, I might. I think it's because of their non-command non-structure; 'go after these guys do' is a real easy rule. And it does mean that to some extent they support each other, and maybe it's so the first one to get past me can focus on blocking me while the others get in.

"But anyway, assuming Heather got the truth out of them, the plan is, I match their schedule, hitting them with spoiling attacks down the Ohio and up the Wabash." His arm swept over the map in a crooked L shape. "They'll be most vulnerable just before they're ready to attack—greatest troop concentrations and smallest remaining supplies. If I beat them to *every* punch, it can be eleven massacres instead of eleven battles, but they only need to be lucky once, and I have to be lucky eleven times. Luckier than Braddock, at least."

"If you need to be very, very lucky, then we're in good shape, because you are." Jenny rubbed her hair with a towel again, pretending to dry it while making sure she was disheveled the way he liked; the motion stretched her just enough to slightly open her bathrobe. *Jeff's arrogance is his armor, and I can't let there be a hole in his armor.* "This time be gentle, 'kay, baby?"

AN HOUR LATER. PUEBLO, COLORADO. 3:35 PM MOUNTAIN TIME. THURSDAY, DECEMBER 25, 2025.

The Christmas tree in the corner of Heather's living quarters hypnotized Leo; he gurgled happily whenever she put him close to it.

I'll need to get rid of that fire hazard before the New Year, even though Leo loves it.

While she waited for James, she redid her master chart, the layout of file cards, slips of paper, thumbtacks, and string by which she tracked her efforts to—

Leo had gotten a body width closer to the tree by rolling onto his back, the first time he'd ever done that, and was now grabbing for the ornaments just out of his reach. Heather propelled all six-feet-one of herself around the table to her son, who fortunately had not yet acquired or ingested anything. "So," she said, "you've got a new trick, turning over. Wait till I tell MaryBeth. She'll get such a kick out of telling me that you're a normal kid and I worry too much."

"Ah!"

She moved him farther from the tree, and returned to her chart.

A knock. "Heather, it's James, they've apparently decided I can be trusted to climb stairs by myself."

"You must feel practically human." She opened the door.

James unloaded a bulging pack onto her table. "Eggnog, made with the last of my pre-Daybreak Jack Daniel's, and I wrapped the jar so it's still warm. Also quiche, trout bisque, and some appalling Mesa County wine, pre-Daybreak, that someone must have given me as a joke."

"James, this is why you're perfect."

They sat and enjoyed the warmth and the company, as the sun sank into the mountains, just visible from this high window, in a spectacular burst of reds and golds. "I can almost forget," Heather said, "that those colors are the dust of billions of people, thousands of cities, all of civilization—"

"Eggnog," James said. "Warm eggnog."

They clinked cups. "Merry Christmas. And that's not a rebuttal, oh chief advisor."

"There's truth in warm eggnog, too, and the colors are beautiful, however they got there."

Sunset was a streak of vivid purple with a deep red egg half nested in it, behind the black teeth of the mountains, when they heard the group of people singing "Adeste Fidelis." "That hymn must have accompanied some bleak Christmases since the Romans first sang it," Heather said.

"It's not *nearly* that old," James said. "They were still writing hymns in Latin down almost to 1900, because Latin sings better than English."

"How did you—don't tell me the government had a *pamphlet* on that?"

"You bet. *Recreating historic holidays, a teacher's guide*, 1950s booklet from the Park Service's history guides series. 'Adeste Fidelis' would be okay for a grade-school production of *Christmas at Valley Forge*, but not much earlier, and even for *Christmas at the Lincoln White House*, only snooty Episcopalians would know it. If you want common soldiers singing it, go to the Bulge or Chosin."

"I was visualizing Roman Britain, brave old legionaries and half-trained boys surrounded by Saxons, you know. Anyway, it sounds brave against the darkness."

"'Brave against the darkness' probably counts more than archival-librarian accuracy."

She nodded and they sat quietly until she asked, "James, are we expecting too much, too soon, for putting the country back together? There's so much to do in this next year."

He squatted by the fire, surprisingly agile, held his hands to the warmth, and seemed to listen to some voice. At last he said, "Right now, a few million loyal Americans—not Daybreakers, I mean good people who do their jobs and who we need—have just begun noticing that a restored United States might not be so good for them."

Taken aback, Heather blurted, "Who *wouldn't* it be good for, besides Daybreak? Why not?" She could hear indignation in her own voice and wasn't sure she intended it.

James spread his hands. "Lots of people. The guy who created a business out of property that was just lying around, who has never paid taxes, and doesn't want to start. The teacher who teaches what she likes, how she likes. The farmer who has access to all the land he can plow.

"Right now, if people put resources back into productive use, good enough, and we let them keep it; the real owner is almost certainly dead and if not, unable to get back to the property. But what if the roads and the courts re-open, and people can come back and prove they're the old owners? Then add in that once it's set back up, there'll be taxes again.

And that old folk figure of evil, The Book-Smart Man From Washington That Don't Know Shit, will begin to reappear at the doors of hardworking people."

"There's no more Washington. There's a lake where it was."

"You know what I mean. And you can bet that if we do carry out our plan and get a Federal government going again, 'Springfield' will mean pretty much what 'Washington' used to, well within our lifetimes. We'd have some people losing things they've worked for, and many people remembering things they didn't like. So some of them are catching on, right now, that the Restored Republic of the United States is a nice idea but it's not necessarily the best thing for them."

"But, James, *who*?"

"How many people with a spending problem sleep better at night because their debt is gone, with no one to extend more credit to them and nothing to buy with it? Why would they want to bring back the world of consolidation, bankruptcy, and foreclosure, especially if they have to work at it? How many people played dead, and got a fresh start, by just walking away from lovers or families in the chaos? How many people were in jobs they hated back then and have lucked into jobs they like, now?"

"Oh, there are some like that, I'm sure, but come on, James, what about an ex-desk jockey who's shoveling mud? Won't he—"

"Everybody doesn't have to be better off for there to be a movement. Think how many big causes in history turned out to benefit *nobody*. And the benefits of the new world are not illusory, Heather. Re-creating the Federal government is going to be a net *cost* to a lot of people who won't want to pay that bill."

"Then should we just give up? Are we too late already?"

"I think we're still in time, but only just. Right now, I think most people haven't yet admitted how much they have to lose if the United States comes back.

"But if we give them a year or two, they'll see all kinds of practical reasons to put off the Restored Republic for another year, or another decade, or their grandchildren's generation. My advice as your consigliere is *now*."

He stirred the pot, the red glow bathing his bald spot and sagging cheeks, making him look a thousand years old. "All in the timing. Like the moment for this bisque, and the moment to just enjoy Christmas with company, and every other moment that matters. Hold out your bowl and no more gloomy talk till we've finished."

TWO:
WE ALL FEED OFF THE WRECKAGE

Jenny Whilmire Grayson thanked the crowd and left the rostrum on the
steps of the First National Church (the former University of Georgia chapel) knowing that she had given one of her best speeches, ever: just Christian enough so that her father's disciples would not feel deserted; heavy on
Army, patriotism, and honor for Jeff's home crowd; enough quotes about
restoring the Constitution for the Provi audience that would read the
speech in the *Pueblo Post-Times* next week. And she'd written some good
catchy phrases, and delivered them well.

Her father's expression brought her up short. "Honey, I'm proud of
you, of course—"

"But . . . ?"

"As we move deeper into the Tribulation, we also move the saving remnant of America toward its union with the Lord, and—"

"Daddy, I can tell you're not speaking as my father, you're intoning as
the Chief Bishop of the Post Raptural Church—"

"Jenny, I *am* your father. You were always my smart, beautiful daughter, and I love you, but if you are going to be our First Lady, you have to be
more than smart and beautiful."

"What else did you have in mind?"

"America needs a First Lady who is a model Christian woman, because the President and First Lady, in a very important symbolic way, are the national mother and father—"

"Daddy, Jeff has had a vasectomy and nowadays there's no way to reverse it." *Sorry about lying to Daddy, Jesus, but we will just have to wait for the ten-year shot that Mama got me when I went off to college to wear off, because there's no counter-shot anymore. I guess once it does wear off we'll say we'd been praying and the Lord saw fit to reload Jeff's musket.*

"I don't mean literally, physically parents, I mean that you represent motherhood and fatherhood, in the same way that the President himself represents not just fatherhood but our Father in heaven, too. Ever since Kennedy, America has responded to filth in the White House like the boy who saw his father with a prostitute—"

"And you think I'm behaving like a prostitute around the National Daddy?"

It was a calculated tantrum; before he could gather himself to protest that he hadn't meant that, she had pushed past him, and the guards had waved her into her husband's inner office.

Jeffrey Grayson looked up. "Well. Your speech was brilliant, and you look unhappy, so I guess you talked to your father."

Her chuckle was humorless. "Do *you* want me to be more of a good National Mommy?"

He shook his head. "I want you around. And in love with me. That's first and second. Third, I want to know I've done my duty as an officer. And then, way down the list, but still on it, I want to be president."

"And you think all that might conflict?"

"I think you're already angry and I didn't cause it."

"True. But do you think I should go bake cookies like what's-her-name?"

"Hillary Clinton? *She* got in trouble for saying that people *expected* her to. I'll win with you the way you are. Or if I don't, keeping your love is what matters to me anyway. Everything else is just what I do for a living." He drew a breath and was watching her intently when he added, "Okay?"

He wants my *approval.* She smiled, and relished the relief in his eyes.

5 HOURS LATER. MANBROOKSTAT (FORMERLY THE AREAS SURROUNDING NEW YORK HARBOR). 8:30 PM EASTERN TIME. THURSDAY, JANUARY 8, 2026.

The shiny cylinders and dull spheres resembled heavy children's toys or mathematical demonstrations, but Jamayu Rollings felt like he was spreading out diamonds on the black velvet drape that covered the folding table.

Like the pale-skinned, smiling men facing him, Rollings wore a tuxedo. Beside him, the Commandant and his two Special Assistants were in dress uniform. The Special Assistants wore their shoulder holsters ostentatiously, as if to deter the Galway trade negotiators from lunging across the table and grabbing the ferromolybdenum, tungsten, and palladium. "We hope to have use for all these materials, soon, ourselves," Rollings said, "but for the moment, truthfully, our labs and factories aren't ready.

"These were all found in a specialty metals workshop just a bit up the river from Albany, undisturbed in their containers, with full paperwork. I don't need to tell you that for the next ten years at least, no one on Earth will be able to refine any more, and if, let's say, you have any people working on hydrogen-based energy tech, there's no substitute for palladium.

"Gold, silver, or special barter are acceptable, but I won't give credit. I'll await your offer with interest, gentlemen. Anything else you'd like me to be looking out for?"

Dr. O'Ryan, who had spoken little till now, said, "We have a very acute interest in titanium, especially in sheets, but any piece larger than five kilograms. If you should happen to find anything like that on any future salvage expedition, you can notify the trade mission and have them send a message to my attention at the Recovered Technology Project in Galway."

Rollings made a note in his pad. "Anything else, gentlemen? I should get out of Captain Carton's way, as he has a lot of good stuff to show you too."

"Excellent stuff, Captain Rollings." Doyle, the Irish trade delegation leader, extended a firm handshake and a warm smile. "You'll be hearing our offer within a few days."

Rollings's younger son Whorf stepped up beside him and slipped the samples into velvet jeweler's bags with flair and reverence. *I could have brought Geordie but he'd just have shoved our samples into bags, and never met the eyes of the Irishmen. Whorf's got the* I am the keeper of tungsten, and who are you? *condescending stare down perfect.*

God, I'm going to miss him so much. Time to tell him, though, keeping him in suspense wouldn't be fair to anyone.

As Whorf took up the cloth from the table, Carton came in with his samples of salvage timber.

The Commandant walked Rollings to the ballroom. "Nice job, Captain Rollings. I think we'll have a deal for your metals with them."

"If they beat *Discovery*'s offer, sure. We'll take the best deal we can get."

"An excellent principle." At the ballroom door, the Commandant added, "But I think it will turn out the Galway men can offer us far more than the rednecks for Jesus. Enjoy the party." He clapped Rollings on the shoulder too heartily, and headed back to the conference room. The Special Assistants at his heels wheeled and closed up behind him. Over his shoulder, he added, "If you can persuade Uhura to save me a dance, it will be much appreciated."

And if I can keep Uhura away from you, she'll appreciate that, Rollings thought.

The Commandant's engineering team had rigged the Ritz-Carlton ballroom with producer-gas lighting. The warm, brilliant glow, after so many months of candles and oil lanterns, could almost make you forget the sharp, dirty odor and the soot streaks on the wall above each light.

At his side, Whorf said, "Wow, a whole room full of people with clean clothes and a recent bath."

Rollings choked on a laugh. "Thanks for that. The Commandant dropped me a big hint about your little sis."

"I'd be just as happy if Uhura went home early," Whorf muttered, looking down at the floor so no one could read his lips.

"Me too," Jamayu said, also looking down. When he looked up, he was smiling again. "Let's grab some free chow and then take a short walk outside; there're details I'd like to go over. Unless, of course, I'm spoiling your chances to hustle the local ladies?"

Whorf snorted. "Dad, look around. The single ladies my age are *not* here to have fun. Any more than I am. Let's get some of that stew."

They found a table back in the shadows, and, wary of being overheard, concentrated on eating, watching their neighbors in tuxedos and long dresses dancing not-very-well to a still-not-very-good band. Rollings glanced sideways; Whorf had grown into a big, strong young man with a piercing, alert expression. Both men wore dreads, but whereas Jamayu's were gray and rough, Whorf's were black and glistening.

He's not going to want to spend his good, vigorous years mining junk, Rollings thought, and resisting sadness, smiled broadly when he asked, "So, about that walk . . . ?"

In the lobby, they pulled on heavy coats against the fierce cold.

They were silent until they stood in the dark, far from where anyone could hear them, looking at the flaring gaslights and lanterns in the harbor. Outside that yellow-orange pool of light, beyond what had once been the western boundary of Battery Park, Rollings finally spoke, his voice low, his face pointed down at the icy rubble around his feet. "The Temper offer is *real* good," he said, softly. "I didn't tell the Commandant, but Captain Halleck sent a guy by on the down low this afternoon, and *Discovery* is offering cash and carry—they're carrying enough gold and silver to pay for all our specialty metals, and they want to take them to Savannah once their repairs are done at the end of the month."

"And it's a good offer?"

"It's *excellent.* I want to take it without bothering to hear what Doyle and his people offer. I'd rather be selling to the government of America than to those slick Irishmen."

"Athens is *one* government of America," Whorf pointed out. "They'll want our metals for their labs at Castle Newberry. The Provis are just as American, Hanford probably needs those metals just as bad, and when a coffee clipper comes—"

"*Discovery* will leave before any other American ship comes in. And once I've got that metal on board *Discovery*, I won't have it in my possession, for the Commandant to seize and tell me who's buying it." Rollings kicked at a scrap of steel. "That metal came from a government lab, so it belongs to *some* American government, and *not this one*. Because it's obvious that the Commandant wants some deal with the Irish. Like he can just decide what to do after we did the work, and with stuff we retrieved at our own risk, from . . ." He shook his head, his arms rising with his shrug under his thick coat. "Back before, he was a plain old cadet at West Point."

"Pop, back before, you were a dentist with an expensive boat, and I was a freshman in African-American Studies," Whorf pointed out. "Daybreak hit, you had a schooner, and we made a good life. The Commandant had a military force, and he's made himself a great life. We *all* feed off the wreckage."

"True." Rollings sighed, listening to the crackle of the water vapor in his breath freezing. "Cold out here. Let's not stay too long. Look, if the metal is in my possession and hasn't been sold yet, the Commandant can push that deal onto me with his thugs and their guns. I already might have to make some bad trades to avoid having him for a son-in-law. For that matter, he might want Uhura for something a lot less than a wife." Rollings kicked the ground with his heel as if trying to bury the thought. "So, they've offered you a spot on *Discovery*."

The name had magic. They both turned to look to where the handsome three-master was moored, gleaming in the ruddy gaslights on the pier. The ship was taller to the eye even than most tall ships, with her hull long and low and her superstructure raking back in a series of smoothed out, oblique steps; most of her was freshly painted a gleaming white that glowed gold in the gaslights, and her masts seemed to reach right up into the stars.

USS *Discovery* had been SS *l'Esprit de Brest*, offering the priciest of Caribbean sailing cruises. Back before, she'd been just finishing an overhaul, awaiting the crew that would never fly in to Savannah.

The TNG had rechristened *Discovery* as a science ship, because she had been designed for a minimal sailing crew and the old recreational spaces made decent labs, libraries, and sample storage. In addition she had ample room for a staff of fifty, who came from every intellectual center on the continent: the RRC at Pueblo, the Oregon Exploration Center at Eugene, the Scholar's League at Santa Fe, the NASA remnant at Houston, and Stone Lab up in the Erie Islands.

On *Discovery*'s shakedown cruise up the coast to map the Atlantic shore of the Dead Belt, the winter weather had shaken her harder than they'd expected. Repairs would take a few weeks. Some crew were too injured or sick to continue; Captain Halleck had offered Whorf a chance to take over a berth as a "scholar-sailor," bluntly describing it as "a chance to work as an Able Seaman and do homework, too."

"So, do you think Halleck offered me the job because he wanted our metals?"

Rollings shook his head emphatically, stamping his feet to warm them. "Halleck made the offer to you before he ever saw or even heard about the metal. And he's not a man to link a deal or take advantage, that Halleck. I've always prided myself on sharp unsentimental dealing, but now I find I'd rather deal with an honest Yankee who had a real commission in the old Navy than a passel of slick Irishmen and ambitious kay-dets." Rollings tracked Whorf's gaze as it reached out to *Discovery*. "Got to admit it," Rollings said, softly, "I mean, *look* at her, she's *gorgeous*."

"Yeah." Whorf sounded choked up.

"Whorf, I'm thinking about the family here. You know how we keep *Ferengi* stocked and ready to go, and we all know we might have to run for it any time. Geordie's a good guy, but—and don't you ever quote this to your brother—even though he can take *Ferengi* anywhere with enough water under her keel, I think he will always need someone to tell him where.

"Deanna's no sailor and never will be, but she'll run Ferengi Enterprises some day—from an office, someplace, like it should be run. If I'm gone, and your brother pulls any oldest-male privilege bullshit, you take Deanna's back and make sure she keeps the company. So Deanna needs to stay here to inherit the company, Geordie needs to stay here to sail *Ferengi*, and Uhura needs to stay here because she's young yet. And that leaves you, Whorf."

"Yeah, I guess it does." Whorf sighed.

"If anything happens to me, Deanna'll need your judgment and maybe your gun. So promise me you'll come home as fast as you can—*if* you hear of that kind of trouble."

"You knew before you asked I'd—Wait, *come home?*" Whorf's stare was almost comic. "Where am I going to be, Pop?"

Rollings thought, *in my heart, like always*, but he said, "The family needs somebody away from Manbrookstat, 'specially if we get into a major thing with the Commandant. You've got a fine mind and you'd like to see the big world before you settle down, and I understand that being the biggest junk man on the Hudson is not your idea of the good life. So *all* I'm going to ask is for you to haul ass home if you hear we need you.

"But meanwhile, it's a big world, and *Discovery* is a beautiful ship. Halleck's a skipper I trust. You'll never get a better chance. Besides as soon as your Moms heard that you can get a bachelor's degree from being a scholar-sailor, she was ready to tie you up and throw you on board."

"Oh, man, she would, wouldn't she? Pop, I don't know how to say it—"

"You don't have to, I already know." Rollings thumped his son on the back, and somehow that turned into an awkward bear hug between the men. "Hell, *yeah*, sign on with *Discovery*. I wouldn't want to be the man who kept you home." The men held each other in the icy dark for a long time. "All right, let's get back in and try to keep that creepy white boy's eyes off your sister."

"I don't worry about his *eyes*, Pop."

They were settled at a table with warmed wine punch, and Uhura had just joined them, when the band played a brassy, clumsy fanfare and the Commandant strode in, half a dozen Special Assistants at his heels, followed by the Galway trade delegation.

The Commandant spoke first, and at length; his gift for an inflated phrase had them half stupefied when finally Doyle strode forward to speak.

"Well, with the fine food, and warmth and light on a cold winter's night, and it's good to be here," he said, "so I won't detain you long. From here on, you'll be seeing a great deal of us. A bit like what happened after Rome fell, once again we Irish were a well-educated people far away from the worst of it. And because of how the wind blows, and being so far west and north, and a certain amount of luck in beating back our tribals, Galway was hardly scathed at all.

"So we've got everything to make a new world, except natural resources and sheer space. But New England is empty now, and has all we need, and more. Empty cities, forests, and fields. Fast steep rivers for hydropower, brisk winds to turn mills, and though the regrown forest is mostly dead at the moment, that makes it all the better fuel for the next fifty years. New England is stony but it fed itself before, for centuries, with horse-drawn farming. We've got the people, and Manbrookstat has the land—so your country'll be seeing a great deal of us, and we'll be seeing a great deal of your country."

Looking down at the floor, Whorf muttered, "So now the Commandant has all of New England to trade away."

Uhura said, "I'm kind of tired and feeling a little headachy, Pop, can we go home?"

They emerged from the cloakroom to make their excuses to the two Special Assistants who had been looking for them, and after some fast talk from Rollings, and a couple of realistic dry heaves from Uhura, they were back out in the clean, icy chill of the winter night.

Out of earshot of the Ritz-Carlton, Uhura "revived," and she and Whorf chattered eagerly about his shipping out. She seemed to say, "I want to go too!" with every other breath.

Passing the pier, looking up along *Discovery*'s masts deep into the field of stars, and then down to the open road of water reaching south toward the Atlantic, Rollings thought, *I wish we all were going.*

3 HOURS LATER. CHRISTIANSTED NAVAL OBSERVATORY, ST. CROIX, US VIRGIN ISLANDS. ABOUT 2 AM ATLANTIC TIME. FRIDAY, JANUARY 9, 2026.

Tarantina Highbotham was enjoying her crab cake sandwich, watching waves roll in, slow, low, and dark, their crests silvered by the light of the waning gibbous moon that stood high in the sky.

Peggy barked, "Got it!" and Abby crowed, "Yes! Oh, yes!"

Highbotham turned; her five observers were sliding from their telescope stools to the desks beside them, opening candle lanterns shielded in red glass. Behind the scribbling, hunched silhouettes of the observers, the parapet wall looked like a grainy, dull black-and-white photograph. Their faces and hands, close to the lanterns, glowed vivid red, like ghosts half-emerging into the living world. The sea was so quiet that Highbotham could hear pencils scratching.

Richard was chief recorder tonight. "Times are 2:08:09, 2:08:12, 2:08:08, and 2:08:05, with an outlier at 2:08:17. How'd everyone do on location?" He had been a pudgy old drunken beach bum, retired early from an architecture practice. Nowadays muscles moved under Richard's loose baggy skin, and he spoke crisply and precisely.

Highbotham reminded herself not to think *he's better off because of Daybreak*. According to the Jamesgrams from Pueblo, that was an entry path for the mind to catch Daybreak.

"I've *got* 'em," Peggy said. Lit with red from below, and framed by her too-dark homemade lipstick, her maniacal grin beneath her charcoal-darkened eyelids gave her the look of Mrs. Joker.

Highbotham and Richard hurried to look. Peggy proudly showed them her pencil lines on her painstakingly hand-copied map of the moon. "I saw the flash itself directly, first time Fecunditatis has been dark on a flash in *months*. And I marked six good shadows. And look at that." Six pencil lines from her shadow marks converged on her marked flash site. "A closure error smaller than the thickness of the pencil line."

"Same here, Peggy, with five shadow lines, and it looks like we agree." Abby, a tall young woman, had been an alt-tech engineer before Daybreak. Highbotham privately worried that in a fight, Abby's waist-length ash-blonde ponytail might get her shot for a Daybreaker.

Gilead, slim, dark, at one time a Miami stock analyst, clicked his tongue. "Same spot but with one out of six shadow lines that was a little off. Looks like girls rule today."

Henry, who had been a math grad student, was nodding too. "On this scale a pencil line is about 667 meters wide. We can't get any more precise than that with the instruments we have. We've got the moon gun *nailed*." The hand-whittled frames and hand-ground lenses of his glasses in the moonlight looked like an outsized silver domino mask.

"Unless when we combine all our observations," Richard said, "it turns out we have it nailed to more than one place."

"Two pitchers of beer and good meal say the CEP will be less than a click," Henry said.

"You're on."

"Well, now that you all have food and beer riding on it," Highbotham said, "I *know* I can trust you with the calculations you're about to get to."

The team bent to the job of combining all their observations into one best result with pencil, abacus, adding machine, and slide rule; the process would take till well past dawn.

Highbotham scribbled Morse for a brief radiogram to alert the world that another EMP bomb was coming in, but her pencil stopped after two lines. She stared out to sea, listening hard. *Something's wrong.*

She sat back. *So why now?*

The moon gun launched an EMP weapon to burst over any strong radio source. There were half a dozen hypotheses about how Daybreak had placed it there, but for the foreseeable future those questions were merely interesting. The more significant question was how much the operators, if any, of the moon gun were able to communicate with the leadership, if any, of Daybreak. Arnie Yang's experiments, before he himself had been seduced by Daybreak, had demonstrated that to some extent it responded to the content of the messages as much as the strength of the signal, and that it had some ability to coordinate with the tribes on the ground, suggesting that the moon gun, like the tribes, had been ready to go sometime back before.

As recently as last May, they had hoped to cobble together something out of existing nuclear gear and rocket engines at sea, and Christiansted and the other observatories had been working to locate the moon gun to within a kilometer, which they were estimating would be the necessary accuracy since they were only getting one shot.

But nanospawn and biotes had beaten them to the punch; the last, crumbling nuclear carrier had barely made it home to ground on a Georgia beach two months ago, its inventory of rocket and jet fuel already turning to slimy, stinking soap and its computers and communications gear turning to crumbly white powder. Nothing remained of the old Navy and Air Force; probably nothing on Earth now could get as high as 20,000 feet above the ground, let alone to the moon.

Highbotham drummed her fingers. *That's why it doesn't make any sense for us to bother about them. Not the issue.* The Temper government at Athens's first exploration mission to Europe was going by *sailing ship,* for the love of god, barely a step up from Provi explorers and scientists who went out from Puget Sound as paying passengers on coffee clippers. Pueblo's "aerial reconnaissance" was almost entirely mailplane pilots' hand-written notes and maps.

Heather's RRC in Pueblo just archived Highbotham's reports; *nothing they can do. Right now we'd have a hard time attacking the moon gun if it was in Vermont.*

But no one had told Highbotham's team to stop, and they needed something to do besides feeding and educating the Academy kids, so for now, they carried on.

But that was what was normal, now. *The new normal,* they'd have called it when she was a young commander on an old destroyer. *The tech of 1850 or 1900 is the new normal.*

But normal *was the wrong place to look for an answer.*

This particular moon gun shot was utterly abnormal.

Since May, the moon gun had fired only when it was in bright sunlight; yet tonight, the moon was waning gibbous, so Fecunditatis was in full darkness, and all the observers had a good fix on the flash. And why fire at all? Till now the moon gun had always targeted large, fixed radio stations, but there were none of those left.

Yet something was wrong. She was sure of it. Was the clue on Earth, or on the moon?

Shit.

The moon was slightly south of bang overhead. *High tide here comes about three hours after lunar transit, so the tide's about half run in.* High-botham's last few commands before retirement had been in the perpetual overseas wars of the 20-teens, in small surface warships. She had planned dozens of raids, invasions, and landings, both in staff college and for real, *and sea raids come in with the tide and go out with it. And that gigantic tribal raid that destroyed the West Texas Research Center used the moon gun as a diversion.*

"Raiders," she said. Her observer team turned and stared at her. "Raiders have probably already landed somewhere on the island."

Not questioning, not panicking, they moved faster than Highbotham could rattle off reminders. "Henry, Peggy, blinker to the regular watch-towers and Christiansted militia. Signal *Cuppa Joe* too—Fanchion's ships travel well-armed and they'll give us a hand. Richard, Abby—"

"Kids," Abby said.

"Right. Keep them quiet. Little ones to shelters along with the books—"

"Big ones to battle stations. On our way, Captain." Richard bolted like a bull with bees on its butt; Abby ran after him, hair and long skirts streaming.

"Gilead—"

"—charts and plots into the safe," he said, not looking up from his quick folding and stacking.

Henry yanked up and slammed down with the whole force of his scrawny body on the long lever linked to a line of modified tire pumps, making a deafening clatter. Air and methane flowed; Peggy lit the torch and adjusted it to play on the stick of calcite, then closed the door on the steel drum. The limelight blazed to life. Peggy chopped the light on and off with the slatted wooden blind covering the open end. The wooden pieces rattled and thumped despite all the lard lubricating them, adding to the din of Henry's gasping and pumping and the fierce deep hiss of gas on calcite. Peggy swung the blinker to signal Christiansted, then the watchtower chains east and south of them, and—

"*Cuppa Joe* is already signaling," Peggy said. "They must have read our blinker to Christiansted. They're weighing anchor and moving out for sea room, requesting any info we have on the raiders' position. Answering with—"

A blinker flashed far down the eastern shore. Henry said, "Chenay Bay reports all quiet, they've relayed to Prune Bay and are waiting for—"

The flashing dot went out; a huge orange flame leapt up. Chenay Bay watchtower must have had just time to throw a signaling lantern against the pre-laid warning fire.

Highbotham held her voice low and even. "Peggy, is Murcheson on line now?"

"They just said so."

"Good. Message: RAIDERS AT CHENAY BAY, TOWER DOWN, EXPECTING ATTACK HERE. Same to the south tower chain. Same to *Cuppa Joe* but add: RAIDERS PROBABLY LANDED COAKLEY BAY. Make sure you include 'probably.'"

"Sure." She began flashing, not pausing as she asked, "Why Coakley?"

"That's all low ground, the road's close to the sea, and if they surprised the Coakley watchtower, they would have had good cover to surprise every station before Chenay. It's what I'd've done. We were just lucky that Chenay is higher up and better defended." *Was,* she thought.

Cuppa Joe's mainsail was unfurling; lights flickered all over Christiansted and blinkers flashed from the towers on the hills to the south. Highbotham could see motion in the streets—militia running to their posts, everyone else to cover.

It was more noise than Highbotham had heard in many nights. Peggy's hands worked the clattering, banging wooden slats with crisp precision. Henry's furious pumping added gasps, thuds, rattles, and slurps. Across the harbor, church bells rang and snare drums beat "To Quarters."

But above all the uproar, they heard the distant chant on the wind:

All we are doing,
Is to set Gaia free.

Abby said, "The Academy's Company is all present, armed, and ready, Captain."

Highbotham turned around and sternly ordered herself not to smile at the raggedness of the CAM kids' fighting clothes; what mattered was the people inside them, after all. Months of drill had paid off; some kids looked afraid, but none looked panicked, and they held their spears, leaf-spring crossbows, and plumbing-pipe muskets with confident competence.

"All right then," she said. "You are going to shoot, or load and clean, or run and carry, whatever your job is, just like in drills. If the enemy penetrate the compound, use your knife, hatchet, or spear. Don't hesitate, hit hard, and keep hitting till they stop moving. Let's go."

That, she thought, *has to be the lamest pre-battle speech ever.*

Henry, Gilead, and three of the older kids led their squads down the gentle slope of the promontory to their assigned firing pits, on a low rise overlooking the six-foot stone fence across the small peninsula. During countless hours building the fence over the summer, the children had covered its outer surface with broken-off bottles, steak knife blades whose plastic handles had dissolved, and scraps of old barbed wire, and systematically cleared everything out of the fifty yards between the pits and the fence. If it worked as intended, the fence would force the attackers to come over it slowly enough for the firing pits to butcher them.

Of course if they ever learn to make decent bows or slings, or start using guns, that fence is cover for them, and we'll be in deep shit. But you have to take your bet and play it.

Abby spoke beside her. "Captain, rockets are—"

"Boats! Coming around the point to the east!" a voice shouted from the tower.

Abby whirled and ran toward the beach.

Highbotham looked over the reserve force on the patio. *Confidence comes from seeing confidence,* she reminded herself, and took an extra moment to tuck her dreads under her kerchief and tie it tighter. "Reminders, people," she said. "Hair where it can't fall into your eyes. Shoes on tight. Check all weapons *again*. Stick close to your squad leader; if you get separated, regroup here. If it all turns to—uh, if it all goes into the soup, this is where we'll make our stand."

They were all looking past her, down toward the landward fence. She turned to see a stream of tribals coming up the road, still too far away for the rifles or crossbows in the firing pits.

When she turned back, she saw boats rowing in across Punnett Bay. "All right, our guests are arriving," she said to her reserve squads. "Showtime soon, but nothing we can do till the range closes. Stay loose till we're needed, breathe, relax, check your weapon."

Shit, how did Jebby Surdyke get into Squad Nine? She's only twelve, she should have gone with the little ones.

Most of the kids at the Caribbean Academy of Mathematics were orphaned or separated from their families in the chaos after Daybreak; some had been street kids, back before. CAM offered hot meals, a safe place to sleep, and as much instruction as they could manage to children with mathematical talent. Highbotham privately defined "mathematical talent" as "homelessness and hunger," but she thought phrasing it as a scholarship helped the kids find the pride they needed to work at their studies.

"One more order, everyone. No matter what happens tonight, *live*. The world needs your brains."

"Br-r-rains," an unidentifiable voice said, like a movie zombie.

She saw many of them freeze, anticipating one of the Captain's famous tirades. *Not tonight, guys.* "Right. Keep yours, don't let anyone spill them. A famous general pointed out that you don't win by dying for your country, you win by making the other son of a bitch die for his. He was right, despite his being Army and a West Pointer and a bigoted old asshole." *And I hope he was right that you use language like that to people going into battle.*

The landward mob of Daybreakers was fanning out from the road as they rushed the fence. As they came into range of the firing pits, Newberry Standard rifles flared and banged. A few leaders carrying spirit sticks fell.

The Daybreaker swarm kept coming. Crossbow bolts flicked into the front ranks, now, and more fell, but still, losing leaders did nothing to slow the raiders. They all knew the plan: *move toward the plaztatic enemies of Gaia and kill them where you find them.*

At the fence, the first wave didn't even try to take cover, grabbing and climbing till they hung up on wire, blades, and bottles. The ones behind piled against them until the human wave stalled, and bolts and bullets stabbed into the accumulating crowd.

If the Daybreakers had numbered in the thousands, as they had in the human waves that had swept away WTRC and threatened Pullman and Athens, they might have carried the fence and destroyed the observatory and CAM in a matter of minutes, but counting and guessing, Highbotham thought there were only four hundred at most. Still, that was enough sheer pressure to begin to crack the stone fence from its foundation, toppling stones set in the poorly cured, inadequate mortar.

Henry and two of his team leapt from their pit and ran toward the fence, each carrying a bottle bomb. Those had been Henry's idea: guncotton made and dried in the bottle. While the guncotton was still wet and therefore safe, the little ones had scratched the glass all over with a cutter. Then they had dipped the bottle in animal glue, and rolled it in shredded metal, gravel, and broken glass as if breading a deadly chicken leg. A paper-wrapped squib of black powder—really just a big firecracker—glued into the neck a couple of weeks later, after long drying in the sun, had completed the process.

At about twenty yards from the wall, all three of them struck matches,

touched the fuses, and threw the bottles into a high arc toward the screaming mob. One bottle bomb burst impressively, knocking down half a dozen
people; in two seconds, the Daybreakers behind the dead and wounded
stepped over and closed up the hole. Another bomb disappeared into the
crowd without any effect. Henry threw so hard that his bomb sailed over
the heads of the crowd, bounced, tumbled, ignited without bursting, and
scooted around trailing hot white exhaust like a firework.

As Henry and his two grenadiers ran back to their pit, one fell, clutching her leg; Henry, turning back, fell beside her.

Instantly the other CAM students in Henry's pit rushed forward. *Shit,
that's a hole, gotta plug it.* "Squads Nine, Ten, Eleven, follow me! Twelve
and Thirteen, watch for Abby's signal in case she needs you!"

Highbotham ran down the grassy slope with three squads just behind
her. The pits on either side were firing, but Henry's pit had been the center
of the line, and Henry had been commanding this whole side of the
defense. *I hope he's still alive so I can chew him out about excessive personal
initiative.*

A Daybreaker rose atop the stone fence, drawing his bow; he fell backward with a crossbow bolt in the eye. But the bowman that followed him
leapt down into the cleared space and loosed an arrow into the press of
Henry's squad; someone screamed.

Highbotham's small force flung themselves prone in the firing pit and
wriggled forward to the mounded dirt at the front. Several Daybreaker bowmen were over the fence and shooting, and more were climbing in over their
dead.

She drew her black-powder revolver, leveled it on crossed wrists, and
brought down two bowmen on four shots. *Homing missiles were a lot easier.* Beside her, little Jebby was working her crossbow with grim efficiency.
Okay, kid, from now on you can kill with the grown-ups.

"Squad Ten, hold this pit and keep up firing," Highbotham's voice was
as unnaturally clear and calm as a language lesson. "Squad Nine! Squad
Eleven! We're going down there to bring our people in. Stick together.
Nobody leaves early and nobody gets left. On my call, three, two, one,
now." She jumped, and felt them jump beside her.

With her revolver emptied and no time to reload, she pulled the cutlass from her scabbard. An old martial arts freak named Bobby had taught her the *dhao*, which was similar; she hoped—

On her right.

Raising an ax over his head.

Her hands were already moving in the bamboo cut. The blade tip bit into his neck and broke through his collarbone; he fell over backward, almost dragging her cutlass out of her hand. She glanced back, saw a man behind her raising a poleax to strike Jebby, and her cutlass turned in her hand as it passed low across her front, flew back past her thigh, and struck upward into the man's lower ribs faster than she could think any of those words, jarring against her hand as if she'd hit a sandbag with a mallet. He froze and stared. Her blade continued up and around, the tip parting shirt and skin all the way to his shoulder, rose past his head, and came back in a neck-high slash that cut his windpipe and carotids. It felt like parting a rope.

Staying with her blade, she faced forward again, and seeing the way clear, advanced to Henry in two big leaps. Her cutlass beat down an enemy spear tip on her flank; in a two-handed grip, she let the cutlass ride up beside her body, then whipped it full force down across the man's skull. She wrenched her sword clear of his head and whirled toward something moving in the corner of her eye.

The man raising a hatchet was being pushed over backwards by Jebby's spear in his throat. Highbotham swept his foot, stepped forward, and chopped between his eyes. Her wrists ached; those had been some forceful shocks.

Henry was at her feet, Jebby at her side, the rest of her squads and the survivors from Henry's Squad Three in a cluster around her. Looking down the slope, she saw the last tribal bowmen fleeing toward the wall. As a space opened between friend and foe, crossbow bolts whizzed after the few surviving raiders, bringing several down.

Henry better live. I owe him props on the crossbows. They were his idea, from that Nantucket book he was always talking about. Is always *talking about.*

Highbotham ordered, "Crossbowmen, cover us, everyone else, carry the wounded, back to the center pit. Two runners!"

Two survivors from Henry's team stepped forward. "You, go to Squads

One and Two. You, Four and Five. Let Gilead know he's in command now, and Squad Ten will hold the center pit. Bartie commands Squad Ten and he's Gilead's second in command. Tell them this is an order: No one is to rush the fence or try to carry the attack beyond it. Hold *this* side of the fence till the town militia relieves us. Do not charge into the enemy like some crazy-ass hero. Repeat that."

They did, *crazy-ass hero* and all. She nodded, and the runners were off across the thick lawn.

"My fault," Henry said, as two boys lifted him from the ground at her feet. "Bombs didn't—"

"Rest," she said. "And your crossbows are *great*." A few more steps brought them back to the center firing pit. "Anyone left from Squad Three—"

"Sorry—"

"Shut *up*, Henry. I said *rest*. Squad Three survivors, you're in Squad Ten, under Bartie's orders, now. Bartie, hold the center pit for me, and you're Gilead's second in command for the whole force."

Whooshes and booms resounded from the sea side of the big house; flashes of light flickered behind the low rise. "Squads Nine and Eleven, back to the rally point and we'll probably keep running when we get there."

It was not a long run—back before, a high school runner would have called it "middle distance"—and they were warmed up and well into second wind, so it seemed to Highbotham that she and her little force almost flew up the hill and onto the patio. Abby had just signaled, and squads Twelve and Thirteen were running down to the beach ahead of them.

They put on a burst of speed and caught up, racing into well-rehearsed positions on the first rise above the water, between the rocket squads and the incoming boats. "Everyone down! Prone firing position!"

The force lay down instantly, wriggling forward, weapons pointed down the beach, checking mechanisms and laying out ammunition within easy reach without being ordered to.

Highbotham stayed on her feet to look the situation over. Rockets had set the lead boat on fire, but most of its crew had made it to shore; the other two were just landing, and already there were almost as many raiders as defenders. Three more boats had already rounded the point.

The voice of a long-ago instructor echoed in her head: *The first rule of repelling invasions is* act now, *because it won't get better. If you screw that one up, there is no second rule.*

Highbotham turned and shouted to Abby and Richard behind her. "Three-rocket volley into their landing! Then concentrate on the ones further out!"

Abby and Richard were yelling to their squads as Highbotham spoke quietly. "Squads Nine, Eleven, Twelve, and Thirteen, form up. Make sure you're reloaded. Stay down till the rockets go over, then we're going to rush them. Be ready." She stretched out prone. Her hands busied themselves reloading her revolver. She had just pushed the last paper cartridge in, topped it with a percussion cap, and swung the cylinder back into place when three roars of thunder overlapped scant yards above them, the white glare lighting the beach like an old-time flashbulb.

"Now!"

She felt more than saw two dozen CAM kids jump up and race forward with her. The tail flames of the three rockets shot out beyond them, wobbling and spiraling like footballs through the 200 yards.

In less than two seconds, one rocket augered into the sand about 20 feet short, exploding in a big burst that sprayed the raiders with grit and gravel but hurt them very little. The second bent upward, tumbled, and sailed out over the water.

The third hit a jackpot. Before the Daybreakers had recovered from the blinding explosion and spray of gravel, the lucky rocket's short fuse set off its 15 pounds of crude dynamite less than 10 feet off the ground, directly above the main body of Daybreakers. The rocket had flown only a fifth of its normal range, so the dynamite set off most of the fuel—a saltpeter/tallow/powdered-aluminum slurry—in a fireball 50 feet across, which flared and went black in the time of one gasp. The reeling, groping figures emerged from it with clothes and hair on fire where blazing tallow clung to them.

"Follow me!" Highbotham and her reserve squads raced down the beach. Some of the Daybreakers dove into the water, extinguishing the flames, but exposing themselves to bullets and bolts when they stood. Others ran screaming, to be run down and chopped, stabbed, or clubbed, as the islanders drove all the way to the water's edge in that first charge.

It was victory for the moment, but the additional three longboats were now close enough for a bowman in the lead one to launch inaccurate, wobbly arrows onto the shore. Abby's voice carried on the wind behind them. *"Everybody down!"*

"Down!" Highbotham echoed, and dove onto the sand. All around her she could hear the kids doing the same. Three more rockets roared over them. The beach and sea were briefly brighter than day.

One splashed to extinction without detonating. One burst early, scattering blobs of burning tallow onto the water. The last lost a fin, looped once, and fizzled into brief pathetic fire as it fell harmlessly into the sea. The Daybreakers cheered, rowing as hard as they could, much closer, now, because the rockets had taken up time when snipers might have been working.

"Crossbowmen and riflemen," Highbotham said, "pick *one* target—a helmsman or a bowman—and on my count of three, take *one* real good shot. Squads Nine and Eleven, as soon as those shots are fired, move back into a line fifty yards back. Twelve and Thirteen, fifty yards behind the first line. Backwards leapfrog, like in drills; we've *got* to give the rocketeers time to reload. All right, on—"

A *boom!* shockingly loud and close.

Highbotham looked and laughed, a little madly. "Belay all that! Pick targets and fire at will, we're winning."

Cuppa Joe, under full sail in the light land breeze, was sailing into Punnett Bay; a shot from her bow chaser had capsized the longboat nearest shore. The cannon boomed again, making a big splash in front of the next boat, which then veered when a crossbow bolt struck the steersman in the face, knocking him backwards into the sea. Another shot from *Cuppa Joe* holed the boat, sinking it in seconds.

The last boat was pulling south, either running away or trying for a flank attack. *Cuppa Joe* fired again, capsizing it.

As heads bobbed up in the bay, crossbowmen began picking them off. *We really should talk about taking prisoners, soon.*

Morse blinked from the stern of *Cuppa Joe*; it wasn't encrypted, so Highbotham and everyone read it together. TOWN MILITIA ARRIVING. CJ PROCEEDING COAKLEY. GOOD HUNTING.

Highbotham walked slowly back up the beach. The sounds from the landward side were no longer of battle but of rout. The absence of chanting and drums, and the rhythm of volley fire, told her that the Daybreakers who had overstayed were trapped between the fence and the town militia.

As she arrived at Abby's rocket station, she heard no more volleys, just wailing from the few Daybreakers left alive. A few of those could be rehabilitated in their seizure-recovery phases, according to the latest Jamesgram; the Christiansted town council had voted to try it the next time they had prisoners. Scattered distant shots meant pursuit continued.

Highbotham couldn't hear waves hissing down the shore, and some people's mouths were moving without her being able to understand them; *ear protection for everyone, one more thing to think about soon.* Right now she just needed to report to Murcheson, who commanded overall island defense, and "get everyone to bed, Abby, as soon as you can."

Abby looked up from where they were swabbing out rocket tubes. "Right, Captain. Richard's already taken a party to go bring the little kids back."

"Good job on the rockets," Highbotham said. "Good job on everything."

Abby nodded; in the moonlight her hair was almost phosphorescent, and her face was streaked ghostly white and black from the soot of her rocket launching. "We can do everything here now. You'll want to get the land side squared away, and then get down to C-sted for the commanders' meeting."

"Yeah. Tired."

"Well, we were fighting for nearly four hours, Captain. That's false dawn over east." Abby took a deep drink from her water bottle.

That reminded Highbotham to drink from her own. "I'm kind of disturbed that none of our kids gives any of the enemy a chance to surrender."

Abby shook her head. "You spent too many years hanging out with the boys, Captain. This is a woman kind of fight—if you're going to kill each other, *kill* each other, no good-sport bullshit like it's a football game or a deer hunt." Among the smears of soot on her face, a toothy grin glinted in the dim light. "Besides, you haven't seen yourself yet, but you've been wiping that cutlass on your pants, and your shirt's got so much black-powder smoke and blood on it, you look like something straight out of hell. At least wash up before you try to teach the kids about the Geneva Conventions."

As she walked back to the main house, Highbotham noticed Jebby Surdyke holding her hand. "I waan learn dat Ge-ne-va Con-vic-tion," she said, "if you waan me a learn."

Highbotham smiled. "Later, honey, but you'll learn it, I promise. It's part of that civilization thing we're working on bringing back. And speaking of civilization, we all need some breakfast and cleanup. Shouldn't you be with Squad Nine?"

"They don gimme no squad so I go wid yah." Jebby's hand closed on hers a little tighter.

Highbotham thought, *Well, I'm not going to scold a first-rate bodyguard for not following procedure. Some parts of civilization can wait.*

3 HOURS LATER. PUEBLO. ABOUT 6:30 AM MOUNTAIN TIME. FRIDAY, JANUARY 9, 2026.

When James Hendrix heard the knock at the door, he had just pulled two trays of muffins from the oven. *Patrick and Ntale, of course.* Lately Patrick had been teasing him every day with *Don't shoot, it's me, oh wait, where's your gun?* so this time he carefully took his pistol from its rack by the door, pointed to the side to avoid accidents, and opened the door.

Patrick grinned at seeing the pistol. "Hey, Ms. O'Grainne was right, Mister Hendrix, we're finally getting you trained."

James racked the pistol again. "Enter, my young trainer."

"Lock that door," Ntale said, following her brother in. "If tribals barge in here and kill us all, no more muffins."

"Excellent point," James said. *Back before I was always a little intimi-*

dated by how fast kids picked up new technology; now it's the same thing with security. "Nothing new this time," he said, apologetically, "just oat-and-corn muffins with some dried apple again, and some leftover elk stew."

Patrick, tall for fifteen and seeming to be mostly head and feet, laughed. "Mister Hendrix, it's *hot breakfast.*"

"And help on the homework," Ntale added.

While the brother and sister ate, James scanned through the overnight dispatches; the excuse for Patrick and Ntale to come here every morning was to deliver the first package of received radio messages from Incoming Crypto. *Besides, nothing is better for a cook's ego than a teenage appetite,* he thought, watching the food vanish into the kids.

First item on the top priority list: the moon gun had fired again. Word would already be going out everywhere to prepare for an EMP sometime Monday, and normally it would have been no more than a small nuisance to think about, but Captain Highbotham's note made him stop and think; there weren't any big stationary radio stations anymore. What the hell had they shot at?

Red Dog, in Athens, reported that Jenny Whilmire Grayson was clearly siding with her husband and against her father, and people had overheard her quarreling with Reverend Whilmire in public. James rated that a plus; if the Army won its struggle with the Church, Constitutional restoration became easier.

White Fang in Manbrookstat had details about the Commandant's deal granting away everything from Cape Cod to Niagara to Halifax to the Irish. The Commandant's handpicked judge had refused habeas corpus for a jailed opposition newspaper editor. *Not good.*

Bambi and Quattro wanted his thoughts about their scheme to hand over taxing authority to a legislature, *not easy when you're already a Duke and a Duchess and most Californians would be happy to make you the King and Queen.*

Blue Heeler said he saw no prospect of avoiding the Provi government in Olympia declaring a deliberate policy of genocide against the tribes. Allie Sok Banh had left all idea of restraint behind after fighting off Day-break's assault on her mind just a few months ago, and since she was First Lady, Chief of Staff, Secretary of State, and almost any other job she wanted, only her opinion really mattered. President Weisbrod was too weak and tired, and General Norm McIntyre too afraid, to restrain her.

Five pieces moved, James thought. *The Commandant moves for more power, the Duke and Duchess move for less, Allie Sok Banh moves for vengeance, Jenny Grayson moves for independence, and Daybreak moves, but I don't know why. It's a big, complicated board.*

He looked up to see the last of breakfast disappearing into his brother-and-sister messengers. "So," he said, "how's that *Hamlet* thing doing, Patrick?"

"I just wish I could figure out why that guy does anything."

"You have all the evidence anyone else does."

"Anyone else doesn't have to be graded by Mrs. Thrammer. And how can there be so much evidence and no conclusion, anyway?"

"Get used to that question," James said. "Expect to be asking it forever."

THREE:
NINETEEN RED CARDS

3 DAYS LATER. PUEBLO. 6:30 AM MOUNTAIN TIME.
MONDAY, JANUARY 12, 2026.

In Pueblo, the lockdown against the impending EMP had begun at 8:00 Sunday night and would continue until 2:00 this afternoon. For most people in the still-civilized parts of the Earth a lockdown was a chance to sleep in, with nothing to do but wait to hear that the EMP had fallen somewhere else before disconnecting all the protective grounds, taking the precious surviving gear out of its metal boxes, and resuming work. For a few people the lockdown meant a tense fire watch, but probably their concern was unnecessary: Pueblo went on and off the air briefly, at low power, much less than had ever been known to draw the moon gun's fire before.

So this should have been sort of a nuclear-electronic snow day, Heather thought. *Too bad Leo's not verbal yet, so he missed the memo, and still expects his feeding on time.*

Heather poked up the fire, and her little room underneath her office was cozy as she dragged her rocking chair over to the west window, perfect for watching the sunlight creep down the Wet Mountains.

She had been rocking for a few minutes, humming something silly to Leo, watching the stars fade and the sky creep from black to indigo, when the snow on the far-off mountains turned for an instant to burning silver, and the twilight-muted red, yellow, and brown bricks of Pueblo flashed in a second of full color.

Heather was already on her feet before she realized she'd heard crackling and smelled ozone. She set Leo down in his crib, grabbed the bucket, and poured sand over the glowing-red ground wire that connected her old metal filing cabinet to a water pipe. Watching to see that the wire didn't smolder or flare, standing well back in case of a residual charge, she pulled her sweater down and picked up the wailing Leo. "Brekkers is interrupted, buddy, we gotta—"

A knock. "Ms. O'Grainne, sorry, but we're evacuating—"

"On my way."

She pulled on her boots, coat, and hat, put another blanket around Leo. In the stairwell, the ozone odor was strong, but without much smoke—yet, anyway.

Outside, the sun was still not quite above the horizon; the last upper edge of the crescent moon was a parenthesis enclosing the mountains. The first whispers of the east dawn wind were crisply chilly. She squeezed her tube of documents under her arm, freeing a hand to tuck Leo's blanket.

"This is *really* bad news." Ruth Odawa, her Chief of Cryptography, was standing beside her. "They've never targeted Pueblo before; they always just aimed at radio sources, and we were careful to stay fairly quiet. So now the moon gun knows we're important."

Lyndon Phat joined them. "Wow, it's cold out here this—"

"People, listen up!" Kendall, the area's Emergency Action Coordinator, was a stocky African-American woman who had been an MP at Fort Carson back before. "Mister Mendoza from the railroad says they've got a locomotive spot-welded into place on the main narrow gauge track, and they need a lot of hands on ropes and levers—"

Gunshot.

Phat said, "Down," and guided Heather onto the hard-packed snow, her body sheltering Leo.

Two more shots. A man shouted, "Mother Earth! Mother *Earth*! *Mother*—"

Another shot.

Yells and shrieks. She clutched Leo close and stayed down, trying to look around, but seeing only hurrying feet and huddled backs.

An eternity later, Phat helped her to her feet. "Captain Kendall wants us to go to a safe house under guard," General Phat said. "She is perturbed because I tackled the shooter."

Heather smothered her exasperated scream into a croak. "Has it occurred to you that that was probably an *assassin*, and *you* are the most assassinatable person here, and you ran *toward* him?"

"I thought of that just after I took him down."

"May I quote you on that?"

They turned and saw Cassie Cartland, the editor of the *Pueblo Post-Times*. Her brown hair had grown out from a practical pixie to an expedient shag in the last year, so that now she looked her actual age—seventeen—rather than several years younger. When Chris Manckiewicz had gone with Mensche on the long traverse of the Lost Quarter last fall, she'd taken over and run the *Post-Times* well enough so that on his return, he'd just left Cassie in charge. "Any tips for your fans about how to take down terrorists bare-handed, General Phat?"

"It was an act of complete irresponsible idiocy."

She grinned. "Just let me get that down and read it back."

Heather said, "Wow, the world has changed. Back before, nobody running for president would have dared to say anything like that."

"Also," Phat said, "an ugly runt, to quote my ex-wife, has a chance of winning a presidential election. You can quote that too, Cassie—on one condition. I want a news story that says 'General urges common sense in walling city,' and run it alongside a map I'll lay out for you. It's a disgrace we don't have a city wall yet, and City Council is a bunch of whistleheads who need to get their job done. Quote me on that too, or the deal is off. Clear?"

"Clear." She shook her head and brought her pencil back to her pad. "Now, what do you all see as the role of Pueblo under the Restored Republic, and do you think there will be more job opportunities locally?"

**5 DAYS LATER. MOSCOW, IDAHO. 2:30 PM MOUNTAIN TIME.
SATURDAY, JANUARY 17, 2026.**

Darcage heard footsteps. The door opened, sudden bright light hurting his eyes. Guards unbound him from his bunk, dragged him from the train, shoved him along the broken pavement of the platform. Big hands grabbed his arms and dragged him onto his back in the bed of a wagon.

As he rode through the streets, he pressed his bound hands awkwardly against his face to block the sunlight, sobbing to recover his breath, until his eyes adjusted; as soon as he could bear it he stared into the deep blue sky and let himself feel sun on his face, sucking in the freezing air. It had been so long.

When the wagon halted, they flung him headlong off the tail-gate, catching him with his face barely off the pavement, laughing at his wince.

He was pushed up a flight of stairs and through a building door. Inside, they yanked him by the arms up three more flights of stairs and through several doors till, without pity or apology, they dropped him onto the floor near the rostrum of a college lecture hall.

She was there.

Beautiful and elegant as ever, Allie Sok Banh wore a handmade linen suit that must have taken someone two weeks to sew. "Take the gag off. Turn him to face the room."

The people chained to the seats were leaders, counselors, and shamans among the tribes of the Hells Canyon area. Darcage had met most of them when he carried messages to them from the Guardian on the Moon. If anyone had been going to rescue him, it would have been ordered by one of these—

"I am so glad you are all here," Allie said from the podium. "I only wish the rest of your tribes were, as well." She barked a forced laugh through bared teeth. "When I invited you to negotiate, I was lying. We do lie to terrorists, criminals, and traitors, but here's the truth: you are here to witness that the United States does not negotiate with criminals or terrorists, regardless of what silly stories you make up about yourselves. The United

States and the Constitution are real. Mother Gaia and the tribes are made up. We're here to show you that."

"Now, Mister Darcage here, as you know, was my controller during the time when Daybreak invaded my mind. I am paying him back for that, *personally*—when someone attempts to seize my personality, that is *personal*."

She held out her hand. A guard put a pistol into it. She walked to Darcage and held it a handsbreadth from his head, pointed directly into his left eye. "Darcage, you will say, 'Daybreak is a lie,' before I count down from five. Five." She paused, drew a breath, and with curious gentleness, brushed the muzzle of the gun against his eyelids, making him blink, before pulling it back a bare inch. "Three-*one!*" The hammer slapped closed.

The inside of his head rang with a high-pitched whistle, drowning out every other sound. Everything in his vision had a bright blinding rainbow-hued halo. His mouth opened so far it hurt his jaw, and his vocal cords were in dry agony as he forced all his air back and forth through them with all his strength. The world rolled madly.

He woke with his face chafed and sore from weeping, thinking, *She fast counted, then dry-fired.*

He had probably only been out for a minute or two. Allison Sok Banh was explaining, "—no use to us; he does not exhibit the brief lucid post-seizure period that less thoroughly indoctrinated Daybreakers do, so we cannot free him from Daybreak. We will try to induce a Daybreak seizure in all of you. If you emerge like Darcage here, without enough of your old self for our doctors to work with, we will hold a short, fair trial and hang you. We'll do the same if you successfully resist going into a seizure. But if you emerge able to communicate, we will attempt rehabilitation."

Somewhere out in the seats, someone asked, "And our proposals—"

"You may take this as our answer."

Darcage's mind retreated toward the gentle, cool press of linoleum against his face, crossing over into the schoolroom smell of remembered childhood, and down into deep unconsciousness.

THE NEXT DAY. CASTLE LARSEN (NEAR THE FORMER JENNER, CALIFORNIA). 3:30 PM PACIFIC TIME. SUNDAY, JANUARY 18, 2026.

Five days before their coronation as Duke and Duchess of California—a consolidation of fiefs and titles for their hypothetical future children to inherit—the Countess of the South Coast and the Earl of the Russian River were walking together on the rammed-earth fortress wall of Castle Larsen, *laying some awe and majesty on the locals*, as Quattro called it. "What I don't get is the way they act like they *like* it," he said. "Before Daybreak I'd ride my bicycle down to Sandy's place for a hamburger and ice cream, and she'd be, like, 'What'll it be, Quattro?' all friendly but nothing special. Now she yells at her help to set up the private room for the Earl, and you can tell she's getting off on how grand that is, and once they Duke me, she'll probably roll out a literal red carpet with a bunch of guys in tights blowing horns." He stopped to watch a Newberry Dieselplane taxi down the runway, turn around, and taxi back; his technicians were testing ND-3, the third one built. "Nowadays I can't even test-fly my own new airplanes."

"Quattro, they'd rather bet their families' lives on the Earl of the Russian River, or better yet the Duke of California, than on that rich surfer dude up the road, you know?"

"Yeah, I do know. I just hate having to be the most responsible man in California when there are airplanes to fly and adventures to have."

"Me too. But Heather needs a loyal Duck and a trustworthy Doochess to get the country glued back together, and like it or not, that's us. Now keep laying on the awe."

She guided him away from the side of the parapet that faced the airfield; no sense rubbing his nose in his frustrations. From the sea side, they watched the Russian River pour down between the snow-covered, deep green banks. The chilly wet long winter had been good for grass, but the extra rain had brought down huge loads of mud.

Quattro looked out over the new land forming in the sea. "With the grass and brush to secure all this silt, Goat Rock Beach will end up as a lea, but there'll be another beach beyond it, and people will love that too. This is going to be a good place."

THE LAST PRESIDENT 57

"As far as I'm concerned it already is."

"Yeah." He pulled his cloak closer around him. "Bambi, it's so beautiful here, and I'm so proud of what we've been able to do." His arm extended toward the fields of snow-spattered deep green, then swung out to encompass the docks along the river, the many smoking chimneys in Jenner, and back to the awe-inspiring ocean and coast. "If anything happens to me—"

Against the spitting wind, Bambi shielded her face on his chest. "Morbid morbid morbid."

A big slow wave curled in, breaking over the new sandbars. Sea lions hurried out of the way.

He sighed, and folded his arm back over Bambi. "You're right, I'm being morbid. And I've got no reason to. Just, right this second, I'm not feeling lucky."

15 HOURS LATER. SAVANNAH, GEORGIA. 11:15 AM EASTERN TIME. MONDAY, JANUARY 19, 2026.

"Back before, I hated to admit I knew what a sailboat *was*. *Ferengi* was like Pop incarnate—a Hudson River schooner, *much too* authentic of a replica," Whorf said, "every bit as much heavy physical labor as the original. It was what you'd expect from a super-achieving overcompensating Nerd of Color. I mean, good god, he named his kids Deanna, Geordie, Whorf, and Uhura, even if Mom made him compromise about how he spelled a couple of them so it wouldn't be so obvious."

Whorf was splitting a fish-and-okra pizza, the only thing on the menu, with Ihor Reshetnyk, the other scholar-sailor who had joined the ship in Manbrookstat. Not to be outpaced, Whorf took a large piece and took another couple of bites before continuing. "It embarrassed the shit out of a five-A like me, the most humiliating—"

"Whoa up, homie." Ihor was working on his American slang. "What is a five-A?"

"From a TV series a few years ago. Affluent artistic achiever African-American. Snobby black teenager who pretends not to know pop culture, talks a lot about being authentic, into jazz and the Harlem Renaissance and Spike Lee and all that. Looking back it was strictly a pose to piss off Pop." He took another bite of the hot, chewy pizza. "I'm horrified at how good this is."

"*And* we don't have to wash dishes!" Ihor tore off another slice. "Sailing wasn't no hobby with my whole family, we *all* followed the sea. That's how you say it, like Conrad?"

"'Followed the sea' is right, but that should be something like 'wasn't just' or 'wasn't merely.'"

"Sailing *wasn't merely* a hobby to my family. I like 'merely.' We all followed the sea. We followed it right out of Odessa—you live in Odessa, you figure out real young, *out* is the direction you want to go. And now I'm away from my family. That Captain Halleck, he's strict, right?"

"'Strict' is the word."

"But he don't—*doesn't*—hit and he says what it's about. How I know I'm not with my family, eh? I was surprised my old man, he said, go with my blessing. Like he liked me."

Whorf thought, *If I don't change the subject away from family I'm going to be homesick.* He checked his pocket watch. "We should probably start walking. Some policeman might decide he doesn't care about our uniforms, and decide to notice we don't have a Chapel Pass."

"Right." Ihor rose and gazed at the scattered crumbs that were all that was left of the pizza. "The tide'll turn in three hours, and I don't think the Captain will want to bail us out of the slutter."

"The slut—oh, the *slammer*. I can sure tell where *your* mind is, dude. You *wish* they'd throw us in the slutter." That was the only area of endeavor valued by young men in which Whorf felt superior to Ihor.

Ihor laughed. "If they were going to do *that*, they should've did it—should have *done* it first thing this week so we'd have time to enjoy it. Anyhow, I don't know English, but I do know tides, and it's time to go, eh?"

The white ship gleamed at the far end of the street like the future itself. "With you all the way."

**3 DAYS LATER. PUEBLO. 12:15 PM MOUNTAIN TIME.
THURSDAY, JANUARY 22, 2026.**

Back before, Johanna Schrenck had run a diner in downtown Pueblo for twenty years, sold it when her husband retired, and spent ten years working on a fresh-game cookbook by cooking all the things her husband caught or shot. But when the modern world had stopped working, so had Kurt Schrenck's pacemaker.

Johanna had come home from the funeral, hauled up the old hand tools from the basement, paid orphaned kids with food and worked harder than any of them, and in a few weeks had converted her big old house back to a wood-fired kitchen, gravity coal furnace, and candle sconces. Just after the first EMP had destroyed the tech center at Pittsburgh, she had opened Johanna's What There Is.

Since the Reconstruction Research Center had opened half a mile away, "this old frame house has hosted a lot of history," Heather remarked as she sat down to dinner with James Hendrix and Lyndon Phat. "Today what there is, is elk stroganoff and trout cakes on polenta."

James beamed. "History and current events in one convenient lunch—"

"Oh, god, you brought the critic," Johanna said, stopping at their table; she generally waited the exclusive upstairs back room herself.

James protested. "I've never said—"

"You think loudly. When I finally give you what you deserve, your last thoughts will be 'needs more coriander to balance the strychnine.' First course today is raccoon bisque, coming up." She hurried away.

"Listen." Phat held up a palm. Rumble and clatter in the distance. "They started knocking down old buildings for the wall this morning. In a few weeks, I'll be able to go to bed knowing ten guys on horses can't ride in, shoot the watch, and throw a bomb through my window."

"Except the Daybreakers don't like horses or guns," Heather said.

"It's not just Daybreakers. Grayson might send someone; he assassinated poor old Cam Nguyen-Peters. I certainly would not put it past Allie Sok Banh. And there are rich men here in Pueblo angry about where I put the wall."

"But they're *inside* the wall—"

"Once the wall is built, it'll be obvious if it's an inside job. And a rich man without a fall guy is a cowardly thing indeed, as Thucydides could tell you."

Heather laughed. "You and Graham Weisbrod would have understood each other. He wanted all us policy wonks to be able to debate the tax code by teasing out the wisdom in something Marcus Aurelius said to Socrates—"

"Ouch," James said.

"What?"

"Marcus Aurelius lived about as long after Socrates as we do after Columbus."

"Whatever. I'm still thinking about what you guys said about the ancient rhythm coming back. I liked it better when the past was history."

Phat seemed to be listening to a faint, far away voice, perhaps from the distant mountains. "Maybe the past still is history, but the great joke on all of us is that it is, maybe, not the history it was before."

4 DAYS LATER. CASTLE EARTHSTONE (NEAR THE FORMER TOWNS OF PALESTINE AND WARSAW, KOSCIUSKO COUNTY, INDIANA). 11:30 AM LOCAL SOLAR. MONDAY, JANUARY 26, 2026.

Robert had to love it: this time, Daybreak had sent him a chick. The first Council of Daybreak herald, just before Christmas, had been a rude young guy with a bushy beard who came in giving orders like a highway cop ticketing your expired plate. The second herald, a couple weeks ago, had looked and dressed like Gandalf in the movies. And old Karl, who had founded this place, had *looked like fuckin' Santy Claus. Wonder why Daybreak hates razors?*

But Daybreak-Enchantress-Chickie's red-blonde hair, worn long and loose, looked clean and unratty. The soft white dress underneath her hooded cloak was clean and form-fitting. *And my god, that's a rack. Well, let's get the talking part done and move on to the fun part.*

They stood facing her at the outer gate of Castle Earthstone, where the barbed wire came up to a spline-curve wooden arch festooned with skulls, capped with a sign:

CASTLE EARTHSTONE
BLESS DAYBREAK
SAVE MOTHER GAIA

Robert was flanked by Bernstein, his chief steward, and Nathanson, who commanded his soldiers; behind them was an honor guard of six soldiers.

She nodded in a snotty who-are-you-anyway fashion that set his teeth on edge, even before she asked, "You are Robert Cheranko?"

"I am Lord Robert of Castle Earthstone. You may call me Lord Robert. What is your name and what is your business?" His thoughts added, *And why don't you fuckin' mind it?*

"The Council of Daybreak has charged me with a mission of grave import," she said. "Word has reached even to the Guardian on the Moon that we have heard nothing from this Castle, Mister Cheranko—"

"Lord Robert," he said.

There was a long pause. "Lord Robert, then." She drew a breath and returned to her memorized text. "Two missions have been sent, and neither has returned. We on the Council of Daybreak have heard strange stories since the death of Lord Karl, and so I am sent to demand"—she saw him touch his belt knife—"uh, to ask, uh, Lord Robert to inform us—"

"Walk into the Castle with me," he said. Carefully not looking to see if she followed, he turned and walked. A moment later, flustered, pretending she hadn't just run to catch up with him, she was walking beside him.

He glanced sideways. *Yeah, make'em bounce, baby.* He wondered how Daybreak decided who to send out. First that bush-hippie cop, then that boogie-boogie wizard man, now this big-tits spirit girl. *I guess they tried discipline, then spookiness, and now what? Sweet mama nature?*

He smiled, and saw her notice and relax slightly. *Wait till you find out.*

When the bushy-bearded cop type had started right off giving orders, and Robert had told him to shut up, he'd raised his spirit stick and spoken some gibberish, and all of Robert's men had had some kind of spaz attack.

But not Robert. He just threw a straight, hard punch, knocked the herald down, jumped on him, pulled his knife, and sliced the man's carotid. By the time Robert's deputies came out of their spaz attacks, he'd already picked out where to display the herald's head.

Not long after, one of his scouts had brought back a brochure by some Pueblo guy named James Hendrix, *A procedure for the negation of Daybreak-originated deep suggestions*, which apparently they were using in the Provi and Temper states.

He made Bernstein, Nathanson, and the rest of his inner circle practice the resisting-Daybreak tricks daily. By the time old Gandalf came along, and launched into the religious-y spiritualisticalish intoning bullshit like he was going to fucking change Robert into a fucking frog, Robert just said, "Fuck Daybreak, it's a load of shit." The herald's eyes opened in surprise, the two men escorting him reached for weapons, but Robert's men had already been on them with knives and hatchets.

He really wanted to see how this one would go.

It went *great*. When Little Miss Shamaness saw the heads of the previous heralds on posts by Robert's private drinking patio, she raised the spirit stick, but Robert plucked it from her hand and broke it over his knee. She came out of her seizure nearly mindless, the way the more severe Daybreakers tended to, and lay quietly weeping on the table while they cut her robe off.

When everyone had finished, Robert told his officers, "Give her a blanket and some moccasins and put her out on the road."

Nathanson looked startled. "We gonna let her go?"

"Yeah." To the shamaness, Robert said, "Go back to the Council, and tell them what we did to you and what we did to the ones before you. Tell them Lord Robert rules at Castle Earthstone, and Daybreak don't say he do or he don't." He grabbed her face and pointed it toward himself. "Repeat."

She did, voice low, eyes shut.

At the gate, when she didn't begin to walk right away, he hit her ass with his walking stick. That got her going; she ran up the mud-and-snow trail, blanket and hair streaming behind her pale nakedness, like a deer that feels the hounds' breath on its flanks.

"Why'd you let her go?" Bernstein asked.

"Do you think *any* of us will ever be forgiven, or allowed to come back into Daybreak, after that?" Robert asked. "Will Daybreak ever stop trying to catch us and kill us?"

Bernstein shuddered. "God, never."

"Then we're all in it together, ain't we, for good, now?" Robert clapped the shorter, older man around the shoulders. "Walk with me. We have things to talk about."

3 DAYS LATER. SOUTH OF MIAMI. 6:00 AM EASTERN TIME. THURSDAY, JANUARY 29, 2026.

"Steady, Whorf, but stay alert. The charts are pretty near worthless from Key Biscayne south," Captain Halleck said. He was comparing the air photo prints taken by the very last reconnaissance planes from USS *Bush*, two months before, with the old paper charts.

At the helm, Whorf was bringing *Discovery* into Biscayne Bay on the last of the high tide, letting it carry them in so that later the receding tide could help pull them back out. Sounding lines brought up so much muck and junk that all they really knew was that about thirty feet below them, thick muddy water became thin watery mud.

Morning wore on; when the wind shifted, the stench from the land was overpowering. Jorge relieved Whorf at eight. Not quite ready for his bunk, he went forward to see what the scientists were doing. Lisa Reyes, from Stone Lab, was fiddling with a microscope, the sort of thing that might have been a toy for a brainy eight-year-old a few decades ago. Satisfied with the light the mirror sent through the slide, she looked up, shoving stray black curls back under her bandanna. "Take a look, Whorf, and please draw." She opened her record pad beside the microscope.

Whorf stretched his shoulder, a little stiff from four hours at the wheel, and flexed his hand. He bent carefully to look without disturbing anything; one eye saw through the scope and the other saw the page. He barely had to compensate for the rise and fall of the gentle sea. Quickly, he copied the dots, whorls, smears, and blobs his left eye saw onto the pad his right eye saw.

"Beautiful," she said, as he finished. "Now, do you know what it's a picture of?"

"It's better if I don't think of words while I draw. But that looks like—hunh. Are those E. coli?"

"Well, their ancestors were. I suspect Daybreak used them because they could pass through the human gut and spread rapidly." She tapped the page. "And these?"

"A filament of pennate diatoms, right?"

"Right. I'm calling them *Phaeodactylum morticomedentis incognans*. I think I have the genus right—it's pretty similar, anyway, to the Phaeodactylum that genetic engineers had been working with for a long time, so there would have been easily available commercial versions for Daybreak to modify. The species name just means 'unknown dead-stuff-eater.' The one thing we've established in the tanks so far is that coral love them, and that at least partly solves the mystery of what's not here."

Whorf asked, "What's *not* here?"

"Yeah. Right over the horizon, we have a few million decaying bodies, plus hundreds of square miles of fertilized lawns and burned real estate, plus all those artificial materials that decayed—tires and gasoline, plastics and nylon, all that lawn furniture and all the polyester on the old people. All those nutrients lying out in the rain on soft, shifting soil must have washed down here. Biscayne Bay should be pretty much a brackish sewage lagoon, crawling with conventional decay bacteria and buried under algal blooms. Instead, those nutrients are being snaffled up by these diatoms that fast-track it into coral."

"You think Daybreak meant to do that?"

"Well, it sure looks like in the next thousand years, Florida is going to get much bigger, as all those dead people and their stuff turn into coral reefs. Doesn't that sound like a Daybreaker program?"

Whorf looked out over the barely-moving green sea. The overpowering reek brought home the realization that there was a thousand-square-mile mausoleum just over the horizon. Almost, he could imagine bony hands reaching out from the land, empty skulls staring out to sea and looking for him. "You sound like you approve."

"I don't approve of people being dead," Reyes said. "Or the world being a wreck. But I do like seeing things grow."

THE NEXT DAY. CASTLE EARTHSTONE. 7:15 AM LOCAL SOLAR. FRIDAY, JANUARY 30, 2026.

Roger Jackson had been followed for ten days, ever since walking northeast out of Pale Bluff, the last secure town on the frontier with the Lost Quarter. He was used to the shadow extending beyond the tree, the flicker of motion at the corner of his eye that wasn't a feral dog, the creak of a low branch in still air. He felt their eyes on him as he walked the empty streets of burned-out towns along the Wabash, and crossed the big bridge into the ruins of Terre Haute. When he walked along the brushy overgrown trail that followed the Tippecanoe they were still there.

He had seen no one till the sentries challenged him at the skull-festooned outer gate. After almost an hour of too many sentries, skulls, and pompous Shakespeare-Tolkienesque greetings, he now stood before Lord Robert and his . . . lordlings? flunkies? *Flunklings*, Roger decided.

Lord Robert smiled. "The door is closed, and everyone in here is past that ritual ceremony bullshit, 'kay? Let's deal. So Daybreak is your enemy. It ain't ours but it's not exactly our friend either, and we don't want it to own us like it does the tribes, got me? We've been using your James Hendrix's pamphlet about turning off the seizures, and we want whatever else you know."

Roger said, "You don't need to trade for any of that information, and you won't even if we go to war with you later. We *want* people to free themselves."

Lord Robert tightened his lips and bared his teeth. "We've broke with Daybreak, and put all our necks in the noose. We'd like to ally with the biggest thug on the block."

Roger made himself speak calmly. "Lord Robert, as long as we are being truthful, we know you, *you personally*, tortured our agent Steve Ecco to death. You're asking us to forgive a lot."

"Yeah, it's a lot to forgive." In the warm, flicking lantern light, Lord Robert's face was as innocent of lines as a little boy's. "But *you* need allies too."

After a long silence, Roger Jackson said, "What did you have in mind?" He felt slightly sick.

**4 DAYS LATER. CASTLE EARTHSTONE. 1:00 PM
LOCAL SOLAR TIME. MONDAY, FEBRUARY 2, 2026.**

Roger Jackson crouched comfortably in the slave shack where they had hidden him from view, trying not to listen to Lord Robert's speech to the people of Castle Earthstone outside in the main yard. *He's not much of a speaker, but then supposedly Moses wasn't either.*

So far it had been an hour-long bragalogue on the career of Lord Robert, Mighty in Battle. *Quite a promotion for Robert Cheranko, electric company lineman less than two years ago, to Lord Robert, Torturer and Slayer of the Tied Up and Helpless.*

The slave shack in which Roger was concealed was a lean-to against the main wall. Clean rugs and blankets were laid carefully over the pea-gravel floor; the fire pan from an old outdoor grill was embedded in one corner, with a chimney-duct making a Z shape across the ceiling to the high corner above the door. *Probably fairly efficient,* he thought. He smiled at himself for that; you could make an engineering student into a scout but you couldn't make him not be an engineering student.

When Lord Robert finished bragging about what a brave guy he was, he revealed that he was also the true interpreter of the True Daybreak of Lord Karl, which had been perverted by the Council of Daybreak. True Daybreak was opposed to poverty, misery, slavery, and forced infanticide.

I notice rape is still okay, though, Roger thought.

In a few sentences, Lord Robert freed all the slaves, granted them rights to marry and raise children, and commanded a cleanup for the boneyard of dead slaves and exposed newborns, with proper graves, a memorial, and freedom for everyone to pray and leave flowers.

Of course "for the duration of this emergency, my officers and I will still need your complete loyalty—"

The roar of applause made Roger wonder if Robert had arranged for claques. *Probably; he thought of everything else. Still, around here, a plain old feudal tyranny is reform.*

He watched through a crack in the shed as the crowd's passion and joy mounted; at the height of it, Lord Robert raised the Castle Earthstone spirit stick into the air, and the crowd shrieked with pure ecstasy.

"I free you! Follow the True Daybreak!" Robert smashed the spirit stick across his thigh, breaking it in half.

A Daybreak seizure struck two thousand people in the courtyard simultaneously, the soldiers as helpless as the slaves. Ignoring the thrashing, writhing bodies at their feet, Lord Robert's officers walked quickly to positions in the courtyard, and stood waiting for the first ones to come out of the seizure.

Lord Robert walked directly from the rostrum to Roger. "You'll want to get going before they revive." His slight smile was barely a twitch. "Tell that fat bitch in Pueblo that we'll keep talking with you. Central heat, clean sheets, and antibiotics would kind of put the fun back into being a lord, you know?"

3 DAYS LATER. PORT ST. JOE, FLORIDA. 10:15 AM CENTRAL TIME. THURSDAY, FEBRUARY 5, 2026.

Whorf held his voice low and even. "Doctor Reyes, don't move."

"Hmm?" she asked, intent on lowering her sampling jar into the pond.

The cobra reared fractionally higher, intent on her leg. Whorf said, "Don't—"

A black-powder pistol roared beside Whorf; the cobra's head vanished and the body thrashed in the grass. Reyes jumped. Ihor said, "Sorry if I startled you."

Reyes was staring at the writhing body in the brush. "Startle all you want."

"Good shot," Whorf said.

"Just had to be careful, 'cause I was only going to get one shot. Do we got—*have*—to worry about a . . . wife?"

"*Mate.* Maybe," Reyes said. "But everything I know about cobras I got from *Rikki-Tikki-Tavi.* I don't want to stay here, anyway."

They watched the brush and their feet all the way back to the crumbling pavement, where Pembrooke, their local guide, arrived huffing and panting. Running in the heat had turned him an even deeper brick red than his normal sunburn, in contrast to his white mustache, eyebrows, and soaking-wet wisps of hair slipping out from under his straw hat. "I heard a shot." He bent over, hands on his knees, to catch his breath.

Reyes said, "You said people had seen cobras near that pond? Ihor just shot one that was getting ready to strike me."

"You're sure you got it?"

Ihor nodded. "These big pistols take the head right off. It was maybe a meter, maybe more—look, he's got it!"

An eagle rose from the thicket back by the pond, something black and writhing in its talons.

Pembrooke nodded. "All fresh and wiggly, yum yum."

Whorf asked, "What are cobras doing in Florida?"

Pembrooke grimaced. "Back before, idiot collectors and dumbasses who wanted a scary pet smuggled them in. Now with Daybreak they've gotten loose. *Officially*."

Reyes nodded. "But unofficially?"

"Well, walk with me." On their way back to his house, they walked slowly because of the heat. "Since March, I've had eleven dead cobras brought in; Fish and Wildlife doesn't send me a paycheck anymore but people are used to me being the guy for invasive species. Now, the mayor used to sell used cars, and the city council's all his cousins, and the big local business was always tourism, so they want me to tell everybody we got two escaped pets out there making babies. But the old print encyclopedia I have says there's ten to thirty in a litter, they don't roam far from where they're hatched, and they're kind of shy—people would go months or years before finding out they had a pair under the house. Now I've seen eleven dead—twelve counting what that eagle was carrying off—and we've had two hundred and nine sightings, as much as forty miles apart. And three of my dead ones didn't have that spectacle pattern on the hood; based on more old paper encyclopedia research, those were Chinese cobras.

"So the official position, I guess, must be that we've got one multispecies litter of exhibitionist cobras who decided to go on tour."

"What do *you* think?" Reyes asked.

"I *would* think it was Daybreak making it hard to restart civilization, except it doesn't make sense to me that a bunch of save-Mother-Earth types would introduce invasive species."

Whorf shrugged. "They used giant H-bombs. Their moon gun is probably the highest tech still working in the solar system. And Daybreak itself was coordinated and maybe created on the Internet. They *aren't* environmentalists, at least not as we used to know them, and if they're back-to-nature it's not necessarily nature's idea of nature."

Reyes frowned, looking at her wristwatch. "Based on what we've seen all along the Florida coast, we need to assemble a report on the possibility that Daybreak is trying to re-shape the environment to make it more human-hostile. Unfortunately most of the supporting material belongs to Mister Pembrooke, who will need to keep it here for further research, so Whorf, you copy drawings, and Ihor, you copy text. We'll need to be getting back aboard when the tide turns, in six hours."

"On the other hand," Pembrooke said, "your working conditions include a fresh boiled crab lunch and nearly unlimited lemonade—warm, though, I'm afraid."

"And I suddenly realized I really should stay and help," Reyes said. "We all make sacrifices."

2 DAYS LATER. PUEBLO. 9:00 AM MOUNTAIN TIME. SATURDAY, FEBRUARY 7, 2026.

When Heather carried the big, flat object, draped in cloth, into what had once been the judge's chambers, there were three knots of people around the big table.

At one corner, the scouts lounged in their Walmart/mountain-man mixture of deerskin shirts, heavy jeans, slouch hats, and knee-high moccasin boots. Larry and Debbie Mensche, father and daughter, sat on the table; Dan Samson leaned back in a chair with his feet almost on Larry, and Freddie Pranger and Roger Jackson draped themselves sideways over the arms of the chairs.

Conveniently near the luxury of the coffee urn, Quattro, Bambi, Nancy

Teirson, Sally Overhaus, and Bret Duquesne, the aviators, stood in leather jackets, scarves, coveralls, soft moccasins, and confident wide stances, with their leather helmets under their arms or dangling by straps from their hands. Bret was explaining something complex about the southern route to Mobile Bay.

At the far end of the table from the scouts were Heather's wizards: Ruth Odawa and her academic group of codebreakers, and analysts like Chris Manckiewicz and Jason Nemarec, and librarians and archivists like Leslie Antonowicz. In old, worn suit jackets, pullover shirts, and rumpled pants, they looked like a shabby faculty club that shopped at Salvation Army. They were mostly scribbling and muttering to each other, making lists and notes, starting sentences that other people finished. All of them were constantly checking everything with James, who sat at the center of the group. *The way Arnie Yang used to,* Heather thought, with a pang. James had grown to be a close friend and he was quite possibly better at the Chief of Intel job than Arnie had been—at least he wasn't a traitor—but the lack of Arnie still felt like a missing limb. *How many times did I stop him from explaining something that we're only realizing now we needed to know? How many clues to our situation was he holding in his head, how many insights were there because our best analyst had been all the way inside Daybreak, and how much irreplaceable knowledge went through the trap in the scaffold and out of our reach forever? We were always so crazy to do something, anything, that we wouldn't listen to him. It's a miracle he ever got to tell us anything besides "I told you so."*

She had let Arnie himself talk her into hanging him, and though his reasoning had seemed right at the time, and emotionally it had made sense to execute the biggest traitor they'd ever caught, she and James had concluded later that it might have been Daybreak they had been talking to, and that it was protecting itself by eliminating the most valuable witness they had in custody.

James was in Arnie's spot; she just had to hope that neither he nor she would ever be in his situation.

She looked around again: *scouts, aviators, wizards. Like characters from too many different movies.*

Carefully, she lifted the three-by-six-foot chart onto the table, gently because she wasn't completely confident of every thumbtack and drop of glue. "Only James and General Phat have seen this before, though it's not *officially* secret. Some of you will recognize this as a grandchild, or maybe a cousin, of a critical path chart," she said. "I started it in March, when the RRC moved into Pueblo. Up here at the top is where we started from: May 2025. Here we are today in February, and down there at the bottom where it says DONE is where we're going: the day when a fully Constitutional elected government takes over, on January 20, 2027.

"These ribbons running the length of the chart are the critical paths, the connected series of things that need to be done by a certain date. Green ribbons are clear sailing, nothing blocking the path; yellow ribbons are ones where there's trouble, which usually means they end at a red card that names the trouble; red ribbons are ribbons that continue on beyond a red card, the roads we can't get to right now."

"There are no green ribbons touching DONE," Quattro Larsen observed.

"*Yet*," Heather said, quietly.

"Nineteen red cards," Leslie Antonowicz said, counting. "And none of them is trivial. SECURE BORDER OF LOST QUARTER. DISRUPT OTHER TRIBAL-HELD AREAS. EMERGENCE OF NATIONAL CONSENSUS CANDIDATE FOR PRESIDENT. GRAYSON RENOUNCES TITLE NCCC. WEISBROD RENOUNCES TITLE ACTING PRESIDENT. MANBROOKSTAT JOINS AS NEW STATE. And I hate to point this out but a lot of the worst things happening aren't on here."

"Red cards aren't necessarily the worst things happening, or the best things not happening," Heather said. "Red cards are just the things that most interfere with putting a new President and Congress in place under the Constitution. We're going to relaunch the Federal government in the middle of a famine, a civil war, and maybe the collapse of civilization.

"Objectively any of those are worse than not having a Federal government. The most comfortable parts of the country are back to about 1910 for standard of living, and in the worst-off areas we hold, it's more like 1810, and in tribal territory, it's the Dark Ages, at best. *But none of that is the RRC's concern right now.* Our job is setting up and handing off to the Restored Republic. Once we do, dealing with the mess is *their* job.

"So I have red cards about tribals, not because they're crazy, evil, and destructive bastards—although they are!—but because they will make the election difficult. I have red cards for getting Grayson to quit calling himself the NCCC, and the same deal about Weisbrod calling himself Acting President, because that makes either one of them a rallying point for sore losers to rebel against the Restored Republic in the name of the extinct one. That's also why there's a red card for finding someone that the whole country can vote for—because we also can't afford too many sore losers, and we really can't afford to have any important region with a majority of sore losers." She purposely did not look at General Phat, but she could feel everyone else did. "So this chart has nothing about collapsing dams in Nevada and Arizona, or that cattle epidemic on the Great Plains, but I have a great big red card here for the Post Raptural Church because the Tempers declared them the National Church, and another one for Manbrookstat, because they have secret police, tribunal courts, and a state monopoly on exports. An established church and a fascist police state are not necessarily worse, or better for that matter, than collapsing dams and dying cattle, but they are not allowed under the Constitution, so we can't have any such thing on January 20, 2027.

"Now, this is probably the last time we can all be together here, because we're going to be busy. We have nineteen red cards to take off this chart, somehow, in the next nine months, so that twenty-four streams of green can flow down to that magic word DONE. I have you all here because it's our last chance to talk, all together, before we plunge into it. Do we all still agree that Daybreak is planning a major tribal surge in the spring?"

Nancy Teirson spoke first. "Flying the Ohio Valley between the mouth of the Wabash and Fort Norcross, it's one big camp after another. They're packed."

Roger Jackson said, "Coming back from Castle Earthstone I saw boat and canoe convoys on the rivers, some a mile long, all headed down to the camps."

Heather took a deep breath. "Then does anyone see any reason to modify General Grayson's plan to roll spoiling attacks down the Ohio and up the Wabash?"

Phat said, "I think General Patton said it best. 'A good plan violently executed now is better than a perfect plan executed next week.'"

Heather nodded. "Grayson is already at Fort Norcross as of today."

"I flew him there on my way here," Bret Duquesne explained. "Him and his wife. Picked him up outside Athens, after they faked a departure for a vacation on the Gulf Coast."

Chris Manckiewicz added, "We don't think that deception can hold more than three days."

Heather asked Malcolm Cornwall, the only remaining meteorologist, "Forecast for the Ohio Valley for the next few days?"

"Clear and warming. Ground should stay hard another ten days; it froze pretty deep this winter. Ice will be breaking up below Uniontown in a week or two at most."

"Last chance to say stop." Heather looked around from face to face. "Ruth?"

"Everything from crypto looks like the tribals are not quite ready, and we are."

"Freddie?"

Freddie Pranger drawled, "Wabash Valley's quiet, right now. Ohio's closer to ready to move. Just a matter of they gotta carry more stuff further to set up on the Wabash, like we always figured."

"Roger?"

"No guarantees on what Lord Robert will do. He's freakin' nuts, Ms. O'Grainne. But he did just do several things that must've ticked Daybreak off pretty badly; they won't be eager to be buddies with him again for a while."

James Hendrix said, softly, "Agents in Athens, Olympia, Manbrook-stat, San Antonio, and Tallahassee are reporting all the major decision makers are either with the program or at least won't interfere. We're as united as we are ever likely to be."

"One more time, do I hear a 'wait'?" Heather asked.

She watched the clock on the mantel, whose second hand was just crossing the two, and told herself *wait, listen, give them a chance.* It was so quiet that she heard every tick of the clock.

Just as the second hand crossed eight, Phat spoke. "So we don't wait. Time to go. The die is cast."

Slowly, emphatically, loudly, Larry Mensche began to clap, and the rest joined in.

FOUR:
HOW BEAUTIFUL ARE THE FEET

The eight pilots arrived in a group, as had been agreed; silently, Ruth Odawa handed each of them a batch of encrypted messages, and working together, they all verified, one more time, where each encrypted message was to go. When they finished, the pilots rode to the airfield in two wagons, each escorted by a squad of militia. No one spoke an unnecessary word.

At the field, there were handshakes, taps on the shoulder, pats on the back, and then each pilot walked to a plane.

Three hours before dawn, Pueblo was bitter cold but windless. Nancy Teirson's homebuilt Acro Sport led the taxiing parade of aircraft around to the wait point. *This will tell everyone that something is up,* she thought. *Eight planes all taking off one after the other.* And *they've turned the runway lights on; they'll be wiping them with lye for weeks after this. Must've been at least a year since anyone in America saw a mass takeoff at night.*

She turned for a moment and waved at Bambi Castro, in the Curtiss JNE in line behind her; Bambi waved back. It helped Nancy feel slightly less alone.

Then the first flagger advanced to the line, raised both flags, and lowered them in parallel to point down the runway. Nancy opened the throttle slightly and depressed the left rudder pedal. Her tiny biplane waddled toward the next flagger, who held up his left flag and motioned downward with his right. Nancy watched the flagger, who watched the tower.

In the corner of her eye, Nancy saw a light flash in the tower window.

Facing Nancy, the flagger brought his left flag to his side and raised his right with the elbow bent at a right angle. With both flags in his left hand at his side, he saluted.

Nancy opened the throttle and roared along the runway, the oiled-linen tires feeling squishy and draggy even when freshly inflated. The Acro Sport seemed to bound forward and up from the pavement; in a shallow climb as the end of the runway passed 300 feet below, she banked to head east.

The slightly-more-than-half moon behind her, halfway down the western sky, shed more than enough light to distinguish US-24 and follow it through the snowy plains to Garden City; now and then there were other lights. A few windows shone in the walled towns. Dark blobs of cattle herds surrounded the fires in the cowboy camps. Twice she saw makeshift camps that might have been tribals or refugees, and made notes to help cavalry patrols locate them, but tonight she did not circle and sketch; she held her course, east over the old highway, and the moon slowly sank till it was on her tail.

In the pre-dawn twilight, she came in over the earthen ramparts of Garden City, waving back to the night sentry in his rooftop shelter.

The crew dragged the little red and yellow biplane into the hangar. They would refuel it, wipe its engine with lye, and go over every inch of it looking for crusty white nanospawn. Another day she might have gone with them to help, but today she hurried to the old stone house across the airfield, the local Jayhawk Guard commander's office.

He opened the door with a broad smile, and gestured for her to sit at the table pulled up close to the fireplace; she gulped a bowl of shredded beef chili with eggs over cornmeal mush while he worked the coding. "How beautiful are the feet," he muttered, looking at the message.

"Unh?"

He grinned. "Preacher's kid can't help quoting. It's from Isaiah. 'How beautiful upon the mountains are the feet of him that bringeth good tidings, that publisheth peace.' But I kind of like the blasphemous version, 'How beautiful over Kansas is the biplane of she that bringeth good tidings, that declareth war.' Take this message back to them: RECEIVED BREAK 'BOUT TIME BREAK MOVING ASAP FULL STOP. They might not know Isaiah."

In less than half an hour, she took off again, climbing into the light, fitful west wind, wheeling around toward sunrise in a wide semicircle.

As she flew on, the sun ascended between columns of smoke from the chimneys of newly reoccupied farmhouses; it looked more like 1876 than 2026. Farmyards bustled with people feeding poultry, chopping wood, and pumping water. Wagons bumped over potholed roads. Herders on horseback in heavy cloaks drove cattle and sheep out into the winter pasture. *At least, only flying at a quarter of the speed and altitude that planes used to, I get to see it all.* A stream of coal smoke revealed a train passing far to her north.

The sun was high when the Ozarks rose beneath her. In Springfield, Missouri, lunch was noodles and rabbit with hot, milky tea, in the kitchen of the RRC's new station chief, Paul Ferrier.

As Nancy finished her meal, he looked up from his code pad. "Tell Heather that it's crazy busy here, but the Ozark and Ouachita tribals have pulled some pretty gruesome shit in raids lately. I think I can get public opinion behind calling up the militia and sending out some big punitive raids into tribal country in early March. Sorry we can't do it sooner—we're up to our ass in alligators with trying to get ready for having the whole Federal government move in by the end of the year."

"We all do what we can," Nancy said. James had given the pilots that generic response for any message recipient who sounded less than enthusiastic, and besides, in Ferrier's case, it was true.

Airborne again in the early afternoon, she flew over the wooded hills of southern Missouri to Poplar Bluff. The country grew less harsh and richer; spring was greening the land and lifting it out of the snow below her.

In Poplar Bluff the militia commander was out with a cavalry detachment, intercepting a tribal incursion coming up from Arkansas. She tried to explain that when their commander read the message, he would understand why she hadn't been able to take a few hours out and go scout for them, but they seemed unconvinced and resentful, so she took off again as soon as she could, firmly telling them that the message needed to be decrypted as soon as possible, and everything would be clearer once it was.

Crossing the Mississippi, with Cairo just to her left, Nancy saw big floes of ice coming down the Ohio, groaning and booming as they collided with floes from the upper Mississippi and the Missouri above St. Charles Rock, and scribbled a note to alert the downstream towns that still had standing bridges; the radio operator at Pale Bluff could send that for her.

Up the Ohio Valley, snow still lay deep and the river was still frozen. At the Uniontown Dam, she turned north-by-northeast, and descended over the winter-bare apple orchards into Pale Bluff just before 4 p.m. Carol May Kloster, the RRC station chief there, ran the central station for the whole Wabash front, and also reported for the *Pueblo Post-Times*, so she was probably the busiest person on this frontier of civilization. But she had found time to make a quiche and a dried-apple pie, and most of both went into Nancy, along with an unexpected treat: a whole pot of real, fresh coffee. "I have plenty," Carol May said. "And you look tired."

"I love my Acro Sport with all my heart," Nancy said, "built it all with my own hands after Daybreak, and it gets me out of militia drill and digging ditches, so I don't feel like I can complain about it. But it does feel like being shaken inside a kite with a running lawnmower engine in my lap. And with no hydraulics, I feel every bit of the wind I touch." She drank deeply from her coffee cup. "This stuff puts heart into you; no wonder our first post-Daybreak plutocrat is Lisa Fanchion. I usually only get coffee when I pass through Pueblo, every couple of weeks."

Carol May smiled. "I'm just glad to see it go to good use. Quattro keeps me supplied, every week when he passes through in the Gooney Express, and I use it to lure the local Temper and Provi spies in here; a little access to good coffee and they blab everything they know."

Carol May's pencil played over the decoding grid as she copied numbers from the one-time pad, added, and wrote the string of new numbers into the green strip for the clear message. When she read it, she said, "I was going to suggest that you just hold off flying to Put-In-Bay and stay the night in my guest room, but now that I see what this is about, I guess not. You'll want to get moving while it's light."

Shadows grew long below her as Nancy flew northwest across the Lost Quarter. No light shone from the abandoned farms and burned-out towns of what had been Indiana and Ohio. Here and there, she saw a wide trampled track in the late afternoon sunlight, rising smoke from campfires, or a still-standing bridge, and would lock the controls and make reconnaissance notes; those were much more important here, over hostile territory, than they had been in Kansas.

It was deep twilight when she passed over the lights of Catawba Point and the little settlements around Sandusky Bay. To her left, Lake Erie was still frozen over, with occasional patches of dark, open water. She circled wide to come into Put-In-Bay with a headwind; from a few hundred feet up, she could clearly see the burned sleds and huts on the ice where the islanders had intercepted a tribal attack across the frozen lake.

The runway was freshly shoveled and graveled, a good thing since she was landing in late twilight; when she killed the engine on the tiny Acro Sport, and saw the ground crew running up to tow it into the hangar, she realized her shoulder blades were sore from tension and her clothes under her flying leathers were soaked with sweat. *Just like running a marathon, it's the last long haul that kicks your ass.*

Fred Rhodes, the head of Stone Lab, was an old friend, and he was waiting with the ground crew. With his very dark skin, dreads, chest-length beard, and multiple colorful sweaters and caps, he looked like a Rastafarian with a compulsively-knitting Dadaist grandmother. "Right this way," he said. "You're here, you're alive, so by modern standards I guess you had a good flight." They walked across the field to his horse-drawn sleigh. She accepted blankets and a towel-wrapped pot of hot mulled wine gratefully. "Drink it all," he said, "I need to stay sober to do my calculations. I brought my one-time pad with me, and I want to confirm that this is what I think it is."

As they clopped along and Nancy sank into the warmth inside and outside, she noticed that Fred wasn't bothering to look at the road, and a little bit of a tune from childhood came to mind—*the horse knows the way to carry the sleigh.* It made her think of the smell of an overheated school-room, and she wondered if anywhere smelled like that anymore, or ever would again.

Rhodes finished his calculations as they were pulling up at the Edge-water Hotel. "You go check in, they're expecting you," Rhodes said. "I'll give you an hour to freshen if you need it."

"Make that half an hour," she said, "so I can stagger to bed sooner."

"Fair enough. You're having dinner with me, Rosie and Barb Rosen-stern, and Scott and Ruth Niskala. It won't go long but we need to pull our intel together." He grabbed her bag before she could. "Do you know what's in the message?"

"They kept the details from us in case we were forced down." Exhausted, and relaxed by the wine, Nancy shuffled after him. "My notes are pretty clear, maybe I could give them to—"

"Did they tell you we're starting *now*?"

The lobby of the Edgewater, lit by soft yellow oil lamp light, abruptly sprang into harsh relief, and she felt herself stand straight, as if with a click. "I'll throw my bag into the room. Give me five minutes for the bath-room, then let's get your planning dinner started."

ABOUT THE SAME TIME. FORT NORCROSS (ON THE OHIO RIVER, NEAR WARSAW, KENTUCKY). 6:30 PM EASTERN TIME. SUNDAY, FEBRUARY 8, 2026.

In the clear twilight, Bambi Castro could see the runway, a black slash of carefully cleared and graveled highway, while she was still several miles from Grayson's camp. The JNE seemed to like the chilly, wet, dense air, which made the engine run well and gave the wings a little extra lift. *Of course, that's till it freezes the fuel line and ices the wings, which it would be doing if it were any colder. Glad I'm landing now.*

As the ground crew took over the plane, General Grayson rode up on a white stallion. *Well, now, that's putting your symbolism in order,* Bambi thought. Behind him, his wife, Jenny, rode a palomino that Bambi immediately pegged as *the horse every girl wanted when she was twelve*, and led a gray-and-white pinto, already saddled.

Feeling like she should salute—the general was in faultless-as-far-as-Bambi-could-tell uniform—she handed over the message. He accepted with that annoying, mocking smile of his. "Are you going to make me wait till it's processed through crypto, or can you just tell me if it's what I've been expecting?"

Security violation be damned, Bambi thought, *give him every spare second we can*. "Yes, it's exactly what you're expecting."

"In that case," he said, "I'll turn you over to Jenny, who will entertain you for dinner; I've got a long night ahead of me. Thank you for bringing such good news." He mounted again and rode off at a fast trot.

Bambi had met Jenny Whilmire Grayson a few times before, and tried hard not to detest her because she understood her so well: they had both been the beloved, brainy, spoiled-but-pushed, beautiful daughters of famous, spectacularly wealthy fathers. *But I used the head start Daddy gave me to become a Fed and go bust bad guys for thrills, and Jenny used those boobs and that hair for a shot at being the First Lady.*

Meow, and stop that, Bambi reminded herself sternly.

Jenny said, "I told Jeff that there was no way that Harrison Castro's daughter wouldn't be an expert horsewoman, so I just brought along Splash here, but I thought you'd have more recent practice on airplanes, so in case I was wrong I brought a horse that's more docile than most armchairs."

"Daddy made me learn to ride," Bambi said, "but the truth is I was a lot more in love with the Porsche and the sailboat than I ever was with the horse."

"Oh yeah. I would *so* have agreed with you when I was sixteen. If there were still Porsches, I'd *still* agree with you. But since you can ride, let's get to dinner. Our cook Luther is kind of a genius, and he won't have many more chances to show off till the campaign's over."

They rode for several minutes in silence. At the gate to the airfield, one of the younger soldiers started to salute and caught himself. Jenny grinned. "You go saluting the wrong person too often and my husband'll catch you."

"Yes, ma'am, I'm sorry, won't happen again."

After another block, safely out of earshot of the sentries, Jenny sighed and said, "The regular Army held together pretty well down south around the big bases, but as for the militia, Jeff says we're back to recruiting cannon fodder, and forget esprit de corps, they're just thrilled to have a job, regular food, and someone to tell them what to do. The regular Army sergeants that are all captains now have terrified the militia boys into saluting, but they're not so good on who or what yet."

"Pbbt. It's a different world. I go to grab a sandwich in the kitchen and fifteen bowing fools are there to tell me a duchess can't slice her own bread," Bambi said. "See your salutes and raise."

Jenny laughed. "Fold. At least they don't expect me to go around in a tiara."

"Part of why I insist on flying so much—that leather helmet precludes even sillier hats. Quattro *loves* the hats, though."

Dinner was everything Jenny had implied; "Luther is not 'kind of' a genius, he's a genius," Bambi said.

"Let me write that down." Jenny grinned. "He keeps a quote book of things famous people say about his food. He'll love getting a quote from a duchess."

"In that case," Bambi said, "write down that I said that if I'd known about him, I'd've had him cook for my coronation." She let Jenny have a moment to scribble before asking, "So was the general just being a workaholic, or did he really need to ride off in a hurry like that?"

Jenny smiled. "Both, always. Jeff only relaxes when I shame him into it, but I only do that when he's falling-down non-functionally tired, because he really does need to be that busy. We've been talking with Heather about Operation Full Court Press since Cameron Nguyen-Peters proposed it last fall."

"It's a shame he's not here to see it bear fruit," Bambi said, staying carefully neutral in tone. She had only met the last regular NCCC of the United States a couple of times, briefly, and hadn't liked him at all, but he had been one of two indisputably legitimate links to the old United States government, his assassination had made everything far more difficult, and Heather was absolutely certain the Graysons had been behind it.

THE LAST PRESIDENT   83

Jenny sighed, not taking the bait. "Jeff says, at least ten times a day, that he wishes he had Cam at the other end of the supply lines."

Gosh, do you mean now he thinks that shooting Cam was a bad *thing?* Bambi wanted to ask. Red Dog's report had said that Grayson had actually done it personally, and that Jenny had not only known it was going to happen, but had urged Grayson to go through with it. Bambi remembered James's briefing about Jenny Whilmire Grayson: *Looks like Barbie but under that plastic is the brass heart of Lady Macbeth, and don't forget it.* "So I guess there's a lot on his mind and a lot to take care of."

Jenny grinned fiercely. "We've been doing everything we can to convince everyone *below* battalion commanders that it'll take us ten days to execute an order to start. Everybody thinks they're in the very first advance guard and that other troops will be catching up with them for days, but most people aren't dumb enough to talk about what their own unit is doing. But an 'obvious problem' for the whole army, though, well, that doesn't seem like much of a secret, and so the cover story about the ten days has been leaking like crazy."

"How do the tribals hear any rumors from our side of the river?"

"Oh, there's a huge black market across the Ohio. Tribals aren't supposed to but lots of their scouts trade looted jewelry and tools for canned food and real bread. So by now everyone at the first big tribal encampment, just downriver from here, is dead certain that they have a week at least before we even start to move."

"So how long do they really have?"

"Jeff was riding off to tell the engineers to start putting a temporary bridge across the ice right here; it's all preplaced ready-to-go pieces. That will be done by about two in the morning, he hopes. Meanwhile the tribal spies and scouts won't be meeting the people they expect, and their regular patrols are going to have some real bad luck; we've been following but not taking them for weeks. So with a little luck, almost none of them will make it back to the tribal encampment before our army is on top of them, right about dawn. If Jeff's plan works, the first tribal horde will be gone before lunch tomorrow." Her eyes, reflecting the candlelight, seemed feral and vicious, but her smile was still a beauty-pageant dazzler.

"Brilliant," Bambi said, meaning it. *Lady, you scare me just a little, but right now we need scary people on our side.*

THE NEXT DAY. OLYMPIA, NEW DISTRICT OF COLUMBIA (FORMERLY OLYMPIA, WASHINGTON). 12:30 PM PACIFIC TIME. MONDAY, FEBRUARY 9, 2026.

It amused Quattro Larsen that nobody was there to meet him at the airport. *No perqs for the Duke.*

He did what he usually did on his regular route—made sure the right people would be working on the Gooney, then swapped his leather flying helmet for his trademark floppy hat with a feather, slung up his bag, and flagged down a taxi, a museum-piece buggy that had probably been in the business of giving romantic rides around a park somewhere, back before. "The New White House, please."

The driver nodded. "Little White House, right."

Quattro paid the cabbie with one of the new California Eagles, the twenty-dollar gold coins that he and Bambi had begun minting privately, and told him to keep the change. The cabbie managed a sketchy bow that amused Quattro, but he returned it gravely. *Wish more people got that all this Duck and Doochess stuff is a joke,* he thought. *Laying on the awe and majesty is kind of fun in a silly ironic way but I'm starting to worry about the number of people taking it seriously. Hate to admit that to Bambi, though, she'll say she told me so, and she's been worrying about it for ages already.*

Inside the New White House there was a great deal more bowing and saluting in the foyer before Quattro was allowed to just proceed into the plain office to his right. The moment the door closed, he sighed and relaxed, and his three old friends rose to greet him.

Graham Weisbrod, the last living person with any claim to be President of the United States, was scrawny and short, and the stress of the last couple of years had removed most of his white hair, stooped his shoulders, and shrunk his hips and belly to slackness, but he still had the same lopsided cynic's grin that had terrified generations of grad students.

Next to Weisbrod, General Norm McIntyre, tall, iron-gray hair, wearing plain fatigues, the highest-ranking surviving officer from the old army, was almost expressionless; *we've all aged a lot in the last sixteen months,* Quattro thought, *but it's like Norm was cut off from all his life force. Norm's not the type to start over; his head's too full of what he did back before.*

Allie Sok Banh, half the age of either man, scrawled one more thing on the pad on her desk before she rushed to Quattro, giving him a quick phony hug and air-kiss. The last year had probably been harder on her than either of the men, but she was a generation younger and had adapted better. "I hope it's the package we've been expecting," she said.

"Well, it's not new Federal standards for laundry detergents."

Weisbrod said, "Allie, you're faster than either of us with a coding pad, so if you wouldn't mind? Quattro, while she works, can we offer you coffee?"

The men chatted quietly while Allie scribbled swiftly through the hundreds of two-digit additions on her coding pad.

Quattro did his best to concentrate on Graham's talk of building a new rail line over the Upper Peninsula and across the Mackinac Bridge to connect the whole New State of Superior, and McIntyre's elaborate plans for re-merging the mostly-former-National Guard Provi Army with the mostly-former-regular Temper Army so that everyone's seniority was respected and the required promotions and demotions could be fairly distributed. Quattro could not forget that what was happening on Allie's coding pad was capital-h History; *maybe they can't either and that's why they're talking about procedural crap like mid-level postal clerks.*

When she looked up, they were all instantly silent.

"Operation Full Court Press is set to begin as fast as we can begin it," she said. "Apparently everyone is jumping on it; if he's on plan, Grayson is already across the Ohio and has attacked the first horde."

"Well, we can put it on the agenda for the Cabinet meeting for next week," Graham said, "and see what everyone says."

McIntyre nodded. "That'll give me a chance to assess the impact of all the requests for troop commitments—"

"There are only two, for right now," Allie said. "Grayson wants the six regiments you already promised, especially the President's Own Rangers, for the Wabash Valley campaign, rendezvous at Pale Bluff, early May. And Utah, even though they're still declining to take their seats in our Congress, wants to coordinate so that when they slam the tribals in their northwest corner, we'll be ready to close the trap in southern Idaho and western Wyoming. We've already got the requested regiments preparing to join Grayson, and the forts in the Yellowstone are ready for the reinforcements. So all we need to do—"

"I'm sure all that can be pulled together at the Cabinet meeting—" Graham began.

Allie showed neither irritation nor impatience, apparently taking their agreement for granted. "Well, I'll start the things rolling that can't wait, and I'll clear everyone's calendar so we can move that meeting up to tomorrow morning. You'll want to review the planned deployments before we finalize them, General." She stood. "Quattro, I am guessing no one has fed you, you're probably starving, and so am I. Are you too tired for dinner?"

"Never."

"Well, then," she said to the two older men, who looked stunned, "I'll do my Chief of Staffly thing on the calendar when I get back; meanwhile, the full document and all the addenda are right here on the pad, and you both should read all through it. Quattro and I will eat in the Secure Dining Room. Are you sure you won't join us?"

"I, um, I don't think—" McIntyre said.

Graham Weisbrod looked mildly annoyed. "There are some serious political issues to discuss—"

"Well, of course," Allie said. "That's what Quattro and I will be discussing—are you sure you gents don't want to join us?"

Graham Weisbrod froze like a listening rabbit, then sagged. "Well, I guess we can iron out details after you get back."

The Secure Dining Room was located in the attic space; as they passed by the kitchen at the back of the house, Allie leaned in to say, "Bobbi? Secure Dining Room, just two, for lunch—"

"Of course, ma'am. Today it's chowder, fresh bread, and greens, need anything special?"

"Got a pot of coffee we can take up?"

"Right here."

Allie led the way upstairs. "Craig?"

"Yes, ma'am," the Ranger sergeant replied.

"We'll be talking and eating in the Secure Dining Room. Could you have a guard come up with Bobbi? We'll stick to small talk till the food comes."

"Sure thing, ma'am."

The Secure Dining Room seated eight at a central table and three at a smaller table by the window, which looked out over Puget Sound. Allie sat at the small table, gesturing Quattro into the chair facing the window. "Best view in the New District," she said. "I often bring a notepad and a pot of coffee up here when I need to work."

"Wow, I've got a better view, but you've got reliable coffee."

"It's Lisa Fanchion's bribe to us, in exchange for a friendly, low-tax, no-regs port to operate from."

"I think if we heard she was unhappy with you at noon, we'd be rolling out the red carpet at San Diego before one."

The food and coffee arrived, and the guard took up his post outside the door. When they had finished, Allie gestured toward the harbor again. "The country is going to regrow in some other shape this time. Probably much more facing the Pacific than we did before; it's the quick way to Australia and India, and that's the friendly two-thirds of the Big Three."

"You think we're going to have trouble with the Argies?"

"Wish we wouldn't but . . . too much says we will. They've already signed special arrangements with ports all over South America, and they're pushing into Central America and the Caribbean. The surviving national governments wouldn't run without Argie advisors and loans, and sometimes their troops. Given how beat up Daybreak left Mexico, and how little we can do for them right away, I think we'll lose them to the Argentine orbit too. The RRC espionage teams over in Manbrookstat say that Argentine ships are already sniffing around at the Chesapeake and making offers to the Commandant for stuff he doesn't own."

"Stuff like—"

"Like the Delmarva, and maybe the Potomac Valley. I don't really like the idea that the site of DC might be inside an Argentine colony in the next generation. Besides being our capital, it's my home town, and if anything is ever built there again, I want it to be American. I thought I was an internationalist with a broad perspective, back before, and maybe I was, but nowadays: not one inch of dirt to outsiders. Hell, I even resent the Texans talking about secession, and I'll miss those cranky impossible hicks if they do.

"And the Commandant really pisses me off most of all. An ex-cadet selling off the upper right corner of the country! The minute we settle the tribals, whether the next president is Phat, Grayson, or Weisbrod, I want to send a fleet to plug up New York Harbor and an expeditionary force to go in and arrest him, put Manbrookstat under martial law, hold a fast election, and bring them in as another New State in the Union."

"Grayson would go for that."

"Yep, I hate the son of a bitch and he hates me more, but we'd both rather live in the other one's complete America than see it torn up by these petty shithead wannabe kings."

Quattro grinned. "That's *Duke* Petty Shithead to you."

"Oh, bah." She flipped her hair away from her face. "We know perfectly well that you're holding California to bring it back into the Union whenever you can make sure it'll come back and stay back."

Quattro nodded, acknowledging it, and tried a slightly riskier question. "Why all the foot-dragging from Graham and Norm?"

"Half them. Half me." Allie sighed. "Graham is old and a liberal, and since we're tied with Russia, Europe, and China for biggest basket case, he wants to focus on rebuilding, not fight a long big war, especially not against what he still thinks of as American citizens. Norm liked fighting when he was younger and running an army when he got older; his heart's not in it, because as far as he's concerned, the real America is back before, and he can't fight for that. So he's going through the motions of being a good administrator, because he took an oath, but in his heart he just wants to die somewhere quietly. Still, they'd both probably be more enthusiastic about settling the tribal problem if they weren't dealing with me all the time. Sometimes I think my husband and the general are the only people who understand that when I say I want to wipe the tribes out, I mean that.

Ever since Graham brought me back from a mostly-complete takeover by Daybreak, knowing what Daybreak's grip on the mind feels like, and feeling what Daybreak really wants to do, I cannot imagine any way we can rehabilitate more than a handful of the tribals.

"Graham and Norm think they can solve the tribal problem the same way they think they can solve everything else: by concentrating on reconstruction. They think if we can get enough food, and running water, and schools and roads and all that bullshit, why, those naughty tribals will come begging us to take them back, because their having destroyed modern civilization was surely just a silly mistake.

"I, on the other hand, agree with Heather, and Grayson, and everyone else with half a brain. So I'll get you as many men and guns as I can squeeze out of the Provisional Constitutional Government, but it'll take some desk pounding and some whining to push them into doing the right thing. Grayson'll have the whole regiment of the President's Own Rangers, and everything else I've promised. More if I can." She was staring intently. "But here's what I have to have: no criticism and no attempt to block what we're going to be doing in our own tribal pockets."

"What are you going to be doing?"

"Eliminating the problem for good and forever. No waiting, no rehabilitating, no more chances."

"No quarter. No survivors."

She beamed at him. "*Almost* none. Our tribals will be given a window of opportunity for mercy—just not open very far or for very long." She reached out and stroked his hand with one long nail, polished blood-red, almost hard enough to scratch. "Just tell Heather and James that I *insist* on giving them more than they asked for."

2 HOURS LATER. MANBROOKSTAT. 4:15 PM EASTERN TIME. MONDAY, FEBRUARY 9, 2026.

Huddling around the upper harbor in the ruins of old New York, the puny city-state of Manbrookstat might be headed for great things, but currently they lived by trading usable wreckage for food. Yet to get the Commandant even to look at this message, Heather had had to promise him more and deeper reconnaissance than was usual. Bambi had come in ninety minutes north of the usual mailplane route, swinging much deeper into the Lost Quarter than she liked. At least those hours of anxiety were safely over; now she was flying in over the abandoned zones of Queens and Brooklyn, descending toward the southern tip of Manhattan. At almost any other airfield, she would be looking forward to a good meal, a comfortable room, and some major attention; in post-Daybreak America, a mail pilot was at least as big a celebrity as a Duchess.

Having flown into Manbrookstat before, she expected to be treated as a nuisance at best, but Heather had emphasized that she was to pick no quarrels with the Commandant.

The tail wheel touched down. The JNE's squishy tires grabbed FDR Drive. Now she was rolling rather than flying. At the flagger's signal she cut the engine and braked the prop. The ground crew chief who came to help her down from the cockpit was Knox, an old friend from the early days just after Daybreak. "Welcome, Countess, we don't see enough of you here."

"It's good to be back," she lied, smiling back at him. "Take good care of the Jenny."

Knox nodded. "Like always." Then, so softly Bambi might have missed it, he added, "Keep your eyes open. There's a lot you oughta see but you gotta look."

Bambi listened without expression, remembered carefully, and reacted not at all. She slung up her flight bag and walked toward where the Commandant waited with his entourage. *At least the son of a bitch saw fit to meet me himself. Maybe he's only ninety percent of the asshole I always thought he was.* Twenty feet before they were in reach of each other, she extended her hand so he could not bow to extort a bow in return.

Dinner that night was in the Ritz-Carlton by a southeast-facing window. The deep red sunset, filtered through the haze that still hung over the burned continent, lit the sad stump of the Statue of Liberty.

"The arm with the torch fell off on Christmas Day," the Commandant said, following her gaze. "Something about the big electric currents that ran through the steel made it super-vulnerable to rust, that's what one of my engineers guessed, but I wonder if it wasn't the ice load that built up on the upper part for a month; it looked like she was holding a big load of cotton candy just before it went."

Bambi nodded. "I traveled a lot, back before, when I was a Fed, and now I fly everywhere. I see things like this all the time . . . still, somehow, it's different when it's the Lady, isn't it?"

The Commandant shrugged. "As soon as there's less floating ice around the island, we'll cut up the arm and torch, probably trade it to Argentina for tinned beef. Life goes on and a statue doesn't need to eat."

Bambi changed the subject. "Since you asked me to come in over the Dead Belt and give you some recon, first of all, it's still dead but showing signs of life."

The Dead Belt was the lumpy strip across Michigan, lower Ontario, upstate New York, and New England where the fallout from the Chicago superbomb had killed everything except grass and bugs. The 250-megaton bomb had been a pure-fusion weapon, so its mostly-light-metals fallout had been intensely radioactive but very short lived. For a few weeks after the detonation, it had been enough to kill nearly all vertebrates and trees, leaving only corpses and mud under the deep snow, and forests of mere upright logs; now radiation was almost completely returned to background levels.

Bambi summed up. "Dead cities, empty land, not one column of smoke horizon to horizon, washouts miles across that cut right through roads and subdivisions. Big drifts of silt in all the rivers, and the rivers themselves are cutting snaky, complicated channels and forming new lakes— everything the Mensche expedition saw a few months ago, but more so after so much rain and snow. Big parts of it won't be farmable again for thousands of years, it's going to be some kind of a badlands. But all those empty snowfields did make it easy to see five big Daybreaker trails, and one of your Special Assistants is copying my notes about those; it looks like each trail represents a horde of at least four thousand tribals moving south and west."

"None coming this way, though?"

"No. But remember I didn't overfly New England."

"We have sources of our own up that way," he said. He snapped his fingers; a young girl, eyes downcast, came and poured more wine for him. Bambi declined. The Commandant ran his finger slowly around the edge of the wineglass. "Would the RRC—and you—like some advice?"

Since I'll undoubtedly get it anyway . . . "Always. We listen to anyone."

"I wonder. The message Heather O'Grainne sent makes me wonder about the quality of your intel or maybe the wisdom you apply to it. Of course, it's obvious that the tribals are planning some big raids this summer, so it makes sense for you to attack the tribals, pre-emptively, at a few points, to help their attack fizzle—but don't you realize it's going to fizzle anyway? When are you going to consider that you don't have to have a war unless you want one? The tribals are starving and getting weaker. They aren't farmers—most of them are trying to end farming, and they only survived this long because canned and boxed food in the Dead Belt stayed edible, the people who would have eaten it were all dead, and the tribes could move in and mine for food. Sure, a horde of twenty thousand people sounds like a lot, but coming out of areas that had *how many* millions in them, back before?

"So what if the tribals surge this summer, or even two or three more? They lose thousands on every surge, and more to starvation and disease over the winter. Bribe or talk them into staying put a couple more years, and eventually you can walk back into the empty land, because the tribals will be irrelevant."

"Isn't that pretty hard on the people that will be burned out, looted from, maybe slaughtered, to wait for the tribals to 'become irrelevant'?"

"Almost the whole world's irrelevant already, because it's dead. And without planes and radio, whatever is left is mostly far away. Which brings me to my advice to you personally. You used to be a Fed, you took an oath, I understand all that, I was a senior at West Point, after all, back before. It's hard to change old mental habits. But . . . here we are. I own New York Harbor, because of a few things I did right after Daybreak day. You own San Diego Harbor, because of what your father did. For that matter that silly bastard Lord Robert with his mud-hut empire did a couple things right, and he's at least got the best hut in the whole empire of mud. We're alike."

"You're suggesting something," Bambi said. She was watching the last blood-red light fade from the Statue of Liberty; the contrast between the blackened areas and the reflection from the flows of resmelted copper on the lump turned it into a red and black abstraction. She knew what the Commandant's suggestion would be, but she waited for it anyway.

"The old world is gone. We're powerless to bring it back. Most people who would benefit from that are already dead, aren't they? Do we owe them anything?" He drank deeply, and set his glass down in a prissy way that Bambi realized was probably a twenty-three-year-old's idea of sophistication. "Someday, at a summit conference, you and I will say 'United States' just as we now do 'Soviet Union' or 'Roman Empire,' and probably no more frequently."

"So Operation Full Court Press—"

"Although it is regrettable that the tribes are smashing up civilized areas a long way from here . . . well, 'a long way from here' covers it."

"You're part of the same country."

"That's the issue, isn't it?"

FIVE:
HOW A GENERAL SLEEPS

Jeff's voice was flat and expressionless, but his hand held Jenny's arm as if he were afraid she would run. "It smells like that because they were planning to die before summer, so they didn't see much point in camp sanitation. Besides, all that uncovered crap and piles of corpses will keep pathogen counts high in the Ohio and the lower Mississippi for another year, poisoning more of us wicked Gaia-rapers. We can't stay a month to cover and burn it all, so we're just piling the corpses and building an earthen dike around them for now."

The heap of bodies in front of them was a congeries of gray faces with livid lips and white staring eyes, reaching hands like driftwood branches, swaths of wadded hair, rag-wrapped feet black with mud and blood; the pile came about up to his chest. From the other side, lines of men were passing corpses in a grim bucket-brigade, flinging them along hand to hand onto a taller mound in the center. "Most of them probably didn't join Daybreak till they'd been enslaved, and we just killed them all for having a contagious mental illness."

"Are you going to do anything—"

"We put down a layer of brush and scrapwood, and some coal from rail cars, under that pile. When the dike is finished the engineers will try to light it, but good luck with that in all this mud and snow. Probably be next year before anyone can come back here to do something about it." He squeezed her arm tighter. "We'll have to keep doing this about once a week, well into summer." She could feel the tremor in his grip.

Jenny closed her notebook, put it into her pack, and took Grayson's hands. "Let's get you away from all this for a little while. You have good officers and they'll take it from here."

"I just keep thinking how we'd have them surrounded, and be chopping into the crowd with poleaxes, and then I'd see so many of them just drop their weapons and stare around them, like they wanted to ask, 'Where am I? How did I get here?' And then they'd go into seizures. They *couldn't* have surrendered to us even if we had been taking prisoners."

"This way, dinner, bed." She clamped her hand on his wrist and turned at the waist, tugging him away from that pile studded with faces, feet, and hands. "Dinner, bed, I'm gonna take care of you."

He stumbled, found his balance, and trailed along, holding her right hand in his left, constantly returning salutes, nodding when people said things to him. She wasn't sure whether he saw or heard anything; as soon as she got him to bed she'd write down everything important she could remember.

The sun was setting as they reached their tent. Towers said, "I'll tell the cook to bring around your meal."

"Thank you. Get some rest and food yourself."

"My relief should be here any minute," the guard said. "And your father and his people don't have access tonight."

"You're the best, Mister Towers."

"Just remember that when you're calculating my next raise, ma'am. Take care of the general."

"Count on it."

Jeff sat motionless on their folding bed, by the woodstove. She pulled off his boots, made him put on slippers, and had him sitting at the table when an orderly brought dense, warming pot pies and a thick soup with rice.

They ate silently until he seemed to wake up abruptly, halfway through the meal, began to wolf it down in great messy slurps, and finally caught himself, looking up from his plate, dabbing at his face with his napkin. He took another bite of pot pie, sipped at his water, and looked straight into her eyes. "Massacre is so different from battle. And it sounds stupid, but I wish this had been a battle."

3 HOURS LATER. OLYMPIA. 6:30 PM PACIFIC TIME. FRIDAY, FEBRUARY 13, 2026.

"How often do you think about back before?" Allie asked Graham, as they sat by the warm fire in the New White House.

"Are you asking your husband, your old professor, or the President of the United States?"

"I'm not sure. How about you identify which one you are when you give the answer?"

He stretched, hands over his head, twisting with surprising vigor.

Right now it's hard to believe he remembers Vietnam and the moon landings, but catch him in another hour and it'll be hard to believe he's still alive. He comes and goes so unpredictably.

"You're staring at me that funny way again," he said. "The main thing I think about 'back before' is that the words are revealing. For almost a year after Daybreak there was no one standard way to say, 'In the time before Daybreak.' Now everyone says, 'back before'—"

"Very professorial and not what I meant. I was thinking how, if we'd caught Daybreak and stopped it, right now you'd be working on figuring out your post-Washington life."

"If this new era is anything, Allie, it's post-Washington."

She froze. "My whole family disappeared with Washington."

"Sorry. I didn't mean—"

"Shit, shit, sorry, I was enjoying just getting some time together and then I had to go and snap at you. Forgive?" She grasped his arm as if he might bolt.

With his free hand he brushed her hair to the side and looked into her eyes. "I could tell that demonstration this afternoon was getting on your nerves."

"Yeah. 'This is America—no genocide!' This is why there should be an

IQ test and a current events quiz before people are allowed to have demonstrations. Don't look at me that way, Graham, I'm kidding, but still, I mean, come on, what the Khmer Rouge did to *my* people was genocide. What we're doing is *necessary*. I don't want to commit genocide. I just don't want there to be any more tribals."

"'Acts committed with intent to destroy, in whole or part, a national, ethnical, racial or religious—'"

"I read the Solicitor General's report too," she said. *Whereas you just skimmed the executive summary and then fell asleep with your head on it.* "Even if you call that made-up shit a culture—and I sure as hell don't, I call it a mishmash of heavy metal, comic books, and New Age—it can't be a heritage, they haven't had time for anybody to inherit it since they made it up," Allie pointed out. "Anyway, what they are is, is . . ."

"People."

"All *right*. People. So regrettably, killing them is murder. But not genocide, Graham."

He drew a breath as if to shout, then let it flow back out. When he spoke his voice was soft and even. "We're both products of the old Washington; we worry too much about what to call things. Allie, it just looks to me like this is your revenge on Daybreak for having infected you, and it's like this passion for revenge is taking over your personality—"

"Not like Daybreak did. Don't you dare say that."

"I wasn't going to." He sounded angry for the first time. "I just meant, I put a lot of work into getting you back, and, hell, I love you—you okay?" He was staring at her strangely.

She reached up and touched her own cheek; it was wet with tears. "Aw, shit."

"You hardly ever cry."

"Yeah." She wiped her face, hard. "Graham, you just might be the first guy who acted like he *loved* me, not just valued me as an asset or a trophy. The whole time I was recovering from the Daybreak infection, I never once heard anything about you needing me to be your secretary of state, or your chief of staff, or the way things were falling apart in the White House without me—"

"Oh, boy, were they, though. I just didn't want to worry you about it."

"See? That's what I mean." She took a handkerchief and dried her face. "Love can sure do weird shit to a person. Anyway, I guess I brought all this up and then bit your head off for talking about it because I wanted to know if you were pining for back before—"

"Back before I didn't have you? Never."

They sat and watched the fire until time for bed. Allie stayed pressed close against him, relishing how far away she felt from everything.

8 DAYS LATER. JEFFERSONVILLE, INDIANA. 3:25 PM EASTERN TIME. SATURDAY, FEBRUARY 21, 2026.

Even across the Ohio, the burned smell from the ruins of Louisville filled Jenny's mouth and nostrils and squeezed her throat. Louisville had burned even before the giant bombs, one of the first big fires after Daybreak. Nanospawn had turned off the electricity to pump water. Biotes had eaten the hoses, tires, and fuel for the fire department. When a fire had broken out in the industrial area around Camp Ground Road, there had been nothing to stop its upward climb till it spewed burning debris on the helpless remainder of the city. The eastward flow of blowtorch-hot flames had blasted across the city to the Ohio in less than an hour, killing tens of thousands.

Two cold wet winters had washed away soot and toppled building frames, leaving heaps of rust on a plain of vitrified soil, but the smell lingered anyway.

Here, on the Jeffersonville side, residents and refugees had saved the town with four days of nonstop bucket chains and shovel work, only to be overrun by the Shine Forth Gaia People last May. The Louisville side looked like Hiroshima; the Jeffersonville side, like Beirut.

Although scouts had turned up relatively few tribals in their path, Jeff had chosen to follow the river road on the Indiana side, hoping to tempt the Daybreakers to break their discipline and come out and fight in smaller, less organized, more numerous groups. "If we can make those big hordes melt away before we reach them, so much the better."

"But we haven't had a quiet night since we crossed," she pointed out.

"I'd like to sleep through a night without waking up to screaming and shooting."

"Well, yeah, a night human wave attack by a hundred of them *is* scary. It's meant to be, and that's why they do it." He gazed across the bridge at the ruins of Louisville. "But so far, scary is *all* they've been able to be. We can rotate troops through night guard duty so nobody has to cope with it for more than one night at a time, and our guys have the discipline to stay safe in their positions, keep shooting quickly and accurately, and break the wave before it gets to our lines. It's ugly but we get through it fine. And this way we capture a lot more of the other side alive for the wizards at Pueblo. Call me squeamish, but I prefer converts to corpses. Besides, there—"

A rider galloped up to them, saluted, and handed over a note. Jeff looked, read, and pulled out his order pad, scribbling with quick accuracy. "Messenger!"

He sent off the three riders who had been sitting quietly by, his always-ready communication system, then apologetically said to the rider who had brought the dispatch, "Sorry to make you and your mount work so hard but this needs to go to the TexICs commander, Colonel Prewitt, right now. They're on wide patrol north and west of us—"

"I'll find them, sir."

"Good."

The messenger rode off at a pace that made Jenny fear for his horse. "He's the only one that knows what his message is about, and he's riding like a maniac," she ventured.

"Very observant and absolutely right." Jeff nodded grimly, and set off at a trot. "Ride with me back to HQ. Scouts from the Alabama Mounted found the enemy breaking camp and retreating north. We've got to catch up with them and close them off *now*. I had four messengers available and I needed six, so I prioritized, and we *are* the fifth message, to HQ—"

"Jeff, we can gallop—I ride at least as well as you."

He picked up the pace but kept to a trot; Jenny decided not to argue. "Are there more messengers at HQ?"

"Yes if I'm lucky, but it's being a busy day."

"Where were you going to send the sixth message?"

He glanced at her, thought for an instant, and said, "Okay, you can do it. I'm nearly certain you'll be riding away from the enemy anyway." He reined in and grabbed his order pad. "You'll be as safe as you'd be at HQ and this is important."

"You're not going to tell me I can't—"

"There's no time to argue," he said, lettering fast and hard into the pad. "And you'd win the argument. Now listen up, because you have to understand this as you carry the message—things could change fast and the officers will need to know what I was thinking, not just my orders, if they have to improvise.

"Right now we're laid out kind of like a scorpion making a right turn—two wings of cavalry out front like claws, big mass of infantry in the middle, and then a long string of mixed units that went out on side missions all day, and are catching up now, with a little cavalry force at the end as a rearguard. Or a stinger.

"The four messengers I sent went to the units that form the claws; they need to swing in to harass the tribals' retreat, slow them down and keep them from opening up the distance.

"But that cavalry is not enough to block their retreat and besides, the first place we can get ahead of them is just about the last place we can stop them at all. What will make them stop moving is pushing some infantry up against them to make them stand and fight. I'll be taking charge of that from HQ.

"Your job is to make our long tail whip around to come in behind the tribals, once they stop moving. I want them to secure the Grant Line Road south of St. Joseph, all the way down to the junction with Chapel Lane if possible. These orders tell each commander to use his or her own judgment and head for the junction by the quickest route they can figure out, and then the senior officer present will allocate forces along the road as they arrive, till I can get there.

"They are on no account to allow any tribal forces to escape northward if it's in their power to prevent it. I'll be coming up to join them as quick as I can but the key thing is to grab that road, close it to the enemy, and secure the flanks. Show this message to the colonel of every regiment and the major of every free-standing battalion in the column. Make sure he knows he's going to Grant Line Road between St. Joseph and Chapel Lane. Then take that same message to the next one." He thought for a moment and added one more note. "I'm adding, 'Maintain contact with friendly forces on your left flank if possible, but do not delay under any circumstances.'" He glanced up at her. "Repeat the part of it that's orders; the scorpion was just to help you remember."

She stammered and felt flustered and foolish, but she managed it.

He nodded. "Excellent. Don't let any officious wiener take the message copy from you, and if the CO isn't available right away, tell it to the highest-ranking person and move on. No delays. Good luck. And come back safe." He mounted and rode off with a wave.

Jenny zipped the message into the pocket of her leather jacket and rode off to the northeast on Market Street. She leaned forward and told Buttermilk, "Well, for once, we've got something to fight besides boredom."

AN HOUR LATER. JEFFERSONVILLE, INDIANA. 5:45 PM EASTERN TIME. SATURDAY, FEBRUARY 21, 2026.

As the most distinctive-looking person traveling with the Army, Jenny encountered no questions or arguments. *Maybe it's even* better *than having a regular messenger on this job; I'll have to mention that to Jeff.* Every colonel and major on the way had immediately issued a flurry of orders to the officers around him or her. (*Of course, how would I know if they were* the right *orders?* she thought.)

She was riding fast and hard, promising Buttermilk they could just walk after this last one, picking along the debris-choked Utica Pike toward the rearguard company of the rearguard battalion. Definitely, this beat hell out sitting next to her father while he prayed for victory, being steered around by polite young men from the invalid list, or watching in a lady-like manner from a distant hilltop.

Delta Company, Third Battalion, Fourth Iowa Provisional Volunteers, was the rear-of-the-rearguard. Captain Shirley Mendoza listened to the orders from battalion and nodded. "Makes sense. We'll take Port Road, it's close and goes the way we're going. And tell the general he's in our prayers, and I'm voting for him for president."

"Let's win the war first," Jenny said. *That'll make for a good little story for them to hear up in Provi country.*

She considered traveling along with Mendoza's company, but after all they were moving toward battle to the north and west; if she stayed on the south side of the scorpion's tail swinging north, she would probably be closer to obeying Jeff's order to stay safe, and besides, Buttermilk was tiring.

She had ridden only about a hundred yards back toward the main body of the rearguard when a man jumped out from behind a burned-out SUV and threw an ax at her. She ducked sideways and the ax flew past; Buttermilk went light to the front, preparing to rear, but Jenny leaned forward, put her arms around the horse's neck, and pressed with her legs, urging Buttermilk forward.

She drew her pistol from her sash. The man had followed his ax in, and was two steps away with his drawn knife when she shot him, putting a hole where his nose had been and scattering bloody meat on the road behind him.

Buttermilk had heard gunfire before, and smelled blood, but had not been trained to it; she started to rear again, and Jenny leaned far forward, pressing down on the neck, letting the reins go slack and urging, "Come on, baby, come on, chill out now." Buttermilk took a tentative step forward, but Jenny could feel the mare's terror.

When she spared a moment to look up, more tribals were swarming out from between the row of old apartment buildings. She turned Buttermilk and galloped back toward Delta Company; rifles roared around her as she reached them. Mendoza ran up to her. "Look at that," she said. "They're coming out of hiding all along the road. And the army is scattered all over the town, with all that behind it."

Jenny nodded. "Right now our side's in a big arc to the northwest. I'll try to ride along it and let everyone know what's happening, follow it all the way back to HQ if I have to. Thanks for the backup. I gotta run."

If there was anything Buttermilk was happy to do now, it was *run*. That was good, because Jenny found that all along the tail, there had been harassing attacks from the north and east. From officer to officer, unit to unit, Jenny rode as fast as she dared in the swiftly failing light. Luckily most of the units had managed to stay in touch with their flanks, and knew approximately where the next unit in the arc was.

Shortly, she had evolved a single long, fast, clear sentence that summed up where the tribal counterattacks were coming in. It was growing darker, but not full dark yet, and while she could keep up this pace, she wanted to cover as much ground as she could.

Once, a tribal arrow flew past Jenny, but she didn't see where it came from, and just rode on faster. By an old junkyard, a man stepped out from behind a fence with a spear, and she shot him before she even knew she had drawn her pistol; a few times she saw tribals in the distance. It was clear that they were "ambushed, surrounded, and infiltrated," as she said to Jeff, who had come out of his improvised headquarters in an old Burger King to see what the shouting was about.

He looked like he'd received an electric shock, but he managed to say, "Well, thank God you're safe. Sergeant, have Mrs. Grayson's horse seen to. Jenny, come on in here and let's get everything you can remember onto the map as quick as we can. We have a lot of figuring out to do. Meanwhile, messenger!" He was scrawling but looked up in amusement as Jenny had begun to open her mouth and step forward. "Not you, Jenny, the only recent source of intel I have is in your invaluable head, and anyway Buttermilk doesn't have any reserve left. I'm through trying to keep you out of things, and you've more than proved you can be useful, but I get to decide where and when you're most useful. It's one of those general-privileges."

With his hand on her shoulder, he guided her to the chart table; realizing he was right, Jenny complied, answering his rapid-fire questions as clearly and quickly as she could.

At least this part of Jeff's memoirs is going to be vivid. She gratefully accepted a sandwich and a mug of Sherpa tea. When Jeff seemed satisfied with what he'd extracted and was quickly sketching out his plan to his officers, she did not look for a way to leave, but hung around in the shadows and watched the swarm of scouts and messengers flowing in and out as Jeff re-established his grip on his army and moved forces up to hold the junction, and struck back at the many small harassing attacks.

Those solder soldiers that he had brought along slid back and forth over the map as he tracked where he had closed some escapes, where he needed to move to close the others, and where the parts of the trap closed around the tribals.

As the crescent moon was setting, well before midnight, the diversionary attackers had been pinned down, and were being captured or wiped out, or had fled back toward the main tribal force, adding to the chaos there. With too many choices and too much disparate information flooding in from all sides, the tribal system of cooperative, cellular organization was collapsing into paralytic thrashing. The confused mass of several thousand tribals stalled south of the junction was now encircled, but in the deeper darkness it was difficult to tighten up lines enough to keep them from exfiltrating. Desperate little squad-sized struggles were happening everywhere by starlight; between them, Daybreakers crept away quietly, and the haul in the trap was decreasing by the hour.

Grayson stood up from the table, nodding, and rubbing his neck. "Most of our officers have watches and clocks, correct?"

"All of them, sir, as far as we know. Might have been some breakage—"

"This doesn't have to be perfect. All right, tell everyone we want fires, but controlled fires, for visibility, all along the line, everywhere around the pocket. Bonfires in cleared areas, isolated buildings, I don't care what, we want light everywhere. It's not like the enemy doesn't know where we are."

"Sir, we can't light enough fires to light up the whole pocket, it's at least two miles across—"

"No, but we can make more of them afraid to try. In fact . . ." He smiled. "Tell them that as much as possible, without taking men out of combat, they're to cook something that smells good on those fires. Conceal nothing as they prepare for a big assault at dawn, but make sure it looks like everyone's getting a good meal first."

"Sir, everyone is exhausted and—"

"I know that. I'm thinking that the Daybreakers are in even worse shape, and we need to help them see that. Less than forty-eight hours ago, they were in their nice safe dirtbag encampment, with the comforting smell of their shit and body odor, and at least they had something to eat, anyway. Now they're out there trying to sneak around in the dark and find somewhere to lie up till day, and they've run all day, with only what they could carry. Let's see if a night staying awake, cold and hungry and surrounded, makes a difference." He nodded, liking his own idea. "Let's set up surrender poles where they can turn themselves in and get some soup, a safe place to lie down, and some handcuffs. At least the less-willing slaves will come in to us that way. But the most important thing is, make it look like our forces are just waiting for dawn."

"Won't more of them get away?"

"All the ones that really want to and have some initiative, sure. I could be wrong but I'm betting that's a small fraction. I think this might be our first chance to capture most of a Daybreaker horde alive." He smiled. "I don't like the idea of being the general who wouldn't take that chance. Anyway, meanwhile, I'm going to get some rest, and everyone who can is to do the same."

Back in their tent, gulping some boiled corn and unidentified meat, they fell onto the bed together; Jenny looked sideways at Jeff, and caught him looking back. Without a word, they grabbed each other, shoving bodies together, frantic to put him inside her, and went at each other maniacally for a few minutes, nails scratching both their skin, biting hard enough to bruise, clutching and slapping each other until they fell back on the bed next to each other, holding hands.

Now what in Jesus's sweet name was that all about? Jenny thought, before realizing, *Hunh. I killed two men. Apparently Jeff isn't the only one that gets horny from that.* She thought perhaps she should pray, but *Well, Lord, you already saw everything, so as they teach the young soldiers to say, "No excuse, sir!"* She plunged into such a deep sleep that it seemed only a moment before Towers awoke them with more boiled corn and mugs of chicory and milk, and they staggered back to headquarters in the freezing, sullen gray pre-dawn.

THE NEXT DAY. FACILITY 1, PUEBLO. 10 AM MOUNTAIN TIME. SUNDAY, FEBRUARY 22, 2026.

James had brought Jason this time because seizures tended to be particularly violent when Daybreak was losing. Since the seizures also provided windows of clarity, periods of a few minutes when Daybreak's control of 162 was imperfect, James wanted 162 to have the seizure; he just didn't want to be hit or kicked.

He sprang the news of the victory at Jeffersonville on 162 very suddenly, just walking into the room and announcing it. A moment later they were both tackling the man, who bumped his head a couple of times on the concrete table harder than James would have wanted him to. Whether the blows to the head helped him fall asleep without talking, or he was too deep into Daybreak, he had nothing to say. "Frustrating session," he said to Jason.

"Can't always be a breakthrough. It's funny, I was in Daybreak a lot longer, and voluntarily, and I was never anywhere near as resistant as this guy."

"Well, he had three of the things known to strengthen the effect—sustained study of Daybreak for its own sake. Professional training at being open-minded. And, don't take this wrong, but being an intellectual."

Jason grinned at him. "So I wasn't smart enough to catch Daybreak as deeply as, um, 162 did?"

"There's a difference between being smart and being intellectual. An intellectual thinks ideas, in and of themselves, are the most important thing in the world. And Daybreak, despite all its other scary properties, really is an idea. The difference is, if something is going on with the ideas, 162 has to put his whole mind on it. Whereas a poet like you can be distracted by real things that seem more important than ideas—like having a great marriage and a kid on the way—how is Beth?"

"Awesome as ever. Also healthy, and Doctor MaryBeth is telling us it looks great for the baby. Thanks for asking."

The two men shook hands and went about their day, each bothered somewhat differently by the picture of a man screaming and fainting when told about a military operation a thousand miles away.

THAT AFTERNOON. CHRISTIANSTED. 2:30 PM ATLANTIC TIME. SUNDAY, FEBRUARY 22, 2026.

"Here it comes—" Although the roaring seaplane was at least fifty feet above them, Whorf, Ihor, and the other sailor-scholars ducked instinctively as it passed over, before rowing frantically toward where it descended into a towering white spray.

"Wow, smells like a fire at McDonald's," Whorf said.

Pulling hard on his oar, Ihor said, "Our kids will say, 'Smells like an airplane,' the first time they have French fries."

"Put your backs into it," Jorge shouted from the tiller. The sailor-scholars stopped jabbering and bent to the job. Rowing was always hard work, but dragging a long cable was much more so.

The pilot brought the seaplane about and killed the prop; the plane settled onto the gentle waves just within Christiansted harbor. Whorf, Ihor, Polly, Felicia, Sendhar, and Pablo couldn't see behind themselves while rowing, but Jorge, at the tiller, announced, "it says NSP-8 on the side."

After interminably more rowing, Jorge brought them alongside, and the pilot climbed out on the short lower wing, picking his way between the struts and wires. "Hey, chief, what do you call this contraption?" Polly asked, passing him the tow rope from Jorge.

The pilot glanced back from where he was securing the cable to the thwart that ran just under and behind the prop, between the pontoons. "Technically, it's a sesqui-seaplane. High tech if this was 1910. The NSP stands for Newberry Scratch Plane—it's the eighth plane we've built from scratch at Castle Newberry, where I'm the freeholder." He was a muscular, young sandy blond with what, back before, had been called movie-star looks. "And who are the hecklers whose acquaintance I am making?"

Jorge, as the senior, introduced them all, explaining, "We're sailor-scholars on *Discovery*. That means sailors with homework. The plain old sailors decided it would develop our character if we were put in charge of rowing the line out to you. Captain Highbotham sends her compliments from the observatory. She said she'll work out a regular landing area and anchorage for you ASAP, but she only found out you were coming yesterday, so we had you land out here where there's nothing to run into. You'll ride with us in the boat back to *Discovery*, they'll winch the plane in close and tow you into the harbor for the night, and Highbotham'll get everything figured out while you eat and sleep."

"I like Captain Highbotham already," the man said. "Do I ask for permission to come aboard the boat?"

"Well, how about you tell us your name?"

"Whoops. Sorry. Bret Duquesne. Pilot, Federal Aviation Service—"

"Or maybe Earl of the Broad River," Polly said. Daughter of a high-ranking reverend, she had come down from Athens to join *Discovery* at Savannah, and knew the TNG's higher social circles well.

Climbing down to join Jorge, Duquesne made a face. "Stupid title. When my dad was alive he made fun of that. We're not California. I'm the freeholder of Castle Newberry and that's a big enough job and title for anybody. Would any of the ladies like me to take your oar?"

"Not a chance," Polly said. "I had to fight my way through five colonels, ten bureaucrats, twenty reverends, and a hundred Bible verses to get it."

No longer dragging the heavy tow rope, they were back on *Discovery* soon enough to be sent to the capstan to help winch the seaplane in.

When NSP-8 was in close enough for towing, and *Discovery* was headed back into the harbor, Captain Halleck came around to thank the interns for the extra work. "Pair up, and we'll roll dice for an extra shore leave. First one's tonight, if the pair that draws it isn't too tired."

To their delighted shock, Ihor and Whorf won the roll, which also carried with it the privilege of an on-deck shower, a change into clean clothes just returned from the laundry on shore, and a round-trip pass on a row-taxi.

"Life is pretty sweet," Whorf said, as they walked into the streets of the little nineteenth-century town nestled in a tropical harbor.

"For once, I don't need no—*any*—translation. Did you see the girls that smiled at us back there?"

"I'm not blind or dead."

"I am thinking this place is almost perfect."

"*Almost?* Unlike any place we've been recently, it's not a totalitarian dictatorship. It's not a few hundred desperate people hanging on in the middle of an ecological disaster. And it's still in the States and they speak English. How is Christiansted only *almost* perfect?" Whorf asked.

Ihor snorted. "Well, the girls that smiled at us back there? A bar that was cheap and had girls like that in it, that would make it perfect."

Whorf shook his head. "I've never seen a place like this before and I don't want to try to see it drunk."

"Ah, in Ukraine we would say, you have the soul of a poet. But not the thirst."

"I'll try Christiansted for reals first," Whorf said. "I can blur it out later if it turns out to suck."

"Sailors have changed since my day." The voice from behind them was warm with amusement.

They turned and snapped to attention. "Captain Highbotham!" Whorf said.

She returned the salute but she was smiling. "I'm afraid I was eavesdropping, which was rude of me, and discovered young men who are in something resembling a real conversation, and was so startled I spoke out loud. I was about to ask, though, if you'd like to come up to the observatory? It should be a pretty slow night, the moon is setting before midnight, and we always have a late supper on evenings like this. I'm afraid you've already walked right through the closest thing we have to a vice district," she said.

"You mean both bars are on this street?"

"And as your cohort was noting, they're pricey; the local liquor industry will need a while longer to get properly going. I'm afraid they really are about all we offer in the way of fleshpots. Can I interest you in a pleasant evening chatting with mathematicians, followed by some pretty good island cooking?"

Whorf admired the way that it sounded like a pleasant invitation while clearly being a command. It wasn't far out of line with what he preferred, either, and even better, it probably *was* out of line with what Ihor preferred.

Shortly, they were being shown the wonders of pen-and-paper launch monitoring, and of graphical computational methods on the backs of old posters. Despite themselves, they became interested, and really enjoyed eating with the observers, though Whorf thought the pirate attack stories were considerably more interesting than the discussion of trigonometric corrections.

Walking back to the harbor, where they would share a row-taxi taking them back to the ship, Ihor said, "Why do you think she did that?"

Whorf laughed. "Small-town life, Ihor. Same reason my folks moved out to a tiny village on Long Island and dragged me and my brother and sisters all around introducing us to everyone. How would you feel about being drunk and rowdy and stupid in front of Abby, or Peggy, or even Henry, now that you know each other?"

"I see." He shook his head. "Good trick, and so much for my career as a pervert, eh?"

"You could just as easy say she made us feel at home. The thing is, there's stuff you don't do at home."

"It was nicer than the way my uncle the first mate did that. He just told me if I ever done anything he didn't like he hitten my head till it rang like a gong."

"He would *be hitting*," Whorf said.

"*Be*. Silly word. I don't use it enough."

"That's okay, I'll use your share for you." They found one row-taxi right away, and the gentle rise and fall of the boat as it cut across the smooth harbor to their ship, the exceeding peace of a town where the only light was the single lamp of the watch, and the feeling of safety after a full day's work and a long walk, had them half asleep before they were home.

Jorge had deck watch. "So how was shore leave?"

Whorf said, "Ihor met an older woman with a lot of interesting experience, and he spent the whole evening with her."

Jorge sighed. "Oh, and me with the deck tonight."

"Actually," Ihor said, "Whorf and I shared the experience. And it was truly an experience I think you can only have in Christiansted."

"Oh, you guys are killin' me."

"Well," Ihor said, "you have leave tomorrow, right? When I've got deck and Whorf's on the bridge? If you just get off the row-taxi and take a long slow walk up the main drag, you can have a very similar experience."

"And it was . . . good?"

"Probably the best experience available locally," Whorf said. "Pending further research."

Below, in their berths, they were so tired that after only two fits of mutual giggles—one when Whorf said, "older woman," and the other when Ihor said, "pending further research?"—they were sound asleep in their hammocks.

SIX:
ON PAR WITH BYZANTIUM

THE NEXT DAY. PUEBLO. 6:15 PM MOUNTAIN TIME.
MONDAY, FEBRUARY 23, 2026.

"You always said you don't even *like* kids," Leslie Antonowicz said. She had always been the practical one in the partnership.

Under the table, Wonder, her immense dog, made a whimpering sound that was uncannily like agreement.

"These would be teenagers," James Hendrix pointed out. "Nearly-finished pre-people, like Patrick and his sister." He wore his best apron.

Leslie had been coming to James's house for dinner every Monday for years before Daybreak. James loved to cook and she loved to eat, with her constant outdoor sports, running, swimming, climbing, "all the amusements of a ten-year-old boy" as he liked to tease her. It had begun just after she had gently, painfully let him know that they were friends forever but a twenty-five-year age gap was just too much; now, both their distant families had been missing since Daybreak, and each was as much family as the other had.

"So," Leslie asked again, "all right, granted, not kids, *teenagers*. But why?"

James shrugged. "Why does the RRC do anything? I hope because we think in the long run it's for the good of the country, right? Well, weird though it is, and even knowing that Daybreak took him over, the best plan we've got for eradicating Daybreak and recreating our country is poor old Arnie Yang's plan."

"What about that string-and-card thing Heather has?"

"Who do you think figured out what should be on it? Arnie did the strategy and the rationale; that's just Heather's bureaucratic way of implementing it, and we just have to hope we don't need a major strategic adjustment between now and January 20, 2027. The more I think about it, the more I think we screwed up royally in letting the politicians and cops execute Arnie Yang. I even suspect that his telling us it was the best way and we had to do it might have been Daybreak talking; the advantages of having him alive now really outweigh anything we gained by making an example out of him."

"The public wanted his blood."

"Oh, I know, democracy loves melodrama; that's why it's always a little stupid at best. But killing the only guy who could tell us how things worked or what might be going on—let alone the author of the only strategy we've got—was bone stupid."

Leslie folded her arms. "He was in process of framing me for what he was doing, and I was close to going to the gallows in his place."

"Well, I'm not saying he was perfect."

After a long pause, they both laughed. James grinned. "Of course I would rather have you to laugh about it with. And maybe Arnie was right anyway, the night before we executed him, when he said that he thought the next twenty years would be mostly a matter of getting symbolic things right, and to just keep asking ourselves what Hollywood would do. Which brings me back to why I'm going to launch this Academy of the United States idea, and right away."

"Arnie told you to?"

"He said a new nation—which we're going to be, starting over from scratch—needs living heroes, and if it doesn't have them it will make them. So I think we have to raise some, here, because if we don't, they will be raised elsewhere and we can only guess at what sort of people they're going to be." He lowered the door on the woodstove and drew out the baked trout to go over polenta with asparagus in a butter and pot cheese sauce. "Now, we are at perfection. There will be silent and deeply appreciative reverence for this food until it is consumed."

"There will be," Leslie agreed.

Wonder snored, too experienced to worry about people-dinner till it became dog-scraps.

When they had finished and were enjoying the bucket of beer from Dell's Brew that Leslie had brought along, she said, "You know, the strange thing is, you could argue I was almost born for the world after Daybreak, and I guess I can see why until you caught Arnie everyone else thought I was the Daybreak mole here. I mean, I like hard physical work, I like being out in the bush running around and doing that hard work, I don't mind being uncomfortable if it's a chance to be outside, all of that. I guess some ways my attitude was already halfway to Daybreak.

"But you, James, you like comfort and clean sheets and you don't go outside if you don't have to, you loved cooking and classical music and guided tours to museums and all that . . . and I'm still convinced that if I didn't drag you out for walks you'd be too huge to get through your own door—"

"An accusation which is base, scurrilous, and almost certainly true."

"Well, yeah. I mean, put that all together. Anybody'd think you'd be just barely functioning if you were even alive, and I'd be the Jungle Queen of Daybreak. But look at us."

"You've done very well," James said. "On the RRC Board. Important missions completed. You're a blazing success in this new world."

"And you're Heather O'Grainne's good right hand." She drained her glass and poured another. "And brilliant at it. So I understand you are proposing this weird mix of Hogwarts and Starfleet Academy, but why do you want to run it personally?"

He shrugged. "Probably what you've always called my silent arrogance. There's no one else I trust to understand that it might be the most important thing we do. Right now we have a core of young-to-middle-aged scouts and agents who remember the old United States in their bones, who get up every morning half-expecting civilization and a President and Congress and a United States, and feel how abnormal it is not to have that.

"But give it twenty years and you'll have adults raising kids and voting who kind of remember central heating, and airports, but the republic will be a vague concept out of the past, on par with Byzantium—all they'll know is that there was one. We have to make sure they see what it has to do with them; as long as there are people who remember that we were all one nation once, and what it was that bound us together, then we might not be winning but we won't have altogether lost, either."

"So the Academy is like that kid at the end of *Camelot* that King Arthur says is his victory?"

"Well, Pueblo is not exactly Camelot—"

"You're telling me. Just try finding a knight in shining armor locally—"

"Hush, shameless. Not so much our last-ditch not-beaten-yet try at a win as much as it's support for all the other plans; almost everything else would have to fail before that became our main hope. Meanwhile the Academy of the United States will probably be useful, isn't likely to do any harm, and it's one of those things like a garden or a life preserver—get it before you need it."

They sat in silence for a long time, and when they did talk again, it was about the ongoing search through the pamphlet files, looking for things people could use in this wild new age.

4 DAYS LATER. MAUCKPORT, INDIANA. 8:30 AM EASTERN TIME. FRIDAY, FEBRUARY 27, 2026.

Jenny sternly squelched her envy when the messenger rode up; Jeff had made it abundantly clear that as much as he had appreciated her being a volunteer messenger at the battle of Jeffersonville, and although it had undoubtedly boosted both of their popularity, there would be no repetitions "unless there's another big mess, and I'd just as soon not have any more of them." At least he had conceded that since she had remained completely quiet and unobtrusive in his headquarters, it was silly to pretend she'd be in the way there, or more out of danger elsewhere.

So she knew what was going on, which was better, but every messenger seemed to come in from the big, interesting world outside, and she couldn't help thinking how much more interesting it was out there.

And just in case of another big mess, she'd equipped Buttermilk with two saddlebags: one with rations, canteen, and extra ammo, and the other empty, in case someone happened to hand her a dispatch. *Can't hurt to be prepared.*

This messenger wore regular-Army Rorschach jammies and a Stetson he'd probably gotten from the TexICs. He was slim and short, and had a strange band of tattoos around his eyes, something a rebellious high school student might have sported back before. Jenny wondered if he'd lied about his age, or if anyone even checked age anymore. *Maybe he just looks young because of the tattoo, or that bewildered expression.*

Jeff read the dispatch. "Corporal, what's your name?"

"Dave McWaine, sir."

"I'm asking because we'll be talking a little while. Try to relax, you're doing your job, and don't worry about what I might prefer to hear. Did you come directly from Colonel Prewitt?"

"Yes, sir."

"Did he tell you what the dispatch was about?"

"No, sir, but I did guess it. He was standing right there looking at where their campsite had been, and they're gone. Nothing left but the spots of yellow grass where their tents were, the paths they trampled, a few big piles of bodies, and the charred spots where they had cookfires. Not a trace."

Grayson nodded. "And those were the things I was going to ask about. Any other evidence that you remember or comes to your mind?"

"It was, well, cleaner than a Daybreaker camp usually is, sir. I think that just means they left a while ago, 'cause we had that big rainstorm yesterday, and it probably washed away a lot of the shit. Sorry, sir."

Grayson smiled. "I am aware that soldiers sometimes use the word 'shit,' Corporal. I was just thinking of using it myself."

Late that afternoon Bambi Castro flew low over the camp and dropped a reconnaissance dispatch: the whole Daybreaker horde had fled more than thirty miles northward, past Palmyra, and was still moving at a near run, leaving their dead and exhausted behind on the road.

Grayson looked from face to face in the darkening room, and said, "Well, that's why the patrols didn't catch them and won't catch them. Those men will be coming in all night; make sure they're fed and they get a decent place to sleep, since I made them ride so hard all day for nothing. We'll send a fast advance guard downstream—have them go out at dawn, and see if it's the same situation at the next camp. I have an awful feeling it will be."

"Why 'awful,' sir?" The militia colonel who asked that looked like she should be someone's grandmother. "It puts us ahead of schedule if nothing else."

"Our schedule was built around being ahead of their schedule. Now they've changed it. They won't have changed it to put themselves behind. Have the tech people set up a radio, for keyed transmission, and give me the voice option too, in case General Phat wants to call back."

If he's in a hurry to talk to Shorty Phat, Jenny thought, *the situation is much more serious than it's ever been before.*

THE NEXT DAY. FACILITY 1, PUEBLO. 7:15 AM MOUNTAIN TIME. SATURDAY, FEBRUARY 28, 2026.

James had a meeting later that day, and if he could get anything out of 162, he needed it for the meeting. He knew this had been happening a great deal, lately, but he didn't see any way around it. Jason was grumpy about coming out to be the backup and stabilizer, but there was apt to be violence, and Izzy was just too small and Beth was pregnant.

Jason understood that as well as James, but seemed to feel entitled to be grouchy anyway.

This time, however, Interrogation Subject 162 was wide awake when they got there. They ran through several exercises which should have triggered seizures, and none did; to all appearances, Daybreak was not active in 162 today.

At last, seeing no clever approach, James asked directly. "So here's what we are wondering about. Not only did the tribals pull out of Mauckport before we got there, but air reconnaissance shows that they're pulling back all the way along the line, everywhere, not only abandoning the camps where they were living for months, but scattering and taking different ways home to their tribal camps, traveling in groups of a couple dozen or so. And very often the camps are emptying out too, with tribals heading north and east. It looks like a wide area retreat."

"Daybreak is sort of a living thing. That's probably why it's less active in my mind today; it's trying to hide, retreat, crawl back under its rock like an octopus, you see? It's been burned badly and it's scared and trying to back up. If you press it now—especially if you drive right at the head—you might might might—"

162 began to wave his arms around and fell thrashing to the floor. When he emerged from the seizure, he seemed even more lucid. "Look, you do more than just establish that Daybreak is in retreat. This is where you can turn the war against Daybreak into part of the new national mythology for the Restored Republic. And that mythology is truly vital; you can't just give people 2023 back in 2028 and say, here we are, everything is normal, sorry about nine-tenths of you dying off in the last five years. The Restored Republic won't be the old one, and it needs myths of its own, stories like Lexington and Shiloh and the Bulge that define it, that have heroes who can be held up as models, not because the children will really model themselves after them, but because everyone can have the experience of agreeing about the greatness. Well, 'we beat them up and they backed off and went home for the summer' is not a great myth, and it won't make any heroes. 'We drove right to the enemy capital and smashed it till not stone stood upon stone,' that's a myth, and one that's going to have some heroes. So pick a target—this Castle Earthstone sounds like a good one—and pour it all into taking it and smashing it. Make yourself some heroes."

Jason must have felt strange about all this, because he ran Interrogation Suspect 162 through half a dozen more seizure-inducing routines, but he passed without difficulty, complained of being sleepy, and curled up under the blankets as soon as they said he was done for this session.

AN HOUR LATER. PUEBLO. 9:15 AM MOUNTAIN TIME. SATURDAY, FEBRUARY 28, 2026.

"If I win the election there is going to be an executive order that all national security personnel be able to bake." General Phat spread butter on the thick slice of fresh bread, slid the poached egg onto it, lifted it, and ate reverently; it had only been in the past couple of months that they had gotten egg production up to satisfactory levels, and though they were becoming common again, eggs still tasted like a treat.

A snow-rain mix of big damp flakes and stinging, spitting droplets flung itself against James Hendrix's windows, but inside, the woodstove had been fired up for hours, and the house was warm and comfortable. Heather sprawled on the couch, with Leo on her lap; Hendrix and Phat leaned back in the armchairs.

When they had finished, Phat said, "All right. Look, I don't have any more idea than Grayson does what the enemy is up to, but he's right. The hordes pulling back from the rivers doesn't look like a retreat; it looks like they're going to try something different. Whatever it is, Grayson'll handle it."

James said, "I've got some intel from one of our best interrogation sources that might be relevant."

Phat nodded, and James explained, "Two things, really. One is that Daybreak apparently can do foolish things just like a more conventional person. Right now it's overreacting because we've scared it and hurt it so it's pulling back. I guess once you get the momentum going, they're not likely to stop running. The other is that this campaign is very likely to produce some heroes, if we deliberately create some big battles deep in their territory that really make our people look like conquerors."

Phat nodded. "Assuming that it's not a trap. Or that we couldn't just let them go back to their inadequate farming and hunting and count on starvation to do the job this winter. But your source recommends against that?"

"The argument seems to be that we have them on the ropes and now we should knock them out," James said.

"Well, since Grayson is the theater commander for this, I don't intend to second-guess him. I'll mention the possibility of a knockout, and of course if he's serious about winning the presidential election, being a bold hero instead of a prudent winner-on-points won't hurt either. But he can make those decisions himself. I'm not worried about his competence. I am worried about what's going on inside him, and what's going to happen if he is handed a big bad surprise, like a major defeat or reversal."

Heather and James just looked at him, quietly, for a while, until finally Heather said, "Look, he's a pushy jerk. He's an entitled spawn of the old ruling class. He's a deeply weird guy who married a really smart woman who chooses to look like a porno star, and cut a deal to sell out our republic to a bunch of dumbass hick just-barely-graduates of Bible college, and most of all, he assassinated a friend of yours—and mine!—for reasons of purely personal ambition. So you and I both detest him, no question. But for some reason you also think he's—what? the weak reed? the defective cog in the machine? You talk and act like you expect him to crack up and destroy everything, any minute. And every now and then you hint that you know something really bad about him. Normally I'd regard that as your business and his, but we've got the whole future of our country bet on that asshole, and I think we're entitled to know more than that you don't like him and don't really trust him but you think he's the best we can do. Now for the love of God, tell us what it is. We sure as shit have a right to know."

Phat turned toward the window, and then seemed to realize, himself, that it was a melodramatic gesture. He raised a hand as if to make a point, then let it flop uselessly at his side. At last he obviously forced himself to look Heather, and then all the others, in the eye, before he blurted out, "I didn't think I'd ever tell this story.

"Grayson and I were in the same entering class of second lieutenants, back in 1996. Busiest generation of officers with more combat time in more places than any since World War Two, maybe since the Indian Wars. Grayson and I happened to be posted to the same places, more than once. He was an old-family Southerner, ancestors on both sides of the Civil War, too many uniforms to count in the family tree, a trust fund back there someplace he never touched, the kind that saluted when the doctor slapped his bottom.

"My folks thought I was going to be a concert pianist or maybe a brain surgeon, or ideally both, though they'd have settled for CEO of IBM. Remember that stupid old saying that the last people who believed in America were Asians? Well, maybe there was some truth in it. At least we believed in all the work hard and get ahead stuff.

"It was a big rebellion for me to go to West Point; the fact that Uncle

Sam paid for it all meant my parents couldn't cut me off, and they had no connections from which they could pull strings for my career. For Chinese-American parents that's like being fired. So Grayson belonged there from birth, and I was there in defiance of my upbringing, and we were going to *not* mix about as thoroughly as any two men were ever going to not mix. We never socialized, only ate at the same table when we happened to land there because of a mutual friend, that sort of thing. I don't think we traded fifty words before the story I'm about to tell you happened. We went our ways, at the Point, and after graduation, and through the beginnings of our careers. And, like I said, just purely at random, we drew a lot of assignments where we were around each other, but we didn't get to be friends and we barely interacted.

"Then one night a sergeant named Trimble that I barely knew came to me about something that had happened at a very-out-of-bounds party with, among other things, a couple teenage hookers, and officers fraternizing with enlisted, and some pretty serious drug issues. One of the prostitutes had been hurt badly enough to go to the emergency room—not anything lethal but, well, bad enough for an emergency room.

"By the time I was hearing about it from Trimble, it had already gone to the County Prosecutor. After a night of everybody-take-a-turn-on-the-drunk-girl, somebody had beat her bad enough to crack ribs and put a major hematoma in each breast and buttock, then dumped her in the emergency room.

"Since she left the party with Trimble, it was a real good circumstantial case, but probably not good enough to convict. It was a small-town ER and nobody saw Trimble bring her in; literally the desk attendant came out of the bathroom and there the girl was on the floor, whoever dropped her already gone, and the place was so backwoods there was no surveillance camera.

"Two, the party was in a hotel room, and although Trimble had said he'd take his turn with her and then take her home, witnesses thought they remembered Trimble asleep at the party after, but no one remembered him coming back; only one person remembered him leaving.

"If he kept his mouth shut, probably the judge would dismiss the charges, and he'd leave the Army with a general discharge. And he was even willing to accept the punishment, because . . . well, the Trimbles of this world seem to think it balances out between what they never get caught doing, which is a lot, and what they get blamed for that they didn't do. It was just that he wanted one officer to know he didn't do it."

Phat turned back toward the window and watched the foul weather.

James Hendrix asked very softly, "Grayson did it?"

Phat nodded. "According to Trimble, he and the girl went down to the parking lot and she realized he was way too drunk to drive, and while they were arguing, Grayson came up and offered to give her a ride if she'd put out on the way home. Trimble said he especially remembered because it gave him the creeps that Grayson had to humiliate the girl, making her agree to trade sex for a ride in front of someone else; he said, come on, of course, she was a hooker, she'd been used all night, one more for a ride home, of course she would, but Grayson made her stand there crying and say exactly what she'd do for a ride, and that made Trimble a little sick.

"Anyway they went off in Grayson's car, which was the last Trimble ever saw of either of them."

Heather said, "I was a cop for a long time. I can tell which witness you believe."

Phat made a face and balanced his hand. "I'm a lousy judge of people and situations. If I'd taken two minutes to put a spine into Norm McIntyre, make Cam Nguyen-Peters back down, and backed up Graham Weisbrod when I had the chance, none of this would matter and we'd have a functioning national government today. I misread all those men right when it was critical to get it right.

"So any judgment I make about people, you shouldn't be too quick to accept. Still, I still think Trimble was telling the truth, and I wasn't surprised to hear that about Grayson. Maybe I just disliked him because he'd inherited most of what I worked for, or maybe because he acts weird around Asians, though I'm not sure anyone else would even notice. But whatever. I believed Trimble.

"The case never came to trial. The girl didn't want to testify, and took off to go live with relatives in another state. By the time I heard about it, the girl had already gone across the state line and Trimble knew he wouldn't be tried, or court-martialed, but he asked me to put in a word for him; like I said, he just didn't want all of the officers to think he was that particular kind of monster, 'just see if you can put in a word for me so people don't think the worst, okay?' with a little rising whine on the 'okay' that made me want to shake him.

"So I went to my CO and told him, and he took me up to the major, who listened carefully, and made a couple of phone calls.

"I have a lot more experience now. I'd recognize that major as a guy who had decayed slowly on stateside duty.

"You might say there was something in the air. 9/11 hadn't happened yet, but things nobody remembers anymore like the car bomb in the World Trade Center and the attack on USS *Cole* had. Without anybody quite knowing or saying why, guys like that major were being routed into time-serving jobs where they'd finish out without doing much more harm.

"Well, maybe he *didn't* do much harm. He just told us that Grayson had a lot of family connections and political pull, and we could get into a sticky mess that would hang up everyone's career, but he'd do it if we wanted to pursue it. Or we could quietly take Trimble's word and he'd personally do his best to make sure Trimble didn't get burned."

"Which meant Grayson would get away with it," Heather said. *Funny, she thought, as a Fed, I saw clowns walk when we just couldn't get the right guy into a cell for something we knew damned well he did, and I learned to shrug about that, but this story is getting to me.*

"Yeah. Some years later Trimble—I kept track of him—was killed instantly by a sniper in Fallujah. The major was allowed to retire at a time when the Army was trying to retain anyone of any value, and I guess that says it all right there, eh?

"And time passed and Grayson and I made general. I can't prove that Grayson was sidetracked or I was fast-tracked, but I did get it three full years ahead of him, and a couple of times I was his commanding officer. Relations with him always had a little prickle in them, like he was waiting for me to do something obviously unfair, or I was waiting for him to complain about something he had no right to. After a while, I came to think that he knew that I knew. Maybe I couldn't quite conceal my contempt and distrust, or maybe I treated him like a guilty man and a weak reed, or maybe he'd found out I was Trimble's protector, but Grayson took it. It felt like, on some weird level, he agreed with me that he was a piece of shit."

Wind spattered a spray of sleet against the window. The stovepipe moaned. James tented his hands. "Quite a story."

Heather nodded. "Isn't it possible that he's different now?"

Phat shrugged. "We're modern Americans. We believe in redemption and second chances. But in my experience, some people hug the evil they did inside themselves until it takes them over, like somehow they are always saying 'This thing I did, and got away with, is the real me, and I'm still getting away with it, and it owns me, and it has a right to' down inside. I think that Grayson believes, with all his heart, that he's the kind of phony who does something repulsive and lets another man take the fall for it."

James's mouth distorted into a lopsided wince. "If Dickens had written him, he'd set him up with a moment of redemption. 'It is a far, far better thing I do,' and so on. Maybe Grayson will surprise himself that way, too."

"I sincerely hope that happens—and it brings him peace," Phat said, rising from his chair. "Well. We all have duties."

Heather looked up from bundling up Leo. "Ambitious, flawed guy with a young sexy wife he has to keep up with. And his boss, who knows his secret, is coming for a visit. Let's *hope* he's being scripted by Dickens. What if it's Shakespeare?"

James and Phat shared the experience of forcing a laugh.

ABOUT 2 WEEKS LATER. ON BOARD USS *DISCOVERY*, IN CHRISTIANSTED HARBOR. 6:15 AM ATLANTIC TIME. THURSDAY, MARCH 12, 2026.

The rising sun turned the thin fog in Christiansted harbor a soft gold, and then dissipated it. Red roofs, white walls, a perfect Caribbean sky, and the deep green low hills pulled the eye from one warm, eye-pleasing color to the next. The light breeze from the west smelled clean and fine; the tide was almost fully in.

Highbotham had rowed out to see them off. She and Halleck were reviewing everything that had been settled for at least a week. They paused for a moment by the group of sailor-scholars waiting by the railing, and Halleck said, "Captain Highbotham informs me that there is an opportunity I really should share with all of my junior seamen; I think she's trying to steal some of my crew."

Highbotham shook her head. "Couldn't be done, and besides I wouldn't be the one stealing you and this wouldn't be where you'd go. I just got a note from James Hendrix at RRC, the guy who writes the Jamesgrams. They are opening an Academy of the United States in Pueblo, first classes starting in January." Highbotham shrugged. "For many young people it's a golden opportunity, I'm sure. Sounds like it would beat being a farmer learning the hard way, or a refugee, or a foot soldier, which are the growth fields right now. But the crewmen on *Discovery* already have a better start than that. And maybe I flatter myself but I think the Caribbean Academy of Mathematics can take care of local needs for a while. If anyone wants to go a thousand miles inland to enjoy Rocky Mountain weather and spend all their time in a classroom, and live on noodles and potatoes and beef jerky all winter, instead of . . ." The sweep of her arm took in the town, the harbor, the island, perhaps the whole Caribbean. "Well, it seemed only fair for people to know the chance was available. I just think you'd have to be somewhere well beyond crazy to take it. And since time and tide waiteth et cetera, I'll wish you bon voyage and get myself off your deck, Captain. My prayers and envy are with you."

For the next hour, Whorf, Ihor, and every other sailor-scholar were far too busy with all the business of taking a sailing ship out of a harbor to look around much; by the time they had a moment to catch their breath, St. Croix was a low, lumpy green line on the horizon behind them.

2 DAYS LATER. PULLMAN, WASHINGTON. 1:00 PM PACIFIC TIME. SATURDAY, MARCH 14, 2026.

"Did they hurt your mouth bad this time?" Thompson asked, as soon as the other guards had gone. He was just outside the door, opening it a bare crack and keeping his foot planted against it. *Not quite ready yet*, Darcage thought, *but still, he asked without being prompted.* He nodded his head, slowly and carefully, as if changing the tension in the straps of the ball gag was hurting his teeth.

His teeth did hurt, but not because he was being beaten in the face, the idea he had been planting in Thompson. It was just that the mouthpiece they gave him could not fully protect him from the Daybreak seizures that they were triggering as a sort of daily ritual. He was not being tortured for the three hours a day he was absent; all that happened, every day, was that they brought him into the padded room, put the mouthpiece and a padded helmet on him, strapped him carefully to the floor, and threatened to force him to repudiate Daybreak. Instantly the world would become dark and confusing; three hours later he would wake up still in the restraints.

But over time he had convinced Thompson that he was being punched in the face for hours. A smarter boy than Thompson might have wondered why his face was never bruised, or why they were injuring a man's mouth if they wanted him to talk, but then a smarter boy than Thompson would never have opened the door or undone the gag in response to Darcage's tears, sighs, and whimpers.

"Skootch on over here," Thompson said, "and I'll let you out of that gag so's you can rest your mouth a little."

Making sure it looked like he was aching all over, Darcage crab-scooted on his ass, pushing with hands that he pretended were tender, and pushed his face upward so that Thompson could undo the gag; as Thompson removed it, Darcage stretched and flexed his jaw. He really was tired and sore there; it didn't take much acting.

"I'm just as glad to have somebody to talk to," Thompson said, "but we got to keep it real quiet. You heard 'bout Norman the Spanker?"

Darcage slowly shook his head, though he had overheard, and waited to see if he could learn anything new.

Thompson's whisper was furious and urgent. "That son of a bitch General Norman McIntyre, a.k.a. The Biggest Fuckin' Fag in the Army, he got this bug up his ass 'cause he figured out some of us that's on half-week duty, we been getting ourselves busted and stockaded just at the end of every shift, so's we wouldn't have to go home to our civilian jobs canning fish or digging potatoes and all that bullshit, instead we'd draw stockade time, and serve that here for a couple days, hell, it's a bed and food and no work, just pushups and shit, and then come round to we got out of the stockade, it was time for us to do regular duty here again. If he'd just let us militia soldiers be regulars when we want to he wouldn't have none of this trouble, but no, he made this big fuckin' deal out of it and so now there ain't no stockade no more. Stead of that it's a caning, like a fuckin' little kid, they just beat your ass with a stick and send you off to work, sore and all."

Darcage raised an eyebrow; Thompson made a wincing half-smile. "Yeah, I got my ass caught in that," he admitted. "Fuckin' crazy fuckin' General McIntyre. All them rules and all that bullshit and I can tell you it's just a pain in the ass. Something weird about a gay guy like that, you know, I mean like, there's not nothing wrong with it, I had some bosses and some friends in school, usually it ain't nothing, but some of'em, like McIntyre you know, I think they just like to hurt people. Like tearing skin off my butt for havin' a beer an hour before I was off duty. Like what they're doing to you."

"Makes sense to me," Darcage murmured, slurring his speech. "I don't think I can sleep, and it helps to have something to listen to. If you just need to vent, I can listen."

"Thanks. I really shouldn't be doing this, you know."

"You have a kind heart. Don't let it get you into trouble, but if you need to talk, I'm sure not going anywhere."

"Guess you got that right, anyway." Thompson began his litany of complaints slowly; today it was all reruns, but a lot of them. Darcage agreed sympathetically whenever it seemed reasonable, muttering and slurring to force Thompson to listen more and more closely. After a time he found the man's rhythm and began to reinforce it, fighting down his mounting excitement; he hadn't gotten this far with any guard before.

Thompson dropped the like-I-just-saids and the and-anothers and all the other acknowledgments of repetition. He began to repeat himself without knowing he was doing it, and the phrases became more and more alike, as Darcage reinforced them with his rhythmic, almost meaningless murmurs.

Ideally he'd have preferred to spend a week working on Thompson, but he didn't know how soon they would realize what he was and rotate him away. Probably soon; Thompson was probably like this everywhere, with everyone, all the time, whenever he wasn't actually being shouted at or beaten, and therefore he might be noticed and moved at any time.

Darcage pushed his luck and mumbled something about eye contact and a friendly face and just having a sense that they could have a real rapport, talk about the really important things, and Thompson did it: sat right down on the floor in the doorway, with the door partly open.

Fighting down the excitement he was afraid might leak into his voice, Darcage made more soothing and agreeing noises, and in less than an hour, Thompson was deeply asleep.

Darcage stood cautiously, trying not to clink. They had sewn the chains that joined behind his back to the seat of his pants, but with enough squirming, he pushed his pants down, slid the pant legs up the chain, and sat through so that he could join hands in front of himself. He had nothing to cut the chain, but standing on the pants and sawing back and forth, he quickly rid himself of the pants. He looked at the soles of his feet; after months of not walking much, he would definitely need Thompson's shoes.

He kept muttering the rhythmic suggestions so that Thompson barely woke as the chain wrapped his throat. As he pinned Thompson to the floor, tightening the chain to prevent any noise, he looked into the dying man's eyes and caught a miserable expression of betrayal. Darcage laughed so hard he began to fear he would make a noise, but he didn't, not while Thompson died, not while claiming his shoes and soiled but workable pants, not even when he noticed that the strangulation had given the poor dumbshit an erection that wobbled around like a failing flagpole when he gave the corpse a final kick.

2 DAYS LATER. PULLMAN, WASHINGTON. 1:15 PM PACIFIC TIME. SATURDAY, MARCH 14, 2026.

"All right, war crimes are bad, but clearing out tribals really shouldn't be counted as war, it's more of a public service like sewage or trash removal." Allie was losing all patience with her husband and with Norm McIntyre; she didn't mind the exclamations of outrage but the constant disappointed little winces were getting on her nerves. "Tribals get a chance to surrender, a brief one because they're dangerous and treacherous, and if they surrender we help them through an initial seizure. If they don't come out of it able to talk to us freely, then they don't have enough mind to be set free, so we just put them down like any dangerous nuisance animal. If they do come out talking like people, we send them to re-education camp—at taxpayer expense, mind you. Then either they recover and return to society minus certain rights like voting, owning property, and carrying weapons, or they revert, which proves they can't be rehabbed, and we put them down. I'm not looking to be gruesome but the spike in the back of the head is escape-proof, doesn't waste precious ammunition and powder, and with this etherizing jig that Doctor Jolly has invented, the process is literally fast and painless. So if we catch'em we convert'em or kill'em, and after a while, there are no more tribals."

McIntyre said, "I don't love'em either, but whether they recognize America or not, they are American citizens, and freedom of belief—"

"Daybreak isn't a *belief*. It's contagious evil that eats your soul. You've seen Darcage—"

President Weisbrod's voice was soft and calm as ever. "And what *are* you going to do with the ones like Darcage?"

"Weren't you listening? Doctor Jolly's neat little device. Which any decent blacksmith can build and which requires only a little ether, which we're already set up to make in industrial quantities."

Norm McIntyre leaned forward. "Because you intend to do all this to American citizens in 'industrial quantities'?"

"Well, yes. Mass production is efficient and quick. A few years' unpleasantness and we won't have to do it again."

Graham Weisbrod slid his wire-rimmed glasses up his nose. "More than seven billion dead, less than a billion left alive, and you think we need more killing?" He watched her like a fencer looking for an opening.

She shrugged. "The percentages are even worse in the US than they are worldwide, Graham. We were more dependent on technology, *and* we had more Daybreakers releasing nanospawn and biotes on Daybreak day, *and* we got hit with two superbombs. Three, really, if you count the way the California radiological bomb killed everything including cockroaches and moss between Irvine and Oakland. The rest of the world lost maybe eighty-five percent of the population, with us and China and Russia it was more like ninety-five, Europe probably ninety-seven. There are places that had worse death rates than us, and places that had much better. So what? You don't win a moral prize either way, and if you did—"

McIntyre seemed to be gaining confidence, and he asserted firmly, "In a country that has lost so many, every life should be precious."

"But that's where you're wrong. Every life that makes things better, or tries to, or will try to as soon as they can, or even would if they could, is precious, sure. But we've got a solid couple million or so trying to kill or at least immiserate the rest of us, because they have something the First Amendment was never *ever* intended to cover—a contagious madness—"

Weisbrod shook his head. "Even the most conservative Supreme Court justices ruled that—"

"Under the Old Republic. Nowadays—"

"Ms. Sok Banh!" They all jumped at the pounding on the door.

"Yes, Brianna?"

"Darcage has escaped!"

She rushed through the door and down the hall; she could straighten these two old men out later.

SEVEN:
A MONTH OF SURPRISES

The uproar far behind him, toward town, probably meant the little boys in their soldier costumes had found the place on the city wall where Darcage had flipped one of their emergency stairs down. A couple of sentries who had been playing cards in the shade rather than watching from the wall would be bending over for Norman the Spanker, but that was a tiny benefit compared to the sheer pleasure of standing here, bent over, deep in the shade of a wrecked plaztatic little burb-house, sucking in cool sweet free air.

He could catch his breath more safely inside. The window opened at his upward yank. He balled the chain up in his hands and threw himself upward, catching himself on the sill with his elbows. From there, he wriggled his head and shoulders inside. Raising and curling his legs, he toppled head first onto the floor. He rolled over, stood, grasped the sash, and pulled the window closed. Now the only signs of his passage were dented spots in the dirt by the outside wall, and a clean patch on the windowsill where his shirt had rubbed.

He dropped to all fours and crawled to the kitchen, since it was closest, in search of tools.

Shouting close by.

He crawled as fast as he could in his chains, staying low, avoiding windows. Unfortunately the people who had lived here had had artificial fabric drapes and plastic miniblinds, which had all fallen in crusty, rotten heaps, so there was little cover and anyone could look through any window.

The initial burst of yelling had died down, but the searchers still sounded close. At least there was no barking; a trained dog would have been leaping and barking at the window by now.

The kitchen windows faced the back yard, which had a privacy fence, so by staying low, he was able to search through drawers and cabinets. He found only a can opener, which he pocketed in the hope of finding something to open, and a carving knife.

Motion caught his eye; a man rode by the back fence on horseback, but at the angle, Darcage doubted that he could see in through the glass, and anyway he'd been moving too fast for a good look. Nevertheless, he hastily peeked behind the closed doors, all the while watching and listening for any motion near the house, especially outside the kitchen window. He found an already-emptied pantry, a coat closet with zippers and buttons lying in congealed goo on the floor, and stairs to the basement.

Nerving himself, staying on all fours, he slipped through the door and pulled it closed behind him. If they just didn't see the wiped sill and the footprints in the old flower bed . . . as he crept down into the basement, he kept his carving knife in hand, where it comforted him with a promise that if they found him, he had either his defense or his exit.

The basement stank of mold. Striations of water damage marked the walls, but the floor was dry. At the workbench, he found bolt cutters and a hacksaw; pausing to listen every few seconds, he freed himself, and then put the chains and tools under the stairs by the water heater, sweeping with the broom to get the shiny fresh metal swarf under the stairs as well.

As he finished sweeping, he heard distant hoofbeats approach, then recede, then approach again; silence, and then another pass. Apparently they were still riding around, oppressing the filthy destructive horses, human-tainted animals who would make a fine feast for some tribe someday, a cleaner and better use than in suppressing Mother Earth's righteous wrath.

Still, the sentimental little boy he had once been was glad that he would probably not have to hurt a horse to get away; unlike people they were at least pretty, and in a couple generations the survivors could be wild again.

There was nothing to do but stay where he was; the windows were down in wells so unless someone came right up to one, they wouldn't see him. If he could find a corner with no line of sight to a window, he'd curl up there with his knife beside him, and rest while he gave the hunt time to spread out and move farther away.

Meanwhile, what else might be useful?

When he opened one closet door, he suppressed a gasp of pure joy; ranks of cans filled the shelves on one side, and there was room to sit in the closet itself, completely out of sight of all the windows.

A moment later he was laughing at his own hopes; the rest of the shelves were piled with the glass and metal parts of home wine- and beer-making equipment. All the cans held wine-making grapes. Still, it was food, and he was hungry. He stepped forward and his foot found a rolling bottle.

When he looked down he saw the corpse.

The floods and the mice had stripped the face off the skull. The shirt had been artificial-fiber and had decayed into slime over the rib cage and the emptied abdomen, but the denim jeans, and the pile of gray hair remained in surprisingly good shape. The leather belt had been gnawed through and lay in pieces.

At least a dozen empty bottles lay around the body. Probably he or she had sat here and drunk till it was all gone, and then died in any of the ways a really drunk passed-out person dies: choking, alcohol poisoning, diabetic coma, stroke.

Darcage pushed the mostly skeletal corpse up to lean face-first against the door; if anyone opened that, they were in for a surprise and would probably make some noise, giving him time to react. At the back of the closet, he sat on a metal stool, and opened one of the big cans of grapes, then held it aloft in a thankful toast. *I'm not sorry for what happened to you at all, but I appreciate your being my guard, and I am glad that you found an exit via something you love.*

ABOUT 2 WEEKS LATER. ON LAKE ERIE, NORTH OF LONG POINT, ONTARIO. 3:30 PM EASTERN TIME. SUNDAY, MARCH 29, 2026.

"We're here," Rosie said. "That's Pottohawk Point on the horizon, across the big ice sheet, just like the escaped slaves described." He handed his field glasses to Scott Niskala, shivering beside him in the crows'-nest of *Kelleys Dancer.*

Niskala looked, adjusting the binoculars for his eighty-year-old eyes. The moon, a couple of days short of full, was low in the western sky, silhouetting the tribal camp around the old marina. He counted three of them patrolling, and two groups of soldiers around fires.

The partly smashed and sunken dock led down to a sheet of ice which reached a full mile toward them. On the ice, Niskala counted more than a hundred wooden structures, each about the area of a small house, and maybe a third the height. "Give me and the guys till dawn, but be ready to run as soon as we get back."

. . .

Their canoes moved through the water without sound until they scraped on the pebbles of the beach. They dragged them between two big bushes to be easy to find and hard to see.

"Reminders," Niskala whispered. "Kill two. Plant four. Come back."

The three boys all nodded and slipped into the darkness; Niskala slipped quietly through the darkness towards the tribal encampment. Being out on a night raid-and-rec was as familiar as an old sweater. He had grown up in the Iron Range, where venison was a staple and a rifle was a tool for acquiring it; his father had pushed a military career so hard that Niskala had done most of a tour in LRPs before he'd really considered doing anything else, and even then, he'd gone straight into the Forest Service and spent his life in the woods, often carrying a weapon. *Wonder if I'm the only Vietnam vet currently serving in the US Armed Forces?*

Wonder if the Wapak Scouts Company of the Stone Laboratory Militia Battalion counts as US Armed Forces?

Wonder if it's still the US?

Shut up, old man.

That last thought was by far the most comforting.

His first kill was easy; the man was bent over a frying pan on the little fire, poking at his dinner with a stick. Niskala slid in beside him and hatcheted the back of his head so hard that the blade went in up to the shaft. Letting the body lie facedown across the fire, he planted a foot on the neck and wrenched the hatchet back out.

The second was almost trouble; he glimpsed motion on the far side of a tent, crept around slowly, and looked into the wide, white eyes of a man squatting to crap on the ground. His hatchet lashed out in a hard backhand, knocking the man over sideways, but embedding itself in his jaw.

The tribal screamed through his shattered mouth, a bubbling inarticulate sound, and Niskala stepped over the thrashing body, pulled a garrote from his pocket, and wrapped the man's neck, but not before his target moaned again. "That's right," Niskala said, loud enough to carry. "Take it all the way, bitch, take it *all* the way."

He heard laughter from the surrounding tents. *Weird thing about tribals, they're communal but there's no community spirit. I guess people that are all planning to die anyway don't get so attached.* He tightened the garrote more, hampered a little by the hatchet handle still sticking sideways out of the man's jaw. A moment later his victim went limp. The damp night air reeked of warm shit and blood.

Niskala pulled out the hatchet and set about planting his four "little bottles of surprise," as Fred Rhodes, back at Stone Laboratory, had called them. Each was a bottle of wood alcohol; to set them, Niskala inserted a test tube into the neck, filled the test tube with acid from the flask he carried, dropped in a gelatin capsule of whatever it was that Fred had brewed up, inserted the narrow part of an oversized cork into the test tube, and pushed the tube and cork down into the bottle till the outer edge of the cork seated.

When the acid ate through the gelatin, an hour or two from now, there would be a small hot explosion to set the alcohol on fire and scatter it around. For the last half hour before detonation, the thinning gelatin capsule would be less and less stable, so that a light touch might set it off; if they found it right away, the Daybreakers might disarm it, but after half an hour it would be on a hair trigger until it blew spontaneously.

Keeping to shadows, Niskala crept down to the old pre-Daybreak buildings, figuring they would have been reserved for something important. They were up a couple of feet on pilings, so he rolled a bottle in under the first one; he realized there were people sleeping under the second, so he crawled in and wedged the bottle into the brace of a floor joist, less than a yard from a particularly dense huddle; when the blazing liquid hit their blankets, with them trapped in this low space, that ought to be good for plenty of chaos and panic, which was what the mission was all about. *Like I tell the boys, try to exceed specs on the core mission.*

Following the marked path to the nearest raft on the ice, he found it was sitting up on concrete blocks. *Sort of clever. Bottom and sides don't get frozen in. Then when it thaws, it just settles into the water, and the blocks sink away.*

A snore alerted him; peering over the gunwale cautiously, he saw that several of them were bunched together in an open-fronted cabin, piled onto each other like stacked cordwood. *Probably the crew-to-be.* He felt along the gunwale and found several oarlocks. *All right, and they're planning on rowing. Enough intel, let's go to ops.*

Rather than chance climbing in, after preparing his bottle, he reached over the gunwale and wedged it into the external corner of the aft cabin. *That'll make another wakeup call.*

That left one bottle and plenty of time to go. He thought about it for a moment, and decided to leave it in the sailboat with the tallest mast, moored in the pool of kept-open water by the pier. Quietly, he crept out on the pier; by the moon, he still had more than an hour.

Something was subtly wrong. A dark smear on the deck led his eye to a hand stretched outside a doorway.

His shoulder was gently squeezed with the Morse for 73—"friend." He turned.

It was Kyle, who pointed at the boat and drew a finger across his throat. Niskala held up the bottle; Kyle gestured that there was already one aboard the boat.

Lying prone and leaning out, with Kyle holding his feet, he planted it on the crossbeam closest to shore under the pier; if the pier itself burned, it might take several boats with it.

Still not having spoken, they crept in the shadows of the trees by the shore back to the canoes, where Derek and Marty were already waiting. As they pushed off and glided away, Niskala thought, *I really ought to do something about getting these boys their Eagles. This is one hell of a service project and I think we can waive a merit badge or two.*

. . .

The moment they had swung their canoes aboard *Kelleys Dancer* and tied them down, Rosie whispered, "Ready? Everyone back aboard?"

"Yep," Niskala said. "Went real well."

"Need two of you on the lines and two working the anchor winch."

In less than a minute, they were moving, with Rosie going aft to take the tiller from Barbara. The wind was light but steady. In an hour the rising sun would raise a land breeze against them. "We might have to make you all row, so stay dressed," Barbara warned. "Meanwhile I've got some hot broth and not-too-awful biscuits."

The biscuits were delicious and abundant. As they finished wolfing them down, Barbara leaned in to say, "Rosie says something you should see on deck."

The bruise-red sun rose from the lake in front of them, turning the snow-covered ice a dozen shades of crimson, pink, and orange. The dim peninsular shore to their south, shrouded in dense mist, bent around west behind them, and Niskala watched that way, waiting for sounds or light.

After a little while, the low clouds were lit with orange flickers, and sounds of screaming and shouting came to them through the fog. Abruptly, flames reached above that black horizon.

"The ground at Pottohawk would've been just out of sight from the crows'-nest about now," Rosie observed. "So the flames are about that high, which is forty-nine feet. One of you sure hit the jackpot."

"Any chance any of them saw our sail?" Niskala asked.

"Maybe. But even if they try to run all the way to the tip of Long Point to cut us off, we'll get there before they do."

"What's burning that high?" Niskala asked. "I bombed a raft, the old pier, and a couple of the main buildings. Nothing I'd've thought would go up like that."

Derek laughed. "That was probably me. They had this massive wood-fired still, and a big pyramid, of barrels of booze. I shoved one bomb way deep into the middle of that pyramid. So if that booze was distilled enough to burn, the whole thing probably went off in one big whoosh."

A big, blazing orange ball of flames climbed out of the tribal camp, and the screaming became wailing.

Marty and Kyle laughed with obvious admiration, and clapped Derek on the back, telling him he had the bragging rights for the op.

Not exactly the kind of scouts I used to produce, Niskala thought. He wished he were already back with Ruth.

THE NEXT DAY. GIBRALTAR. 11:45 AM CENTRAL EUROPEAN TIME. MONDAY, MARCH 30, 2026.

"First time I saw the Rock," Ihor said, "I was fourteen, and my papers said I was eighteen, and they were working me so hard I felt like I was a hundred. But it was beautiful, and just like all the pictures."

"It's a big white rock," Whorf said. It sounded stupid to him even as he said it.

As usual when coming into a port, they were standing by with nothing to do, waiting to be madly busy. On their way across the Atlantic, all the scholar-sailors had had plenty of time for study, and everyone else had been happy to help them fill it. Whorf had drawn images from the microscope for Lisa Reyes till his hand was sore, and then until it was strong, and finally till it was indefatigable. Ihor's knack for languages had made him the pet of their three language-and-linguistics specialists, so he had spent his time cramming Portuguese, Arabic, Catalan, and Italian.

"This is nice, just waiting to pull on a rope," Whorf said. "My brain's about ready for a rest."

"Yours and mine both," Ihor said. "That *is* how you say it?"

"That is. You sound Old New York already."

"Someday when we are old, nobody will believe we remember Old New York, before it was Manbrookstat, and the kids—"

Then Halleck's bellowed orders set them scrambling, as *Discovery* worked her way into the harbor under sail alone, the immense white rock larger whenever Whorf had time to look.

THE NEXT DAY. CASTLE SUNSNAKE, HOME OF THE PEOPLE OF GAIA'S DAWN, IN THE FORMER HELLS CANYON NATIONAL RECREATIONAL PARK. 8:30 PM LOCAL SOLAR TIME. TUESDAY, MARCH 31, 2026.

Darcage had watched the entire *Play of Daybreak* with tears of joy pouring over his face just to be home.

He knew he was believing, totally and utterly, something he had not always believed. Of course, once he had been someone else and had a different name. His memories overlapped peculiarly.

One of the most hateful of all the hateful things in his involuntary stay in alleged civilization had been the cruelty and relish with which they had repeatedly forced Darcage to confront those inconsistencies. They had dug into his mind like painful little burrs: how could he remember both his initiation as a man into his tribe, at age fourteen, and first hearing of Daybreak when a girl he was hot for took him to a warehouse dance-and-chant in south Queens? Why could he be tricked into crossing himself if he had been raised as the son of a Teaching Shaman of the Guardian on the Moon? Why did he insist on pronouncing his name dar-SAHJ like some phony Frenchman when his memories did not include France, and why, when they asked him the question in French, had he started to answer it?

Every little burr of conflict had been the seed of a tooth-rattling seizure, from which he had emerged to worse questions, uglier threats, more abuse of himself and his tribe and Mother Gaia, between mocking, laughing visits from the Horrid Bitch.

Now, he simply wallowed in the way that he could just accept all the pieces of the contradiction, knowing that he had always been destined for a special shamanhood, conducting diplomacy between the tribes by leading them all to the correct and real Daybreak, and knowing that he had lived off the grid but on the net in a Daybreaker nest filled with computers and fabricators until Daybreak day in 2024, when they had picked up the buckets of biote culture and nanospawn from the benches, climbed to the roof to throw them into the early morning breeze, broken the doors off, and left forever.

His mind held his first Sun Dance and his first Sundance Festival comfortably next to each other, and that was one of the finest comforts of home. Now he relaxed and accepted all those dreams of memories and memories of dreams, drifting graceful and untouched between the horns of the dilemma and into its friendly, gentle, toothless mouth.

The Play of Daybreak was the tribe's weekly enactment of the story he had always known, loved, and lived. Mother Gaia's seven daughters lovingly seduced the servants of the Seven Misters, and brought forth the nanospawn and biotes to end the plaztatic world; if somehow it seemed to overlie or exist at the same time as *Star Wars* and First Communion, that was not anything to worry about right now. Eventually, the world would be consistent.

Daybreak loved him.

Every terrifying moment of his captivity, escape, and flight was now worth it just to be back here in the sanity.

His heart leapt up at the final dance by the whole cast, as the Servant of Mister Atom proclaimed that he was going to live on the moon and hurl his thunderbolts against anyone who tried to resurrect deadly Mister Electron again, and for a moment, he did not realize that the Servant of Mister Atom had just asked, "Would Darcage, of the New Green World People, please come forward?"

Darcage stood and walked slowly down the aisle; the people around him rose and cheered, welcoming him, loving him, making him feel he belonged there. He approached the Servant of Mister Atom slowly and tentatively, much like the first time a very young child knows who Santa is. "Kneel, Darcage, for I have a blessing for you."

Applause thundered through the crowd, for everyone knew the story of the horrors Darcage had witnessed in the last holdouts of the plaztatic world. The People of Gaia's Dawn themselves had lost a shaman and a war leader to the Provis's brutal regime within the last two months. "Will Crystal Vision please come forward to assist Darcage?"

He felt her strong, cool hands on his shoulders, but did not look back at the chief shamaness.

"I speak now as the representative of the Guardian on the Moon." The actor's voice took on the slow, precisely articulated quality that marked a direct message from Daybreak itself. "Blessed are you, Darcage, for a mighty work is prepared for you as soon as you are strong and well. One task remains in your life before you go to dwell with the Guardian on the Moon, and for this task, you will be known forever to all the tribes who keep true faith with Mother Earth. Crystal Priestess, you may whisper his mission to him now."

He felt the soft touch of her lips by his ear, and realized she had taken a moment to kiss his neck first. She whispered, "You have been chosen to slay the last President of the United States of America, and free the world from the shadow of plaztatic empire. Come to my sleeping place for the details tonight. And then"—her tongue ran slowly over his earlobe—"stay there, in the bed, for I want to bear the child of the Great Slayer."

The surge of joy in his heart was accompanied by a more primal surge in another organ.

She led him to the front of the stage where he took several bows while the crowd roared at him in a glorious, joyous thunder of approval. They guided him to a seat of honor with the chiefs and shamans, and the play resumed.

The Servant of Mister Atom declared that his exposure to evil plaztatic radiation had made him unfit to father children, and therefore he would take no spouse. He proclaimed that he would fly to the moon, there to listen for the whisperings of Mister Electron trying to rise from the grave, and hurling the fire he had taken from Mister Atom and the lightning of Mister Electron himself against them whenever he heard the least trace, being ever vigilant and ready to strike.

The burial of Mister Smart, everyone was assured, would be forever permanent.

After a last choral hymn to Mother Earth, Crystal Priestess came forward to lead him to her home, but they had to stop first and delay a while, because the whole tribe wanted to hug Darcage. At last, however, he was free to go home with her, where he accepted both the spiritual and physical gifts of the priestess with immense enthusiasm.

2 DAYS LATER. CASTLE EARTHSTONE. 3:30 PM LOCAL SOLAR TIME. THURSDAY, APRIL 2, 2026.

Robert watched the man's eyes widen at the sight of the heads on sticks. *First, they sent the Cop; then Gandalf; then Enchantress Woo Woo. They must be running low on quality people to sacrifice, because what they've sent me here is Scared Little Man.*

"Well," Robert said. "You have a message to deliver. Maybe you should."

The little gray man, in his oversized T-shirt, blanket poncho, and pigskin moccasins said, "Daybreak has commanded me to ask a favor."

"Whether I do anything for Daybreak, or not, and whether I accept your message, or not," Robert said, "stay with us. We will help you through withdrawal from that wrong and untrue version of Daybreak that your tribe uses to control you. And we'll give you the True Daybreak, and make you a better and happier man here than you ever were there."

"I was chosen because I am of little value," the man said, tears running down his face, "and I want—I want—" He fainted.

"Now what, boss?" Bernstein asked.

"He's having one of those seizures, obviously."

Bernstein was already kneeling by the little man, turning him so he wouldn't choke and firmly pushing his flailing limbs down. "I know that, boss, I've seen as many as you have. I mean, why'd you do it?"

"Just a wild hair up my ass, maybe. I have an idea, maybe a good one. We'll see when he comes out. Talk nice to him when he does, gentle him, you know how we did with the slaves."

When the man's eyes opened and Bernstein had made some soothing sounds and given him a drink of water, Robert said, "You are welcome to stay; it may be rough for a few days. But I won't throw you away the way Daybreak did you. All my people here matter to me. We don't keep slaves. Everyone can get married, and I don't make them kill their babies. Everybody has a name and we're not looking for a way to use you all up and kill you. You're going to like it here. For now, though, I guess we should hear your message."

The little man, seen close up and helpless on the floor, looked even smaller and less prepossessing; the sort of fellow that, back before, had worked a counter, pushed a mop, or guarded a building that didn't need guarding, and been nearly invisible. He gasped and more tears gushed; his mouth worked but no sound came out.

Robert knelt on one knee and said, "If your message pisses us off, we know it ain't your message, so you got the same deal whether we love it or hate it. Now stay with us, let us take you out of the false Daybreak and make you one of us, and we will *never* say that you are 'of little value.' But for right now, just tell us the message. We know it ain't from you, but it'll be better if we hear it while you ain't in the Daybreak trance, so's you can tell us the truth about it." He made himself smile; the little man was crying hard now.

Studying him, Robert could see that he was probably younger than the sixty or so he looked; the deep wrinkles and chapping from two winters outdoors, plus the gray skin from eating badly and rarely washing, had made him old, tired, and sick. *I don't think I have ever felt a drop of pity for anyone in my whole life, but if I did, this is the one I'd start on,* Robert thought, and forced himself to speak gently. "Now, just tell your message. It's your job. Don't be afraid. And as soon as we hear it, we'll see about what we can do for you. You are more important to me than the ones who sent you."

The little man sat up, drew a deep breath, and looked down at his feet. "The words they made, made, made me memorize were 'The evil Armies of the Old Plaztatic Order have joined together, forces from the pretender empires at Athens and Olympia, from the treacherous genocidal Duchy of California, and from the very heart of Black and Vile Plaztatic Technology at Pueblo. They have attacked the tribes preparing to carry Daybreak into Kentucky, and by cruel brutality, evil tricks, and sheer—'"

Robert said, "Okay, so the prelude, without all the spinny bullshit is that General Grayson and the army, which Daybreak would have been expecting if it had known crap or understood anything, came over the river in the middle of the night, and because they're a disciplined force with guns and horse cavalry and a few airplanes, they surrounded the big mob of tribals that was supposed to wreck Kentucky, and wrecked them first, then moved down the Ohio like a lawnmower for people, ripping the guts out of Daybreak's spring offensive before it could launch. The tribes have been running north like deer out of a forest fire, Daybreak has lost the north bank of the Ohio, and right now they look like they'll run all the way to Indianapolis, maybe further. What's Daybreak want me to do about that?"

He gasped, choked, and forced out, "Daybreak Council told me to say if you let them be swept away and destroyed over the summer, next summer you will have to fight the Restored Republic all by yourself."

"They have a point," Robert said. "Were you gonna bring back a message?"

"I was told to bring one back if you gave me one and if you let me go."

"We ain't sending you back after what they've done to you. Unless you want to go back."

"No, no, no—" The little man fell sideways, kicking and struggling.

"Bernstein, keep an eye on him. Nathanson, find me the rudest guy with balls you've got that you'd like to get rid of."

"I got twenty of those at least. Ever since you freed the slaves. What d'you need a guy to do, chief?"

"Give me someone to go insult the Daybreak leaders to their ugly faces. If they kill him I can be all aggrieved and give them shit and demand more from them, and if they take shit from him, it means they're weak and I'll have a list of more shit for him to demand. Either way we get as much as we can and they get shit."

"I have the perfect man in mind." Nathanson grinned.

"Is it Calhoun?"

"Yeah. I warn you, though, Lord Robert, he'll be twice as impossible if he comes back alive."

Robert shrugged. "If we can't fix the impossible, we can always fix the alive."

Nathanson nodded and was gone. Robert turned back to where Bernstein was attending to the little man spasming on the ground.

"He's really fighting it now, chief. We can send in a couple people to carry him to bed and have the usual people do the deprogramming."

"That's what I was thinking. Make that happen."

As they left the inner courtyard, Bernstein added, "Well, this is your day for not doing things I expect, Lord Robert. You want to share what's on your mind?"

Robert nodded. "Remember right after Lord Karl died, when you threw in with me and helped make me the Lord?"

"Of course."

"Well, so do I. Little Mister Scared will be loyal to whoever stops him being afraid. Calhoun will be loyal to the man who gives him a chance to get killed doing something impossible. Loyal people generally work out for me, one way or another." He patted Bernstein's shoulder. "Beer time yet?"

"With you, Lord Robert, always."

12 DAYS LATER. LUNA PIER, NEW STATE OF SUPERIOR (FORMERLY MICHIGAN). 5:30 AM EASTERN TIME. TUESDAY, APRIL 14, 2026.

The moon was a thin crescent like a bow bent toward the not-yet-risen sun. It back-lit more than a hundred low rafts coming in to the sand beaches south of the pier. Lookouts lit the fires and rang the bells.

Outnumbered twenty to one, the town militia still mustered behind the crude breastwork, just a row of sawhorses with corrugated iron sheets nailed to them, arranged in a line on each side of their single rocket launcher.

The old people, children, and others unable to fight picked up what they could carry in backpacks and wheelbarrows and set off north toward Allen Cove; there was little question the Daybreakers could chase them down if they wanted to, but perhaps they would choose to do something else. As the rafts neared, they could hear the singing and the drums, then the splashes of the oars, and finally the grunting of the rowers.

"Canoe with a truce flag!" one of the lookouts shouted, and a moment later, another cried, "They're shipping oars."

Still out of rocket range, the tribal armada paused in the water; a lone canoe, with a single passenger holding up a white flag, moved swiftly toward the beach.

On the sand still spattered with ice and snow, the mayor of Luna Pier confronted the Daybreaker representative. The mayor looked like what she was, a civic-minded grandmother, dressed in baggy pants and multiple sweaters, her helmet under her arm. The tribal representative wore a buffalo-horn hat that must have been stolen from some fraternal lodge; it was festooned with feathers, bits of metal, jewelry, and—the mayor saw to her disgust—a dried human hand. Below that he wore an old minister's or professor's gown, the three stripes of the doctorate still attached. He crossed his arms inside the big sleeves, mandarin-style, and bowed low.

"I shall begin by asking you to concede one obvious fact: if we storm your town and take it by force, we will get everything that doesn't burn, we can kill all of you, and you not only won't be able to stop us, you won't even be able to hurt us much," the Daybreaker said. "Therefore, by contrast, my offer is going to be generous."

"I came here to hear it," she pointed out, holding her voice level though she felt her bowels wanting to slither out of her and down into the ground.

Buffalo Hat turned and pointedly stared out into the lake, at the long column of rafts crowded with Daybreaker spearmen, stretching clear to the horizon along the red road the just-rising sun made on the smooth water. "Normally," he said, "of course we would burn your plaztatic little town and end your brutal seizure of resources from Mother Gaia. Normally we would remove the filthy curse of your presence from the face of the Earth, and take away your children to be raised in harmony with the Earth. Normally we would do all those things. But." He drew another breath, let it escape, turned back, and smiled slightly. "We're in a hurry. I will send five hundred of our people into your city to carry out all the food, clothes, and blankets they can carry. Your people will open any door they are told to. If one shot is fired, if one hand is raised against us, if anyone even mutters one word of protest, we will butcher all of you like pigs, burn every building, knock down every wall, and pile your corpses right here where you and I stand. But if you stand quietly by while we take everything we want, we will march on and leave you alive and unharmed, with whatever is left.

"That is our offer. Make your people take it if you can."

"I will." Some impulse made her stick out her hand to shake on the deal.

The man in the buffalo horned hat looked at her hand as if she were holding out a piece of spoiled meat. "This is not an agreement. We will do one thing if you cooperate and another if you resist. That is all. Go talk to your people."

EIGHT:
ONE VERY LONG DAY

6 DAYS LATER. MAÓ, MENORCA, BALEARIC ISLANDS (FORMERLY PART OF SPAIN). 11:00 AM CENTRAL EUROPEAN TIME. MONDAY, APRIL 20, 2026.

"Mister Rollings, Mister Reshetnyk, before you go, I'd like a word with you both in my cabin," Halleck said. "Don't worry, the boat won't leave without you."

Considering we're half of the propulsion system, Whorf footnoted mentally. He glanced at Ihor, whose shoulder twitched in an all but invisible shrug. They followed the captain inside.

Halleck shut the door and turned to face them. "You are the first scholar-sailors to go ashore, and I think you should know why. One, I know you've got each other's backs and you're capable of staying focused on the mission. Two, in related news"—he winced at his habitual back-before reference—"you're the only sailor-scholars I haven't had to bail out of jail, rescue from a mob, or sober up after a shore leave. We're a long way from home and something doesn't feel right about this whole setup. Three—and mainly—you both look much younger and dumber than you really are, which may help them get careless about whatever they don't want you to see."

Whorf said, "Yes, sir. Is there anything we should be looking for?"

"Whatever they're hiding. If I already knew, this wouldn't be the conversation we're having. Maybe I'm just bitter about the fact that this place looks so unscathed; I'm from Maine myself, and all my people and everything I remember are pretty well lost forever. I might just feel like nobody's entitled to be that lucky, so there must be corruption or evil at the bottom of it."

"What's their story, sir?" Ihor asked.

"Well, according to the harbormaster, Mister Quintana, for more than a week after the North Sea superbomb, the east wind held enough to keep the Dead-Zone level fallout over mainland Spain, but not strong enough to pull much in from the stream that flowed through Provence down to Sicily, so although they had quite a bit of radiation poisoning later and many deaths, it didn't disrupt or destroy much infrastructure. Now, that part, I believe; it's consistent with the radiosodium and tritium that the reconnaissance planes picked up, when we had them. Then he says the town government decided not to set up a radio transmitter until their defenses were in better shape, so they were still in listen-only mode when the EMP-bombs came down, and they didn't get hit with any up close; the nearest one to them was that one over Ireland in the spring.

"And then there's the one that sounds really hokey. He says they were lucky that almost all the tourists and retirees found passage on sailboats back to the mainland, so they didn't have too many mouths to feed."

"That don't—doesn't seem lucky to me," Ihor said. "Look at Christiansted, they were very lucky to get off-islanders like Henry or retirees like Captain Highbotham trapped there."

"Yeah," Halleck had said. "Something is not right with their definition of 'lucky.' I want to know what. Also, Quintana said it would be fine if I just gave leave to the whole ship's company and let them go exploring for a couple of days. Very casually, as if it were a matter of course that we would want to and they wouldn't mind having us."

"Maybe we all have honest faces, Captain," Whorf said.

Halleck laughed. "Well, that's part of why I'm sending you two. Hide behind your honest faces, find the story we haven't heard, and bring it back. And yourselves. Especially, and yourselves. Have as good a time as you can, but come back knowing what they're hiding. Good luck."

Rowing to shore was a matter of a few minutes; a local militia officer waved them through without bothering to do more than look closely at them once.

Maó was quintessentially a Mediterranean seaside town. Whorf guessed that he'd seen these sun-washed and stuccoed buildings, probably during his Euromovie phase, behind couples holding hands and babbling, or pouting girls walking away from flailing guys, below the barrel-tiled roofs and just above the subtitles. Despite the captain's premonitions, he was delighted to spend a fine warm spring day walking along the crumbling asphalt streets between the blocky white and tan stores and houses, occasionally interrupted by older columned, gingerbreadish villas. Maó was warm, clean, sunny, and *inhabited* in a world that had become cold, filthy, dark, and hideously empty.

Now, after an hour of walking the winding streets of Maó, they had seen most of the city, physically, but not talked to anyone. Whorf asked, "Do you suppose the real secret is that the place is even duller than it looks?"

Ihor said, "It's just a town, you know? We were spoiled rotten by Christiansted and Gib, I think. Do we want to climb this hill for the view of the whole port? Such as it is, of course."

"Something to do, anyway. But I was just about to ask if your knack for languages would be up to bartering for a fish sandwich." Whorf nodded toward the only open booth on the street, whose sign offered

SANDWICH DES POISSONS—PAIN—CONFITURE
BOCADILLO DE LOS PESCADOS—PAN—MERMELADA
FISH SANDWICH—BREAD—JAM
SANDWICH DEI PESCI—PANE—OSTRUZIONE

Noticing their gaze, the lady behind the cart waved and smiled shyly, the first real greeting they'd had since getting off *Discovery*. She was late-middle-aged, with brownish skin and black eyes; her cheerful wariness reminded Whorf, slightly, of his mother.

"It looks like there will be language we communicate in," Ihor said, "but I would like to start in Catalan."

Ihor always said that part of his supposed linguistic gift was just that he was fearless about mispronouncing things and accosting strangers. He stepped up to the booth with a confidence Whorf could only envy and said, *"Bona tarda. Meu amic i jo volem comprar dues entrepans. Acceptaria una moneda de plata d'Amèrica?"*

The woman's smile was quick and welcoming; she spoke quickly and eagerly. After a moment, Ihor translated. "The bread is fresh from the oven this morning, the cheese she bought at a farm on her way to town, the fish she got off the boat an hour ago, and her grill is ready to go. And, get this, with fresh mayo she made this morning. She says they invented it here, it's the only real mayonnaise in the world."

"Now, that's a sales pitch."

"She says she loves silver, takes it all the time, but she'll want to weigh ours; her prices are in grams."

Ihor and the woman negotiated as they played around with an old postal scale, vociferously but both obviously having fun, before settling on three ship's dimes.

Trying to invent money that was spendable anywhere, the planners at Athens had coined silver into the traditional American denominations from 10 cents up to 10 dollars; they each were issued 2 dollars in silver for a day's shore leave. "You didn't push her too hard?" Whorf asked.

"He is very fair," she said, in perfect, lightly accented English. "But if you want to tip, you could add one more dime."

Ihor shook his head sadly. "And that means we're back to the original price. Whorf, I love you like a brother but I am going to have to gag you every time I'm talking money."

The woman grinned. "Bring him along anytime. I am Ruth. Let me show you that the sandwiches are up to the price."

They were: the bread was fine-grained, dark, and chewy; the fish, onions, and peppers fresh; the thick slabs of tomato firm but juicy; the cheese soft and sticky but pleasantly sharp; the mayonnaise thick, creamy, and indisputably real.

"That was the best first-thing-off-the-ship food I've ever had," Whorf declared, shaking her hand.

"It will even be good when you've been here a month." Ruth smiled warmly; Whorf decided not to point out that this was a one-week-at-most visit.

They started up the road toward the tall hill west of town. As they ascended, the vivid hundred-shades-of-blue of Fornelis Bay, and the deep green of the trees around it, drew the eye away from everything man-made, so that the modern town and the medieval and Roman ruins near it all faded together. But the top of the hill revealed only what they had already known: Maó was unsacked, unburned, and apparently content to have life go on. In the surrounding countryside there were brown, blue, and gray streams of woodsmoke from some chimneys. Between the stone walls, crops grew in neat rows and plots, and sheep, goats, and horses stood in fields; in the sea beyond, dozens of fishing boats were out work-ing. "Like someone asked for a painting in the style of Mediterranean Dull," Whorf said. "Well, whatever the big secret that Captain Halleck wants us to find might be, apparently we can't see it from this hill. Let's go back down and see if we can get into more conversations."

"Thanks to the tip we gave Ruth," Ihor said, "I betcha many, many people will want to talk to us."

The descent, facing the harbor, was also pretty in a conventional way, but they hurried. "I really want to know, too, what the secret of this place is," Ihor said. "Maybe because I really want to be the one that finds it out for Captain Halleck. Funny how a request from him makes me try harder than my uncle yelling at me. I don't want to come back not knowing nothing."

"Anything. Yeah, Halleck's got that same make-you-want-to trick my Pops does. I think they issue it to some old guys on their fortieth birthday or something."

Back in town, they realized that an hour and a half of going up and forty minutes of coming down had left them hungry again. "I suppose we could go looking for other food," Whorf said, "but let's see if Ruth's still open. I could definitely see another one of those sandwiches."

"Adding 'definitely see' for 'am in favor of' to my English idioms," Ihor said, "and right with you."

They had come down a different road from the one they had climbed. In the tangle of narrow streets it took a little time for them to find Ruth's booth again. Three large, muscular men were talking to her.

Their hair was long, worn in loose ponytails, and their beards were full but trimmed. Their baggy pirate pantaloons, tied with twine at the mid-calf cuffs, and their loose, long-sleeved canvas T-shirts were adorned, on every side they could see, with a sewn-on yellow circle-and-eight-wavy-rays sun. Their boots were heavy leather soles attached to long knit socks that continued up under their pantaloons.

"Like very clean tribals," Ihor muttered.

"What I was thinking," Whorf murmured. They stepped a little wide of each other, to free up space in case of trouble but keep close in case of real trouble, and approached slowly; the large men right in front of Ruth blocked her view of them.

As they drew near, one of the men shouted, *"Lliurar tots els diners i menjar, o li tallaré els pits vells fastigosos."*

Ihor sped up into a fast, silent trot, and Whorf kept pace. Ihor prison-muttered, "He said 'Give us all your food and money, or we'll cut off your something.' Sounds like a robbery."

Whorf was about to urge caution—maybe the guy was just quoting some old book or something—when the three big men turned around as one, and fanned out slightly. At a scuffing sound behind him, Whorf glanced back.

Four men in the same clothes were closing in behind them. Ihor's eyes met his. Whorf said, "Go right, get our backs to that wall."

They did; Whorf drew the short flail from between his shoulders and Ihor slid the knives from his sleeve-sheaths. Whorf popped his trouble-whistle into his mouth and blew three-blasts-of-three as loud as he could.

The seven men facing them appeared not to know what to do for an instant, and then one of them clapped the smallest one on the back. *"Digues-los que necessitem arquers."* The small man raced away.

" 'Tell them we need "arquers," ' " which I would bet means 'archers,' " Ihor translated, softly, looking down for a moment. "Whistle again, my friend, just to be sure, and then I say that the two to our left look weak and scared; I'll go that way, you keep the rest off me with your stick, and when I say *run* you follow me."

"Got it." Whorf blew hard, three-of-three again, and was hard on Ihor's heels as they drove to the left. Whether or not Ihor had spotted their weak side, the first man stepped back; the second was reaching for something at his side when Ihor struck with both knives, slashing upward across the man's right shoulder and stabbing straight at his groin, then pivoted into the cat stance, trapping the man's thigh between blade edges.

Whorf grasped both rods of his flail at the open end, driving the chain end up under the retreating man's jaw, and drove forward, sweeping a foot to fling the man over backwards. As he turned, his peripheral vision noted that Ihor's knives continued their slash deep into his opponent's thigh, then rose, crossed, to gash his throat and thrust him back; the man dropped onto the pavement, bleeding in a great gush. Finishing his turn, Whorf backhanded a figure-8 at head height, catching an onrushing man across the mouth and then on the temple, continuing the motion in a great circle to smash the flail into the side of his knee.

"Run!"

Whorf whirled and chased after Ihor; the remaining men, though they were big, didn't seem very fast or eager. The two young men piled down the cobblestone street toward the harbor.

Whorf heard church bells ringing, other crew blowing three-of-three, and the welcome rumble of the ship's drums beating "To Quarters," so help was—

Turning a corner, they looked down a steep alley staircase; at the bottom of it, Jorge and Polly were surrounded by more of the men with the sun insignia. Jorge's arm hung funny and he didn't seem to have a weapon. Polly was swinging a baseball bat back and forth, looking for the first one to come within reach, but though they moved slowly and cautiously, the men were closing in.

Since Whorf was on the right, he moved the flail to his right hand and ran down the steps. His first stroke took a man in the back of the head, and his recovery stroke smashed a second man across the right trapezius and collarbone when he had barely begun to turn.

The free end of Whorf's flail bounced back as if catapulted off rubber; he ducked sideways to keep it from hitting him, yanked hard and down to get control of its spin, and brought the tip around in a hard slap that opened a third man's forehead in a gush of blood.

He could feel Ihor working beside him, striking in the throw-hip-recover-hip rhythm that they'd drilled endlessly on the deck; in his peripheral vision, two more men were down. The enemy had turned their backs on Polly, who brained one with the bat, dropping him. The remaining two opponents fled, shouting.

"Which way?" Whorf gasped.

"Blind alley down here, back up steps," Jorge gasped. He was a very unnatural shade of gray. They hurried up, Polly and Whorf in the lead.

When Ruth popped out at them, Whorf almost let her have it with the flail before she shrieked, "Take me with you!"

"Follow us!" Ihor said.

"This way," Jorge said, and they dropped down another steeply staired alley, Ruth running after them.

They had found the right way this time, because it led them straight to where the ship's company had come ashore and was setting up a perimeter. Glancing behind, Whorf saw that Ruth was still with them.

As the pikemen at the perimeter let them through, one asked, "Her?"

"Maybe a defector, maybe a spy," Ihor gasped.

Arriving just then, Halleck said, "Let her through. Whorf, Ihor, Polly, bind her. Good job. Jorge, Doctor Park is by the boats."

Ruth held out her hands meekly for Polly to fasten the cuffs. "Just so you don't leave me here," she said.

An arrow rattled onto the pavement, not close, and Halleck turned to say something, but two shots had already suppressed the rooftop sniper. He said, "We've got whistles over east, probably near the waterfront or we wouldn't be able to hear them, and no one's gone that way yet. Are you three—"

"On our way," Ihor said.

"One minute more," Halleck said. "Corelli! Get these guys a drink of water, carbines and hatchets. Keep it to one minute, less if you can, it's been a while since we heard the whistles—"

Ten minutes later, with three volleys from their Newberry Carbines and some hard flail and bat work, they drove the cheering mob away from the dangling bodies of their fellow sailor-scholar Felicia and Dr. Darcy Keyes, a microbiologist from Sandia; it wasn't obvious in what order they'd been hanged and mutilated.

"Shit," Polly said. "Shit shit shit."

It was the first time the reverend's daughter had sworn without apologizing, or being teased for it. The worst of the job was guarding the bodies till a bigger party could come to carry them out; it was almost sunset when everyone was finally back on *Discovery*. "Everyone" included two more corpses, besides Felicia and Dr. Keyes: Able Seaman Tranh had been breathing when the crowd kicking him had fled, but he died as the rescue party carried him down to the harbor. Professor Silmarrison had been killed instantly by a flung dart while he stood guard on the perimeter.

Though they could see many watchers on the cliffs above, nothing was fired at *Discovery* and nothing came out to intercept it. As darkness fell, in Halleck's cabin, they interviewed Ruth. She said that the Verdad del Sol tribe had arrived in a huge sailing canoe flotilla even before December 5, and established themselves as the comfortable and pampered lords of the domain.

"Not exactly Daybreakish, is it?" Whorf asked.

"Read the Jamesgrams." In one hard gulp, Ihor knocked back the extra whiskey ration that the doctors had prescribed to help them sleep. "Daybreak is splitting and changing and turning into many things. Someday it will just be a thing, like Jesus Christ or Communism or Ukraine or United States. It will mean so many things it won't mean nothing. Anything. Whatever."

ABOUT THE SAME TIME. PALE BLUFF, NEW STATE OF WABASH (FORMERLY ILLINOIS). 5:00 AM CENTRAL TIME. MONDAY, APRIL 20, 2026.

The MacIntosh Inn, a big old 1920s frame-and-gingerbread house, had been built to display the cider-fueled wealth of its owner during Prohibition. It had successively been the last refuge of his spinster daughters, a real estate agent's cross to bear (and rumored to be haunted), and the retirement project of a chef and her cabinetmaker husband, who had turned it into a highly successful bed-and-breakfast back before. As Pale Bluff had become the key town on the Wabash frontier, they had served increasingly famous and important guests.

For the past week it had been Grayson's main headquarters, and maps, lists, and charts covered every available surface in the main dining room, except for the places at the table where Grayson and Phat ate silently, sharing reverence for hot meals indoors off of plates. By firelight and candlelight, the room was cheery enough, even though the curtains were drawn and the sun had not quite come up yet.

The day before, at Grayson's insistence, Phat had reviewed intelligence, plans, and decisions exhaustively. Once breakfast was cleared and they were savoring the privilege of hot coffee, he said, "Jeff, from everything I can see, you've got it right. You've already shown you're a better general than I am, frankly, at least in this new world; I wouldn't have done nearly as well in the Yough campaign and I am really not sure I could have managed the Ohio Valley at all."

"That wasn't a campaign, that was a series of massacres."

"Sun-Tzu, Jeff. Best way to win is without fighting. You did so well they never had much of a chance to fight. And if they'd had as big an advantage over you, you know they'd have used it, and for what. Now, as for your attack up the Wabash, I stand by my assessment. If there's anything you're missing, it's beyond me to see it too. We both know there's no guarantee of success and no guarantee against surprise, but if things go wrong it is not going to be your fault, and if things go right it will be very fairly to your credit. If anything I say can boost your confidence, consider it said, really, with my whole heart."

Grayson had nodded and extended his hand. Shaking it, Phat thought, *People think that weird little smirk of his is contempt or not taking them seriously, but he does that because he thinks he's a fraud and he's fooled us, and he's ashamed. I wish I'd realized that years ago.*

It might have been a mutual dismissal, but instead the two men sat next to each other in armchairs, huddled close to the fire, holding their coffee cups surrounded by both hands, as if already out in the cold wet field.

Grayson finally said, "I don't know whether to thank you more for coming or more for making such a public show of support for everything I did and said. You've certainly been more than fair and supportive."

"The country needs you to succeed, and you needed the support, and

most importantly, as far as I can tell you have been right about everything." Phat gulped at his coffee as if afraid it might be his last cup ever.
"One thing that hasn't changed, and you'd think would have: we leaders
live in an insulated world. Even in the worst of Daybreak, I don't think any
top officials ever went hungry, or even were at risk of going hungry."

"Do you think we should have? For solidarity with the common people, or whatever you would call it?" Grayson's expression was hard to read;
he seemed to be seeing something a thousand miles beyond the fire. "I've
given specific orders so that I'll never eat if any of my troops have to go
hungry."

"Like any sensible man," Phat said. "Of course you do that. No, I was
just thinking. The world came to an end, people were hungry and cold and
scared, they turned to the institutions that they were used to counting
on—armies, churches, businesses, the government—and *mostly* we all *did*
rise to the occasion, some individuals screwed up, of course, but *mostly*
the armies set about creating order and safety, and the businessmen tried
to get the wheels turning again, and cops and preachers and leaders of
every kind got onto the job as much as they could. But one thing's for sure:
it has consistently been more comfortable to be one of these leaders people
are counting on, than it has been to be one of the people counting on us.
For good or ill we take care of ourselves first."

Grayson nodded. "Remember airplanes? 'If you are traveling with children, put your own oxygen mask on first'?"

"Unh-hunh. That's part of it. Another part is like my old man always
said, it's good to be king."

"Yeah, that too." Grayson finished his coffee. "Most of my troops got
up to big pots of venison-sausage and noodle soup, all the apple fritters
they could eat, and beans-and-rabbit, which they've had so much that they
have new lyrics for 'Caissons,' a cheerful thing called 'The Bunny-fart
Boogie.' But as far as they were concerned, the soup made it a treat and the
fritters were a trip to heaven. If O'Grainne and her wizards are putting the
numbers together right, then if we get a decent harvest in this year, we'll
finally be growing as much as we eat in a year."

"So you think about that too," Phat said.

Grayson shrugged. "Have to. Bet you it's Graham Weisbrod's last thought before he goes to bed and his first when he gets up, too. We're the three people most likely to be president, and our thoughts can't get too far away from food." Grayson stood. "Well, at least we had coffee at breakfast."

"And no dishes to wash."

"Amen. Thank you for coming, and for the support."

"We have differences, and we are not friends, but I have never doubted your competence."

"Isn't that strange? I doubt it all the time. If you're willing, I'd like to go out to meet the others arm in arm, smiling, and looking like the best friends in the world. Really, nobody's ever been able to do much for my confidence, but perhaps we can do something for theirs."

ABOUT THE SAME TIME. PALE BLUFF. 6:00 AM CENTRAL TIME. MONDAY, APRIL 20, 2026.

The warming sun was burning off the last mist, and the view down Chapman Avenue was lengthening by the moment from a gray void into the deep greens and frothy whites of the blossoming orchard. Carol May Kloster, hurrying back with reports from headquarters so that she could read them over breakfast and include the information in her morning report to Heather, stopped to admire the town where she had lived all her life. When people read and wrote history, would they ever just see the nice little town? There must have been people who knew Lexington or Gettysburg this way, for whom they were just "home."

The thought made her feel like welcoming people here, and two young soldiers in the uniforms of Provi militia were shuffling up the street, looking bored and lonesome, so she stopped to say hello. One minute of pleasant conversation established that the scrawny redhead was Jimmy, the small dark East Indian boy was Neville, and they were both now farther from Pullman, Washington, than they had ever been in their lives.

Jimmy attempted to tell a tale of their particular courage and being selected for the mission based on that, but Neville made a disgusted face. "We were playing cards when we were supposed to be guarding the wall, and a Daybreaker prisoner got away because of that," he explained. "And not just any old prisoner, either, some high-level guy they were actually holding on the Allie-train."

"The Allie-train is—"

Jimmy smirked. "The train the First Lady takes around to different towns when she wants to be treated like she's important. She was in our part of the country to impress some tribes and get treated like a queen by the town governments. It kind of worked out embarrassing, and we got stuck holding the bag."

"Because we were away from our posts and playing cards on duty," Neville pointed out, stubbornly.

"Well, yeah, but you keep forgetting, we did real good last summer, especially during the siege, so there was kind of a balance—"

"Yeah, they decided not to drum us out and to only give us a light spanking," Neville said, stubbornly sticking to the truth in a way Carol May was beginning to like. "Just enough so our chocolate and vanilla butts have some strawberry stripes that are never coming off, which eventually stopped hurting, but we realized we'd never be trusted again, and as long as we were in our local militia, we'd be those two assholes—'scuse me, ma'am, can you make that 'jerks'? My mom reads that paper you write for, Mrs. Kloster—those two jerks that screwed up and let the high-level prisoner escape. So when there was a chance to volunteer to come out here and serve with General Grayson's combined army, it looked a lot better than spending the rest of our lives in the militia peeling potatoes and painting barracks. And here we are, all set to serve our country, save civilization, distinguish ourselves heroically, and meet girls."

I suppose I could've found their equivalent at Normandy, or Shiloh, or for that matter at Jericho, Carol May thought.

Half an hour later she was standing on the roadside where Delicious Road led out of town to the east, watching the army pass, with a painful sense that this was more history than she'd ever wanted to see.

"Aunt Carol," Pauline said beside her, "is it wrong that all this is giving me the creeps?"

"War's never been nice, Pauline."

"Not that so much, I mean, I kind of look at the weapons and I think, cool. Kill us some Daybreakers. Go to it, guys." Two improvised caissons, hauling steel-pipe cannons, rolled by on iron-rimmed wheels. Pauline shifted her weight on her cane—though she was only twenty-two, a Day-breaker arrow had ensured she would need it for the rest of her life. "Maybe I just can't help remembering what happened to me over there, even though I thought I was the toughest little bitch that ever lived. Or what happened to Steve Ecco, and he really was strong and tough and brave, but you know, he never came back at all."

The TNG Regular Army regiment going by in Rorschach jammies was carrying four American flags—the plain old fifty-star ones, not the Cross and Eagle TNG flag or the nineteen-star-double-circle of the PCG. Carol May put her hand over her heart; seeing that, so did Pauline.

2 HOURS LATER. PUEBLO. 11:30 AM MOUNTAIN TIME. MONDAY, APRIL 20, 2026.

"Hey, Leo, your prom date's here," MaryBeth Abrams said, sticking her head out the door of the delivery room.

"He seems unimpressed," Heather said, looking down at her sleeping son. "Is this your unique Doctor MaryBeth way to say it's a girl?"

"She is. Very fast delivery, one of those that would make the case for natural childbirth, back before. Beth's fine but exhausted and sore, Jason is ecstatic and will probably come out as soon as you won't see him crying, and Heather Ysabel Nemarec came out with a big gasp before I could even start her breathing, like she'd been holding her breath in there all that time, and is staring at the world like she's totally mad freaked to be here. Don't worry, that terrifying feeling that the world is way too weird usually wears off around a thousand months."

Instinctively, Heather and Ysabel glanced sideways at Debbie Mensche. "Eighty-three years and four months," Deb said. "And I didn't just calcu-late it now, MaryBeth asked me this morning."

MaryBeth grinned broadly. "I'm just a simple country doctor, and out here in Simple Country, we need a never-ending stock of corny jokes. Anyway, I'll be back in a couple minutes and then you can come in; just want to make sure everything is fine before I let the civilians in." She pulled up her mask and ducked inside.

"Guess she wants to make sure she gets *all* the tentacles snipped off," Debbie said.

Ysabel said, "You are an awful person and we really need to spend more time together."

Debbie nodded, accepting the compliment. "So I'm a little surprised you let them name the kid Ysabel instead of Isabel or Izzy. Aren't you worried about being outed anymore?"

"Well, it's a middle name, and the cover story is that they always liked the Spanish version more than the English."

"I just keep thinking we're lucky it wasn't a boy," Debbie said. "Poor kid would've been the only Larry of his generation. Dad would've been impossible, too, practically made the boy a grandson."

"Too late on the only Larry of his generation," Heather said. "Something Chris was telling me about. Baby names come in waves, like plant names for girls—I was in the same generation with a lot of Jasmines, Willows, Aspens, and Roses, and I knew a couple Daisies and an Amaryllis—or Bible names for boys which is why half the boys my age have names ending in –iah. And apparently we were due for a wave giving boys the names of famous people. Thanks to the buildup Chris gave some of my agents in the *Post-Times*, there's a big crop of Freddies and Larrys this year, Chris says, like the late 1800s when there were all those Lincolns, Darwins, Lees, Grants, and Deweys."

"All I can say," Debbie said, "is how grateful I am that at least the Reverend Abner Peet turned out to be a traitor."

4 HOURS LATER. TACOMA DOME, TACOMA, WASHINGTON. 3:00 PM PACIFIC TIME. MONDAY, APRIL 20, 2026.

"I just said that your comment seemed a little *ungracious*," Graham said. "Maybe I should've said *pushy* or *ungentlemanly*. There were two big stories today, two big events, and both on schedules it would not have been easy to change, and Chris Manckiewicz could only be at one of them, so he sent Cassie to cover the other one. And frankly it makes sense for a tough old bird without any family like Chris to go cover a war, and a young woman—hell, a girl, did you know she's only seventeen?—to cover a political party convention. For the love of god, Allie, it's legitimately a big day for Grayson, he's taking his Army of the Wabash out to end the threat of the tribals, I mean, that really is news."

"So is the first political convention in at least seventy-five years where the delegates are actually real live voting representatives with decisions to make," Allie pointed out. "And I can't help resenting that we loaned General Grayson's little circus the only regiment we have that's worth crap, Graham. Plus a bunch of our getting-up-to-decent militia. We put a big part of our own war with our own tribals on hold." Allie was tugging his collar, straightening his tie, fixing him up. *I guess every younger wife of an older man does this all the time, trying to keep your slightly-deteriorated husband from turning into an old wreck while you're still young. Wonder if Jenny Grayson has to make Jeff shine his shoes, or if it's easier with military guys?* Reflexively, she glanced around, hoping no camera would catch him like this.

On Daybreak day the Tacoma Dome had been configured for a touring motivational speaker, which was how it had become the site for the Democratic convention: it was already arranged to accommodate a large meeting in front of a podium and rostrum, requiring no mechanical power to change it to anything else.

Of course, even with mirrors hung to reflect light from the windows down onto the stage, they still could meet only in daylight, still needed candles and lamps, and still only filled the first twenty rows at best, including spectators, demonstrators, and plain old bums. Though their fifteenth-row raised box gave her the best view there was of the whole convention, all that did was allow her to see how small it all was, as if the whole convention was huddled around its few flames at the center of a cave.

It looks so shabby, Allie thought, angrily. Aloud, she said, "*This* is the place where the re-founding of the Republic is really happening. Not that social-parasite-cleanup in the Midwest."

"Allie, something we, and Grayson, and Phat, and a lot of us all agree on is that it's all one country, and it's all one war, and the main threats are the big forces in the Lost Quarter, and the pockets like Hells Canyon and the Ouachitas have to come after. The Lost Quarter is the only place where there are enough of them to break out and do real damage all by themselves. So we have to take that away from them this summer, before they can, so that the next president can go on the offensive and finish the war. That'll be true no matter who the president is. It's Hillel's old saying about if not now, when, and if not us, who? So no more bad-mouthing the Army or the press. Some asshole reporter might hear you and make trouble for us with both, okay?"

"The *only* reporter here is over there." She nodded at Cassie's working table, in the corner seats off to the side of the rostrum. "And really, she looks like such a *kid*. Another note for the first real Weisbrod Administration, we've got to get the child labor laws back in place."

"Don't be so sure about that either, Allie. Seventeen was adult for most of human history, really, for that matter, thirteen or fourteen was adult, more often than not. The child labor laws came in when there wasn't enough work for grown men supporting families, and for the next generation at least what we have is a labor shortage. We *need* everybody who's willing to do something useful—even if they do look like they ran away from cheerleading tryouts."

"*Middle school* cheerleading tryouts. I just don't think someone should be a national media leader till she can prove she's made it through puberty."

"Allie," Graham said, "you are perilously close to judging a person's qualifications for a job by the size of her boobs."

She couldn't help it; that made her laugh at herself. "All right. Fair enough. Maybe I'll even give her an interview and try to get to know her, since she's going to be around." She had long ago given up trying to get Graham to consider a licensed or regulated media for the Restored Republic anyway, despite all the obvious damage that irresponsible private media had done during the Old Republic; there were times when he didn't just seem twentieth-century to her, but maybe nineteenth or eighteenth. Still, Americans wanted their old country back, that was for sure, and maybe Graham was right, maybe that included irresponsible media without any public information policy or regulations. Maybe a compromise? Could they launch something like BBC or NPR with special—

A sudden coalescence of attention spread outward from the podium. Bright quadrilaterals of light swept across the stage as stagehands at the upper windows repositioned the mirrors to bring the reflected light back to the rostrum; the sun had wandered a long way during the three hours of lunch. The reflected sunlight settled around the podium, shimmering vibration slowing as the mirrors were screwed down. Perkins, the chair, mounted the rostrum, waving his gavel in one hand and a sheaf of paper in the other, over his head.

"We will now commence our roll call of the states!" Perkins's unamplified shout did not so much reach the back of the crowd as it started a wave of shushing sounds and the palm-press-down gesture that blanketed the hall in quiet.

He was an older man, close to seventy, with strong-tea-colored skin and wavy black hair. He had said he had an ancestry slightly more mixed than Tiger Woods's. Allie had had to ask Graham who that was, and sure enough it was an old-guy reference; without Goo-22, or even Internet, she'd had to get used to not having heard of things.

Perkins began again. "We will now commence our roll call of the states. Is there a representative here from the great state of Alabama?"

No hands. No one spoke.

"We know," Perkins said, "that this year, Alabama is probably not going to vote for our party, and we realize that they have aligned with the Temporary National Government in Athens. We wish them well and we look forward to joining as one nation with them again in January. We know that some day they will have a strong and vibrant Restored National Democratic Party of their own. Is there anyone here from Alaska?"

Another silence.

"We recognize that the great state of Alaska has exercised its common-law right to secede during the Constitutional interregnum, and is no longer a member of the Union. Of course we hope they'll reconsider and rejoin our Union, but we respect their right to choose their destiny." He hurried on, as if afraid that a second of silence might escalate. "We call on the great state of Arizona!"

The elderly man who rose in response stood erect in a way that proclaimed "ex-military," but he looked as if he might cry. "Arizona was assigned twelve votes. The four votes I've been instructed to vote are from the remainder of Arizona after the secession of four areas. The County of Trans-Mojave has been assigned two votes and will vote those as part of the Duchy of California, to which its Earl and Countess have pledged fealty. The Grand Canyon Temporary Reconstruction Coalition will petition to affiliate with the State of Nevada as soon as possible, and will cast its three votes with Nevada. Apachéria plans to seek admission to the Union as a New State, and asks to cast its one vote independently for Graham Weisbrod. Naabeehó Bináhásdzo intends to seek sovereign international independence and will not cast its two votes."

Naabeehó Bináhásdzo is the Navajo Nation, Allie reminded herself.

Perkins waited a long breath and said, "And how are you voting those four votes?"

"Sorry, Pete. Forgot to say. We're abstaining on this ballot."

Allie was beginning to wonder why she had not brought a book. Arkansas, like Alabama, had sent no one, and would participate in the election entirely through the TNG. Perkins then called upon, "The great state of California!"

A tall, handsome woman, perhaps sixty years old, rose, and said, "The *Duchy* of California, home for more than twenty-five years of Graham Weisbrod, the last President of the Old Republic, soon to be the first President of the Restored Republic, proudly casts all forty-one—sorry, Arizona, I mean forty-*four*—of its votes for Graham Weisbrod!"

Even people who were supporting other candidates jumped up and cheered. *One tiny step toward restoring America in people's imaginations,* Allie thought. *Maybe a bigger deal than I realize.*

Colorado went nine for Weisbrod, four for McIntyre, and one maverick, though yelled at by the rest of his delegation, cast his vote for Lyndon Phat. But then there was, as Graham muttered to Allie, "a real string of bummers." Connecticut and Delaware were swallowed up in the chaos of the Lost Quarter. Florida and Georgia were both TNG-only. Hawaii, embroiled in a many-sided struggle between warlords, bandits, assorted rebels, military units trying to impose martial law, and tribals, was represented by a single observer from a coalition of towns on the Big Island. She had been instructed not to vote.

At last, Idaho broke the chain of bad news with eight for Graham, one for Norm. Indiana and Illinois, the delegates were reminded, would be voted later, as parts of the New State of Wabash.

Iowa went all for Weisbrod and Kansas all for McIntyre, but then there was a ten-state streak of states that had lined up with the TNG, been totally lost to the tribes, or were being reorganized into New States. Perkins tried to hurry through them but there was no missing the sigh of relief throughout the convention when at last Montana, Nebraska, and Nevada were all present and voting. There were more long runs of lost, defected, and reorganized states, until finally they wound down through the Virgin Islands, Wabash, and Washington. When Perkins asked, pro forma, if there were any delegates from West Virginia, the room was pleasantly surprised: three men and a woman stood up.

"We're going to take a little explaining," the oldest man in the group said, nervously taking off the UMW strap-cap repaired with twine he wore, and twisting it in his hands. "There's people in the hall who can vouch for us if you need 'em to. We're a bunch of counties in southern West Virginia and western Virginia that have all been holding out, just barely but we're holding, against the tribals, with our militia, and we retook Wise and Dickinson counties from the tribes last month, which gives us a road open over to Kentucky and down to North Carolina. We're here to announce that we've got a Restored Democrat party, which is hoping to have some members real soon—" Laughter rolled through the convention; grinning, the man explained, "There was about twenty of us that wanted to organize it. Our people back home should've signed up some membership lists while we were traveling, but we've been on the road a month, ain't had communication, so we don't *know* for sure they did.

"Anyway, if things are the way we left 'em, then we'll not only have Democrats, that other party is organizing there too, we're gonna elect a state constitutional convention in November, and we're hoping to apply for admission as a New State in the Restored Republic, if it lets there be any more New States. Last I knew most people seemed to want to come in as the state of Pelissippi, after the river, but there's some that want to call ourselves Appalachia or Clinch River, after the same river. That's gonna be on the ballot this fall, too. So we thought we'd just ask to have two votes, 'cause we think we can get at least enough turnout to justify that, come November."

Perkins grinned. "Well, we're awful glad to see you, even if it's complicated. Maybe *because* it's complicated. Where should we put your two votes down, Probably-Pelissippi?"

"Two more for Graham Weisbrod. We were instructed to just help the front-runner 'cause the party needed a leader more than anything."

"Well, then, two more for Weisbrod, and give it up for another fine New State, people!"

In the midst of the cheering, Norm McIntyre muttered, "Did you ever think people would be excited to find out that part of the country was still there?"

Weisbrod shrugged. "Review the national anthem, Norm. Sometimes still being there is the best news there is."

When Perkins got them quiet again, Wyoming, anticlimactically, cast its two votes for Phat.

Then the panel of judges began to scribble and add; everyone was still relearning hand arithmetic.

They had had to run through the whole roll call because they had not known exactly how many would show up until the convention started that morning. Besides the last-minute appearance by Pelissippi, and the surprise fissions of Arizona and Oklahoma (which hadn't really been expected to attend at all, but had shown up as West Oklahoma plus the Allied First Nations), both the Utah and Texas delegations had arrived within the last twenty-four hours and then had to wait for radiogram instructions about whether to participate or not (both had been told to go ahead). Votes were assigned to each delegation according to the closest guess that could be managed about the number of voters likely to turn out in November, one convention vote per hundred thousand probable voters, and some delegations had been assigned their number of votes only that morning.

The scribbling went on. It was clearly going to take a while to check and reconfirm everything.

Allie noticed Cassie Cartland working at something. "Hunh. Something I want to check out," she said, but since Graham was locked in conversation with McIntyre, she just slipped quietly down to the press table.

Cassie was working a soroban abacus, sliding beads, scribbling on a pad, sliding beads, scribbling, underlining a result just as Allie approached and asked, "What's it look like?"

"Just rechecked," Cassie said. "Surely everyone knew it was going to be Graham; he was a majority with every delegation except Kansas, Montana, North Dakota, Wabash, and Wyoming. Officially Nevada put him over, if you count those Arizona counties that voted with Nevada."

"Actually I was more interested in the abacus."

"Found a pamphlet about it, browsing through the GPO in Pueblo, last year while I was waiting for Chris to make it back from the Mensche Expedition. Knocked one together to have something to do, and found out how fast and accurate they are."

"My uncles and father used to use those."

"Bet I'm not as fast as they were."

"With fifty years of practice like they had, maybe you will be. I was just thinking they might be a good thing in the schools."

Cassie nodded. "Or we could just put the pamphlet out there. Lots of little businesses and farmers are either too old or don't have time for school. I was thinking we might run a series about it in the *Post-Times*."

"About the abacus?"

"Good idea too, but I meant about everyone missing some years of school. We need to figure out some way to get a lot of skills and information out to a lot of people, and you're not going to get people who've been taking care of themselves in this mess to sit down at desks and fill out forms again. Eventually, maybe, but not—here we—"

She probably said *here we go* but the *go* had been swallowed in an immense hoot-to-scream of feedback, as Perkins tried to get the microphone to behave. The young tech types had rigged up a very simple amplifier using jelly-jar vacuum tubes and a treadwheel-powered dynamo; their best guess was that by constantly wiping it with a lye wash they could keep it running long enough for Graham's acceptance speech, if he didn't talk too long. It had bored Allie to death but the young nerds had been so proud of themselves that she had made herself pay warm attention to them.

As one of the young technicians walked inside the treadwheel; the other three crouched around the amp, wiping diligently, and the one in the treadmill signaled Perkins to try again. He announced that Graham Weisbrod was the nominee and, "After our victory, my friends, the first President of the Restored United States! Ladies and gentlemen, Graham Weisbrod!"

In a smaller hall the applause would have been thunderous; it was swallowed up in the dark here.

Graham stepped up to the condenser mike and said, "My friends," triggering another squeal and roar of feedback. The crew fiddled frantically, then flashed him a thumbs-up.

He began again. "My friends and supporters in this room, my opponents and detractors all over the world, my fellow Americans however you feel about me, we're gathered here today to take a long step toward restoring our republic. Of course it is difficult for many of you who have struggled and fought so long for the Provisional Constitutional Government to admit that our struggle is now over; we never attained the full agreement of all citizens that the PCG was the legitimate continuation of the government founded by the Constitution of 1789. But since we did not, a new struggle begins tonight: to establish a new government, which will take office in January 2027, under the same Constitution that was in force until December 5, 2024.

"We have pledged ourselves to work and build for the Restored Republic, beginning with the elections in November. It is fitting enough; it is our 250th anniversary as a nation, this year. Yesterday was the 251st anniversary of the first fighting at Lexington and Concord. In addition to the states that chose to align with the PCG, we have the firm and honest commitments in hand of the Temporary National Government in Athens, and of the sixteen states who have chosen to report to them, to walk with us every step of the way; we have the commitment of the Duchy of California, and we seek to bring in other states such as Manbrookstat and the Virgin Islands. We will refuse or coerce no one, block nothing, accept every territory where people choose to be Americans, sacrifice whatever must be sacrificed except our Constitution and our democratic rights, and we will forge one nation again!"

The crowd did their best to fill the hall with applause.

"More than anything," he said, leaning into the microphone to speak softly, "we need a Restored Republic to which everyone can be loyal, not one that drives away any large part of the population. We need to embrace the idea again that we are one nation.

"And we are going to.

"We held together, in that first 250 years, through good times and bad, through a bloody civil war, through appalling crimes that shocked the world and soaring triumphs that awed it, and through a million things the Framers and Founders could not have imagined, in a great measure because of our commitment to maintain the Constitution, and because so often it called us back to ourselves when we were in danger of losing ourselves.

"So I give my word, to our rival government in Athens, to all the governors, to the Duke and Duchess of California, and to everyone and to almighty God Himself, that we will make this new republic, and make it strong and seat it firmly.

"So let us go forward. As for the Provisional Constitutional Government, let us have faith that our good decisions will be ratified, our bad ones nullified, and our choices in the few months that remain will be as wise as we can make them. I thank you."

The band wheezed to life with "America the Beautiful," and the crowd cheered as wildly as they could manage, a few hundred people in a space designed for tens of thousands. *At least,* Allie thought, *they are drowning out that band.*

Graham thanked them, and because daylight would not last much longer, dismissed them, urging them to be careful and safe going back to wherever they were staying. At least a third of them, Allie knew, were sleeping on floors or cots here in the building.

On their way out Cassie intercepted them. "I'm supposed to tell you that Chris Manckiewicz particularly wants me to extend his apologies; he's covering the war in the Ohio Valley right now, I guess because old guys get to go to everything really cool and young ladies are stuck with politics."

Graham snorted. "You do realize that you are the main correspondent for the most important news source in the country at a national political convention? And that your predecessors would have been amazed that a girl your age could do such a job?"

"My predecessors obviously were too easily amazed," Cassie said.

Allie liked that answer, but *nonetheless I'm still insulted that they decided we were second most important next to General Jeffrey Grayson's Traveling Massacre, Part Two.*

NINE:
ALLE DIE SOLDATEN WOLL NACH HAUS [EVERY SOLDIER JUST WANTS TO GO HOME]

**2 DAYS LATER. PUEBLO. 4:30 PM MOUNTAIN TIME.
THURSDAY, APRIL 23, 2026.**

"Even back before," James Hendrix said, "spring snowstorms weren't unusual around here." Outside, stinging sleet sprayed across the old corn snow and mud patches of James's yard. "Look at that, it's still a couple hours till sunset and it's dark enough for lanterns."

Beside him, Leslie also stared out at the tumbling, billowing gloom, then hefted the jug. "Another round all around? Still an hour and a half till classes start."

"Sure," James said. "It'll lift the mood, or deepen it."

"Sticking to water," Heather said.

"We have that too." Leslie filled their glasses and Phat's. "To being warm and dry, and having something to think about, and sharing it with others." She sat, and Wonder scrabbled around to lay his head in her lap. "Seriously, General Phat, you'll be fine. I'm no kind of a teacher, and James is a dusty old pedant, but the adult students keep coming back because it's a frontier town with too much work to do. Learning stuff is a chance to lift up their heads and feel human now and then. And you've got a great subject. I mean, ancient history, right? They can just listen and read, nobody's life is hanging on whether they remember anything, but they'll feel like today they were more than muscles turning wheels."

Heather looked up from playing with Leo on the floor. "Leslie's right. Everyone is tired after a full day, they've mostly just come from mess hall and bath shift. So their bodies are exhausted but comfortable, and their brains are starved."

Phat yawned. "I still feel like, how is this relevant? An old man's favorite stories about Greeks—"

"Who were cold and hungry and in danger a lot, and trying not to let barbarians smash everything, and making time to enjoy life anyway," James said. "How is that not relevant? And besides, people who work too hard and long don't want to hear more about work, or that life is futile. They want some heroic adventure."

Leslie smiled dreamily. "In books, you mean. That hard work they're escaping from is how we're coping with being in deep shit, a.k.a. *adventure*, and not giving up, a.k.a. being *heroic*."

"Touché, Leslie." Phat shook his head, smiling. "In Peloponnesian War Athens, I'd've wished I could just stay home, read Homer, and ignore Alcibiades, who was as big a character as anyone in the *Iliad*. Now that we *have* a larger-than-life but despicable hero striding around the stage—"

James said, "I don't really know Grayson well enough to despise him—"

"I despise him enough for all of us, and I notice you had no trouble figuring out who I meant."

"But you still think he's a larger-than-life hero?"

"Oh, yeah. That's the problem, and why he scares me."

Heather looked up, frowning. "I thought I was following your chain of thought till right now. You're *worried* about him being heroic?"

"Yeah." Phat's tone seemed like an extension of the icy wet spray, now turning twilight gray, outside James's window. "Despicable, we can deal with. Plenty of our allies are pretty bad human beings but we just use'em and watch'em, same as they do with us. But look at Grayson. Look how he's reorganized his force from a mission to clear two big river valleys to a totally different mission, invading enemy territory and forcing a decisive battle. And he did that in less than eight weeks. That's on par with Alexander, Caesar, or Napoleon, maybe." His gaze was lost in the storm intensifying in the dimming light. "He's been brilliant. People may not have my feel for the technical aspects, but they sense that brilliance.

"When they look at that, they'll think he damned well deserves to be president, and you know, they won't be completely wrong. In any fair election, he's very likely to win. We're impaled on a classic fork—something else Caesar would have recognized. If Grayson hadn't won so far, right now Daybreakers would be cutting the country into vulnerable enclaves full of refugees, and we'd have lost most of our least-damaged areas; nontribal society might not have lasted another five years.

"Now, maybe, thanks to the brutal mauling he gave the Daybreakers in the Ohio Valley, the main danger is past, and he can close the deal by midsummer, get us ready to retake the Lost Quarter the year after, turn all the curves on all those social-welfare graphs back upward.

"But here's the fork: we had to back him to the hilt and make sure he won, because the stakes were pretty much whether or not there would be civilization on this continent. We *still* have to; he broke three tribal hordes but the other eight are only turned back, not gone yet. So he's now our greatest visible hope, and a proven winner. If he confirms that by winning the Wabash campaign—and there is every likelihood he will—then no one, no one, *no one* is going to beat him in the election. You better believe that fork was deliberate.

"And it gets worse. My guess is that Grayson'll be a big success as president, at least if 'big success' is defined as 'getting what he tries to get.' At the end of his first term we'll have an established church, a military that totally ignores the courts and Congress, a political police enforcing blasphemy laws, a licensed press—and clean streets, trains that run on time, and shiny schools full of very polite children. If he loses, we're screwed, but if he wins, we're *really* screwed."

4 HOURS LATER. ANEGADA (FORMERLY ONE OF THE BRITISH VIRGIN ISLANDS). 3:15 AM ATLANTIC TIME. FRIDAY, APRIL 24, 2026.

"What we got to worry about, that coral heads all round inside the reef," Bartholomew said to Captain Highbotham. "You sure you rather not waitin' on sunrise?"

"No, I'm *not* sure," she said, "but I'm guessing they think we can't do this in the dark, so dark will help our attack more than it will help their defense."

Anegada had been a pirate base in the seventeenth and eighteenth centuries, and now it was one again. Highbotham and the St. Croix militia had known the pirate base must be within a hundred miles or so, but the islanders of 2026 had been up against the same problems as those of 1726: once a ship was over the horizon, it could turn to head anywhere.

Besides, for the past eighteen months, the islanders had not had time to chase pirates. Fiberglass and plastic hulls, plus nylon fishing nets, lines, and sails, had turned fuzzy and blue and fallen apart. Magnetos, motors, and antennas had buried themselves in dense white spikes and feathers of metal salts, their spoiled rubber belts and hoses falling off beside them, leaving no way to pump the fuel that had suddenly become foul cheese. Even plywood had broken apart as the glue between the layers deteriorated, and asphalt roads had crumbled as some biotes acquired a taste for bitumen.

People who had spent years demonstrating traditional crafts for tourists back before, but had never had to really live by them, taught as much as they knew to everyone else, and eventually enough skills and knowledge had made it through the harsh sieve, but it had been a hungry time.

NSP-8, along with the loan of Bret Duquesne as pilot/mechanic until he could train enough local crew, and an adequate stock of biodiesel obtained by bartering three tons of scrap metal to an Argentine clipper, had enabled them to start scouting the neighborhood by air—slowly, because NSP-8 cruised at fifty miles per hour, topped out at twelve thousand feet, and could stay aloft for about four hours.

Ten days ago, flying over Anegada at "high altitude" (which would have been low altitude two years ago), Duquesne had spotted the characteristic semicircular outdoor theatre that Daybreaker tribes always built to perform *The Play of Daybreak*, and the burned pile of cars and trucks that had probably been part of an early Daybreak celebration. The next day, with a spyglass from the observer seat, as Duquesne ducked in and out of clouds with the sun at their back, Henry had positively identified three known pirate vessels, confirmed a large tent city around the burned-out tourist area, and found no visible fishing boats.

Strangely, too, a small general cargo ship was grounded on the beach, displaying a sun-faded red cross on its side, like a hospital or aid ship. No other island had been visited by any sort of aid ship, and why would one go to an isolated, barely populated island surrounded by complicated coral reefs, when dozens of equally desperate populations could have been reached more easily?

Just one more mystery to be resolved, along with where the original couple of hundred Anegadans were: Enslaved? Murdered? Joined the pirates?

The possibility of innocent prisoners or hostages, and the impossibility of bombing every important target in less than about fifteen sorties that might take a full week, had forced Highbotham to decide for an invasion that they had to hope would be a surprise. *Because if they get as much warning as we got against them a few months ago, they'll kick our ass at least as bad as we kicked theirs.*

The sea was so calm, and the breeze so light, that they furled sails and deployed long sweeps early. For half an hour, they rowed as swiftly as could be kept silent; then they slowed to use the sounding line. In the bow of each boat, two big guys with poles stood by to keep them off the coral heads, whispering depths back to the boat captains at the helms. At Highbotham's soft drum signals, two boats peeled off and headed for the two pirate ships moored outside the reef.

An hour and a half passed as they worked their way through the reefs. Rowers changed places with resting fighters at twenty-minute intervals; most of the time the rowing was no louder than the breathing. The whispered depths and course corrections were as soft in the ear as a mother rabbit chuckling to the bunnies, but to Highbotham they seemed like screams; her brief backward flashes from a single, shielded candle lantern in the stern seemed like flashbulbs. But nothing moved on the island, and they drew nearer.

The dark line of Anegada along the horizon thickened and expanded into detail until the exposed girders of the never-to-be-finished hotel cut into the stars and the beached cargo ship bulged as a big, dark wedge against the white sand.

Still no alarm.

Perhaps the pirates hadn't set a watch; maybe they were gone. Henry had estimated tent space for more than a thousand of them. Now Highbotham focused on the two pirate ships moored offshore.

On the nearer ship there were bright orange flashes, the dirty flames of big-bored black-powder pistols. An instant later flames roared up along the mainmast of the more distant ship, and now they heard gunfire. On both vessels, fire burst out in a dozen places. Faintly, distantly they heard metal clash on metal, then screaming and wailing.

Highbotham blew her whistle, shatteringly loud after such long anxious silence. Rested rowers moved into seats for the last sprint to the beach. Gunners raced forward to the bow chasers and rocket arrays.

It was almost a relief when they heard shouting and saw torches striking up. Marksmen in the bow of Highbotham's lead boat brought down two of the torch holders.

Cries erupted all over the enemy camp. Shots flashed and cracked from Highbotham's boats as targets silhouetted themselves. As the bottom of her boat shushed softly up the sand of the beach, a mob of pirates, hastily armed and not at all organized, was running down to meet them.

"Bow chaser, fire," Highbotham barked, the final r cut off by the roar of the small cannon. The puff of blue-gray smoke swirled and cleared to reveal that their homemade chainshot had mowed a great swath of dead and the wounded through the howling mob.

Highbotham drew her pistols and held them over her head. "Follow me, stick together, stay awake. Rockets, launch at will, then arm up and catch up with us."

She bounded over the side, pistols still held high in the air, and the blood-warm water came only to her lower ribs. Good, she had some firepower; she kicked forward, planted her feet with the water around her waist, and waded forward.

A few paces onto the beach, a woman came at her, swinging a hatchet wildly. She fired twice from her right pistol and hatchet woman fell, screeching and clutching her guts. Highbotham strode up the beach, her crew around her, those whose pistols had stayed dry during the landing working quickly, using up the four shots in the good hand pistol, switching over the one in the off hand, emptying it too, just like in drill, leaving any wounded behind them for the rest of the crew's machetes and sharpened spades.

Another hatchet woman; were they some kind of cult? Wailing, filthy hair flopping around her, hatchet whirling over her head, the pirate rushed past one of the few remaining pistol shots, and straight at Highbotham.

Highbotham stepped back, pressed the rising hatchet hand back down with the flat of her cutlass, caught the wrist with her free hand, and struck up the arm into the neck in a hard backhand, dragging the blade out and feeling it rasp on the skull and spine. The woman fell dead at her feet.

"Stay close!" Her little force had made its way to the top of the beach already, and they were on the brink of the camp itself.

"Firebombs out!" She untied her own from the back of her belt. She was bellowing over deafening screaming, wailing, gunfire, drums, and horns; when had that started?

Her party rushed forward. Rockets had set many enemy tents and shelters on fire, and Highbotham's crew ran between the blazes, fighting the few pirates who tried to stand against them, igniting any structure not already burning, then standing outside it to capture or slay whatever ran out.

Highbotham paused; her glass jar of paper cartridges was still sealed, so with an old piece of toweling she swabbed out the chambers of her Newberry revolvers and reloaded them. Around her, the night was lit with the orange glow of black powder, the earthy roar of pistols, and the higher, flatter snaps of rifle fire.

Reloaded pistols in her holsters, Highbotham again drew her cutlass and waved it to get the attention of other boat crews. She felt her face constricting into its familiar battle rictus. "Forward, forward, keep them running!" Using her upraised cutlass as a sort of crook, she shepherded her raiders forward into the heart of the pirate camp. *I probably look a bit piratical, myself,* she thought. *Good thing I know we're the good guys.*

When the sun came up, plumes of smoke were rising from everywhere that had been the pirate camp, and from the pirate ships offshore. An American flag flew by the tables where Highbotham and her officers were sorting out prisoners as quickly as they could.

The saddest cases were the relatively uninfected ones with deeply committed friends or relatives. "Protocol would say put the not-too-deeps on our boats," Gilead said, "and as soon as they're over the horizon, hang the incurables and be done with it."

"Reality would say that other forces have triggered riots by doing that," Highbotham pointed out. "Of all the odd things, there was an article about that from Jenny Grayson, that bimbo that's probably going to be the First Lady. She said after they freed a couple big camps along the Ohio, they tried separating out the curables and hanging their incurable relatives, and as it happened some of the curables had only stayed sane in the hope that the troops would show up and rescue their kids, or parents, or lovers, or friends."

"Ouch."

"Yeah. She was headlining it urgent, which I think was right, and it had General Hubby's endorsement, and I think Chris Manckiewicz's, and she did it as an open letter to James Hendrix at Pueblo."

"But there's no reply from him yet?"

"He forwarded it for my consideration with a big underlined *use your judgment.*"

"All right, so what do we do?"

"If someone promises to try to cure them, tie 'em up, I guess, I mean we have room in the boats. Back at St. Croix we'll let families stay together in the re-ed camp. Then we hope they get better. So—"

"Sir."

She turned. She might have reprimanded the messenger's extremely sketchy salute, but considering the boy looked about eleven, she simply returned it very properly. "Message?"

"Sir, Darren at First Platoon says they found a high priority prisoner and—"

"Take me there."

The boy saluted again, with considerably better form and exuberant energy. *Hah. Maybe Abby has a point about the power of example.*

At First Platoon, she found Darren with an emaciated woman with weather-beaten skin. "Carlita," Darren said, "this is Captain Highbotham. She's the one who will be taking us all back to St. Croix to live. She's very nice and you'll be safe telling her everything." His voice was high and a little singsong, the way people who don't have much experience talk to a frightened child.

Carlita nodded, tears streaking down her cheeks. Highbotham realized this *was* a frightened child, just one who had been kept outside, starving and terrified, for two years. Darren said, "Carlita was here on Daybreak day."

The girl wiped her face, nodding. Highbotham squatted down—Abby had taught her to do that with kids, get to their eye level. She waited for the tentative eye contact, and smiled a little, just enough, she hoped, to signal *someday I'll be your friend.* "You know Darren needs you to tell me something, right?" she asked. "Just let it tumble out; don't worry how you say it."

"We were okay, right after Daybreak. We *were*. It was gonna be okay." This was not grief but helpless rage. "Plenty to eat from the lagoon, and stuff still working 'cause we wiped everything good. Dad-daddy was making a thing for fresh water, a thingie, it was a *still, that's* what the word was. And we were gonna, gonna grow vegetables, he said we'd be okay. And then they saw the ship with the red cross, and it was coming in, and our radio still working and they directed it in, and everything, they helped them come in through the reef, and soon, soon, soon as it came up on shore—they were yelling, nobody knew why it kept coming up onto the beach—all those people jumping out, over the sides, swarming out, they killed a lot of people, they said we were all plaztatic, they made us burn all the books and everything, and they dumped stuff from jars all over—"

"I knew you wanted to know what the story was behind that 'Red Cross' ship," Darren said, very softly.

"You were right," Highbotham said, folding the girl within her arms. Into the girl's ear, she murmured, "You're coming with us, and you're going to grow up and help us push Daybreak back." She pressed her hand against the girl's cheek. "I hope you like math, sweetie."

**2 DAYS LATER. CASTLE EARTHSTONE. 5:45 AM
LOCAL SOLAR TIME. SUNDAY, APRIL 26, 2026.**

Lord Robert stood on the platform they had built over the gate in the main wall of his Castle, and raised his arms to salute the sunrise. *Corny as hell,* he thought, *but this new world is pretty corny too.*

On his right, the gathered armies of the tribes stood in their long, silent files, waiting his orders. Directly east of his platform, signaling their privileged position in his kingdom, three thousand of the Lake Erie tribals, who had made the brisk march overland from Luna Pier, raised their weapons as one. South of the platform, the main body, almost ten thousand strong, saluted as well.

He turned west and saluted toward the Old First—a handpicked five hundred of his own Castle Earthstone troops, whom he had built up into some kind of magic sacred band, Jedis, call them whatever you want, but he could sleep safely in the middle of them, and the rest of the tribal army was more afraid of the Old First than they were of the enemy.

Inside Castle Earthstone, the freed slaves and the remaining soldiers sat tensely alert, staying out of sight of the army outside, both to avoid provocation and to hide their numbers; another fifteen hundred Earthstoners would join the combined army as a rearguard, but only once most of it was safely away and headed downriver. It was never far from Lord Robert's mind that Daybreak might yet betray him, and even if they did not, surely in the ranks of his new army of thirteen thousand there might be another Daybreak-immune person with ambitions.

Makes it real important not to snicker while I'm showing 'em all my armpits, too. He stretched out his arms for a few more invocations.

Beside him, Nathanson stood solemnly at attention. It was one of the man's chief talents. *Glad I've got Bernstein to leave in charge.*

"Soldiers!" Robert cried, trying to sound like the barbarian king in one of those silly old computer games. "Soldiers of Daybreak! Hear me!"

They cheered like a bunch of idiots. *Wonder if back before these were the people that used to cheer for sound checks.*

"Daybreak has brought you to me to be freed!" he shouted. "Freed into the True Daybreak, the Daybreak of Castle Earthstone, and because of what we will teach you, you will be victorious in battle, and free in spirit, and you will not just make the clean and healthy world of Daybreak, you will be blessed to live there! You were told you would build paradise, but I tell you now you will live there!"

Now the cheers were wilder and louder, and he had to wait for a while for it to subside. "You have been commanded to follow me and to do as I say, and I say, come and be free. Come and follow willingly, and when you return to your tribes, you will live the life Daybreak promised you."

Robert had read the phrase "deafening applause" a few times; here it was in real life. He wondered if the people in the back rows were even hearing him, or just cheering to cheer.

After a few more shouts and blessings, with the sun full up, he proclaimed, "Follow me, and let's free Mother Gaia once and for all! Follow me!"

A summer of war, be back in time for deer hunting, and then the world the way I always wanted it, he thought, *the way I wanted it before I even knew what I wanted.* Some times, Robert just had to believe some power had grabbed hold of him and was working through him.

The deep blue sky and the green sparkle in the air were like echoes of his soul as he raised his arms over his head, again and again and again, accepting cheers so loud he could feel them pulse against his face and his outspread palms.

THE NEXT DAY. RAS JEBEL (FORMERLY TUNISIA). 8:25 AM CENTRAL EUROPEAN TIME. MONDAY, APRIL 27, 2026.

The officers and social scientists of *Discovery* had thought it was a lucky thing to be invited to a major Monist public service last night; Ras Jebel was a center from which Monism was spreading around the Mediterranean, and here was a chance to hear several of the best-known Monist speakers, teachers, testifiers, and preachers, and to see how the new religion was presenting itself to the world.

Captain Halleck had suggested that anyone who was comfortable with the idea should attend, though after the experience of Menorca he also made sure there was a substantial guard on both the ship and the pier, with enough reserve for a rescue mission to the stadium if need be. But there had been no need. The evening service, lit by bonfires, torches, and lanterns, had been innocuous; the preaching about the love, peace, tolerance, and kindness of the One God, had been more calming than agitating; and the actual applications and commandments that might have roused any passions had been minimal. Most of the crew had been pleasantly bored, tuning it out and just enjoying being in a big public space with occasional music.

Whorf and Ihor, due to their anything-but-exalted position, had been expected to stay attentive and make note of everything. Now, at the breakfast meeting that was part seminar, part debriefing, on deck because the day was beautiful, they were trying to explain a few of the more surprising features.

"Well, we don't really understand how it's organized, but it's more like a network than a hierarchy, and more like a tight-knit community than true anarchy," Whorf said, feeling a bit foolish because he was sure he was wrong somewhere, but not at all sure where. "There's a huge amount of communication going through Monist channels, compared to every other way, from western India and Pakistan all the way to the Atlantic. A lot of it is about conversions and ceremonies that went well and miraculous healings, like you'd expect, but there's also a fair bit of information about everything from soccer and pop songs to epidemics and Daybreak-proof tech. Many people who are not Monist—at least not yet—are hanging around Monist Houses of the One just because it's the best source of business and political news, and fashions and music, that there is."

Ihor took over at that point, as they'd planned, and held up a brownish-yellow pebble of glass. "This is a Jerusalem Tektite." He read a little stiffly from the paper in front of him: "When the Jerusalem superbomb went off, vitrified chunks of Jerusalem rained down all over South Asia. Because of how small atoms are and how thoroughly it was all mixed, a Jerusalem Tektite probably has a few atoms from the Wailing Wall, the Holy Sepulcher, and the Dome of the Rock, and all those other religious sites too. Every good Monist always has his Jerusalem Tektites with him, because they hold one in their right hand when they pray. The market for Jerusalem Tektites might actually be bigger than the coffee or tobacco trade—"

"I would like permission to come aboard and talk to your captain," a voice said, politely enough but quite loudly. They turned to see a bearded, olive-skinned man in a worn-out three piece suit, standing by the guard on the gangplank. Just behind him, a quiet Asian man in a sweatsuit appeared to be staring into space. "Also I could not help overhearing and I wanted to correct something; you hold the Jerusalem Tektite in your *dominant* hand, left if you are left-handed, alternating if you are ambidextrous." The three short, thin stoles, red, blue, and yellow, attested that he was Monist clergy. "I have a matter of some urgency to discuss with your captain. And if it is permissible, I would like to bring my student with me."

"I'm the captain," Halleck said. "Perry, you and these two young guys come along; I need some guidance if this is a religious matter."

In Halleck's cabin, the Monist preacher introduced himself as Samar Rezakhani. "I am in fact a Monist preacher and that is how I have supported myself as I walked and sometimes caught ships to move westward. But it is not about Monism that we need to talk. I was an engineer on the Iranian-Chinese lunar expedition project in 2019, and after Daybreak, until Teheran government collapsed about a year ago, it was my job to investigate whether our expedition was infiltrated or taken over by Daybreak, since so many nations have accused us of this, and since we had found evidence of Daybreak among some of the engineers and scientists.

"My colleague here, Tang Qan Qi, has traveled even farther, from the research center on the island of Hainan, overland through India, because he was trying to find me; before the Shanghai superbomb put an end to them, the Chinese government was very anxious to know if their moon expedition had been corrupted by Daybreak, and because Tang had been the liaison to the Iranian team, he was sent to see what he could find out from us. Alas, we had been shut down and dismissed by the time he arrived."

"I do not actually require you to speak for me," Tang said.

His accent was different from what Whorf had heard; it took him a moment to realize. "You must've gone to school in California."

"Stanford," Tang said. "Yes."

"In any case," Rezakhani continued, apparently trying to take the conversation back, "the important thing is this: the moon expedition did in fact conduct experiments with robotic prospector/samplers, but they were essentially just moving mechanical pigeonhole desks, which loaded a rock into each chamber and recorded where they got the rock. Nothing that was remotely capable of smelting, forging, casting, cutting, or making anything, let alone of self-replication. They were just rock gathering machines that could detect and pick up lumps of something valuable and ignore other rocks. Nothing like that could possibly have built the moon gun, unless it was completely reprogrammed and there were half a dozen other machines for it to work with.

"But the strange thing is, we did find a Trojan horse in the software. After the expedition left the little sampler-miner-prospectors on the moon, and they started roving around looking for resources and bringing things back to the assay labs, we were going to announce that we had a resource map once enough data had come in. But long before we got the chance, something took over the little robots, and they locked us out. And you know, if you look at the mass of one of those EMP bombs, and how often they seem to be able to drop them, it does sort of look like the robots are carrying the rocks to make it out of—the capacities are just about right. Except they couldn't make a moon gun. A hundred good engineers— human ones, anyway—couldn't make one."

"What do you mean, human?" Halleck asked.

Rezakhani shrugged. "Just that. Back before, no power on Earth even had pure-fusion bombs working."

"Let alone being able to build them via robots 400,000 kilometers away," Tang added.

"None of us on the team had ever done anything one tenth as hard as a complex assembly from raw materials on another world. But something apparently could, and did. And it might have hijacked our robots to do it. At least five years before Daybreak day, too.

"Well, we had learned from picking up a couple of radio broadcasts that you have a Doctor Arnold Yang in the States, in the city of Pueblo, Colorado, who is also working on identifying and understanding the moon gun, and since neither of our governments nor our research institutions are still there, and the human race needs this problem figured out . . . here we are. We are quite prepared to work for our passage in order to see Doctor Yang and pool our knowledge with him."

Halleck looked genuinely sad as he explained that Arnold Yang had been corrupted by Daybreak, committed treason on its behalf, and been executed.

Tang frowned. "That is amateurish."

"Amateurish?"

"To have captured a brilliant person with deep knowledge who has been corrupted by Daybreak, and then to execute that person like a petulant child angry at a toy, rather than to keep them and try to turn them and harvest the information. I do not think our political police would ever have made so amateurish a mistake."

Ihor nodded eagerly. Whorf was still trying to decide whether having amateurish political police was a good thing or a bad thing when Halleck said, "Either this is the most outrageous con game and tall tale in the history of Earth, or you're telling the truth. And anybody who could lie that well wouldn't tell *this* lie, I don't think; a thousand more convincing and simpler ones are available that would also have gotten me to take you on board."

"So we're in?" Tang asked.

"You're in. Whorf, Ihor, I think you probably have two more math tutors. Mister Whorf, find Mister Rezakhani some bedding, and put him in berth 104; Mister Reshetnyk, same thing for Mister Tang, berth 88."

2 DAYS LATER. ABOVE THE INTERSECTION OF THE FORMER INDIANA HIGHWAY 14 AND INDIANA HIGHWAY 17. (DOMAIN OF CASTLE EARTHSTONE/NEW STATE OF WABASH). 12:30 PM LOCAL SOLAR TIME/1:15 PM EASTERN TIME. WEDNESDAY, APRIL 29, 2026.

The continuing cold and soggy spring had grounded Nancy Teirson for a couple of days, but today was bright and clear, and there was plenty to see. Two miles below her Acro Sport, Highway 14 was a river of tribals pouring west. She guessed that they extended a little less than seven hundred yards along the road, in loose ranks of six to ten abreast. She circled lower for a better look; rocks and arrows rose toward her, dropping back far below. The tribals were pumping their spears and axes up and down in rhythm; *sorry, guys, the engine's a little loud for me to appreciate all that ooga booga you're doing.*

She thought about buzzing them for fun, but the Acro Sport was unarmed and unarmored, and there was no sense pushing her luck. In the months after Daybreak, it had occurred to her that her old expensive hobby of building kit airplanes might be highly relevant to becoming rich in the new world, and she'd had the kit already, though she'd had to copy many parts in materials that stood up to biotes.

Her "all natural materials" Acro Sport was a great aerobatic biplane, a short-landing tail dragger she could set down on a short stretch of dirt road or even a large building roof, but building it without synthetic fabric, fiberglass, plywood, or plastic had added weight and cost structural strength, and her version of a bio-diesel flathead 8, running on modified kitchen grease in a fog of spraying lye, was badly underpowered. *Poor old Acro, stuck as a mailplane with a part-time job in reconnaissance,* she thought. *Besides, right after Daybreak day, who knew I'd even want a mount point for a gun, let alone a bomb bay?*

She circled, staying up out of arrow range, taking a good look before she turned away from them and headed back to the makeshift airstrip at Terre Haute.

Affectionately, she patted the cowling on the Acro Sport. This coming winter, she was supposed to spend a few months down at Castle Newberry, helping them start building the next-generation copy. *You're going to have grandchildren,* she thought to her plane. *Don't you mind that you're not a war bird; we're going to win the war, get some peace, and go back to being a country where the mail must go through.*

AN HOUR LATER. TERRE HAUTE, NEW STATE OF WABASH (FORMERLY INDIANA). 3:20 PM CENTRAL TIME. WEDNESDAY, APRIL 29, 2026.

"What *did* something like this?" Neville Jawarah asked Jimmy. Most of the old frame houses were burned down to the foundations, and the streets were a tangled maze of wind-drifted debris heaps higher than a man's head with blown-clear pathways between them. The reek of the rotting asphalt was everywhere. But directly in front of them, a circle seemed to have been scoured, with an almost-neat edge; dunes of debris encircled it like rings around a black carbon bull's-eye.

"Firestorms look like this sometimes," a voice said behind them; they jumped into salutes, because it was General Grayson. He returned their salutes absently, talking to the officers around him.

Neville thought, *Please God, don't let anyone notice a general and ten other guys could just walk right up behind us. Also please don't let me be that absentminded when we're fighting. Also please let me get home. Especially also please help Jimmy keep his stupid wiseass mouth shut.*

"... more like a fire *tornado*," Grayson was explaining to the men around him. "Sometimes with so much fuel per acre you get a vortex with winds up to hundreds of miles an hour, and blast-furnace temperatures. I saw something like this one time in Teheran. What makes it so eerie is you never see a really bare space this big in a city, normally, so the sheer scale gets to you. Look at that office building and count windows—five storeys, right? So it's—"

"My dear God." The voice was deep and resonant; Neville recognized Reverend Whilmire from mandatory chapel. "This circle must be ten times as big as it looks."

"Worse than that. Your eye wants it to be about a block across, and it's more like fifteen, and that works out to maybe fifty times as big as your eye tries to estimate." Grayson glanced at the patch on Neville's sleeve. "Pullman Militia?"

"Yes, sir."

"If this firestorm happened in the part of Pullman that's still inhabited, how much would be left?"

"Not much, sir."

"We have to beat these assholes because if we don't"—Grayson's arm swept out toward the empty space in front of them—"somewhere in there, Mom's house. Got that, soldier?"

"Got it, sir."

"Well, I've kept you from working long enough, your sergeant'll be looking for you. Carry on."

"Yes, sir."

The general and his officers were long out of earshot, and Neville and

Jimmy were pounding a post into the strangely soft, crusted black dirt of the circle, before Jimmy said, "You sure said 'Yes, sir,' a lot, there, Nev."

"He's a general. It's what they're for."

"Yeah. Anyone ever tell you you're a kiss-ass?"

"Yeah, you. All the time. But since we got here, nobody's told me I'm getting a lash on the butt or time in the stockade."

. . .

"I do believe you frightened those boys," Whilmire said, as they rode north.

Colonel Goncalves, the commander of the President's Own Rangers, fluffed his long gray beard. "The general also made their day. Frightening attention from authority makes a young man stand straighter and try harder." He grinned.

Grayson thought of Jenny's private nickname for Goncalves, *Santa the Hun*, and grinned back. "Just reminding them that even this far away, they're still defending their town and their family. Which they need help remembering."

Whilmire frowned. "Obviously you saw something else I didn't."

"Those two gave off the not-subtle aroma of having been sent to mark trail as a punishment for doing something stupid," Grayson explained. "They were out away from the main body, and out here that means 'in danger.' But they were slumped over, looking at their feet, and dragging themselves through their work. I mean, honestly, sneaked up on by a whole pack of brass?" Grayson's smirk was as annoying to his father-in-law as it was to anyone else. "I guess I felt sorry for them too. Being sad sacks in a pretty good army must suck. But if loser-ness could be screamed and punished out of them, their CO would've done it by now. So I figure, remind 'em about Mom's house."

THE NEXT DAY. RUINS OF MONTEZUMA, NEW STATE OF WABASH. 3:30 PM EASTERN TIME. THURSDAY, APRIL 30, 2026.

At first Larry Mensche thought someone had tied a piece of firewood to the lamppost on the former US 36 bridge across the Wabash. But it was a naked corpse, covered with pitch.

The eye sockets were empty. The hair was matted into a slick cap on the skull. The face was distorted, as if it saw something horrible on the horizon. A sign had been wired around its legs:

ECCO

RRC

DEATH 2 U ALL

Steve Ecco, scout for the RRC, sent here last summer. Betrayed by Arnie Yang before he ever got here. Captured and tortured to death by that half-ass warlord who now called himself Lord Robert.

The right thumb was missing. Pauline Kloster had described how Robert had battered it off with a hammer and cauterized it with hot solder. The strangely clean emptiness of the eye sockets, so unlike what a bird would do, was probably because they had been burned out with a hot screwdriver while Ecco was alive.

Larry whirled at the soft cough.

Freddie Pranger was there, with Chris Manckiewicz, and Roger Jackson, and other scouts Larry knew less well. "You got here," Freddie said. "We were kind of waiting for you, 'cause we'd heard you were coming this way too, and we knew you knew Steve."

"Yeah, I did. Pretty well. And all of you?"

Roger said, "He was the first guy who trained me as a scout."

Chris Manckiewicz added, "And he wanted to be a great scout more than anything else. If it hadn't been for him, Pauline would never have escaped, and she was our main warning about what was brewing at Castle Earthstone. And we all know Steve was as good as any of us, and it wasn't lack of skill or bad luck." The words "Arnie Yang" seemed wrong to speak here.

"So we were thinking," Freddie said. "They sent us scouts to make sure the bridge was open and secure, and we did that, and to hold it till the army gets here later today, and with no tribals for miles around, we can do that. We have some time on our hands, and Steve Ecco was a scout. Scouts should bury him."

Larry nodded. "Let's put him somewhere where he can rest easy. Maybe facing east, toward the enemy?"

Freddie nodded. "Might make sense, and it would honor him, but I kind of think about times I've been scared and alone, and I thought he might want to face toward Albuquerque."

The other scouts looked at each other.

"Where his kids and their mother live," Freddie said. "Home. Where we all wish we could go."

3 DAYS LATER. PORTA CORSINI (AT THE ENTRANCE TO THE RAVENNA CANAL), ITALY. 4:30 PM CENTRAL EUROPEAN TIME. SUNDAY, MAY 3, 2026.

So far north, and so close to the solstice, the sun rose before 5 a.m., but Whorf was already awake, casting, sounding, and calling as *Discovery* made her way into the canal that joined Ravenna to the coast. A few minutes before the graying light had made it unnecessary to hold the depth line up to the lantern; now at Whorf's call of "five fathoms," Captain Halleck ordered, "Heave to, then, and drop anchor when she's steady."

They were in Ravenna precisely because there was nothing there: the city lay within the southern edge of the Dead Belt produced by the North Sea bomb.

Lisa Reyes found most other radiation sources negligible, and background tritium down to tolerable levels, but recommended they not stay long.

A shore-scouting party came back with an odd request: please detach Whorf from drawing microorganisms for Lisa, and send him to draw what looked like a long list of places that began with "San."

"Feel like I'm in California," Whorf muttered.

Ihor went along to keep watch while Whorf drew.

As Whorf was rolling up his sketch of San Vitale, Ihor asked, "May I look at this one?"

"It's not really finished, I'm going to get some of it done on the ship, but now I remember enough."

"But may I see?"

"Sure, but it's not finished."

Ihor looked for a long time. Then he wanted to see Whorf's sketch of the tomb of Gallia Placidia, and said, "I see it now because you showed it to me, Whorf. It is so good that the first voyage I have where I get to look, I have you to show me how to see."

"Dude, the philosophy is getting deep around here. Our shoes are going to be a mess."

By the end of the day, Whorf had made a few dozen sketches, most not finished but all at the point where he thought he could finish them well enough from memory later. He was surprised how many people wanted to see them. "It's just draftsmanship," he said. "I know just enough about art to know I'm not an artist."

"They're still having a hard time redeveloping cameras with film that works and lasts," Lisa Reyes said. "By the time someone gets back here with a working camera, this might all be lost—tribals might come up from the south to knock it down, more fires might sweep through the city, anything. So this is the last chance humanity gets to see what it looks like, and we all see through your eyes and hand, Whorf. I don't know about art at all, but I know this: you might be our last view of Ravenna. And if you've been listening to your history tutor at all, this was the last place where the Western Roman Empire sort of guttered, gasped, and slid before finally giving up."

"Sort of like Pueblo today," Whorf said.

THE NEXT DAY. RUINS OF LAFAYETTE, NEW STATE OF WABASH. 4:30 PM EASTERN TIME. MONDAY, MAY 4, 2026.

"Sir," the major beside him said, "there's a scout approaching; he just came out of that side street—"

Grayson looked up from the tattered paper street map of Lafayette, Indiana, on which he'd been trying to place the only standing street sign in sight. He did not need to raise his field glasses to see which scout it was; he could pick out Larry Mensche's awkward seat on a horse clear to the horizon, or possibly from the moon. *There's a man with an incentive to see the bicycle redeveloped,* he thought.

As soon as it was practical, Mensche dismounted and walked to them. "Sir, a party of about two hundred tribals is digging in at Battle Ground State Park; looks like they're preparing a fortified camp for a much larger party. As of about three hours ago, they had some breastworks up along the edge of a rise, they were building some fires, and they were clearing junk out where the roof of the visitor center had fallen in, turning it into sort of a fort, I guess. There's a creek—"

"On the west of the hill?" Grayson gave him that strange smile, the one that always made people uncomfortable.

"Exactly, sir."

"I was kind of thinking this might be where they'd meet us. Maybe they have a sense of history, or maybe it's just that it's about the only defensible piece of ground near the confluence of the Tippecanoe and the Wabash, but either way, they are setting up camp exactly where William Henry Harrison defeated Tenskwatawa."

"You think it's on purpose?"

"Definitely. I just don't know what purpose it's on. It's the only high, dry ground around here with covered access to water and there's a ton of symbolism too." Grayson scrawled on a sheet of paper. "Messenger, take this to Colonel Prewitt at the TexICs' HQ, and bring me back word that he's received it. Urgent."

"Sir." The messenger mounted and galloped away.

Goncalves said, "You're sending the TexICs to raid them while they're setting up?"

"Yes. That force of four thousand of them coming down the Tippecanoe that Nancy Teirson has been shadowing was well below Monticello at nine this morning; they'll be down here at the Tippecanoe battlefield before dawn tomorrow. Half a day behind them there's another horde that size, and when Quattro bombed them at Winamac he didn't think he had slowed them up at all, so figure they'll be here by noon tomorrow. Larry, did that force at the battleground park look like they were working hard?"

"They were digging trenches and throwing up breastworks like maniacs, sir."

"Well, there you have it. By noon tomorrow, which is about the soonest our main force could get there, they'll be dug in up there with eight thousand fighters. At logistics and maneuver, this guy Robert is at least a very gifted amateur: he put together two forces the size of back-before divisions, and moved them a long way into a position where they're a serious threat. Just in case he also turns out to have a knack for combat command, we're not going to spot him any more advantages. I think the TexICs can get there by six tonight, and sunset's not till almost eight. Plenty of time to smash up whatever preparations Robert's advance parties have made. But once they do, a short regiment of cavalry doesn't have the firepower to hold it against what's coming down the Tippecanoe."

"Sir," Goncalves said, "I hope this doesn't look like I'm angling for glory—"

"You're ahead of me, Goncalves, and you're right. Whatever it looks like, I need the President's Own Rangers to get there before those first four thousand Daybreakers do, dig in, and hold that hill. I'll push a couple of reserve regiments to try to reinforce you by noon, but I think three is more realistic. You've seen the same things I have: soldiers staggering till they fall asleep wherever they lie down. We'll be lucky to get the main body moving any time before noon tomorrow, and I doubt they'll be able to maintain route step, let alone anything faster. So, if you have to do it alone, can your Rangers get there before the Daybreakers and hold that hill till the main army gets there?"

"I would feel honored—"

"Goncalves, I *know* you'll say 'yes, sir,' if I order you to, and die trying if you have to. If I asked you to take four guys and conquer Asia you'd say 'yes, sir,' and offer to leave two behind for a reserve. But physical reality counts for something too. You started off from Pale Bluff with an official three battalions, but in numbers you're more like two. *And* you were the avant garde coming in here, so your troops are *tired*, even if they show it a lot less than the regulars and the militia. So I don't need the answer from your pride, which I already know. I need your judgment. If I send you to do this, will our side still be holding the hill when I get there with the main army tomorrow evening? And will I still have a functioning President's Own Rangers once you do that?"

Goncalves stroked down his belly-length beard slowly; Grayson had learned to respect it as the *Don't interrupt, I'm thinking hard* gesture.

"Candidly, sir, yes. If it's not any later than sundown tomorrow. Just don't be any later."

"It's a deal. I'll make sure that whenever the TexICs send a report back it goes straight to you. Get going."

Goncalves saluted and thundered away.

Grayson turned back to Mensche. "All right, I'll send you after Goncalves in a minute, to give him the details, but while he's kicking things into motion, you'll have time to tell me the rest. So is anything else unusual about the Daybreaker force?"

"Looked well fed and healthy. No obvious slaves—everyone was armed, looked like they were carrying roughly equal loads, no whipping post. And the few that I got a close look at didn't have that whacked-out expression most Daybreakers do."

"Castle Earthstoners?"

"Roger Jackson's heading over to investigate that right now, since he's seen so many Earthstoners, but yes, sir, it looks like it. We're not the only ones who are sending their best to that field."

. . .

At their main encampment, in the old County Fairgrounds, Larry briefed Colonel Goncalves—though Larry privately thought of it as anything but brief. He was just glad that his memory for roads and terrain in general had become pretty good after more than a year of full-time scouting, because Goncalves and his majors and captains were a demanding audience. In between describing seemingly every tree and wall between here and the Tippecanoe battlefield, and answering even more questions when he failed to be detailed enough, he swallowed about a dozen pancakes and several venison sausages, the rations the cooks were able to put together quickly. "At least we're missing the split peas with corn they're going to lay out for breakfast tomorrow," one of the officers said, cheerfully.

After two hours of interrogatory dinner, Goncalves said, "All right, make sure everyone's ready. Plans to the lieutenants and sergeants. Nap till eleven. Moon'll be up at quarter after eleven, we go as soon as we can see, or as soon as Larry can see and we can see Larry. Kit has to be together by then but make sure they use as much time as they can to sleep. We're going to want to make most of the trip at double time."

At loose ends, Larry drifted toward the "auxiliaries area," which was the polite expression for "where we store all the not-quite military people who have nowhere else to bunk."

Tonight, in the corner of the former dairy barn, the auxiliaries were the Reverend Whilmire, perched with his back to a window to cast the last light of the setting sun on his Bible, and Freddie Pranger, stretched on his back with his arms folded over his chest and his hat pulled over his face.

Larry nodded and lay down near Freddie; Whilmire asked, "Can I ask you something? I'll try to be brief, I know you need to sleep."

"It'll have to be brief."

"A great deal of what my son-in-law was saying to Goncalves went right over my head. I was just wondering what happened at the Battle of Tippecanoe, since it seems Jeff is basing so much of his thinking—"

Freddie Pranger said, "I spent years on all that frontier-history stuff, and I can tell you, so Larry can sleep. I'm not going out till close to dawn but he's only got to moonrise."

"Thank you," Whilmire and Mensche said, simultaneously.

Decades as an FBI agent and more than a year as a scout had taught Larry to fall asleep instantly whenever he could, but he wasn't quite fast enough to avoid hearing Freddie explain, "Well, back in 1811, the Army under Harrison won and the tribes under Tenskwatawa lost, so it's a good site if you're thinking American army and militia versus tribes. But the way Harrison won was, the Americans occupied that hill the tribals are on right now, which made them such a big threat that the Indians had to do something right away. So some of the Indians rushed to take back the hill, and when they got in trouble Tenskwatawa sent more in after them, and the Americans on the hill just kept beating the bigger and bigger forces the Indians brought in, and at the end of the day, the Indiana Militia had taken a lot more casualties than the Indians, but they still had the hill and the Shawnee Confederacy was wrecked forever. So that little hill is also a good place to break an army that's trying to take it away from you. Precedents both ways, I guess you'd say."

Larry firmly told himself the world was no different than it was before he'd heard that, and went to sleep.

. . .

"Am I going to be scared tonight?" Jenny asked.

"Have you ever been?" Grayson was sliding her robe off. "I'm sorry about having to rush, if you'd rather not—"

"It's the night before a battle, baby, I want you, too, what if it's the last chance or something terrible happens? And I don't mind hurrying, I need my sleep too." She turned and caught his hands in hers, moving them down away from her breasts. "But sometimes when you're emotionally wound up, like you're angry or sad or something big just happened, you hurt me, and if you're really wound up, you don't always stop when I say so. The night after you killed Cameron, remember? I had bruises for weeks." She could feel the tension in his forearms, and perhaps he was just wrought up, or did he want to start hurting her? Was her fear making him worse? "I just don't want to be scared tonight," she said. "It was sexy back when I didn't know you or love you yet, but now, I don't want my demon lover anymore. I want Jeff."

Something in his eyes looked so far away and sad that she felt safe letting go of his arms, and stroking his cheek. She felt a tear, and rubbed it gently, and was going in for a soft kiss when he shoved her down onto the pavilion floor, yanking up her nightie.

His eyes were as blank as a Greek statue's or a store mannequin's. He clasped her hair in one fist, forced her head back, and pried her legs apart with his thighs. He pushed in; he was very hard and she wasn't ready yet. She grunted with pain. "Jeff, slow down, that hurts."

He smiled that weird smile, and kept going; the twisted mouth and the flat expressionless eyes seemed like a mask together. The hand clutching her hair pulled her head back farther as he reared up on that arm. *He's watching himself hurt me,* she thought.

With his free hand, he pinched and slapped her all over. She was crying and couldn't breathe, snot running down her throat, making her choke and gasp.

She had no idea how long it took him to finish. As he did, he slapped her in all the sensitive spots, finishing with one on her face that made her head ring.

He pulled out and sat up beside her. She rolled over, curled up, trying to protect her sore body with her hands. "Don't try to tell me you're sorry, this time I'm not buying it, you meant to hurt me."

"All right." His voice sounded mechanical. "I love doing that to you. If you have any sense you'll get rid of me. I will miss you terribly. You're about the only real friend I've ever had. But if we stay together someday I will do something worse, and I think it would be better if you got rid of me."

She shuddered with the force of her sobbing, but she also heard her own voice in her head, calm but desperately urgent. *Jenny, be careful, get away.* She checked to make sure she could move everything, and inside her fetal self-hug, she probed for sore ribs or abdominal pain, and found her cheek bruised but nothing broken. She forced her breathing to calm and began to gather her clothes.

"A long time ago," he said, "I lost control of myself, and almost beat a girl to death. She was a little piece of shit whore, the kind of thing Mama told me I should use for my needs—"

Jenny finished yanking her sweatshirt over her head, afraid for the moment that her head was covered. "And I'm the kind you use for your career. Except when you use me for a piece of shit whore too."

He turned to look at her, and even through her fury, she thought, *Oh, shit, he's Jeff again, now, and if I stay here he'll get to me—and if he gets to me, I'll stay.*

"I really do love you, it scares me and . . . makes me angry, I get angry when I'm scared. I'm sorry."

She thought, *You are a dangerous nut job, and you are in charge of the army that is supposed to save civilization. And you are very likely to be the next President of the United States. And I'm not used to not being in love with you, at least not yet.* "Jeff, I'm not saying I'll stay, but I know you're not dangerous after you have one of these . . . things. Not for a while. Usually. So tonight I'll stay beside you, because I know you won't sleep if I don't, and the whole world is counting on you, and I care what happens to you. I might not ever sleep beside you again, though, are we clear on that?"

He was crying, but nodding. "Whatever you say."

"After the battle, or as soon as there's a spare minute, find a psychiatrist, tell them everything, do whatever they tell you to."

"I promise. I want." He stopped. "I don't want." Stopped again. "I don't know."

"Jeff, all of civilization is depending on you. I might be divorcing you next week, but you've got to win tomorrow. So get up in the morning and just do your duty. Do your best at it. I'll stick around at least till the end of the battle, and I won't go without saying goodbye. Now undress, and lie down here beside me."

She lay fully clothed on top of the covers, holding his hand while he slept. After a while, she slept too.

TEN:
STRANGERS TO TELL THE SPARTANS

"That's why we never heard back from the TexICs," Goncalves breathed. He passed his field glasses to Larry Mensche.

In the bright light of the few-days-past-full moon, Larry made out the breastwork, now much higher, actually a full wall—"Oh, crap." The upper part of the barricade was a heap of dead horses.

Goncalves grunted. "I figure what happened, the tribals were here way ahead of schedule, dug in and waiting. Three hundred against four thousand."

"But the TexICs were on horseback," Larry said. "How come none of them got away?"

The bright, almost-overhead moonlight distorted Goncalves's face into a bitter mask. "If Robert was smart, and we know he is, what he did was put fifteen hundred or so inside the camp, lying along the breastworks, out of sight and waiting. He put another fifteen hundred right where we are now, in all this brush, ready to close the road back, probably with bows and slings to cover the exposed slope, and told them not to make a sound or move a muscle till the TexICs were at the main breastwork. Same orders to another thousand across the creek in the woods northwest of the camp;

a horseman might try to get out that way and then double back, but he wouldn't get far if there were men in the woods.

"So the TexICs arrived, and from right about here—look how torn up the ground is just downslope—they probably saw a couple sentries or a few men working, and went to charge up that steep hill—figuring they'd carry the top of it and then sweep through the camp. Maybe they even split up and sent some around over the creek, by that old visitor center—it would be more effective if they were just on a burn-and-smash raid, they'd damage more stuff faster. Probably they had a minute or so, riding up to the barricade, of thinking this was an easy win.

"But Robert or someone working for him knows what they're doing; they put that wall up right along the top of that railroad embankment, so the last few feet are steep gravel after all the effort of getting up that steep hill. You can bet *that* broke the shock of the charge, created a big jam right there at the wall.

"So as soon as they were all bogged down, in ground that was terrible for horses, Robert's troops inside stood up, the troops back here closed in from behind, and the TexICs were in the bag, exposed on bad ground, and if they broke out on either flank they ran right into that reserve force in the woods across the creek. Horses on a steep hillside, or in a brushy creek, wouldn't have much of a chance. No room to charge or build up momentum. Their horses were pulled down or killed under them, the range was so close that those shitty bows, or just thrown rocks or long poles, would be all it took. Cavalry on foot's pretty helpless and they were outnumbered a dozen to one."

"Shit," Larry said. *And Roger Jackson was with them—Was.* He was already thinking of Roger in the past tense. *Hope it was quick.*

Goncalves said, "Tell Grayson we need him sooner, not later."

"You're still going in?"

"That's what General Grayson's orders were, and it's what I said I'd do. We can take them, I think, or at least take a big toll. There's only four thousand and we've got seven hundred Rangers. We'll get inside their camp and hold at least part of it, make them pay to take it back, tie them up and delay them. But if the next big bunch of tribals gets here before Grayson does, you can count us dead. So tell him to get his ass in gear, and if he gets here in time, I will definitely consider voting for him."

From their vantage point, Mensche ran back along the deer trail through the marshy meadow, zagged onto an old park trail, and angled down toward the river till he struck a road.

In the light of the nearly overhead moon, shadows were sharp and very dark, distances confusing, ambush more than possible, but now that the brush hid him from the fortified camp, he put his whole mind into staying alert and keeping his feet moving.

He kept up his pace, figuring that if he fell down exhausted at the other end they could throw him into an artillery wagon or something, and if he got there too late, he'd have a lot of time to sleep while he was dead. Pace after pace, hill after hill, he pushed the parkland and overgrown fields behind him. At last, when the last mile or so had been warehouses along the river, the sinking moon, now halfway down the western sky, backlit the I-65 bridge, where Larry was planning to re-cross the Wabash. Forcing himself to be as alert as he could be on two days of too much running, too few meals, and about four hours of sleep, he moved forward in the shadows to look over the situation from a low rise in the road.

He looked once, froze, and glided into the shadow of a wall, gulping air silently, pressing it in and out as fast as he could without gasping or making noise. When he had pushed enough oxygen in to stop the spasming of his lungs and silence the burning in his thighs, so that he could again move silently, he began sliding his feet forward, one after the other, in a crescent step, keeping them mostly in each other's tracks, feeling gently in front of him.

Behind the thick weeds that grew from the decayed asphalt at the building corner, he squatted and peered around.

A milling mob of tribals at the far end of the bridge, too indistinct to count. Hundreds of spearpoints stuck up above the dark mass. Below the bridgehead, a vast crowd of rafts and boats had been dragged up onto the bank. Farther upstream, the Wabash danced and twinkled with the phosphorescence of countless oars, paddles, and poles. *Well over ten thousand of them, maybe nearer twenty, not counting at least a thousand at the bridge. We thought the two big forces coming down the Tippecanoe were the main force, but they were a diversion. These must have come down the Wabash.*

No way to reach Grayson with a report.

Then he thought of Mark Twain's favorite pun.

The State Street Bridge should be close enough; he'd need to be up above ground level, so the sound would carry across the river, but he ought to be able to at least get the attention of the scouts on the far side, and maybe the sound would carry as far as the northeast sentries in Grayson's camp.

Quickly, silently, Larry Mensche moved forward, tiredness forgotten for the moment. Because he could only try this once, and it had to be soon, he needed a perfect place right away.

Fifteen minutes later, he had found it—a former supermarket warehouse. The door gave way to prying with his hatchet with only one soft squeal of metal. A more-than-head-high pile of empty cardboard boxes, pallets, and crates covered most of the open space on the first floor; obviously this place had been looted in the early, systematic time right after Daybreak day. He climbed the stairs to the second floor, where he'd seen windows facing the direction he needed. In the office up there, he discovered a family of mummies lying in one corner; smashed skulls on the two largest suggested they had been killed as they were waking up. *More murder victims than I saw in twenty years' FBI service, and nothing to do about them.*

The river-facing window revealed a little gray light creeping onto the eastern horizon. The State Street Bridge, just upstream, didn't rise far above the river; Larry was looking at it almost on the level. The concrete pilings cut the smeary gray pre-dawn into dim rectangles; the facings still shone in the setting moon's light.

He picked up a metal folding chair with a rotted plastic seat and swung it experimentally. *Get this right.* He checked his Newberry Standard by feel, set it on the desk within easy reach, picked up the folding chair again, and smashed the chair into the window, legs first, clearing all the glass with five hard blows in a couple of breaths.

He lifted the rifle to his shoulder and looked through the sights, scanning the bridge from the near to the far side.

A little group of Daybreakers were running across the bridge, drawn by the sound. He aimed for the leader of the group and squeezed the trigger. He didn't seem to have hit anyone but they vanished, diving for the bridge deck.

Another group was gathering at the far bridgehead. He aimed low and sent a shot shrieking off the crumbling pavement in front of them; they also dove to the ground.

The shots might have already alerted Grayson, but to make sure, Mensche re-sighted on the center of the big crowd on the road, perhaps a quarter mile beyond the bridge. Actual sniping would be impossible even for an expert, because a Newberry just wasn't a precision weapon, but he ought to be able to put three bullets at head-to-chest height in a crowd hundreds of yards across. Carefully, but quickly, he fired his last three shots.

Screams, wails, and a sudden milling like a kicked-over anthill told him he'd scored at least once.

The groups moving toward him would not be here for three minutes at least. He used one minute to reload.

Well, that was five *reports, as Mark Twain would have written, and even if the shots couldn't be heard in Grayson's camp, it's for sure that all that screaming was.* Rifle held ready across his chest, Mensche trotted down the stairs to the huge pile of dry wood, paper, and cardboard.

He tore out and crumpled a few pieces of cardboard and paper, then dropped them into a heap at his feet. He struck a match, lit the little pile, let it blaze up, tossed half a dozen cardboard boxes onto it, and sprinted out the door.

At the first alley, he dodged left, then right at the next street, and so forth in a saw-blade pattern to take him north and west.

He glanced back when he heard distant crashes and shouts; a black stream of smoke, lit by orange and red flashes from below, stained the pink dawn sky. *Guess that was pretty ready to go. Well, now they're alert for sure over at camp.*

He kept trotting, beyond exhaustion, hoping to stay alert enough to make them work to catch him.

**ABOUT THE SAME TIME. RUINS OF LAFAYETTE.
5:25 AM EASTERN TIME. TUESDAY, MAY 5, 2026.**

Jenny Whilmire Grayson rose early, dressed hurriedly, and rushed to get to the bathroom, hoping no one would see her awkward walk or the bruise on her cheek. *I am the very model of a modern major general's abused wife, fuck you all very much.*

Fortunately, most of the camp were still sleeping like corpses. The night sentries and patrols recognized her in the dim light of the just-rising sun and didn't stop to question her. She almost ran the last fifty yards to the small concrete-block restroom.

Inside, there was the usual thoughtfully-provided array of buckets of river water for flushing. *One more way for Jeff to show off wealth and power. Some poor loser private had to carry buckets of water half a mile to provide convenient indoor urination for the Great Man's piece of shit whore.*

Still, she was too grateful to feel cynical about the pile of soft rags. She lit the candle in the stall, lowered her jeans, and sat down.

It distinctly stung and ached when she peed. The puddle of urine at the bottom of the dry bowl was pink. A wipe with a light-colored rag confirmed that she was bleeding.

Too soon to be an infection, probably that rough thing he does . . . guiltily, she remembered that it had sometimes gotten her off. *Yeah, okay, so* sometimes *I have* liked it. *When* I *wanted to. When* he *was in control of himself. When my husband wasn't satisfying his need to rape a piece of shit whore.*

She dipped a clean cloth in a bucket of water, and washed her face with gentle thoroughness. When she finished, she sighed, mentally braced herself, and looked into the mirror. She lifted her sweatshirt and lowered her pants, turning to shine the candlelight on the marks on her sides and back.

Jeff had really outdone himself this last time. *I guess once your piece of shit whore flunks her putting-up-with-abuse test and doesn't love you any-more, you might as well use her up before you throw her away.*

She covered up again, and used the cool cloth to soothe her bruised cheek, and catch her tears. *All right. That was the last time I will think that phrase on purpose. The words have done what I needed them to, pissed me off enough to break me away from that son of a bitch. But now I will not think them about myself.*

Also I will not cry when I tell Daddy. And I will not throw anything about this in his face. We were both *ambitious and we thought Jeff Grayson was the ticket to our ambitions. We both trusted him enough to commit murders with him. Maybe I should have known better, maybe I should have guessed more of what was wrong, but, well, Daddy, I* will *still think that useful phrase, "fuck it."*

She thought back to her many arguments with Dr. Otherein in Women's Studies, back at Sarah Lawrence, who had always seemed to enjoy their arguments, even when they became shouting matches. At the time Jenny had thought it was maybe some weird dyke thing about liking to see the hot straight girl so angry she was in tears. *Now all of a sudden, I'm glad you insisted on me understanding that "blaming the victim" concept. You even* said *it didn't matter if I believed it then, just so I understood it.*

All right, no blaming the victim. And in this mess, Daddy would be—

Very far away and faintly, she heard the distant boom of a New-berry Standard—you couldn't mistake that sound for anything else. Another shot.

Three more like a fast drumbeat.

Screaming and shouting in the distance.

Whatever it is, it's starting.

She tucked a soft cloth into her underwear, refastened her pants, patted her face once more with a cloth, poured her wash bucket into the toilet to flush it, and snuffed the candle.

Patrols and sentries were running back and forth in the street, shouting to each other that they didn't know what was going on. Hoping her blonde mane would serve as a pass, she sprinted for HQ, not sure—

Shouts.

Shots.

Metal clashing on metal.

Ahead of her, people were yelling and the words included "HQ!" and "The general!"

A soldier blocked her way. "Mrs. Grayson, you'd better not go—"

She dodged around him and sprinted into the office that still said 4H COMPETITION ADMINISTRATION on the door.

Jeff Grayson lay sprawled, eyes and mouth wide open, across the desk. His throat was a gory mess, a hatchet still embedded there. One arm dangled toward the floor; the other lay by his side as if still reaching for his holster.

Four other corpses: Oxford, Grayson's XO, still clutched his pistol, but lay dead with a knife driven in through one eye. A messenger had had time to draw her pistol as well; her misshapen head was explained by the ax still in the hands of the one tribal, a young man in a black tunic and pants, whose forehead had been torn away; probably Oxford had shot him while he was chopping down the messenger.

"We saw them, we chased them, they got in here before—" the soldier beside her was saying. When had he come in?

"That's all right." Jenny reached out to Jeff's face. *In the movies you just press their eyelids down gently.* Her fingers slipped over his lids and touched the drying surfaces of his eyes, so she pressed a little more firmly and pinched the lids shut; they stayed that way. It did help.

"Get a messenger," she said.

"Yes, ma'am."

She gave Jeff one last long final look, then surprised herself by kissing his already-cooling cheek. "Bye, baby. Hope the next life brings you more peace than this one did. I'm sorry, I *did* promise we'd say goodbye, but I didn't know you'd be going this soon." It seemed terribly sad that now that he could never hurt her again, she was free to admit that she would miss him too.

A messenger gasped in mid-salute.

"Deputize two other messengers and let all the captains and Majors Pilkington and Selniss know that—"

"Ma'am, Pilkington and Selniss have been assassinated and a bunch of captains and lieutenants as well."

Jenny became belatedly aware of how much shouting, screaming, and shooting, she had been hearing. She drew a deep breath. "Deputize *all* messengers. This message to every unit: Your highest surviving rank is now your commander, and if they haven't assumed command yet, do it now. To the new commander, if you are on the line, back up slowly to the nearest position you're sure you can defend. Coordinate with units on each side of you, remain in contact, do not allow a gap. All units not on the line right now, have them do"—she gestured—"I don't know the word for it, a slow outward spiral, say clockwise on the map for consistency, from wherever they are till they reach the line. Kill any Daybreaker they find inside the lines, no prisoners, no time for it. Spiral outward, make sure they cover all the ground. When they get to the line, find the nearest . . . joint, connection, whatever, between two units on the line, and fill in behind to close it up.

"Exceptions to that: nearest company to the hospital, secure the hospital; nearest two companies to the stables, secure those.

"As soon as each unit is in position, have them send a runner back here to report where they are and what the situation is. At . . . nine o'clock, oh nine hundred, I guess, if we're not still under attack, all officers above lieutenant will meet here to sort it out."

The messenger repeated it back—accurately, as near as Jenny could tell, since she wasn't sure she remembered what she had said herself, and he'd translated some of it into military terms she wasn't sure about. When he saluted, she reflexively returned it and then kicked herself mentally, but he didn't seem to notice, already half-gone. A moment later she heard galloping hooves.

At least some messengers are going somewhere, she thought, *and there are some orders, and that is more than we had a few minutes ago.*

Outside headquarters, she found Third Squad, Second Platoon, something or other Company, as a young woman with a single stripe on the arm of her heavy gray flannel shirt started to explain to her. "Never mind that," Jenny said. "Whoever your company may be, are they close by?"

"Yes, ma'am, Sergeant Patel's in command, the officers are dead, Sergeant Patel, he sent us—"

"Run and tell Sergeant Patel that he's a captain now and have him bring the company here; I'm keeping the rest of your squad. You and you"—she pointed to the two biggest ones—"you're my bodyguards till further notice. Stay with me and keep me alive. Don't shoot any of our own people by mistake. Rest of you"—she was down to four—"I need you to go inside and move the bodies you find there out of that room, take them somewhere else and cover them with blankets or something. Part of the building used to be a dairy barn, maybe you can find a clean stall. Try to wipe the maps and charts clean enough to read. Be quick and let me know when you're done."

She stood silently with her guards, hearing the drumming and singing of the tribals, the screams and shouts of fighting, single shots everywhere, companies and platoons hustling past them, and then reassuring volleys of gunfire and shouted orders.

It was growing lighter, and she checked her watch. Twelve minutes had gone by since she'd burst out of the restroom. She would have thought it had been an hour. *Jeff always said time in battle is different.* Her eyes stung, from smoke or dust or something.

ABOUT THE SAME TIME. JEWETTSPORT FORD, JUST UPSTREAM OF PROPHETSTOWN, ON THE WABASH RIVER. 6:55 AM EASTERN TIME. TUESDAY, MAY 5, 2026.

Freddie Pranger was intent on getting across quickly and quietly, and almost missed the leg sticking out of the brush on the little island in the middle of the bridge. Bodies were hardly a novelty anymore, but this one looked fresh. Very carefully, he wrapped an arm around one girder of the bridge truss, placed his feet on an outside strut, lowered himself around the railing, and then dropped the last three feet to the ground.

The body groaned. Freddie drew his knife and, with his other hand, lifted the brushy branch. "Roger!"

The young man lay with a leg folded under him; clearly he'd fallen, jammed a foot in a crack in the rocks, and come down twisting. His pack was pinned beneath him, and his rifle and water bottle lay out of reach.

Roger must have been lying here for at least nine hours—more, if he'd fallen on his way out rather than on his way back. Pranger picked up the water first and said, "Anything hit you in the guts?"

"Just the leg." The voice was barely a croak, but at least he could answer a question. Freddie held the bottle steady so Roger could drink, and then set about figuring out how to get him free. The shores and stream were swarming with tribals, but shadows were still dark under the bridge. They were probably invisible to the tribals, but he dared not strike a light for a better look.

More feeling around revealed that the foot was thoroughly wedged. There would be no pulling it out without moving the broken leg.

"The RRC's first aid kit's got a few morphine sulfate tabs. I'm giving you two, 'scuse my pushing'em into your mouth but we can't waste'em. Now wiggle'em around to get'em on your tongue, and have some more water, and, down the hatch."

Roger swallowed painfully. "They're down."

"Have the rest of the water, it'll do you good and that morphine's gonna need something to dissolve it. It's more than enough to knock you out long enough for me to get your foot free and set and splint your leg. Ain't gonna be any fun, so you're skipping out till I'm done."

"'Preciate it, really do, I really am . . . I'm going to . . ."

Freddie crept away; by the time he had found an old piece of driftwood one-by that seemed like suitable splint material, Roger was completely out.

Freddie's inexpert hands found breaks in both bones in the lower leg, and the knee was at an odd angle, wobbled side to side, and seemed to be wearing its kneecap too low.

He tied Roger to one girder under the bridge by his hands, silently prayed that this didn't dislocate his shoulders too, tied another loop around the unconscious man's ankle (*hope that's not broken too or at least this doesn't make it worse*) and ran a double V of line to pull on it, a sort of caveman block and tackle. The ankle popped free on a hard tug; Freddie decided it felt like most other ankles he'd ever felt.

He re-rigged to tie Roger down across the chest and apply most of the force to pulling the leg straight by the ankle. He tugged and retied over and over until the bones moved easily under his hands, then tied off with a tight timber hitch and slid it a notch tighter.

Pressing things into what seemed like place, comparing it with the good leg, Freddie kept pushing, pulling, and feeling until he couldn't feel any difference. He slowly released the tension, playing the rope out gradually, feeling to make sure nothing popped back out of place, and then tied the splint on with some of the bandaging rags from the kit.

Wish I thought old Hugh Glass couldn't've done better, but I just bet when he *did, it* was *better. And on his* own *leg, at that.*

While Roger slept on, Freddie munched a biscuit, a wedge of cheese, and a cold chop, and considered what he might do. Just after eight, there was a flurry of activity downstream across the river; another big swarm of rafts and boats full of tribals was launching from the Prophetstown area, the swampy stretch below the Tippecanoe battlefield. Lying still in the shadows under the bridge, between the two piers, Freddie didn't think there was much risk of being seen; the enemy had no reason to look upstream for anything, and they were pretty intent on getting all those boats and rafts into the water. He stayed alert, ready to cover Roger's mouth if he woke, but otherwise silent.

Freddie's best estimate was that during the whole launching, there seemed to be fifty boats, rafts, and canoes in sight downstream all the time. The average might have been fifteen tribals per boat or raft, since some of them seemed to be carrying supplies and gear more than people. Maybe half a mile of the river below their launching point was visible from where he was sitting, and they might be going at six miles an hour or so with all that rowing. Not long after nine, the last of them passed around the bend below.

At a guess, that worked out to between seven and ten thousand of them.

He'd heard no gunfire for hours; the army was beaten, or fleeing, or holed up.

About ten, Roger woke slowly, and when Freddie was sure it wouldn't choke him, he gave him another drink. He remembered faintly from somewhere that morphine was dehydrating, and made sure he kept pouring water into the younger man.

Roger explained that he'd gone to take a look at the Daybreakers, per Larry Mensche's orders, and been passed by the TexICs as they rode in. "Gorgeous sight that I'll remember forever," he said. "Like three hundred movie cowboys or Nashville stars, riding like maniacs."

"*C'est magnifique mais ce n'est pas la guerre,*" Freddie said.

"Uh, *my* language in college was Lisperesque-2021," Roger said.

"What a French officer who saw the Charge of the Light Brigade said," Freddie said. "French was the logical language for a frontier-history nut to study. Yeah, it would've been what, almost sunset? Must've been beautiful."

"I was sneaking along on this bank—they crossed on the old I-65 bridge—and I saw them a couple more times, far away, still riding like hell on a broomstick. Then there was a buttload of shots and yelling and everything, from over around the old battlefield, and I came to this bridge. It's kind of perfect because it's so small half the maps don't show it, and without lights it's pretty dark, lots of good shadows to hide in in the moonlight.

"I made it across, went into that swampy area below the battlefield, and found so many Daybreaker patrols and scouts that I realized pretty fast I was gonna have to turn back. I'd heard screaming men and horses, gunshots, all that noise a battle makes, but it had died down to nothing by the time I crossed the bridge the first time; I figured the TexICs had probably ridden straight into a trap. Anyway, there was just too much traffic around in the dark, all Daybreakers, for me to stick around.

"So I started back with my information, taking it real slow and careful because the enemy were everywhere. I stayed in one ditch it seemed like forever, then there was more fighting."

"President's Own," Freddie supplied. "They were supposed to take and hold it in the middle of the night."

"Well, they were hosed pretty bad, Freddie, I don't mean by Grayson or by Goncalves, our guys just didn't know what was happening. But, jesus, dude, the situation. I estimated two thousand Daybreakers outside, and more than that in the fort itself.

"Anyway I snuck along my ditch to the northeast, ran up the embankment, and got onto the bridge. I was right about here when I saw boats coming, and since I was at this little island, I figured I'd just slip under the bridge and let them pass. Slip was the word; I fell and landed wrong, and that's where you found me."

"I would say it could happen to anybody," Freddie said, "except for how much it scares me that that is true."

"Well, the next thing that happened, while I was lying there not quite believing how bad hurt I was, the boats just kept coming, and they were landing all over Prophetstown, and I realized they were closing the trap. The noise got a lot wilder up there and then there was nothing. Then another big force came down the Wabash, I think twice as many as came out of the Tippecanoe, and sometime after that it was sunrise and you were here."

"Yeah, and while you were out, the big force you saw came down the hill and launched; they're all downstream, now, at least eighteen or twenty thousand of them. Grayson's catching all hell—if he's still alive to catch it." Freddie sighed. "On the bright side, *you* look better."

"I'm even hungry."

"I've got some bread and cheese left, let's try you on a little of that and see if you hang onto it."

Roger seemed to have no problem with food, other than getting enough of it; when he had eaten, he said, "Freddie, my leg hurts but not too bad. Why don't you tighten up your splint, and see if I can maybe move with a crutch or something?"

A little experimenting showed that Roger could hop with a driftwood board under his arm and his leg held mostly out in front of him, but climbing back to the bridge looked difficult even with Freddie's help, and it didn't seem likely he could travel either far or fast on his own.

"Don't want to start moving till I know where we're going," Freddie said, "and I don't. No idea where the war is now, and it can't be going well. That black smoke coming up from Lafayette seems more like something that would be happening if *they* were winning than if *we* were."

"Maybe you should leave me here for a while and take a look over toward Prophetstown, even see if you can get to the battlefield. There might be survivors we could link up with, and I'm fine with water and a rifle right in reach, and can move myself around a little if I need to change where I'm hiding or find another angle. You can leave me a couple hours."

Freddie nodded. "Guess you're right." He made sure Roger was as comfortable as possible, and said, "Hey, thanks for not telling me to just abandon you here and go on without you."

Roger snorted. "Thanks for not just deciding to, bro."

ABOUT THE SAME TIME. RUINS OF LAFAYETTE. 9:00 AM EASTERN TIME. TUESDAY, MAY 5, 2026.

Jenny thought, *These people look sick and worried. Bet I do too.* "All right," she said, "my only authority for calling this meeting is that I was here and everyone else was dead. Anything I ordered you to do that was obviously wrong, I certainly hope you did something else instead. Who's the senior officer here?"

Everyone looked nervously at the two surviving captains. Harris, his face still powder-stained and his shirt blood-spattered, said, "Probably me. I don't want the job."

"No one here does." She remembered that back before, Harris had been a state legislator in Idaho, and had joined the National Guard so he could call himself a veteran if he ran for Congress. "But someone's got to do it and your name's at the top of the list."

He rubbed his face. "I can put myself on the sick list and declare I'm not fit to command."

"If you would do that," she said, "I'm sure you're not." *Wow, way to win him over Jenny,* she thought, then decided, *oh, what the hell, it's true.*

Podlewski, the other captain, said, "Ma'am, back before I was a township constable; I've never been—"

"I understand that. *My* previous job was political wife. But we are in the middle of a battle, and we owe it to the troops that trust us to—"

Something roared outside. Metal screamed against bricks.

"What the Jesus fucking hell was that?" Jenny said, shocked at how level her voice was. They all looked stunned, and she said, "Never mind.

Back to your units, *now*. Hold the line or if it's broken close it up and retake it. Send me a situation report as soon as you can. Now! Move!"

They ran out of the office, leaving her alone with her father, who looked at her with an expression of polite, puzzled horror. "You said . . ."

"If they are going to force me to be a soldier, Daddy, I am going to fuck-ing talk like one. I'm just lucky I have the benefit of a modern college education so I already know how." She took two steps toward her father, and looked around the room at the still blood-spattered maps and charts, where she had been marking known positions and recording that she was apparently out of contact with all the President's Own Rangers, the Tex-ICs, her scouts, and one whole battalion of the Missouri militia. "Daddy," she said, "I am so far out of my place. But I haven't given up, and those officers—"

"They were all the rotten branches, Jenny. Daybreak killed all the worthwhile senior officers. Daybreak *knew*. I don't know the army, but I know people and I know administration. Daybreak drew a quality line through the organizational chart and cut off everyone above—"

A man burst in. She read his shirt and realized with relief that she had a real, not post-Daybreak militia, second lieutenant here. He started to salute, shook his head as if to clear the impulse, and said, "Ma'am, the Daybreakers have attacked our whole western line with what's basically a one-shot musket. Piece of pipe with gunpowder at the closed end, jammed down with ball bearings or fishing weights. They light it with a fuse. It's a shitty weapon but our men were used to those lame little bows and thrown rocks, and weren't properly under cover. First volley carried off a lot of our people, lots of serious wounds, and while everyone was screaming and thrashing, the tribals charged. Luckily we had two backup companies in rear enfilade, where you put them, and they moved in, held off the human wave, and we're okay, but we're pretty bashed up. Same report applies all along the western side of camp. I sent runners all around to warn the other sides of the camp."

"Thank you," she said. "And forgive me, you're Lieutenant—"

"Marprelate, ma'am, Calvin Marprelate, used to be of Tenth Mountain back before, spent most of my time after Daybreak as the TNG military liaison for Pale Bluff, long story short your husband assigned me for liaison to the Fourth Washington Militia. With your permission, no one else appears to be willing to do the job, so I'm assuming command."

"You don't need my permission and I'm delighted," she said.

He nodded, and shouted, "Messenger!" Two quick sentences sent the messenger galloping off to bring in a platoon to guard headquarters. He turned back to Jenny and her father. "You two, and Chris Manckiewicz when they bring him in—"

"I'm here," Chris said, bustling in, still tying back his shoulder-length hair and finger-combing his bushy beard. "I was able to pry open a dormer window on one of the livestock barns and get a view up the river. It's solid boats and rafts as far as I can see. At least five, maybe ten times as many tribals as General Grayson expected. I take it you're acting CO, Lieutenant Marprelate?"

"For want of anyone else. Did you get a look toward the stretch of road we've been using for an airfield?"

"Hiatt Drive. Yeah, it's now way outside our lines, the eastern side of the fairgrounds was pretty well overrun before they stopped them at a line of barns, so you've got a big stretch of chain-link fence in the middle of the Daybreakers between you and the runway. Hiatt Drive is like everything else for half a mile around, packed with Daybreakers—"

Marprelate barked again. "Messenger! Word to all units not on the line: I need a platoon of volunteers to retake the landing field."

The messenger saluted and ran out.

To Jenny, Chris, and the Reverend Whilmire, he said, "I'm going to lead that sortie personally. We can't lose our advantage in having command of the air."

"But we don't have to have that landing field," Chris pointed out, "she can fly out of Terre Haute for now, and heliograph to us—"

"That'll be all. While I'm gone, reports will be coming in. Prepare me a set of options for a breakout and a counterattack, and a situation summary." He strode decisively from the room.

Chris said, very quietly, "I don't know whether I'm more afraid that he's doing this because he didn't listen to my report and he's a fool, or because I'm a major newspaper publisher and he's a show-off."

"Quite a choice," Jenny said. "Let's get to work on that situation summary. If Marprelate comes back, he'll want it, and if he doesn't some-body will, even if it's me again."

ABOUT THE SAME TIME. TIPPECANOE BATTLE GROUND, WABASH. 11:00 AM EASTERN TIME. TUESDAY, MAY 5, 2026.

Freddie Pranger had seen the pile of dead children in the McDonald's by Deer Creek Run. He'd seen the dozen bodies hanging from the bridge by Pierce. He'd found the barely covered pile of newborns in the ravine below Castle Greenwood.

This wasn't worse, objectively, he told himself. Just another bad thing as they tried to restore civilization.

But more of this pile were people he knew.

It looked like Goncalves and the President's Own Rangers must have taken the visitor center and held it for a while. Dead Rangers lay by every window, hole, and door, some hacked by blades, a few with arrows pro-truding, some with big holes in their backs.

Freddie knelt, looked, turned the body over, and swore. No mistaking the small, almost round entry wound and the exit wound you could put a fist into; it had been a slug from a heavy firearm. Apparently the Day-breakers were willing to compromise their religious objections to Mis-ter Gun.

Good sweet jesus, if the tribals surprised the army with guns—

*Even if the army had more and better guns, that first shock after almost a year of never having to face anything worse than those lame-ass home-made wooden bows, and those silly little-David rock-and-slings, to be hit with musket volleys—just before the human waves hit—*His heart felt cold and heavy. He would have to push Roger—

Again, he froze: there in the center of the improvised fort, a circle of bodies splayed outward to the compass points from the grim hedge of head-topped spears at the center. Walking forward, he recognized Gon-calves and some others.

They leave us their dead because we want life to go on, so we have to bury or burn them. The tribals don't want life to go on, so to them, usually these

*corpses are just a bioweapon against us, or a burden we have to bear. But
these bodies meant . . . well, shit, I can't leave them this way.*

Pranger wasn't normally a praying man; alone in the forest he often felt
a presence in the loving silence, but seldom saw any reason to spoil that
with yakking.

Nevertheless, when he gently lifted Goncalves's head by the chin and
occiput, letting the blood-matted gray beard stick to his palms like a rag
from a butcher's table, he said, "I'm sorry," and when he set the head carefully beside the big man's corpse, he murmured, "Be at peace" to Goncalves and added "Take care of him," to the presence.

As he placed the last head by the last body, he said, "Help me get this
right, Lord, they deserve—"

"Shit," a voice said.

Freddie drew his hatchet and wheeled. No one. Nothing moved.

He turned slowly around, scanning methodically. Among one pile of
bodies, an arm flopped away from a face. A Daybreaker? The face was tat-
tooed in a domino mask joined to a spiderweb pattern—

But the torn, bloody shirt was fringed, with three stripes on the sleeve,
and the shoulder patch was a star behind crossed lances: a TexIC. He knelt
by the young man. "Scout Freddie Pranger, RRC, attached to Army of the
Wabash. You look like you could use some help."

"All I can get, Scout Pranger. I'm Dave McWaine, Sergeant, Texas Independent Cavalry." Something about the tautness of McWaine's brownish-
bronze skin, or his innocent, stunned expression, implied he wasn't more
than twenty. His deep black hair was bound in a single blood-soaked
braid. He rolled over, looking around. "Shit, not again. This *can't* be happening *twice*."

"Water?" Freddie asked, sticking to practicalities. "No abdominal
wounds?"

"Yes water, no ab wounds, just the worst headache in the history of
everything."

Freddie gave the young man his bottle. "I just filled it at the pump,
there's plenty." He let McWaine drink while he checked for broken bones
and for wounds he might not be feeling yet.

Bad contusions, but no deep wounds. That gash across his scalp probably bled so bad they didn't bother to make sure he was dead. With those dark eyes I can't see his pupils well enough to check for a concussion.

"I gotta get back to camp sometime soon and I already have another wounded guy to take with me. Can you walk?"

The TexIC nodded. "I'm banged up, but not broke nowhere."

"My other wounded man is a scout lying under a bridge with a broken leg a couple miles from here. Come with me, and tell me your story on the way.

"I don't know if nobody gonna believe me." The young man's accent was strange, a hint of border-state south like Pranger's own, but slightly flattened and guttural.

"Probably I will, if it's true."

"True as death, Mister Pranger. True as death."

Freddie approved of the way Dave McWaine told his story while looking around constantly, never letting his voice rise in volume, pausing frequently for them both to listen. Before they reached the bridge, Freddie had heard it all.

. . .

I'm an enrolled Tonkawa; my mom made sure I'as enrolled. But she didn't get along too well with her folks, and I didn't exactly have a dad except biologically, so I didn't grow up near any other Tonkawas, and the little bit that Mom remembered, she remembered all kinda-sorta and scrambled up. On my own later, I learned some of that tribal ways stuff off Goo-22 and Wikimondo on the Internet, but I didn't always know what I'as reading.

Like, first time I got sent up to Corsicana, I had a guy do this tattoo on my face here. They said it was self-mutilating behavior and gave me another two months; I just thought I'as being traditional Tonkawa 'cause there was this thing on a web page about how they had lots of tattoos all over their upper body and face. I didn't even *think* that the tattoo might be, you know, some certain exact thing, or that maybe somebody besides you decided what you should wear, or that maybe they didn't all do that anymore. It was right there on the Internet, you know?

So I'as just back from my second stay at Corsicana, and busting my ass to finish a GED and get something else going because I'as through with the street kid crap and the stuck in a small town forever crap and the everybody knows you're just a piece of crap crap and all the crap in general, and working for this guy Stan Krauss, a horse breeder, 'cause I loved horses, and Daybreak hit and Mister Krauss thought he was gonna be a big old rich guy, and I started working full time for him, 'cause I thought so, too, I mean, engines stop working, people're gonna want horses, right?

So I'as doing okay, had a steady job, Krauss's horse ranch was the most successful business in Grinder's Hole, Texas, orders backed up five years in advance. There I was coming up in the world for the first time even if the world was going down, and then in the spring last year all these bush hippies started coming around by Mister Krauss's place and giving us all this, like, threatening shit, like telling us we needed to free the horses for the wolves to eat, because horses were bred by people to make Mother Earth dirty. I think. Ain't sure I ever got it straight, 'cause they shouted most of it, along with some threats. Well, but you know, that Mister Krauss, he was old school Texas-German, if you know the type, he just told'em to get the fuck off his land.

So one day I'as out chasing Redstone, who was the biggest pain in the ass you ever saw in a stallion and stallions are *born* to be pains in the ass, when I heard noise a long way off, and I came back and there was Mister Krauss and Mrs. Krauss and the other three guys that helped on the place, all dead in the yard, and the buildings burning, and the tribals that did it just a dust cloud going over the hill.

I got all the horses out of the barn—the Daybreakers were just gonna let'em burn alive—and I'as standing in that yard with the horses around me, and me crying like a little kid and talking to Krauss's body like I was right out of my mind, and Redstone stuck his nose in my back, and he's standing there like he's saying "I'm sorry."

So I found a saddle that'd fit him, and him and me got the other horses into a string, and we headed into Grinder's Hole to get the town militia and some help. Got there, and . . . well, there wasn't no help. Shit, there wasn't no Grinder's Hole. The tribals had left some bodies and some burning buildings and taken off north.

So I went south, 'cause I had an idea how to turn those horses into some wealth. The government in Austin was gonna be starting the Texas Independent Cavalry, which a lot of guys wanted to be in 'cause it was like a big deal, but it was bring your own horse, so I figured some guys that wanted to join would want to trade for a horse, and sure enough they did, and pretty soon I had me a big account in the Bank of Texas and the only horse I had left was Redstone, which I'as the only one he'd let ride him.

And I don't know if I'as drunk or 'cause all us rich guys were doing it, but Redstone and me signed up, and damn if I wasn't pretty good at being cavalry, made corporal before we even left Fort Norcross and sergeant by the time we'as at Pale Bluff.

So yesterday the general told us to ride hard and hit'em before the main force of tribals got there. But they got there before us, and unlike your usual Daybreaker hippie dumbshits, these ones had some tricks. Right alongside the other TexICs, we rode in from the creek side. Redstone jumped that breastwork like he had wings. I pulled out two pistols like Buffalo Fuckin' Bill to get it started.

But there'as more of'em around me than I could count, mostly with spears, and one asshole with a two-handed ax brung down Redstone with one hard chop to the face, and the rest drug me off and was beating me, and that was the last I knew for a while.

So I woke up and I'as in a pile of tied up TexICs and they told us we better scream and holler when they put us up on the wall 'cause we'as gonna be human shields. So I made up my mind to keep my mouth shut, but it didn't matter 'cause next thing I know Goncalves and his Rangers come busting into the building where they had us, and a couple of'em cut us loose and found us guns and knives to help out with, I thought us TexICs were hot shit, but the President's Own Rangers're something else, man, something else.

So it seemed like we'as in that building for a million years, we took charge after charge, and a few'd die, and then a few more, and finally one Daybreaker charge got inside. I shot till I had nothing to shoot, I remember running out of ammo, and then it was hatchet work, and then, boom, something on the back of my head, right where I wear my braid, which I think maybe saved my skull and my life.

And that's me.

ABOUT THE SAME TIME. ABOVE LAFAYETTE, WABASH.
12:00 PM EASTERN TIME. TUESDAY, MAY 5, 2026.

Nancy Teirson saw her landing field was overrun with Daybreakers and did not begin a descent. She flew on over the Tippecanoe County Fairgrounds, observing guns flaring in the thin open space between the thick double line of people encircling what had been about a third of the army's encampment. Obviously there was a lot of shit on what remained of the fan.

Staying high, she put the Acro Sport into a several-mile-wide counterclockwise circle to observe, and to give General Grayson a chance to heliograph to her. There was a garrison, a fuel depot, and a radio transmitter back at Terre Haute; she could report the bad news from there. Meanwhile, she needed to make sure she saw as much of it as she could.

The hasty tribal fortifications at the Tippecanoe battlefield were empty, but scattered bodies were everywhere.

She climbed up into the fierce cold, almost to the Acro Sport's 18,000-foot ceiling, for a better look from a distance. No more big tribal forces moving along the Tippecanoe River, so obviously they had arrived. Circling back over the main battle at the fairgrounds, she estimated 23,000 tribals by a radial count and 27,500 by an area count.

The forces she had been tracking before had totaled no more than 8,000. Had all these others come down the Wabash?

Descending to a much warmer 6,000 feet over the camp, she looked for interruptions in the Daybreaker lines, but found none: the army was surrounded.

As she flew a slow circuit, looking for anything unusual or any clue she could take back with her, a heliograph flashed below:

SORTIE 9 QEO 15 **BRK**

QSE 30 **BRK**

They're going to try to break out in 9 minutes, they expect to have the runway clear in 15, and they want me to land in 30? Grayson must have—

no. Not Grayson. *He'd never give an order that dumb. He's dead or uncon-scious, and some real idiot is in command down there.*

She clamped the stick between her knees, got the sun on the position-ing spot, sighted the headquarters signal tower down the scope of her own heliograph, and sent,

DO NOT SORTIE **BRK**

QCI 3X **BRK**

QSP RECCE B4 QRF TH **BRK**

Surely they'd understand *do not sortie,* whether or not they grasped the Q codes for *I will circle three times* and *I will relay reconnaissance infor-mation before returning to Terre Haute.*

They flashed back

QSL

which meant only "signal received."

Well, whatever they do, I'm not landing here. One good look and back to Terre Haute. She moved the stick gently forward, slowly descending for a last pass across the fairgrounds. On the western side of the fairgrounds, she saw flashes and puffs of smoke from both sides of the line.

Tribals using guns.

Has to be the Castle Earthstone heretics, which means—what's that?

She turned sharply to the east, flying straight across the camp, toward the strange object on the other side, near where her landing field had been. The thing was perhaps twenty feet across, like a giant quiver of arrows—no, an array of spears or harpoons—*rotating and tilting toward her—*

She hauled back and to the right on the stick and opened the throttle wide, avoiding flying over it, trying to climb away. A blue-black cloud appeared where the spear-things had been. She kept climbing, wishing the Acro Sport had a lot more engine.

Multiple thudding booms sounded behind her, audible even over the roaring engine. For an instant, she could hope she had been out of range.

The plane jerked and bucked. With a bang, her prop blades flew up and away, carrying off a piece of the upper wing; she leaned forward to see a long piece of wire wrapped around the shaft, one of those spears dangling from it.

Her leg felt funny, but the engine was shrieking with no load to balance it, so she first unlocked the throttle cutoff and slapped it in. In the abrupt silence she looked around, trying to put the plane into as long a glide as she could, hoping to make it back into the besieged army at the fairgrounds. She couldn't seem to work the rudder, and as she gently eased the stick back, instead of leveling off, the plane pulled hard right.

A strange ripping noise made her look; a spear, stuck through both right wings, was pulling loose in the wind, taking fabric, struts, and wires with it, leaving big flapping shreds. Her right side now had far more drag than lift. She compensated with the stick as well as she could, but the rudder pedals—

Something *hurt*. She looked down. A spear was sticking out of the cockpit floor and into her left calf muscle.

The shaft must be trailing down between the landing gear.

A crash was probably more immediately dangerous than blood loss. Nancy pushed on the barbed head, then pulled on the shaft, trying to back it out of her calf. With the torn wing it was already a hard fight to keep the Acro Sport in a straight glide toward the fairgrounds. It was trying so hard to tumble and dive. One hand on the stick and the other pawing at the spearhead, she plunged into a rising cloud of rocks and arrows.

She was still holding it mostly level when, seventy yards short of the fairground fence, the spear butt hit dirt. The spear ripped through her calf muscle, freeing her in a rush of blood. Screaming, she hauled back on the stick, willing the tail wheel to touch first. For a half second it felt almost like merely her hardest landing ever.

But the tail did not come down. The saggy, deflated tires grabbed pavement. Nancy jammed her face between her knees, hands clutching her seat belt.

With a sound like dry sticks crushed in a garbage truck, the Acro Sport flipped over its nose, landing on its upper wing and rudder, crushing and dragging them against the fuselage. When the plane stopped sliding, she was hanging from the belt by her waist. She poked her head downward into the light.

Through a drizzle of spattering blood, she peered between the cockpit edge and the crushed upper wing. Her seat belt buckle was jammed. She fumbled for her knife, concentrating on getting out of the plane.

She found the hilt and undid the snap on the sheath just as she smelled the biodiesel, silently praying *not like this not like this anything but this*. She was sawing on the belt when, through the narrow aperture, she saw a blazing torch laid onto the fuel-drenched fabric of the upper wing.

She sawed as hard as she could, crying *please not like this* as she did, but the belt did not give way before the whole Acro Sport flashed over into a blazing roar.

ELEVEN:
BY THE TIME HISTORY IS WRITTEN, I HOPE NONE OF US WILL RECOGNIZE OURSELVES

ABOUT THE SAME TIME. RUINS OF LAFAYETTE. 12:15 PM EASTERN TIME. TUESDAY, MAY 5, 2026.

"She's dead," Chris said, flatly. "And the plane is already burned beyond repair. Lieutenant Marprelate, there is no reason—"

"I'm in command here," Marprelate said. His voice was terrifyingly calm and reasonable. "American forces depend on air power. We can't lose air superiority."

Jenny looked at the flame towering twenty feet over the heads of the Daybreaker mob, and at Marprelate's little band of thirty volunteers. She thought, *Half of them look like psychos trying to die, and probably are, and the other half look too scared to back out, and I know they are.* Forcing her voice to stay level, low, and calm, she tried once more.

"We don't *have* air power," she said. "We used to have an airplane and a pilot. They're both gone. You'll be taking these men into a pointless—"

"Return to headquarters and have a situation report waiting for me when we return. And we *will* return, with the airfield secured. Go now. If you're part of this force, that's an order, and if you're not, I don't want to waste time arresting you, but I will, and chain you too."

Jenny and Chris caught each other's eyes, and walked away.

Chris said, "Those men could stop the whole thing, just say they don't volunteer after all, anymore, because it's fucking crazy. But they're going right out there with him to die. What makes anyone *do* that?"

"Let's run. If we go up on the roof we can at least get a good view of what happens and I think we'll need to see." She sprinted and Chris chugged and puffed after her. Twenty years and sixty pounds was a big difference. He didn't catch up until he was following her up the ladder from the second floor through the roof access.

Once he stood beside her on the flat roof, she said, quietly, "Jeff said once that some men want to die with honor, and other men will die just to be around them. He was big on honor. Probably, so are these guys. I just wish Marprelate was—"

Chris said, "Here they go."

The platoon waited behind three iron-pipe cannon, which sat behind an old flatbed trailer covered on its far side by a chain-link and barbed-wire gate. At Marprelate's whistle, men dragged the gate aside.

Daybreakers rushed the emerging gap; the iron pipes erupted in a point-blank volley of "Edison shot"—electrical parts from hardware store bins, crushed into juice cans with a perchlorate mix, so that the rotted plastic exploded and burned and the copper and aluminum fragments formed shrapnel. The smoke blew off to reveal ground covered with blood and shattered bodies, almost a third of the way to the downed plane.

Marprelate's scant platoon of volunteers jogged forward, slipping on patches of blood. A few downed Daybreakers were still reaching upward with knives and hatchets; the soldiers clubbed them with rifle butts.

As they reached the tip of that little peninsula of murder sticking into the tribal sea, Marprelate barked orders. Because the volunteers were drawn from a dozen different units and had never worked together, their execution of Street Firing was ragged and slow, but they did put out three volleys, pushing the enemy farther back.

"Reload." Sergeant Patel, on Jenny's other side, spoke it like a prayer. Chris and Jenny turned.

"Marprelate sent me here to guard you because I tried to talk him out of it too." His gaze remained on Marprelate's men, who had drawn hatchets and were charging into the panicked tribals in front of them. "I wish they had reloaded. The enemy was hesitating. Newberrys load quick, wouldn't've taken more than a couple seconds and they might not get—aw, shit."

Tribals were pouring into the space behind Marprelate's party. Patel shook his head. "It's gonna be all hatchets and bayonets from now on. And everybody along the line back here's gonna have to shoot too low to do any good, for fear of hitting them."

All around the little surrounded party, Daybreaker spirit sticks rose high, rattles and whistles sounded, and the crowd pulsed like an amoeba engulfing food. Army snipers from building roofs and windows brought down spirit-stick bearers and silenced booming war-drums, but there were more every second.

Then dozens of spirit sticks rose all at once, drums pounded to a crescendo, and the knot of tribals yanked closed around the surrounded soldiers.

Their first volley was a single disciplined roar, and the attackers staggered back. But instead of trying to break through back to the gate, Marprelate's men surged a couple of yards closer to the burning plane.

Again the sticks rose, the drums thundered, and the tribals leapt in. This time the answering volley was feeble and scattered, and did not even slow the tribals closing around them under the big puffs of blue-black smoke. A few more shots cracked like the last popcorn in a kettle. Hatchets, pikes, and poleaxes rose above the crowd and plunged into the center, too fast to follow.

The tribals ululated exultantly, then fled back toward the still-blazing plane. On the suddenly bare, crumbling pavement, Marprelate's force was now a pile of still bodies at the center of a ring of tribal dead and wounded. A lone young man stood holding Marprelate's severed head aloft, upside down by the beard, singing "Give Gaia Her Rights." Then he fell backwards, hit by a sniper, and Marprelate's head bounced a few feet from him on the pavement.

But it was mere revenge; as the crew slid the gate closed, the war-drums were already thundering again.

Chris turned to Jenny. "Your army now, General."

"I told you, I am not—"

Very softly, Patel said, "Don't let *them* hear you."

She turned to follow his gaze; a little knot of lieutenants and sergeants, the unit commanders she had appointed, were emerging from the opened skylight onto the roof, looking like ashamed children expecting to be spanked. Shoulders drooped, weapons dangled in loose grips, and sooty cheeks had been tracked by tears like snails.

Looking down, Chris murmured, "Remember, two years ago, most of these guys weren't ready to manage a shift at McDonald's. Some of them just made sergeant a month ago. Now they're commanding battalions."

She forced herself to look back at the approaching men and women with a level, expressionless gaze. *I will pretend that I am reading an order to them very clearly, an order from Jeff, the one he'd give if he could, and I see it in my mind's eye. Aaaand . . . I read it, aaaand I say . . .*

"Thank you for coming. We don't have much time. When I send you back to your units, if you're up on the line, give the bastards three good volleys if they're close, or some sustained sniping if they're farther back. We're still far ahead on firepower and both your men and the tribals need reminding.

"Then keep the enemy well back for the next hour." To her surprise, her voice stayed even and controlled. "As I said before, don't spare the shot. Keep sending runners for ammunition till you are up to full stock."

"If your unit is *not* on the line, then appoint company and platoon commanders as you need to, let them pick their XOs, and get ready to go up on the line. Clean and maintain all weapons. Distribute ammunition, food, and water. Make them eat a meal. Be ready to move up to the line and take over from a unit there within an hour and a half. Units on the line, same drill as soon as you're relieved." Jenny felt as if the person Jeff had always wanted to be had taken over her spirit.

"Now, before you go, we're going to figure out who's going where. Walk with me around the roof. This is my XO, Sergeant-now-brevet-Major Patel, and most of you know Chris, my intelligence staff. Chris, get out the notepad."

In a quick circuit of the roof, she assigned everyone to advance or retreat to straighten and contract the line, pressuring them to volunteer and to keep their mouths shut about difficulties or objections.

Back at the access ladder, Jenny halted them all with a glare. "What kind of example are you setting your men? Stand up straight, hold those weapons like they're yours, and when you give orders make them sound like orders. Dismissed!"

The men and women climbing back down through the skylight were still frightened, worried, unsure, even traumatized, but they moved like people who intended to do their duty.

"You were saying, General?" Chris said, smiling slightly.

"You know, right now they'd hang any man I told them to. What if I turned out not to have a sense of humor?" She saw the speculation in his eyes that she might mean it, and scolded herself for enjoying it.

9 HOURS LATER. RUINS OF LAFAYETTE. 10 PM EASTERN TIME. TUESDAY, MAY 5, 2026.

"We're six hours into blackout, ma'am." Adele was a heavyset young woman who had probably been ignored by everyone back before because she was quiet, but there was no problem with her assertiveness now. "If I set up a radio we're risking destroying irreplaceable parts at best, and a fire or an explosion at worst, and anyway chances are no one is on the air to hear us right now. Plus all the parts will have been out of sealed containers and the nanospawn'll start up on them. I'll do it if you order me but you're going to have to order me."

Jenny nodded. "Then I'm ordering it. We'll get you a couple more oil lamps so you have light to work by."

"Don't need the lamps. They'd just be one more thing to burn if the radio blows up. Just give me a clear table and have someone ready to run the antenna out." Adele hoisted the metal file box onto the table and began unpacking parts. From the corner, Chris said, "I'll have the encryption all rechecked in a couple more minutes."

Jenny nodded. "Great, and thanks, both of you. And remember, some folks on the west and south sides of the line did think there was a flash in the sky late this afternoon. Good chance the moon bomb already went off, probably over Pueblo. We weren't monitoring for an all clear at the time."

"We *were* a little busy," Chris muttered. The tribals, having exhausted the possibilities of their crude firearms once the army had re-discovered taking cover, had fallen back on massed charges. It was no more effective than it had been before, but it still had to be coped with and it was still nerve-wracking. For the last hour things had been quiet, and after a quick meeting to assign responsibilities for the night, they were catching up on everything that went into running an army under siege, and preparing a breakout for the next day.

Chris reminded himself that he was alive, behind the lines, and might even get some food and sleep soon. *And thank god or some such person, Jenny banished Reverend Daddy to the supply office, where he's useful, which means I didn't have to add murder of clergy to my sins. I don't think he has any idea how much she's not his little girl anymore. That's going to be—*

"Hey, can I get a message to Heather O'Grainne into that queue?" Larry Mensche said from the door. "I want to tell her I quit."

Chris looked up in shock. "You're alive."

A minute later the two old friends were bear-hugging, pounding each other's backs, and Jenny was explaining to Adele, "It's a beefy old guy thing, I think." Behind Larry's back, Chris shot her the finger.

Larry asked, "Has it been bad in here?"

Chris nodded. "Yeah. Out there?"

"Bad too. Really it's a good thing I *can't* just teleport to Pueblo and collect a pension because I'd do it in a heartbeat, or worse yet I'd think about it, not do it, and curse myself for being an idiot. Anyway, I'm here. Have any other scouts made it in?"

"They have now," Freddie Pranger said. He appeared to be unhurt but looked exhausted; the two young men following him were Roger Jackson, who was hobbling on crutches with a splinted leg, and a man with strange facial tattoos and a bandage wrapped around his head, wearing the grimy and bloody remains of a TexIC uniform, who introduced himself as Dave McWaine. "Got two that should see a doctor soon, and with stories to tell, so if it's okay, Larry, I'd like these guys to report first."

Patel leaned in through the door. "Ma'am, I've got medics for these men and food for everyone on the way; I'm having the cooks make up some of the emergency coffee because I think you'll be up for the night."

Adele looked up from the radio setup and said, "Ma'am, there *was* an EMP strike over Pueblo this afternoon, so they're broadcasting an all clear. We can send out reports as you like, at least till the nanos eat the radio."

Jenny looked around the room, stretched, and yawned. "Gawww," she groaned. "All right, thank you, Major Patel, perfect on everything. Make sure there's a cup for the radio operator." She turned back to the scouts. "You've all heard that General Grayson and the senior leadership were assassinated, and I'm commanding because I'm the one who will?"

They nodded.

"All right. Chris, that message did include a request for a real general and some actual officers ASAP, right?"

"Oh yeah."

"All right, then." She shook her head and rolled her neck; her hair had long since escaped from its ties. Chris couldn't help noticing, in the yellow flicker of the oil lamps, that she was still strikingly beautiful despite her evident exhaustion, and a glance around the room showed that even Roger, broken leg and all, seemed to take an interest. *God, if I get the chance to write that next book, it'll make a great scene but no one will believe it; some future historian will say that men could not notice a thing like that at a time like this. Some future historian who has never seen Jenny or is not a straight man, anyway.*

Jenny seemed to summon full alertness by an act of will and said, "Let's hear everyone's reports, starting with—Roger, correct?—since I want him to get to the medics quick. I'm just glad to see we have some scouts left. What did you see and what's out there?"

Taking turns, the four scouts told a quick, brutal version of the last stands of the TexICs and the President's Own Rangers. Larry Mensche confirmed that it had been he who had fired the shots that alerted the camp; while over on the western bank he had seen most of the gigantic tribal horde pass down the Wabash in rafts and canoes, or moving at a quick march along the river road. The tribal force had escaped them and they had no way of catching up.

On their way in, Freddie, Roger, and Dave had seen all the bridges below the narrow, old one at Prophetstown, knocked down; they had actually witnessed the tribals drag rafts loaded with fifty-five-gallon drums against the pillars of the US-231 bridge and then detonate the rafts, dumping the bridge into the river.

"So if we wanted to cross the river and catch'em, and we had the rested men to do it," Freddie said, "we'd have to go about ten miles the wrong way up to Prophetstown, go over a truss bridge there that's only two lanes, and then the way the river arcs, we'd have another twelve miles or so to get to a point opposite us here. More than a day's march just to be at a point where they've already passed. Makes me sick to think about it but there ain't a thing we can do."

Jenny sighed. "How did you get back to this bank, Larry?"

"I stole one of their canoes, and they had so much traffic on the river right then I'm not sure they even noticed. I probably just looked like another cruddy, worn-out old guy with some mission for Mother Gaia. Paddled into a corner where a lot of them were loading into canoes, said, 'Here's another one,' and took off before they looked too close; walked like I had someplace to be through their camp, yelled 'On my way!' at the edge and charged down into the brush, sneaked this way. They were pretty busy; looks like they loaded twenty-two to twenty-five thousand tribals onto rafts and canoes for the next leg down the Wabash. Closer in than I landed, they've got maybe three thousand still holding south and east of here, to keep us from pursuing them. Had to come around them, which took a while longer."

Jenny leaned across the map and said, "On those rafts and canoes, it's not likely they'll make it through a wrecked dam or bridge. So if they're going to keep wrecking bridges to keep us trapped on this side, they'll have to take their whole force under each bridge first, before they blow it. And the ones still fighting us probably aren't being expended either; Lord Robert doesn't think of all human death as progress the way mainstream Daybreak does. So there should be a bridge across the Wabash open somewhere not far downstream." She called softly, "Patel."

He came in at once, and she said, "Your opinion. Will the troops do something really hard if I ask them?"

"Depends on what you mean by *hard*, and how you ask, ma'am, I think."

"Well, here's what we need to do. We're not under siege anymore; they've lifted the forces east and north of us. I think they're trying to trick us into going twenty miles out of our way to use a bridge up that way, and make it hopeless for us to catch them. So they'll be very encouraged if their scouts see our forces moving out on the east side of camp. But what I want is the fastest-moving forces we can get to go way out around and then attack them from the south side, along the river to pin them against the main force. If our troops have the energy, we might bag that whole Daybreaker force. Then after that—"

"*After that*, ma'am? They're already exhausted."

"—after that, as I was saying, we all head downriver as fast as we can to the first open bridge, and start chasing the enemy main force. Don't tell me whether our troops will be *willing* to try—leave that up to me. Just tell me, physically, if they try, can they do it?"

"I think so, ma'am. They had more than a night's sleep yesterday. They've fought all day today but once you started the rotation they've all had some rest, most have had a hot meal. But you have no officers left to speak of, these are mostly militia or not much better, and—"

"But they *could* do it."

"They *could*."

"Get me battalion and independent company commanders in here, and anyone we have left at regimental level. Half an hour. And kick a medic for me and make sure someone puts Roger into a bed and takes a look at his leg."

"Right away." Patel vanished through the door again.

"All right. Freddie, Larry, Dave, find somewhere to finish your meals, and sack out someplace Patel can find you. You're all the functioning scouts I have left and there's going to be work soon. Adele, any word back from the transmissions?"

"Just a QSL from Pueblo and one from Pale Bluff. So they know what you told them."

"Well, then you might as well take down the station and wipe it and box it for the night, and after that you're dismissed but make sure the messenger pool knows where to find you. Thanks for your help. Chris, I need you to stick around and let's—finally."

Two men carrying a stretcher had arrived, and Roger fell asleep literally as they picked him up; the other three scouts followed along to the infirmary, leaving Jenny and Chris alone.

She turned to him and visibly forced a smile. "Well, chief of intel and staff, what do you think?" Her face hung limp and enervated; she must have seen his worry because there was a brief flicker of her beauty-pageant dazzle when she added, "Don't worry, I'll be all sparkly and vivacious for the captains in a few minutes, but right now, with you, I figure I can rest my face a little."

"You're pretty amazing," he said. "All right, my take on things, bwana-boss-milady, is that you did it. The only reason the tribals left a bridge standing, just barely in reach, was to sucker us into losing more time by going around the back way. They're moving as fast as they can, and the target has to be Pale Bluff."

"Checking our thinking, why Pale Bluff? Why not go all the way down the Wabash, land on the south bank of the Ohio someplace, and put themselves totally out of reach?"

"Because Lord Robert is smart but he's not cold-blooded. He hates Pale Bluff as a symbol; it's the closest town that's still really part of the old order. And if he can shut down the airfield there, and the railroad close to it, that breaks the quickest, easiest links between Tempers and Provis, his two biggest enemies.

"But what worries me more is that now that he's gotten past the army with a horde that size, I doubt anything can stop them before Pueblo. They're going to burn out a big part of the functioning middle of the country and I don't see what we can do about it. Do you see any way we can catch them now?"

She shook her head. "Not really. But I think we have to try, at least till we're sure we can't. Lord Robert and his mob are only mortal, too, and they could run into so many kinds of trouble with what they're trying to pull off. So in case they do, I want to be right there on their back to pull them down right away. So I want to keep up the pursuit, and preserve the possibility of our having some dumb luck." She shook her head and clicked her tongue.

"What?" Chris asked. "You just had a thought."

"I sure did. I just thought *can my army do this?* I hate how much I'm getting to understand poor old Jeff."

Chris Manckiewicz had spent a lifetime doing interviews, and he'd mastered the art of the quizzical look that calls forth more words long ago. Feeling like a little bit of a shit for taking advantage of her vulnerability—she looked so tired—he gave her the quizzical look, and waited.

After a moment she looked away, and stammered, "We quarreled very badly just before he was assassinated, and somehow I keep remembering I'm angry and forgetting he's dead. Uh, I hope that's off the record."

"You know as well as I do—you're one of my best writers, whenever you have time for it—that the *Pueblo Post-Times* is dedicated to printing the legend always, and the truth when it's convenient."

"You're a cynical guy, Mister Manckiewicz. I take it that means that my marital problems—"

"Are your own business. As for General Grayson, *de mortuis nil nisi bonum.* If you haven't figured it out yet, he may have been a hard guy to get along with, and we'll miss some of his talents, but he might be even better as a legend."

"He was still my husband."

"I'm sorry, it's much too soon. I spoke thoughtlessly."

"Don't beat yourself up. You're right, he wasn't an easy man to like, not even—well, especially not—as his wife. It's just, right now when I'm scared stiff, I can't help missing him; he was the only person in the world, including me, ever to have complete confidence in me."

"There's at least one more now, because I do. And when I write it up the way I intend to, the rest of the country will too. By the time it's officially history, everyone will understand that General Grayson was the brightest hope we had, but because his warrior widow rose to the occasion and played the part of the American Joan of Arc—"

"Oh, geahhh, yuck."

"By the time history is written, I hope none of us will recognize ourselves."

THE NEXT DAY. WHITEFISH, MONTANA. 2:00 PM
MOUNTAIN TIME. WEDNESDAY, MAY 6, 2026.

The town square of Whitefish hadn't changed much for almost a hundred years, back before. Two buildings on its perimeter had burned in the last year, victims of the difficulty of fighting fires by nineteenth-century methods; because knocking their charred remains down was not a priority, the blackened timbers still framed the holes in the facade of the town. For similar reasons, the surrounding streets were still lined with abandoned, decaying cars, slowly being picked apart for salvage. But most of the chimneys in town sputtered little gasps of smoke into the brisk spring breeze, staining the bright blue sky, and the snow still clinging in the shadows was trampled and dirty from human traffic. The little town smelled of cold damp, woodsmoke, and outhouses, but it was still recognizably civilized.

Looking at it from the President's Residence car of "Amtrak One," Allie said, "Such a pretty little town. I don't know if I'm more relieved that it's in such good shape, or more heartbroken that it's in such bad shape."

"Eventually we'll put it back into good shape, and you'll just be saying, 'What a pretty little town,' like people did back before," Graham said. "For right now, though, it's not what it looks like, it's what it is. An intact town that's winnable in the fall election, but not in the bag. And they have a newspaper, and regular radio contact with the outside world."

"I still . . . well, I guess it goes back to your grad seminar, doesn't it? I'll never understand why we don't just have the smart people figure out the right answer, and give it to everyone else, and they just do it."

"The technical term is 'democracy,' Allie."

"Yeah, I know." She turned to rest a shoulder on his, and run a hand down his arm. "I've enjoyed this express train ride so much. Just you and me in the car for a whole day, nothing to do but rest and eat and talk. And the ride from Olympia to here . . . well, it's still a beautiful country, isn't it? Mountains and rivers and canyons, and pretty little towns like this—behind fortified walls, and with tribals dangling from gallows by the gates . . ."

"You have a knack for the unpleasant," he said, stroking her hair.

"Yeah. Maybe losing my whole family, maybe having Daybreak take my mind for a while, whatever, I'm not the sunshine girl I was before." But her mouth twitched in a little smile. "You mean you don't think the gallows, and the palisades, are part of the beauty?"

"I'm a sentimental old poop, as you never tire of reminding me, sweetheart. I remember when we Americans did our killing overseas and out of sight except for what was on screens. Anyway, here we are, and—"

A guard stuck his head in and said, "Showtime in two, Mister President."

"Thanks," Weisbrod said. "All right. Quick review. Goals here: electoral, get stories into news media about what nice reasonable answers I give to people who don't agree with me, so that we get some favorable coverage in the Temper states, but we still reassure all our Provi supporters that I haven't sold the side out. Presidential, firm up this area's commitment to staying in the state of Montana and Montana's commitment to the Union, because there's a growing independence movement and a growing federate-with-Alberta movement and we don't want either of them to grow any bigger. What am I forgetting?"

She glanced down at her pad. "National security goal. Firm up the commitment to keep them involved in suppressing the tribals. The Whitefish city government has been conducting covert talks with Daybreakers about a separate peace. There's considerable support in the town for that and local merchants are almost openly trading with tribals. You need to tell them to cut *that* crap right away, as a last warning before we send some muscle out here to *make* them cut it. You'll be doing the nice-doggie part of the program, you might say, because I don't quite have the rock picked up yet." She held her breath a moment as she squeezed his hand, afraid he'd reopen the genocide argument right now, while there wasn't time, or insist on some unacceptable condition at the last moment.

But he nodded. "Slipped my mind. Three sets of goals for 40 towns on this trip is 120 sets of goals. That's a lot for a guy to remember when he's at an age where a more common goal used to be getting through a day without losing my glasses."

Recognizing her cue, she kissed him passionately and said, "You're still in shape to seduce a former student."

"Even if it's a grad student from a quarter century—"

"Poo. The student/seducee rules it's a score and you're a stud. Now, go out there and—"

The door opened again, and Weisbrod said, "Just coming," but the guard said, "Uh, no, sir, sorry, but there's an urgent radiogram that was waiting for you here in town. The mayor's already told the crowd that you'll be delayed at least twenty minutes." He held out three sheets of paper. "You'd better read this right away."

Graham Weisbrod stood up like a much younger man and took the pages. The guard ducked back through the door as if he had seen a bomb with the fuse burning down. Weisbrod glanced at the triple line of decoded message; his eyes widened and the paper crumpled and bent as his grip tightened. Allie rose to stand beside him, reading over his shoulder.

Army beaten at Tippecanoe.

Survivors under command of Jenny Whilmire Grayson & Chris Manckiewicz NOT TYPO under siege.

All senior officers incl. Jeffrey Grayson dead.

TexICs, Presidents Own Rangers, other units wiped out.

Scout plane destroyed. Pilot killed.

Tribal horde of at least 20k under Lord Robert believed headed for Pale Bluff.

Grayson/Manckiewicz attempting breakout today but probably unable to overtake horde before Pale Bluff.

No way to stop them.

"Well," Weisbrod said, "shit."
"Yeah. Are we going—"
He grabbed up a pencil stub, turned the radiogram over, and scrawled a few words.
"What are you doing?" she asked.

"Getting ready to break the news to them."

"You're supposed to just give a quick speech, do a q&a, and get on down the line, Graham, chances are no one will have heard before you're done and out of town, and we'll have a lot more time to think—"

"So, what's to think about? There is terrible news. As a nation we have to face up to it and deal with the consequences. We don't know much yet so we can't say exactly what we're going to do. We'll come through this and we're strong and brave and smart enough to handle it. That's all there is to say, Allie, so I'm trying to find a dignified, respectful way to say it."

"But if we can work on it on the train on the way down to Bigfork—"

"It'll be the same simple problem, and we'll just over-think it. Is there anything to add? As far as you can tell, did I just leave anything out of the analysis?"

Reluctantly she shook her head; he bent to his work with the pencil, muttering as he scrawled, beating cadences with his free hand, satisfied in a few minutes. "Make sure you get this paper back from me. We want to give the local paper a scoop, and breaking the exact text should do it. All right, let's go."

It was clear that the crowd around the platform had not heard the bad news, because they were bouncing up and down, chanting and cheering, and when Weisbrod walked onto the platform there was a great thunder of applause. He waved; Allie remembered that big, infectious Graham-grin, profiled against the distant forested and snowy peaks, for the rest of her life.

Clearly some of the officials had heard the news, because they tried to huddle around Weisbrod as if to shield him, and buzzed with obvious advice delivered fast and low. Weisbrod shrugged them off like an ugly sweater, and said, "I've worked out what I'll say already." He walked to the edge of the platform.

Allie recognized the format of Graham's speech from her PR classes, ages ago. First he asked the crowd for silence because he had bad news, and waited for a wave of shushing and silencing to run through them. Then, simply, in the plainest of plain sentences, he told them as much as he knew. As they collapsed into themselves, absorbing the blow, he said, "This is a terrible blow to all of us, to the Provisional Constitutional Government, to the United States and the people of Earth and to generations not yet born. And we have not seen the last of it, much as I wish I could say we had. The enemy have the advantage, and they are going to press it just as hard as they can, and so we can expect more terrible blows will fall before we are able to recover.

"Nonetheless, the United States and civilization will survive. Nonetheless, ultimately this war will be won. Even if we are not the ones to win it, nonetheless our children or our grandchildren will live in a world that has returned to the upward path, and their children will walk and advance along it, not only all the way back to the level where we stood so recently, but far beyond where anyone has ever been. We begin their long march back to civilization as we knew it, and beyond to something better, at this moment—nonetheless.

"I'm not much of a praying man; as most of you know, I'm a non-observant Jew, which means I only talk to God maybe three times an hour, at most, but I'd like us all to take a moment to pray together, silently, for our country, and our people, for all of our leaders, and for our planet and all its people."

When he had allowed less than a minute to pass, he said, "All right, I was planning to speak briefly and then you would ask me questions. I've already spoken briefly. Please pardon that I probably don't know any more than you do about what's going to be foremost in all our minds. But if you still have questions about anything else, let's go to those."

Hands near the platform waved, and Graham chose one.

The man was small and very thin, with whiskers most of the way down his chest, and he said, "I just wanted to point out that sad as all this is for Grayson and all his men, the truth is, we were invading their territory. In fact for three months the so-called civilized people have been invading tribal lands and slaughtering as many as we can, every chance we get. What's wrong with living in peace? It's a new world now, maybe not a shiny one, but new. Why not just make peace?"

Graham Weisbrod couldn't get an answer out because of all the shouting. People were grabbing the man as he shouted, "It's a question, it's just a question, I only want to know—"

Allie felt more than saw something move in the front row, and then a man in a long dark coat leapt between two of the guards, onto the platform. She had an instant to realize she recognized the face, another to know it was Darcage, but no time at all to scream or raise a hand before Darcage lunged between the mayor and a councilman, shoving them against the guards on either side, and threw his arms around Graham.

She saw her husband jerk back, but his face was away from her. Darcage's gaze seemed to pass through her and go a million miles farther into space; there was no sign of recognition. His hands clenched together around Graham's middle, tightening and pulling the two men close together.

She felt her feet try to fling her forward, when—

A terrible roar.

On her back on gravel. Everything hurt. People all around her. Shouting. Someone wanted a doctor. Someone wanted troops.

Someone always wanted something.

Her mouth wouldn't work well enough to ask what had happened to Graham.

Dark and quiet. It felt like sinking into freezing cold ink. She could not swim back upward. She felt herself trying to come back, over and over, like sparks struck off flint in a cave, until there were no more sparks, just the attempt, and then not even the attempt.

3 HOURS LATER. PUEBLO. 6:30 PM MOUNTAIN TIME. WEDNESDAY, MAY 6, 2026.

"Today's situation report is . . . well, honestly," James Hendrix said, "my main purpose today is to make sure you don't all decide to just give up. We are in a very bad spot, but we may yet reach January 20 with the United States back in place and some hopes for another 250 years. The country has suffered terrible losses, and our side is in more danger than I could have imagined even three months ago, but we're only beaten if we decide to be. So, per Heather's request, I'm going to wade into the bad stuff right away, and then talk about what we've still got going and what our options are."

They were in a conference room that had once been judge's chambers in the Old Pueblo County courthouse. The late afternoon sun provided enough light through the north-facing windows so that the kerosene lanterns on the sideboards were unnecessary. James stood at the end of the long table; behind him there were two easels, one with maps and one with a newsprint pad, and a kerosene lamp on a stand for lighting, since they expected the meeting to run late.

To James's right, Heather sat quietly, her attention seemingly on smoothing the covers around the sleeping Leo. James had asked her to be present for this meeting, but she had said it would be difficult enough even to be there. Graham Weisbrod had been her teacher, friend, and mentor for twenty-five years; the initial radiogram had included the detail that the explosion had cut him in half. Allie Sok Banh had been her rival and her dependable ally, her most-trusted buddy and her debating foil, for nearly as long; the radiogram had said that though she was alive, she had lost her left eye and hand for sure, with cracked ribs and broken pelvis, and a probable severe concussion with high risk of brain damage, adding that they urgently needed tetracycline from the new facility in Pueblo.

Graham was really as much family as Heather ever had, James thought, looking at her, and hated that he had even had to ask her to be present.

Lyndon Phat sat at the opposite end of the table, fingers resting and tented as if he couldn't quite decide whether he was praying. He was gazing out the window right now; James wondered if he was thinking about the strange, sometimes horrible story of Jeffrey Grayson, wondering if he might have done any better or any worse, perhaps wondering if the deep cracks he had perceived in Grayson's character had helped cause the debacle, or if Grayson had gone to his abrupt death without the fatal break. *In any case, now no one will ever know.*

Beside Phat, on the corner of the table, Quattro and Bambi leaned on each other, looking down at the notes Bambi was preparing to take. *Bambi always takes so many notes, and more when she's nervous. She says she needs something to do with her hands, and it's a good habit anyway for someone who ever only really wanted to be a cop.* Her free hand clenched on one of Quattro's; he had both hands pulled against his chest as if cradling a kitten. *Lot of pain there too.*

All the aviators are such a close-knit community, James thought. *And Nancy Teirson was popular, and the way she died is all of their nightmare.*

About halfway along the table, her long, rawboned frame in the careless sprawl of a lifelong athlete, Leslie Antonowicz was the only person that James was sure was really listening. *And not as a favor to me, either,* he thought. As if she'd heard him, she smiled for an instant, just with her mouth. He hoped she was signaling *Go on, we'll get this, James, we'll make it work.*

Having finished his *I am serious* scan of the room with only that encouragement, he suppressed a sigh and launched into details. "Grayson had to strip out every still-functioning unit he could from the Temper states to mount his expedition. That's not blame; he had to bet the works to win, but unfortunately, he didn't win, so we lost most of the works.

"When I say 'most of,' that doesn't mean we have nothing left or can't recover. Red Dog's really wired into the Army at Athens, and that picture is very reliable, even if it's discouraging. What's left down in the Temper corner of the country is mostly jumped-up militia trying to find their way, and some old and disabled officers and sergeants who are trying to turn it into an army. They'll get there but not till late summer.

"It's a little worse in the Northwest, to judge by Blue Heeler's reports. The Provis didn't start with much of an army, just the Rangers and a scattering of cadre and a half-dozen decent National Guard units. Most of those are smashed or stuck in that useless pocket on the Wabash, and the Rangers are gone. The Provis will take even longer to have any really professional, functional units available. The best news might be that our analytics team says there's no risk of a Second Civil War in the next year."

Leslie added, "I *am* that analytics team. Temper and Provi states don't even touch each other at any point anymore, now that the New State of Wabash is lost. Neither of them has an army that will be ready to go on the road for at least a year, so even if we can't bring them together, they can't push themselves farther apart."

Phat cleared his throat. "You're overestimating the time to get both Temper and the Provi forces back on line. They won't be as good as what we've lost but we'll have a functioning army—well, two functioning armies—well before the end of the summer. First of all, a black-powder foot army just doesn't take as long to train, and besides, as soon as we can get the Army of the Wabash onto trains and shipped back to their home territories, that's a lot of men who have lived through combat. Give them a chance to win, and some time to train more militia from back home, and they'll be there for you. Don't sell those old sergeants in Temper territory short; there's a reason why they used to say a good sergeant had to be trilingual, English, Spanish, and Alabaman.

"As for the Provi area, Norm McIntyre was a pencil pusher and a garrison commander all his life, and I wouldn't want him running a war, but he had a knack for training and readiness, and especially without Allie Sok Banh and the Provi Congress riding him to do social work and provide special cushy slots for their relatives, and with a bunch of experienced troops to mix in, he'll turn the new recruits into an army faster than anyone else could. In another hundred days, tops, maybe much sooner, we'll have road-ready armies again. I'm more worried about Manbrookstat and Texas. Can we skip to that part of the report?"

That's good. At least Phat's attention is here in the room, James thought. "Governor Faaj stuck his neck out politically and twisted a lot of arms to loan us the TexICs, which the State of Texas was pretty proud of, and there's *one* survivor. The name of the United States is below mud, and well down into shit, in Austin. The unofficial word from Governor Faaj is that he couldn't hold the legislature back from declaring independence for more than about a week, and anyway . . . he doesn't want to." It made James sick to see the old general look so sad, but some perverse desire to share the full misery made him add, "He told me that Texas has had a good time in the USA, but Texas is Texas first, and the United States has nothing much to offer anymore."

Phat nodded. "And Manbrookstat?"

"White Fang, our main agent there, has asked us to consider active measures."

James saw Leslie tense, though she had known it was coming. Heather glanced up for a moment at him, a bland little smile that reminded him that he was the one who had insisted on bringing this up now. Quattro and Bambi sat back in their chairs. *They're trying to make themselves listen in a fair-minded way. But they also know that what we do to the Comman-*

*dant of Manbrookstat today for good reason, can be done to the Duke and
Duchess of California tomorrow for any old reason. That means it's down to
Phat—*

"'Active measures' means what?" he asked. "I know we can't just
invade, we just finished working that out. So we're talking coup? Revolution? What? And why now?"

"Coup or revolution," James said. "Most likely both together."

"And why now?"

"The Commandant has stayed very, very quiet. But White Fang is far
enough up in the inner circle to hear about most of it, and for what he calls
'personal reasons' which we think means the Commandant is hot for his
daughter, he's been taken into confidence on some of it, so the source is
about as good as you get. The Commandant is currently taking bids to sell
off the depopulated land in the Dead Belt—and not just a little, I mean
parcels as big as Maryland or New Hampshire."

"Sell them off? To whom?"

"Argentine, Irish, Icelandic, or Portuguese settlers—those are just the
ones we know have already put in bids. And that's only problem one.
Problem two, he's the main organizer behind the Atlantic League, which
would be a *sovereign* confederacy of city-states."

"Sovereign as in 'Manbrookstat becomes part of a foreign power'? No
longer even nominally part of the USA?"

"You got it. Then there's problem three. The Commandant is negotiating under the table with Lord Robert and some of the tribes to set up trading posts in the Lost Quarter."

"Trading posts? But they don't trade."

"They didn't. They also didn't use guns till recently. Remember Lord
Robert has created Daybreak 2.0, which is basically all the primitivism
and savagery but with more in it for Lord Robert, and less random agoniz-
ing death for everyone else. A week before the battle, we intercepted the
Commandant's proposal to Lord Robert: tribals will loot metal and anything else useful from the Lost Quarter, in exchange for canned food and
new clothes. How long before it'll be guns, too?"

"And you think a revolution could happen about that?"

"Well, none of that would be popular if it were known. But what's more likely to set off the revolution is that the only people who are better off because the Commandant is in power are maybe thirty families that can see a chance to be the aristocracy of a new nation, and maybe a thousand thugs and bullies lined up behind them. That's it. Everyone else is living with isolation, regulation, forced labor, and obvious favoritism and exploitation. He's pissed a lot of people off. So we topple, kidnap, or assassinate him, chase out his cohorts, and give Manbrookstat space to reorganize."

"What will they do if we do that?"

"Well, White Fang seems to think there's no way they'd elect the Commandant or any of his followers if you gave them a real choice. Maybe they'll join the Tempers as the successor to New York State, maybe apply to be a New State under the Provis, maybe do both like those counties trying to form Pelissippi are doing."

"But you're thinking the coup first, to get him out of the way, and then hoping the revolution will endorse it retroactively?"

James shrugged. "A coup against an illegal government—"

"Wasn't that what Norcross thought when he overthrew Shaunsen on a bunch of Constitutional tricks? And what Cam Nguyen-Peters thought when he locked up Weisbrod to keep him from becoming President? And what Grayson thought when he assassinated Cam? Only a little over a year ago we had four presidents in ninety days and barely averted Civil War Two. Supposedly May 1st was Open Signals Day, a new permanent national holiday to celebrate our avoiding the war, and how did we celebrate the first one? With nothing at all. Not even a proclamation from the Temper Board or the Provi President." Phat was shaking his head slowly, his mind clearly made up. "Now, look, I will acknowledge that having spent most of the last year in a prison cell because I was inconvenient for purposes of changing presidents by coups, and starting civil wars, I *am* probably too personally sensitive. But all the same, here's how I see it: an intelligence agency of extremely dubious Constitutionality, which let's face it is what the RRC is, which got the blessings of two dubious successor governments, is now proposing to overthrow another dubious successor government. That's a *lot* of dubious.

"If there was a revolution underway already in Manbrookstat, and we were just helping out, sure. Recognize the rebels as the government, send them guns, blockade any outside help the Commandant calls on. But Federal officials actually organizing a coup against a local government—no. No way. That's what we're trying to get away from, James. You can't just suspend the rules whenever you feel like it, the whole point of Constitutional government is that you play by the rules when they're inconvenient."

Leslie had been listening intently. "What the Commandant is doing is treason by the standards of Article III, Section 3. If we could arrest him it would be a short trial and a quick hanging."

"And if you could arrest him I would suggest you do it." Phat shook his head sadly. "But you can't send a force big enough to just barge in and lock them all up."

"He could be shot while resisting arrest," Heather said quietly.

Quattro stood up, his face stiff with fury. "Is that the best we can do?"

James froze, taken completely by surprise. Heather and Leslie had turned away from him to face Quattro; they sat perfectly still. Behind Quattro, Phat seemed to be looking for something to say. Bambi rose slowly, reaching tentatively around her husband to take him in her arms, but he gently pushed her away. "My god," he said. "Look what we've gotten into and what we're thinking about. I started wondering about us when we went busting into a family Christmas and murdered the dad. I flew over the camps on the Ohio where Grayson piled tribal bodies ten deep. And now . . . we've had a whole army beaten, surrounded, and saved just because Jenny Whilmire Grayson was too crazy to let them give up. And with only twenty-two airplanes on the whole continent, we let one be shot down, and the pilot—who was also one of the most expert airplane designers we have—was burned alive. And now we're sitting here saying well, we can't do anything for Pale Bluff, one of the most decent civilized places there is and one we've depended on for so many things, and we're going to just let the enemy have it, to murder and loot and burn. And so where do we put our attention? Into getting our army out of there? No. Into avenging Nancy Teirson? Not a bit. Into maybe, just maybe, at least fucking trying to save several thousand civilized people that have been a total bulwark for our side, from being burned out and butchered? Oh, no. No no no. Perish fucking forbid. We're trying to decide how to keep our consciences clear while we kill the leader of one of our few working, functioning port cities. I'm so fucking proud of you all I could just fucking piss my pants.

"So here's my little thought for you. I know I'm not an ex-general or an ex-cop or an ex-librarian or anything cool like that, I know I'm just a rich guy that happened to inherit a fortified house and it's all kind of a bunch of coincidences that a lot of people now think I'm the feudal lord of California, and shit, Heather, it was a joke when you talked me into taking the title, but you know, as a rich man and a guy who owns a lot of land and has sworn vassals that I have to think about and protect, all the way from San Diego up to Crescent City . . . I am very tempted to take my ball and go home. But I won't. What I'm going to do is win this war, the way it needs to be won. You got a message for me, radio me in Pale Bluff. Don't bother appointing me to a command or whatever you want to call it. I'll let them know I'm taking over when I get there. You coming, Duchess Babe?"

Bambi nodded, but her eyes were closed and she was breathing hard. "I'm your wife and your duchess, both. And you're not going into that much foolish danger without taking me along. Just let me talk to these guys for a second, okay? I'll catch up."

He kissed her, said, "Don't be long," and went out the door. They all looked at each other.

"I will try to help this all come out for the best," Bambi said. "If I don't see any of you again, remember me whenever you're drunk and sentimental."

TWELVE:
BODIES IN MOTION, ACTED
UPON BY A FORCE

Pale Bluff had been far too small to have an airport, back when it had first come to the attention of the wider world in December 2024. That had been a pure accident; the very first EMP attack from the moon gun—the one that had destroyed the original recovery center at Pittsburgh—had forced down the Gooney Express that had been carrying Graham Weisbrod in his escape from the TNG prison, on his way to found the PCG.

Now, as Quattro Larsen brought the Gooney back to Pale Bluff for perhaps the thirtieth time, he wished he had Bambi in the co-pilot's seat, so that he could say something like, "Remember when we made our first landing, here, babe?" but she had insisted that if the aviators of the continent were going to converge to win this war, she would want her own plane. At this moment her Stearman was off to his right and a little below him.

That first emergency landing had been on I-64, miles away. *It seemed like such a big deal at the time that Graham Weisbrod was the true President of the United States, so my plane was Air Force One.* Once they were safely on the ground, however, any pretensions Quattro might have had had deflated like the greased linen tires on the plane. Everyone, including the nominal President of the United States, had walked into Pale Bluff with Freddie Pranger, the Township Constable.

Now look at what you did, Gooney, Quattro thought affectionately at his heavily modified DC-3. In a bit over a year, Pale Bluff had grown from a tiny town sleepwalking toward ghostliness, to the important crossroads where Weisbrod had given his Pale Bluff Address, to the most important town, industrial center, and military base on the Wabash frontier.

What one opportune forced landing had wrought was visible on the ground below, now. The old orchard-market town of back before was the center spot of a bull's-eye. Surrounding the old town in a broad circle, where there had been only open fields leading out to the orchards, were newly-built wood-and-scrap metal shacks and cabins, and a profusion of temporary shelters ranging from lean-tos to tents, and every other conceivable arrangement in which people might sleep between shifts of work. Most of the refugees pouring out of the Lost Quarter after the rise of the tribes last spring had kept right on going after a brief stay in Pale Bluff, but enough had stuck to triple the town's population.

The apple orchards, now dense as the spring green darkened to summer, were the next ring, which had a prominent notch in it: an old plot of aged, underproducing trees, surrounding a stretch of serviceable county road, had been sacrificed to create an airfield within the city wall, which outlined the whole bull's-eye.

Quattro leaned back and shouted to his passengers over the thump and thunder of the biodiesel engines. "I'm going to let Bambi land first; she's got less fuel reserve and the Stearman isn't as durable as this old pile of junk." He put the Gooney into a wide circle around the airfield, and enjoyed watching the golden early morning light dance across the green orchards below. When he saw his wife's plane roll to a stop and the ground crews running out to pull her in, he swung down lower by the tower, caught the go-ahead signal from the flagman, and came around to land.

Like so many times before, Carol May Kloster was waiting for Quattro and Bambi, but this time she was joined by the town government and the local militia commander, there to meet the party of officers Quattro was delivering to them. It had been short notice; he had only radioed from Cape Girardeau, about 150 miles away, a couple of hours before, but apparently the radio operator had realized he needed to awaken Carol May, and she'd turned out the officials of the town.

Quattro removed his leather flying helmet with a sweeping bow. "Gentlemen, and lady, I come not to replace your authority but to enhance it." He tucked the helmet under his arm, where his plumed hat had been, and set the hat on his head. "I bring you two lieutenant colonels, four majors, and three captains, all experienced Army and Guard officers from Kansas, Missouri, and Kentucky, who volunteered literally overnight to come here and help you organize your defenses against the expected tribal attack." He made all the introductions, secretly pleased that he'd managed to remember everyone's name. "And aside from their sterling qualities as officers, these are also the winners of the Good Sport Award. While I was on the ground in Cape Girardeau, I got a radio relay from Bret Duquesne, whom some of you may know as the Freeholder of Castle Newberry—the place where all the nice guns come from, and currently the leading aircraft manufacturer in North America.

"Bret had received a message from me and taken it upon himself to round up a cadre of officers for the Army of the Wabash, and he'll be flying them direct to the army on the NSP-12, Newberry's first experiment with an airliner of sorts. They should be arriving within a couple of hours.

"I had been flying these officers to the Army of the Wabash, and in fact they will still be joining it, but when they heard that the Army of the Wabash was going to be all right, but Pale Bluff was still in terrible danger, they agreed to come here and give you a hand. I suppose if you don't need any more officers—"

The local militia colonel shook her head. "Don't you dare take them away. Gentlemen and ladies, you are all very welcome here. If you'd like to follow me, we can start planning our defense."

As the officers walked away, Carol May said, "And those officers were willing to get up in the middle of the night, and get on a plane, just because of your request."

"I was surprised too," Bambi said, "at first. Then I realized that the same charisma that had so gripped me completely into Quattro Larsen's thrall was affecting other people just as strongly, and like a sort of Pied Piper in a silly hat—"

"Aw, shit," Quattro said. "It's just that everybody out there wants to friggin' *do something*. Nobody wants to just hang back and wait for the blow to fall. They were all just fine and in solid with the restore-the-Constitution stuff when it looked like we would just clean up the Lost Quarter, raise the Stars and Stripes over the ruins of Castle Earthstone, go home, vote, and have our nice old familiar United States all back together again.

"Now they're being reminded of the kind of thing that made my parents into libertarians, the stuff that made my old man start building Castle Larsen back in 2013. When minutes count, the national government will need to spend weeks negotiating and deciding; and because they always see the big picture—or that's what the government types always call whatever they see—little details like a town facing a tribal horde get swept to the side as details. So even though a couple of years ago those officers couldn't have imagined being invited to get out of bed and climb into the Duke of California's airplane to go take a stand for civilization, nowadays—"

"They've already believed a hundred other things just as crazy," Bambi finished for him. "I'll admit, 'The Duke summons you to defend a friendly realm from a most desperate foe' has more of a ring to it than 'You have been assigned to maintain a full level of readiness in the Western Kansas Military District.' If any of those officers ever saw *Star Wars* or *The Three Musketeers*, I mean, how could they not be on board with all that romance?"

"Maybe so," Quattro said, "but people are starting to realize that the real world today *is* romantic, and that no matter how much they miss back before, and would like to go back to filling out forms and voting on resolutions, that's no longer their world. So a chance to get in some hard shots at Daybreak, and for it to be just plain personal instead of about all this abstract nation-and-Constitution stuff, well, that gets a lot of people pumped up."

Quattro had always enjoyed arguing with Bambi, but lately arguments were always about this subject and never seemed to go anywhere. Perhaps Carol May saw Bambi's irritation, and decided to intervene before it turned into a public quarrel. She said, "Chris Manckiewicz, and General Phat, and James Hendrix all keep talking about how we're slipping back in time, and I guess as we get more feudal, war gets more personal. I don't know if it's a good thing, or a bad thing, but it's definitely a thing."

Quattro felt vaguely reprimanded, but before he could sort out why, Carol May added, "Nobody else is going to be coming in till late today at earliest. And you've been up all night flying and need some rest. Let's go back to my place, and I'll fill you full of pancakes and dump you into my guest bed."

Quattro had always liked walking through Pale Bluff in the morning; this wasn't even the first time he'd done it while exhausted from a long flight overnight.

Pale Bluff was the most irreplaceable link in the chain of airfields linking Athens and Olympia, but the town proper was a tight little jam of nineteenth-century gingerbread frame houses, interspersed with twentieth-century ranches and brick bungalows. It looked like a set from some historical drama back before, one of those gentle stories about life in a bygone day. Kids were trudging off to school, just as always. Adults were carrying lunch buckets and toolboxes more often than briefcases, and no one had a phone at his ear or a screen in front of her face.

Rounding the corner into the main part of town, they saw a militia company march by; they weren't in uniform but their badges and insignia were all pinned in place, and "they march as if they've done it before," Quattro observed.

"Not by much," Carol May said. "We sent every soldier we could spare with Grayson, and now we have to hope they make it home in time. These aren't raw recruits, but they're not seasoned troops either. More like half-baked recruits. And if the numbers Jenny Whilmire Grayson reported are anything like right, we just don't have anything like enough. We really need the Army of the Wabash to get here before the tribals do, but since I don't see how that's going to happen, we're counting on that handful of militia to hold the tribals off till the A-o-W gets here."

Quattro looked around again, still cheered by the bustling prosperity of the town, but also letting himself realize, "It's hard to imagine we could lose all this."

"Harder to imagine when it's always been home," Carol May said. "Hope you can stand some of the usual apple butter on those pancakes."

"I relate well to apple butter," Bambi said. "Always have. Lead on."

**2 HOURS LATER. NEAR THE BRIDGE OVER WEA CREEK
ON THE FORMER INDIANA HIGHWAY 25, JUST WEST
OF THE FORMER LAFAYETTE. ABOUT 10 AM EASTERN TIME.
THURSDAY, MAY 7, 2026.**

Jenny Whilmire Grayson looked around the camp; she felt like she had utterly emptied her soul. "So it's there," she said. "We guessed right."

"*You* guessed right, *I* said it made sense, and now *Freddie's* confirmed it," Chris Manckiewicz corrected her. "Lord Robert left the bridge standing at Attica because the last horde that was supposed to push us up toward Prophetstown could walk there, crash for the night, and have an easy way to the other bank. And they didn't make any provision to blow it because they figured we would have a way to know what was happening at Prophetstown, but we probably wouldn't have a way to know about Attica. If you'd fallen for that, Mrs. Grayson, we'd be twenty miles further behind them."

Freddie Pranger nodded. "I was never so happy as I was to see that bridge standing, after the two that were blown." At dawn, the morning before, when the battered Army of the Wabash had abruptly wheeled to attack and destroy its tormenters, he had scouted for the two cavalry troops dispatched to find and secure the bridge. He had missed yesterday's battle at the "small" cost of a very long round trip, and his exhaustion showed in the gray pallor and deep lines of his face.

And the man's not thirty-five yet, Jenny thought. *The moment he finishes reporting, we're throwing him into a wagon for a long nap.* After a pause, Freddie added, "When I left the Montana cavalry, they were digging in on both ends of the bridge, and they had sharpshooters covering the river upstream and down. They will still be holding that bridge when the rest of the army gets there. So you're in business as soon as you get moving."

"I have never doubted they'll hold it as long as they have to." Jenny looked around; everywhere, men who had staggered up from their first decent sleep and meals in days were packing up camp, however stiffly and slowly. "That getting moving part might be a while, but I truly don't have the heart to push them."

Yesterday, worn-out by the desperate push to flank, surround, and subdue their besiegers, and even more by the brutal massacre afterward, they had barely marched three miles from the fairgrounds to this more-easily defended space where there was a long stretch of straight road in an open field for a plane to land, abundant water for cooking and cleaning, and plenty of decent grass for the horses to graze.

But though they had staggered into this camp, they had staggered in victorious, with enough spirit to make a proper camp for the night. Most of the soldiers had filled their bellies and had their first real rest in a long time. Today would be a long march—seven hours on the road, they estimated—but at the end of it, they would cross the Wabash at Attica, and be able to make a beeline drive for Pale Bluff.

That'll be about a 170-mile beeline, Jenny thought. *There will be a lot of tired bees at the end of* that. *It's flat ground, mostly along the old interstates, but it's still going to take ten days at the most optimistic. Lord Robert and his horde will be going the long way round because they have to stick close by the river for 210 miles, then drop most of their supplies and march about 40 overland. They have almost two days head start, and we don't really know how fast they move along the river or overland . . . too many unknowns for anyone to come up with a number, as Chris keeps telling me. We don't even know if it's a close race, or we've already lost, or already won.*

A distant droning rumble alerted her, and then it was drowned out in cheers from the camp. What was approaching from the south looked to Jenny something like an Art Deco railroad diner car sandwiched between sections of a circus tent, one low and one high, joined by wooden trusses. Five propellers, one at each wingtip, one close to the body, and one on the nose, were pulling it through the air. Twin pipes stuck up from the middle of her fuselage, looking like—

"Well, shit," Chris said beside her, sounding somewhere between amused and amazed. "Those are the old raised exhaust pipes from some semi rig, but they look a lot like smokestacks. You almost expect it to have paddle wheels."

The ground crew were waiting and flagged the NSP-12 down. As it passed overhead, Jenny's party could see that it had about half again the wingspan of the Gooney Express, "but since that's doubled, on a biplane, figure maybe three times the wing area? Lots of lift but it probably needs all those props to fight drag," Chris said. "I can't wait to hear what Quattro thinks of it."

"Boys and airplanes," Jenny said, "I'm just glad it got here. I'm guessing if we start walking now he'll have finished his taxi and be climbing out by the time we get there."

Bret Duquesne was a handsome young man. When he stepped down from NSP-12 and shoved his flying helmet back off his head, letting his straw-blond forelock flop down between his deep blue eyes, Jenny thought, *Definitely, back before, he could've done underwear ads.*

Introductions were quick; the NeoGoliath, as Bret had dubbed it, had flown here direct from Fort Benning and could loop back to Campbell before needing to refuel. This was "logistically marvelous, but since the design team didn't think to provide the NeoGoliath with a restroom, urologically disastrous," Bret said, returning from claiming a pilot's privilege of being first at the latrine.

"Where did they come up with the design?"

"One of our machinists at Castle Newberry used to build R/C model planes. He had lived a few miles out of Newberry, back before, and it occurred to Dad to send a wagon and some guards to recover his whole model collection, as research material for later. Well, one of his proudest productions was a big honking model of the Farman Goliath, the first real airliner. Not the most aerodynamic or esthetic thing you've ever seen, but at least we knew that airframe would work if we built it out of canvas, wood, and wire. And we'd been working toward a high-powered pure diesel engine, something that wouldn't attract nanospawn or have to be rebuilt after an EMP. The power part was fine, plenty of horsepower, but making that work took such a big engine block that we only wanted one per plane, and that was where someone thought, you know, quite a few early planes had chain-driven props. So the NeoGoliath has four chain-driven and one shaft-driven, and that big diesel can chug away, nice and slow, the way it wants to, without having to spin a high-speed shaft, and still give it plenty of thrust."

Jenny raised an eyebrow toward Chris to remind him of her earlier comment about boys and airplanes, but he appeared to be rapt with Bret's explanation. *Well, I guess that proves my point. Wish I had Bambi here for sympathy.* To break up the conversation, she asked, "So you said this thing is EMP and nanospawn immune?"

"Because it's pure diesel," Bret said. "No spark plugs or alternator, no electricity at all. You just have to preheat the glow plugs, but you can do that in a campfire if you have to. In fact, you probably haven't heard but we've been warned there's a blackout in three days—mid-day till midnight on the tenth—and it'll be our first chance to see how the NeoGoliath does. We expect it'll be fine even if it's right under the EMP bomb, ready to go without any repairs. Even the structural metal, like wires and struts, has been set up not to let big charges or currents form. Then if it rides out an EMP on the ground, we'll actually try flying during one. So they haven't got us grounded forever.

"But I've got some news that's a lot more urgent than the aircraft tech news—and not nearly as fun. We purposely flew along the Wabash as reconnaissance, and Lord Robert's forces are already in Terre Haute."

The punch-in-the-gut feeling must have shown on Jenny's face, because she could see how Bret Duquesne was reacting to it; that was annoying, as if he was regretting have stressed out the little lady, so she snapped at him. "And you couldn't tell us that right away?"

He winced. "I already admitted that I should have."

Chris Manckiewicz broke the awkwardness. "Look, it took us five days to walk here from Terre Haute, and that was with cavalry and air scouting, and a baggage train with wheels and horses and mules. How did a bunch of unorganized hippies on foot and rafts manage to do the same distance in three days?"

"Probably less than two," Bret said. "Major Southern here did a lot of coursework at Fort Lee, back before. Even while we were circling, and trying to figure out what had happened, he started scribbling and arguing things out, and then we did some more reconnaissance by tracking a couple of the rafts against the street grid along the bank. Southern's answer is, we've all been working with the number 0.6 mph, which is about how fast the Wabash flows in normal times. But these aren't normal times; thanks to all the fires and soot in the air and all the rest of it, we've had way over average snow and rainfall, and way more than usual erosion too. All the rivers on the continent are flooding or close to it."

"We should have realized that," Jenny said. "The river was so high that on the way in we never even thought of fording it or stopping to build a temporary bridge. No shallow spots left, and it's way up on its banks."

"Exactly," Duquesne said. "We were surprised too, but in present conditions, the Wabash flows at between three and four miles an hour, five to seven times as fast as normal. And although it's full of trash, it has a deep center channel, and if they stay on that, they're mostly okay. So they just floated all the heavy stuff on rafts, letting the guarding force run along the bank carrying nothing but a little food and water, and switching off between floating and running so they could literally sleep on the march. The force you left behind at Terre Haute probably didn't have any idea what was coming till Lord Robert and his Daybreakers were right on top of them.

"So when we flew over Terre Haute, whatever hadn't been burned before was burning now, and there was a huge encampment of tribals along the river, swarming with boats and rafts. We think he's regrouping, but at this current speed, he's only a day or so by river from St. Francisville, which is the closest landing to Pale Bluff."

"Well, that answers the question," Chris said softly. "We've lost the race before we start. We're ten days from Pale Bluff, minimum; they're only about three or four."

"Ma'am," Patel said, "the new officers are all comfortable, and they're ready for their briefing in the pavilion tent."

"Let's get it done," she said.

Duquesne said, "I've got nothing more to report than what I've already told you, and Major Southern can give better details and a clearer idea about things. If you don't mind, I'd like to look up your dad and maybe talk some things over with him."

"Sure. He's that way, at the Quartermaster's tent; he's been doing a lot of our logistic and organizational work."

"Thanks!" Duquesne almost sprinted away.

"Why is he so eager to see your father?" Chris asked.

"Well, purely personally, that beats me too, but it's probably that he's quite religious, and a lot of people who are like to pray or get a blessing from a particular person they think is wise or holy. Bret Duquesne kind of looks the handsome-playboy type but he's what Daddy calls 'solid Bible all the way down.' When his father was killed in that accident, all of a sudden Castle Newberry went from being a bulwark of the secular types to square in the church's corner. So, I'm guessing, Daddy's been away for a long time, and the Earl of the Broad River, or the Satrap of Carolina, or whatever he's calling himself probably feels a need to get caught up on the spiritual guidance."

"I'm not going to quote any of this till I do a book, years from now," Chris Manckiewicz said, "but you don't sound quite like you used to."

She sighed. "The last few weeks have been an eye-opener. I had no idea how many things were wrong with Jeff Grayson; I think if I'd married him but Daybreak had never happened, I'd never have had anything worse than a creepy feeling about him, which I'd probably have shrugged off as 'Mama told me men were like that.' And I might've just thought my father was a crusty old poop, but very sincere and after all we're both Christians and he just wants what's best for his daughter and . . . well. I found out so much was bullshit that I'm still sorting out what parts aren't. It might take me a while, and I might be a little sarcastic about people who really just believe the same things I did a month ago. Especially Bret, because he's so schizo about it all; he'll be joking and laughing and kind of a dashing young heroic type, reminds me a lot of Quattro Larsen, and then somebody makes a slightly off-color joke or says 'God' or 'Jesus' as an oath, and he'll lose it and go crazy rigid puritan, worse than Daddy. A couple months ago I'd've attributed it to his spiritual struggles but nowadays I just think he's an unpredictable part-time dick."

"Language like that will humanize you in the history, you know."

"Like anyone wants to be human, or has the time." She grinned at him. "Sometimes you just need to call a thing by its right name. Well, let's get the handover to the officers done. After that I'll figure out the rest of my life, or take a nap, or something."

ABOUT THE SAME TIME. MANBROOKSTAT. ABOUT 11 AM EASTERN TIME. THURSDAY, MAY 7, 2026.

Jamayu Rollings had worked hard and consistently to thoroughly establish that he did not permit anyone to interrupt him, ever, during his just-before-lunch daily meeting with his daughter Deanna. Anyone with a really thorough inside knowledge of Ferengi Enterprises might have wondered why an hour-long meeting was needed every day for a company that consisted of a couple of warehouses of high-value salvage cataloged on index cards, an office with four clerks, and a largish yacht that needed a crew of three. But Rollings kept so much of his operations quiet and out of view that no one really knew how little administration Ferengi Enterprises needed or how simple things really were.

The real purpose was not to secure the non-existent meeting, but to make sure that no one who wasn't family would ever walk in while they had the clandestine radio and the one-time pads out in view. The transmission from Pueblo to White Fang was exactly 500 words long, as always, so that if anyone was listening, a change in the length of the message would not provide any hints to the codebreakers.

Private radios were not exactly illegal in Manbrookstat. They were on the list of "Discouraged Activities," and "participation in a discouraged activity" could result in being assigned to a labor gang or preventive detention, and every now and then a preventively detained person simply vanished, leaving behind only a name on the list of subjects about which unnecessary conversation should be avoided. But they were not officially illegal.

Usually the message from the RRC in Pueblo was merely that their report had been received, with perhaps a question or two that James or Heather had about it. But today it concluded with an answer to an earlier question:

RRC Board has overruled us on request for active measures.
No support unless&until events make clear revolt underway,
resistance widespread, coup already planned, or other evidence.

WF, HoG here: basically first steps all you. Board only willing to come in to back success, not initiate, fund, or plan. J/L/me badly outvoted. Sorry, please forgive.

JH append1p3: Situation here could change drastically if situation there did.

There was another brief, appended note:

No transmissions from noon till 11 pm Eastern on 10 May. Moon gun shot detected.

"So we're screwed," Deanna said.

"Sort of. Basically it means we have to stick our neck out, maybe take the chop, but if we start to win, then they'll come in."

"So do we do it, Pops?"

Rollings sat back. "Well, not this afternoon. I've got no connections I trust in the Special Assistants or the militia, so a coup is out. The Special Assistants know they're dead if the regime comes down, so if anyone openly killed the Commandant, the SAs would butcher that person on the scene, at best, and maybe drag them straight to torture."

"So . . ." Deanna leaned back and looked toward the ceiling. Rollings had always liked the way his eldest daughter "thought with her whole face," as his wife described it. After a moment she shook her head. "Unless there's something you haven't told me about, we got no connections, zip, for a more covert kind of assassination. I don't want to try to build a bomb that works right the first time, or cook up a poison, and I'm no sniper and no ninja, and I don't think you or anyone else in the family is."

Rollings nodded. "I'm afraid that in every education there are always some deficiencies."

She made a face at him. "I hate that someday I'll probably quote that and some people will think that meant you were laughing in the face of danger, instead of just couldn't resist a silly joke. Oh, well."

"Yeah, more seriously, that was kind of what I was hoping Pueblo might provide us—some clean, covert way to take him out, and someone untraceable who knew how to use it. But the more I think about it the less useful their help would have been anyway. There's a couple of hungry creepy types that would move right in after an assassination, and the idea is to get rid of the Commandant, not replace him with a clone or worse. So it's going to have to be a revolution . . . or at least a revolt, maybe some serious rioting . . . and right now people are still pretty relieved just to have a roof and food. Any idea what we can get them to rise up about?"

Deanna said, "Well, somewhere back in one of those AP History classes you made me take, I remember the instructor said something about how riots often start on or around holidays. Next big one is Memorial Day—"

"Too soon, and back before, anyway, it was basically the start of barbecue and white shoes, they didn't—hunh. And the next big holiday would be the Fourth of July. Matter of fact, it's the 250th Fourth of July. Should have been one of the biggest of them all, ever, eh?"

"Wasn't it just another day to eat yourself sick and watch fireworks, back before, for most people anyway? Isn't that what it's going to be this year, except with less food and even less fireworks?" she asked.

"What if the Commandant decided to put the Fourth of July on the Discouraged Activities list? Threatened to punish people for celebrating it? Maybe even sent cops to break up a celebration?"

She started to grin. "He'd have to be crazy or stupid."

He was grinning back. "Well, we already know he's crazy. Maybe we can give him some help with the stupid. And here's another thought; we have a blackout day coming up in three days, and that means lots of people on the street with nothing to do. Suppose we help them find something."

ABOUT THE SAME TIME. ARMY OF THE WABASH ENCAMPMENT AT WEA CREEK. ABOUT 12 PM EASTERN TIME. THURSDAY, MAY 7, 2026.

Jenny Whilmire Grayson and Chris Manckiewicz had just finished walking through the Order of Battle, identifying the most in-over-their-heads temporary officers, the best and worst performing units, where each unit was right now, and a bit about what each unit had endured recently. *They're all nodding and I like the way they take notes and ask questions,* Jenny thought. *Sure, it's only been "my army" for a couple of days, but I want to hand it to people with some idea about how to care for it.*

Chris was explaining that the Fourth Washington Volunteers had been surprised on their flank by the pipe-and-fuse muskets. "In that first volley they lost half of one company, all from Pullman, Washington, people who knew each other well. They're all putting off grief but there's a world of pain there, and you'll want to keep an eye on it. Now, turning to the artillery, you have three batteries that didn't even—"

An unmistakable chuffing raced up into a drumbeat, then rose to a rumble outside: a very large engine starting up slowly. They all stared at each other for a moment, then rushed out of the big tent en masse.

The NeoGoliath was already rolling along Indiana 25, gathering speed into the wind, Chris, Jenny, and the officers crowded together, gaping, its spoked, iron-tired landing wheels on their double-bowed axles lifted from the roadway. The tail wheel came up, and the NeoGoliath was airborne and on her way. NSP-12 turned south at once, as if afraid or ashamed to let the officers look more closely, and began a steady climb into the sky.

"Well," Chris said, "there goes your ride, Jenny. I was planning to stick around with the Army of the Wabash, but it would have been nice of them to offer me a choice. I wonder—"

"Let me think, Chris. I don't see—"

Patel approached her, saluted, looked embarrassed because he wasn't sure he was supposed to do that in front of officers, and handed her a folded sheet of paper.

She opened it and read:

My dearest daughter,

The Earl of Broad River has told me of the situation in Athens, and it is grave indeed. The leadership of the National Church, both within itself and as the Christian body that must guide our nation through Tribulation, is in the gravest peril, and it was urgent for me to go there and use the talents with which the Lord has blessed me to ensure that the outcome strengthens the hand of our Lord and King.

How I wish that I could count on your support at this dark and terrible time, or that I could say in my heart that after all, you had only just lost a husband in a terrible murder, and therefore must be excused. But I am afraid that I cannot afford, in so dire a situation, to be less than honest with myself, with you, or with the Christ whom I hope we both serve: you have shown far too little willingness to submit, far too much drive toward your own goals.

You have in fact said that you do not even believe we are in Tribulation, despite all the obvious signs, and you have not only expressed ideas and goals contrary to church teachings but you appear to be willing to endorse those who would re-secularize our government, just as if the terrible lessons of the last year had never been learned.

So with so much teetering on the brink in Athens, to be blunt, Jenny, though you are my daughter and I love you, God's Own Nation cannot afford to have you anywhere near its capital until proper authority is re-established.

In Christ,
Daddy

She turned to face Chris and the officers, and with her voice even and level, priding herself on never falling into sarcasm, she read the whole letter aloud, and when she finished, she said, "Now, are you all a part of whatever my father was talking about, or if you are not, can you tell me what the fuck it is?"

Colonel Irwin, the seniormost officer with them, said, "Well, ma'am, we're mostly here because we're *not* a part of it. At least that's what I think, anyone else?"

All the other heads were nodding.

"Well, that's the start of an answer. Part of what?" Jenny said.

"I guess it started back early in the Ohio Valley campaign, ma'am. Your dad, he, uh, well, he thought he was being excluded from a lot of decisions. Like he wanted to spare a lot of lives and get preachers in here to convert the Daybreakers, he thought you could kind of pray them out of it or heal them like they were possessed or something, and he wanted the Board to order General Grayson to try to do that, he thought that . . . well, he thought the massacres were un-Christian. And he wanted the Board to remove General Grayson as the NCCC, he was arguing all the time that they had the power to do that if they wanted, and a lot of different things. But he was the leader of the Church side of the Board, and General Grayson was more the leader of the Army side, and not only was there already kind of a balance, but nobody really wanted to stick their neck out and make big decisions with the main guy on each side so far away, especially not with it being a war and all. So . . . this is kind of embarrassing . . . well, to put it delicately—"

"Please *don't* put it delicately," Jenny said. "I have feelings about this because we are talking about both my father and my husband, but I really need to know what's going on."

Irwin's lips pressed together, and he said, "Two days ago when we received word that your husband had passed on, and the army was surrounded, some of the Church people made a really big move; they tried to vote about half the military officers off the Board and replace them with ministers, they were going to declare their independence as a Christian nation, declare peace with the Lost Quarter tribes, and call the Army home.

"Well, that didn't set well with the Army, and it turned out there were a lot of people that didn't want the nation to be any more Christian than it was, so there were protests and demonstrations outside the government buildings in Athens, people demanding to stay in the US and backing the Army against the Church, and the Army was called in from Fort Benning to break them up and most of us here were among the group that refused the order, said it was against our oaths. And it was starting to look like a real revolution against the National Church, in Athens, a lot of officers muttering they didn't like Graham Weisbrod or liberals or the Provis much, but now that General McIntyre is President up there, they'd a lot rather be dealing with a gay three-star three thousand miles away, than with a bunch of ignorant-ass crazy preachers right on top of them, if you'll pardon my putting it that way."

"I've been having similar thoughts," Jenny said, smiling a little.

"So things were hanging in the balance, with the old Board and the

Church holding most of the government buildings in Athens, and the crowds outside chanting for 'Restore the Constitution!', and churchers and rebels fighting each other everywhere. Most of us in the Army were figuring the rebels would win and invite us to restore order, sometime in the next few days, and we needed to stay out of it, because that's what we've been trained to do, stay out of civilian politics.

"Well, but here you were surrounded and without officers, so let's just say many of us were worried about you. Then that Bret Duquesne, you know, he's nothing like his dad who was the biggest independent on the Board, well, Duquesne offered to fly twenty officers up here, and naturally the ones that were in favor of reunification and winning the war with the tribals were the ones who volunteered. And I am seeing now that we have possibly all been had, ma'am, because we all thought he'd be taking you back there, because our side could sure use someone to rally around— actually both sides could—and now Duquesne has maneuvered things so we're up here, you're up here, and the Reverend Whilmire is down there."

Jenny nodded. "Pure Daddy. Political from the ground up but he always thinks he's doing it for God. Well, the Army is almost ready to move, and we have the assignments worked out, so is this the place where we all shake hands and you go to your different commands?"

"Yeah. I just wish we had a way to get you to Athens; it won't do us much good to pull the Army back together, relieve Pale Bluff, and then all be called home after the Board sends a note of apology to Lord Robert for annoying him."

Chris spoke up. "Isn't the radio rig still up? Let me talk to the RRC and see if something can happen."

THIRTEEN:
A DEAL WITH A REASONABLE DEVIL

Carol May tapped her finger on the map at St. Francisville. "Everywhere else with a decent place to land is at least seven miles further walk to Pale Bluff. And if they land at one of the not-so-good places it will take them a lot longer to get onto shore and set up. So we're looking at sending a few men on mules over there to wreck St. Francisville, but it's two days to get there and then the question would be, what could they do to make it really useless to the Daybreakers? Anything ten guys could pile up on the ramps, ten thousand guys could take off the ramps pretty fast. And just burning the old buildings wouldn't accomplish much. Lord Robert might like to sleep under a roof, but he won't let it slow him down if he can't. And most of his force will be camping out anyway."

"You couldn't mine anything, or booby trap it?"

"Not so it would mean anything. We might set up a few black-powder bombs or some tripwire deadfalls, but at best you might kill or injure a couple dozen tribals, and we figure we'll be facing tens of thousands of them. And the only one that would really count is Lord Robert, and we will not get a shot at him, I think. It's just . . . we know where they'll be coming ashore and we could probably get a few troops there first, but we can't think of anything useful for the troops to do once they get there."

Bambi said, "What about trees along the bank upstream? Cut them down so they fall in the river, create snags?"

"Maybe, but—"

A chime from the other room announced a radio message coming in. Carol May put on her headphones, charged the capacitor, set the spark, and keyed QRZ, "who is calling?" She listened a moment and said, "Bambi, my one-time pad is in the drawer at your right. Key 310, please."

Bambi handed her the sheet printed with triple rows divided into neat boxes; the middle row was typed in with random numbers, the top row blank for recording the incoming message, the lower row for the decrypt. Carol May set the sheet in front of her, put a fresh pencil beside it, and keyed QRV—go ahead.

"Apparently whatever it is, it's a big deal, because Pueblo is calling way off their regular schedule, and they—" She picked up the pencil and took down a string of letters and numbers. When the page was about half full, she set down her pencil, keyed an acknowledgment, and shut down the transmitter. "Hunh. And they repeated the clear-code for DECIPHER IMMEDIATELY at the end of the message. Like anyone would get an emergency message and not decipher it ASAP. Whatever it is they really want us to know right away."

After the first sentence, Carol May said, "All right, you finish the decryption. I'm going to make you a bag of sandwiches and a big thermos of coffee."

"Am I going somewhere?"

"Ninety-nine percent chance, I'd say, if when you decrypt the rest of it, it's like that first sentence. I'll get your food packed. Good thing you got as much sleep as you did."

Carol May had the sandwiches and thermos ready to go in a sturdy cardboard box when Bambi emerged from the radio room. "You were right. Thanks so much, and I hope you packed enough for two."

"Of course. I've already put up my TAXI YES flag, so—there we are."

A pedicab was pulling up at the front of the house. "Just a sec while I grab my flight bag and gear," Bambi said. By the time that Claudia, the pedicabbie, was knocking on the door, Bambi had returned to the front room, bag slung over her shoulder, in her fur-lined moccasins, jacket, scarf, and goggled helmet. Claudia gaped for a moment, and Carol May couldn't resist teasing, "Have you never seen a pilot before, or never carried a duchess?"

Sheepishly, Claudia said, "Actually, I've been looking for that pattern to knit a scarf for my husband."

Bambi grinned. "Get me to the airfield in less than ten minutes, and since I have a spare scarf in the plane, you can have this one to copy. Just remember I'll want it back; a tough thug of an FBI agent named Terry Bolton made it for me as a wedding present."

"With my life," Claudia said. "And I'll see if we can make the airfield in five."

At the airfield, the Stearman was ready—local ground crew were efficient—so Bambi just tossed her things into the forward cockpit, switched scarves with her spare, tossed the other to Claudia, and hugged the cabbie. "What's the fee?"

"Carol May keeps me on retainer, and the loan of your scarf is the best tip I'm getting all year. Thanks, your, uh, Duchessness? That can't be right."

"Don't get too good at titles. Doesn't look good on an American. Thanks, Claudia, see you soon I hope."

She felt like she really shouldn't take the time, but she trotted over to the black and yellow checkerboard-patterned Gooney Express. Quattro was in the rear. He had already removed the passenger door and bolted the S-shaped, hand-fed bomb rack to the underside. Now he was reinstalling the black-powder Gatling as a door gun.

When he saw Bambi, he dropped the tools and jumped down to hug her. "Where to, Duchess Babe?"

"There's a revolution forming in Athens and we might be able to replace the goofy religious nuts with an only slightly crazy right-winger, which is Jenny Whilmire Grayson, so I'm going to pick her up from the Army of the Wabash and plunk her down in Athens."

"Charming company."

"She's not so bad, really, and we understand each other. We both were brainy hot chick trophy daughters for power-mad fathers."

"So you're in the same support group?"

"Yeah, and we both know the secret handshake. No shit, she'd piss you off and she'd drive Heather or James bugfuck crazy, but I can relate to her. I'm sure that's a character flaw of some kind."

"Well, better you than me. And while you're gone I'll have the Gooney to play with. By the time Lord Robert gets here, we'll be set up to surprise the shit out of him."

"Eahh. That's another piece of bad news. Estimated time of arrival is *way* sooner, according to Heather's emergency message. Carol May can fill you in on that. But if I were you I'd never leave the Gooney unflyable overnight."

"Then I won't. I'm just a flyguy with some charisma. You're the one that knows how to do all this danger and fighting stuff. Think I should sleep out here?"

"Well, you might need to take off in a hurry any time, but you should be okay for a day or two. Maybe after tonight. Carol May's place isn't that far away, and mostly I'm just paranoid these days, and I worry about you. Also there might be some delay about me getting back here; I'll be picking up some high-priority secure communications at Athens and delivering them to General Phat at Paducah, and I kind of think he'll have more work for a pilot and plane, and then there's a blackout on the tenth—the moon gun went off this morning—so I might be grounded someplace for a while."

"Bambi, hon, being apart sucks, and I want you back as soon as you can be, but I'll be fine. I'm going to be inside a wall, and guarded by armed troops, and my plane will be safe on the ground when the EMP hits. You're flying over hundreds of miles of tribal territory in something that isn't much more than a powered kite, and you know how when there's a big military operation, like the one you're visiting in Paducah, they always want you to fly right till the second before blackout starts."

"Well, I'll tell them no if they ask."

"You better. You've already had one force-down in tribal country, and whatever it was for you, it was the scariest week of my life till we got you back. So *you* are not going to worry about *me*." He held her a long time, and hugged extra hard. "Be back soon, Bambi, okay? I like the world better when you're close."

**4 HOURS LATER. RICHMOND, KENTUCKY. ABOUT 8:30 PM
EASTERN TIME. THURSDAY, MAY 7, 2026.**

Conversation was impossible between the open cockpits. Bambi and Jenny
could communicate in very occasional shouts over the roar of the engine,
but that was all. So Bambi's view of Richmond at sunset—a little town
with lights coming on, the guard changing on the city walls, and people
trudging home from work—was all her own. They had built a new landing
strip within the walls, and she flew low to take a look at it. They were just
hoisting the white-circle-on-blue that meant "We have clean fuel," and the
long pennon that meant "Welcome, you were not expected." Bambi wag-
gled her wings to indicate she'd understood, then came around and
brought the Stearman in for a smooth landing, or as smooth as you could
do on partially deflated greased-linen tires. She taxied over to the recep-
tion area and killed the engine.

As they climbed out, Jenny said, "Whenever you and Quattro get a
chance you should take a look at that NeoGoliath's landing gear. Chris
was all impressed that they used a double-spring axle like on an old-time
covered wagon, with iron-rimmed wheels."

"Yeah, interesting. I wonder what that lands like—"

A light cough nearby made them turn to see an older man in a somewhat lumpy, probably handmade blue uniform, sort of an inexpert copy of
a police patrolman's uniform, with the Cross and Eagle insignia on both
shoulders. On his chest, he wore a metal disk with the words "Airfield
Master—On Duty" stenciled in black paint. "Uh, I'm supposed to ask you
to identify yourselves and what you're doing here."

"Of course. Bambi Castro Larsen. Pilot, RRC courier service."

"Jenny Whilmire Grayson, urgent government business, en route to
Athens."

"Uh. Well, that is, uh. I have orders to detain you. I mean you, Ms.
Grayson. I have no orders about you, Ms. Larsen."

"I would like to see that order," Bambi said, and held out her hand.

"Um, I don't think—"

"Would you like me to demand it as an RRC courier who has an abso-
lute right anywhere in the United States to protect my passengers from

harassment? Or as a senior RRC agent who could call in troops to occupy this airfield if I don't like the answer? Or as the Duchess of California, so that this can be an international incident? Because I'll be happy to play it any of those ways. Or all of them."

The man looked terrified, which was exactly what Bambi had intended, and handed over a transcribed radiogram. Without asking, Bambi also reached out and took the lantern from the man's hand, holding it up to read. "'All stations, Jenny Whilmire Grayson is to be detained but not harmed, for reasons necessary to the government.' And then it adds 'This order has been authorized by Reverend Donald Whilmire, National Constitutional Continuity Board Chairman and Acting NCCC.' This doesn't give an appropriate and specific description of the reasons, it doesn't specify anything that you would need for an arrest warrant, and it's signed by an authority that isn't recognized in the rest of the United States."

"They say I have to hold her."

"They can say you have to shoot down the moon, depose God, or kill all the firstborn males in Kentucky, and you're still the one who has to decide whether to try to comply or not."

"I'm a Federal official—"

"What were you back before?"

"Ain't got nothing to—"

"Because, buddy, I was a Federal agent and we learned about warrants, since screwing one up, or using an invalid one, could cost us a job or the Attorney General a conviction. And this is not a valid warrant. Now, you can point that gun at us and see if you can make us take orders that you have no power to give, on behalf of people who also had no power to give them, or you can shut up and do your job as Airfield Master, which I would bet you're a lot better at than you are at playing cop." She had been walking closer to him as she spoke, holding the lantern up so it shone in his eyes. "Now are you going to be a real Airfield Master or a fake cop?"

As she asked that question, she reached forward and lifted the man's pistol from its holster, gently, not grabbing, and held it out in her open hand, so it pointed at neither of them, but he could reach for it easily. "You need this for routine protection on your job, I know. Do I have your word you aren't going to go any further with this arrest nonsense, you're not going to radio anywhere for orders or instructions, and you'll get us a maintenance and fuel wagon out here? If you'll give me your word about that, then I'll fix things up tonight, we'll sleep by the plane, and we'll take off at first light. And you can always say I took your gun away from you and you had no choice."

The man had seemed to shrink the whole time Bambi had been talking to him. "I don't know what—"

"Exactly. I took your gun, I had the authority, and you didn't know what to do so you just did your job as Airfield Master. Now take the deal—and your gun back. Just say, 'Yes, ma'am.'"

He mumbled, "Yes, ma'am," and took the gun as if afraid it might go off, sliding it uncomfortably back into his holster, then slouched off toward the main buildings.

"Think he'll keep his word?"

"Probably, at least for a while. One of those things I've learned to have a feel for, spotting the people Daddy used to call 'Natural omegas,' people who are just looking for someone to tell them what to do. He probably really is a good Airfield Master and he'll feel a lot more comfortable doing that than he did trying to be the KGB. So I think we're all right. And anyway, I just volunteered us into sleeping under the wing, so we're right where we need to be if trouble starts."

"Good thing it looks like a warm night," Jenny said.

"And thank god for Carol May's sandwiches. My plan is, sandwiches now, get the checkout and fuel done right after, sack out, then open the coffee thermos when we get up and take off just as the sun rises."

"Sounds good to me."

The meal was good, no repairs were needed, and after fuel, tire air, oil, and lye were all topped up, they stretched out in blankets next to each other under the wing. Bambi said, "Hope you didn't mind being a mechanic's helper before bedtime."

Jenny snorted. "I'm only afraid I might like the job so much I decide to give up on politics and become a full-time mechanic. You ever think about being just a pilot instead of a duchess?"

"Only about every other breath."

"Well, good, it's nice when you take a flying trip to know that the pilot isn't crazy."

From the sound of her breathing, Bambi knew that Jenny fell asleep almost immediately. *Well, compared to what she's been through recently, I guess sleeping under a plane wing and hoping you won't be arrested in the middle of the night is probably pretty restful. For that matter when I consider what's happened to her, I realize how lucky I am.* A moment later, Bambi fell asleep too.

AN HOUR LATER. RUINS OF TERRE HAUTE, THE DOMAIN. 11:30 PM CENTRAL TIME. THURSDAY, MAY 7, 2026.

Terre Haute had grown into a sizable town, back before, because it was a good landing at the big bend of the Wabash; the same fact, plus the convergence of road and rail in the area, had been in Grayson's mind when he had decided to make it the main supply base for his reconquest of the Lost Quarter.

The garrison, just a short battalion of militia, had had almost no warning before the first big flotilla of canoes and rafts had begun landing just upstream of them. The first human wave of tribals—mostly fanatical types that Lord Robert didn't like much anyway—had torn through the waterfront side of the garrison's camp, cutting them off from escape and enabling forces to land downstream of them. Within three hours, well before the full force arrived, Lord Robert's personal guard had been hanging the last of the captured and wounded, while the tribals drummed and celebrated. It had been a good little party, Lord Robert thought. *And these guys really needed to blow off some steam considering how hard they're working and how much they've accomplished.*

Terre Haute was a good place for the forces to get some rest and to reorganize for the next phase, and the heap of supplies was so large that it took a couple of days for Bernstein and his quartermasters to take inventory and divvy up.

"I still don't get why this is a good idea," Nathanson was saying to Lord

Robert, who was stretched out on an antique couch that had apparently had no synthetic materials, in the main room of a big old mansion he'd made his headquarters.

"Why *what* is a good idea?" Lord Robert took another sip of the high-priced fancy-ass brandy they had found, and decided that it really did taste like cough syrup and he would switch back to bourbon when he wanted another drink, which need not be soon. *Got this sweet life going, not going to lose it because I'm drunk when a guy shows up with a knife.*

"This," Nathanson said, waving vaguely around himself. He drank rarely but always to get drunk, with no interest in adjusting his mood but apparently an occasional desire to get stupid and helpless. He was well on his way right now, but this was about the safest situation for it. "This. The big house. The cognac. The jewelry for the house bitches, the fancy shit like eating caviar, all that stuff that says we're rich and better than anyone else. Don't you think that's gonna be bad for morale, sooner or later?"

"Just the opposite. I mean my followers are not going to be impressed with just any old cheap ass junk. I need to keep a little awe going, you know, and the living-rich stuff helps with that."

Nathanson made a face; maybe the cognac was catching up with him too. "Lord Robert, doesn't that sound kind of like a reason you made up on the spot?"

"Well," Robert said, "I did. But the truth is, if I tell'em they feel that way, they'll feel that way. That's one of the things that you gotta realize, that these Daybreaker types, the fundamental thing about Daybreakers, whether they came in from fundamentalist churches or whether they came in from environmental groups or wherever they came from, the one thing they really had in common was they sure did love to be told what to do. There's lots of people like that, always been. Hell, I don't think people have revolutions 'cause they want freedom, that's bullshit they tell themselves afterward 'cause they're proud of themselves, I think what makes revolutions, is, is, whenever people want to be told what to do more by the opposition than they want to be told what to do by the government." He was pleased with having had the thought, though he wasn't sure it was true.

"In fact," Robert said, "I been setting aside some of the good stuff and

I'm gonna make public presents of it to you guys, big ceremony and all, and you're going to accept it in front of the crowd, and that's an order."

"An order?"

"Sure. If this crowd ever turns on me for having made myself comfortable, you are going to have your head as far into the trap as I do. That way I don't have to worry about you being able to sell me out to them. So what'd you rather have, Nathanson? A couple nice rugs, pricey booze from back before, maybe some canned goods?"

"Whatever. I was gonna show you a surprise from me, too, but then you invited me in and we got to drinking. Can you stand to look at something that's not purely personal?"

"What's the funny grin about?"

Nathanson held a finger up, walked back to the front entryway, and came in carrying a gun with a short stock, short barrel, and enormous drum magazine. On the magazine it bore the stamp "Newberry Tech Works, Castle Newberry, South Carolina."

Lord Robert realized at once what it was. "Oh, yeah," he said. "You're fucking kidding me, right? I mean I'm dreaming? They went upriver to the war and they left behind a fucking machine gun?"

"Ten crates of them, and a mountain of ammo. It's a Newberry SMG Model 1." Nathanson pronounced that with careful reverence. "And they left them behind 'cause they had some big problems with them. There was a letter in an envelope tacked onto the crate that had broken ones in it. They were returning all the rest of them unused. Seems they blow up around the tenth time you use them—really blow up, blow up, I mean, like a round'll jam in the barrel, flash gets around someplace, and the whole mag goes off. And they're complaining too that they ain't all that accurate, you have to be almost on top of a mob of enemy packed pretty thick to do you any good.

"So we test-fired one, and, yeah, it makes a mess of itself and probably jams like an old dog farts. The auto mechanism kind of looks like it was copied from a cuckoo clock, too, bet it breaks pretty often, and it doesn't fire very fast when you hold the trigger down. Maybe two rounds a second. *And* you have to hand-load both the drum magazine and the little chain of caps. So they were getting rid of it before it got some of their guys killed, and it's a lousy weapon for them because they want something that'll work every time and be reliable and some guy can carry it through a whole war."

"But for a weapon that you throw away . . . because you're gonna throw the guy carrying it away . . ." Robert said. "And if you have slaves to do the loading . . . Yeah. Yeah."

Nathanson beamed. "Just what I thought. Especially if we can trick or force some people we don't want to take back with us into using it. Then it would be one of those win-all-around Daybreak situations."

Bernstein came in from the foyer, and said, "Inventory's coming along."

"Grab some cognac, it tastes like shit but it's good for Nathanson to get drunk on."

"Naw, I need to be sober. So do you, Lord Robert."

"I am. It's General Drunk-ass here who has to worry, I'm just buzzed. So what's up that I need to be sober for?"

"Guess who's back and wanting to talk."

"Did they send us anybody hot this time?"

Bernstein shrugged. "No, but they sent four people that are real whiny and polite and trying not to piss us off."

"We ought to make them suck up to Little Joey," Lord Robert mused, thinking of the terrified little man they had sent him before, who was now his devoted personal valet. "That would be entertaining. But I guess we should hear what they have to say, just in case it's something nice."

The three gray, tired-looking middle-aged men came in literally with hats in their hands. Those hats were functional, without feathers, jewels, or machine parts. Their shirts, sweaters, and pants were plain cheap cotton or wool, and they wore the lumpy semi-moccasins that many tribals made by sewing deerhide to old canvas sneakers to replace the rotted rubber soles. "Lord Robert, in the name of all the tribes and their Councils, and on behalf of the Guardian on the Moon, we would like to ask you for a favor."

"Well, then," Lord Robert said. "You must know there is not a whole lot of love between us, and I don't see any reason why I should be doing you any favors."

The man in the center of the delegation bowed very low and said, "We understand that. Some of us did not want to ask a favor at all. Some of us wanted to propose it to you as something with possible mutual benefit."

"Mutual benefit is always of interest," Lord Robert said. "Nathanson, Bernstein, let's meet with our guests around the big table upstairs, where everyone can sit down."

Lord Robert extended the small hospitality of offering water, and then added, "The cook might be able to find us all something, should we do that?"

The leader of the delegation visibly swallowed hard. "Um, yes, that would be good."

Bernstein said, "I think the cook's got fresh squirrel and rabbit, some wild carrots, and maybe some spring greens and he's doing something up. Be right back."

While he was gone, Lord Robert said, "I trust all is well with you? I have been very pleased with the people you sent me. In particular those ones from Lake Erie knew a lot about boats and rafts and stuff and we couldn't've done this without them. I should probably warn you they mostly say they're going to stay with me at Castle Earthstone afterward. That isn't the issue you want to talk about, is it? Because I have told everyone you've sent me that they are free to join me, and even we have been surprised how many of them take us up on it."

The quiet man on the left said, "Of course the Council will be displeased when we report that, but that's not what we came here about."

"Well, good then."

Bernstein returned with two of the kitchen workers, bearing wild-game-and-vegetable stew. Someone must have found an unlooted stock of spices, as well, for it had a rich, tongue-stinging blend of pepper and mustard. Lord Robert ate his casually, watching his guests; after a couple of bites had not resulted in any of them falling over choking, they dove into the stew, eating as if starving. *Which they probably are,* Lord Robert thought. *So even high-ranking people with important missions aren't getting enough to eat out there in the tribal boons. Even with so many people dead, and the way Daybreak arranged for looting and hoarding right after Daybreak day, they must have finally run out of canned and dried stuff, and most of them probably never really learned how to hunt, fish, or grow much of anything. Too busy doing oogie-boogie ceremonies and robbing their neighbors.*

He offered them seconds, and was amused that they accepted so quickly.

When he judged that they were finally more afraid than hungry, he smiled nicely. "Well, at least now we're all more comfortable. This proposition you were thinking of making? Proposition me."

Their leader said, "We will not contest your possession of your territory; in fact we will concede you all the lands east of the Wabash and the Tippecanoe, south of the Maumee, west of the Miami, and north of the Ohio. All tribes with claims in those areas will renounce them forever. Furthermore we will not try to create new tribes in the lands between Lake Michigan, the Ohio, the Wabash, and the Mississippi; if you conquer any of that land in this summer's war, it is yours, as far as we are concerned."

"But since you don't hold it now it ain't hardly yours to give away," Lord Robert drawled. Beside him, Nathanson chuckled, and Bernstein smiled at them.

"That is true, but it also carries our pledge that we will not go to war for it or seek to gain it for tribes in the future."

"Did any of you ever promise the plaztatic world—isn't that what you call it—that you wouldn't kill most of the people on Earth and send us all back to the Stone Age? It's worth something to hear you say you'll pull whatever is left of the tribes out of the Domain, which is what you can call my territory from now on. Promising that if I conquer more you won't try to steal it—that's pretty fuckin' abstract, you know? So . . . you got any more for me or are you about to tell me what you want?"

The leader seemed to be trying to control his temper. *Don't suppose he liked being told that to his face. Don't suppose I care what he likes, either.* "We ask that this summer, you raid as deeply into the remainder of the plaztatic world as you can, destroy everything you can, especially anything that will be hard for them to replace, smash them down so that there is less chance that they will come back up. We would like you to take as many of our warriors with you as you can."

Robert shrugged. "If I decide to do that, I will take along as many as you send me. And I will use them first; no reason to kill my own people, if you're giving me people to kill in place of them."

"We expected an answer somewhat in this kind. We're prepared to send you much larger forces, and to call up the tribes from other areas like the Ouachitas and the southern mountains, to support your effort. But we are giving them to you so that you can conduct this great raid."

"And because you're out of resources and you need to get rid of them before they get too hungry. This way they can either eat by raiding all summer, or die raiding, but either way they're not at home to be disillusioned with Daybreak, the way my people got to be, before I gave them the version that works."

"As you wish to say it, let it be said. We will not argue about words."

"So the real offer is, you'll send me a lot of people, and you'll make me a couple real vague promises, and coordinate some other attacks in other parts of the country, and in return, I tear the holy fuck out of everything between the Mississippi and the Rockies that I can get my hands on?"

"We would . . . that is close enough for us to agree with."

"All right, three ways you have to sweeten the deal. One, that moon gun thing of yours drops a big old EMP over Pale Bluff sometime in the next few days, and you tell me *exactly* when it's coming. Two, after that your moon gun just keeps dropping'em, steady as rain, on Pueblo, till I tell them to stop—but when I tell them to stop, they stop. Three, any of your troops that want to join my True Daybreak, and break away from you, they're mine, no arguments, no take backs. Do me all those three and we got us a deal."

The leader nodded, apparently taking no offense at Lord Robert's tone, and said, "As for the Guardian on the Moon, we will do what we can but we don't like to make promises on which we cannot deliver. We will say to those who communicate with the Guardian on the Moon that if the Guardian does these things, our agreement will take effect, and that if it does not, we do not have an agreement, and hope that the Guardian on the Moon thinks that reaching an agreement is as important as we do."

Ha. Now I'm learning things. Robert asked, "You don't really know who or what is running the moon gun, yourselves, do you?"

"We only know that the Guardian on the Moon is a force for good and helps us in ending the plaztatic world. None of us has ever met anyone who knows anything about the Guardian on the Moon. But though we all know nothing, we are teaching our children, so that when we are all dead, our children will know the Guardian on the Moon for what it really is: the Servant of Mister Atom, visible proof that *The Play of Daybreak* is true and the world is the way we taught them that it is.

"As for your use of our tribes—of course. Do whatever you like, so long as you carry your Great Raid deep and far. In fact, we will send some of the tribes from the Tennessee Valley, the Ouachitas, and Texas—and from the Ozarks too if you get that far—to join you; use them freely as well. We did not want any of them back in any case; strew their bones from Cairo to Seattle, or take them home and feed them yourself, it's all one to us."

"You don't seem to mind our heresy much."

"We don't. Your so-called True Daybreak may offend us personally, just as the computers and technical knowledge we used to bring about Daybreak, back before, offended us. *But we used them.*

"Like everything else that must pass eventually, for the moment, you are a means. We have not compromised on the end. Whatever you may wrongly believe, you are going to help us kill plaztatic civilization. We can tolerate a small empire based on military conquest, the same sort of thing that the world has had many times before, if it hastens the final end of plaztatic civilization. Do as you like; ultimately you work for Gaia. We accept your offer completely, and let me add, personally, all hail Lord Robert of the Domain, for the services he shall perform for Mother Gaia."

After an enthusiastic round of handshaking, the tribals went on their way.

Bernstein said, "Well, someone skunked someone, there, but I'll be damned if I know who."

"That's 'cause we haven't made sure that we are the skunkers and not the skunkees," Robert said, cheerfully. "But we will. I know in my bones we will. Did Nathanson show you those fun toys he found?"

They each took one turn firing a Model 1, which was fun. After that, they sent for a tribal who had rudely refused True Daybreak and talked back to Nathanson. They made him practice fire the SMG a few more times, to see what Grayson's letter to Duquesne had meant by "blow up." It burned his face badly and tore off two fingers. Lord Robert and his advisors all had a good laugh.

THE NEXT DAY. ATHENS, TNG DISTRICT. 10:30 AM EASTERN TIME. FRIDAY, MAY 8, 2026.

Jenny Whilmire Grayson had been slumped, not moving, in the front cockpit of the Stearman, for the last hour or more of the flight. *Well, if she can sleep in that situation, it's not like any of us ever gets enough sleep,* Bambi reflected. She remembered that the first time Quattro had taken her up in this thing, it had been exhilarating, joyful, fascinating—and about fifteen minutes, and for fun. The three hours from Richmond to Athens, on a breakfast of two cups of lukewarm coffee, had been long and tiring for Bambi, and she was just as glad her passenger was probably dozing through most of them.

As they crossed the vast ruin of Atlanta, something in the changed rhythm of the plane must have awakened Jenny, who stirred, leaned back, and shouted, "Can we circle over Athens before we land? So we can see what's up?"

"Sure!" Bambi shouted back. "Good idea! Will there be anyone there if I signal your house?"

"Should be!"

"General Grayson always had us do that! Then they know to bring the carriage!"

Jenny gave her a fairly jaunty thumbs-up, for the circumstances.

In Athens, seen from the air, this morning, the crowds surged through the streets like jellyfish in some absurdist maze, blocked occasionally by lines of troops or cops. At the corner of Baxter and Milledge, there appeared to be a mass brawl going on; downed picket signs and banners along Baxter suggested that one side had been marching on the TNG capital, the old U of Georgia campus, and the other side had ambushed them. Mounted troopers were riding down Milledge and a police line had been set up across Baxter.

They swung south and east to make a low pass over the Grayson house; Bambi was relieved that it was still standing in apparent good shape. She just hoped it wasn't triggering too much for Jenny. *Call me a heartless coward, but she's been through a lot, and I might understand her better than other people, but she's not exactly my BFF, and I'd rather not be the only person there when she starts to cry.*

Bambi banked and descended northeast again, toward the airfield, but as they approached, she saw that there were people—*lots of people, big swarms and herds of people, actually*—on the runway, running back and forth, and . . . *oh, man. Throwing rocks. Slugging each other. It's pretty much a battle down there. And since that Airfield Master probably radioed that we were coming, I am guessing this is about us.*

Many faces were turning up toward them, and there was a puff of smoke that had to be from a handgun; the shooter was immediately mobbed, but Bambi decided this was no time for taking chances, and circled higher. In a few minutes, a cavalry detachment showed up and went down the runway at a slow trot, shoving the crowds aside; infantry appeared and set up police lines, which took another fifteen minutes.

"Is that about us?" Bambi shouted.

"It's about me. I can pick out some Christian symbols on the signs and the other side is waving the old fifty-star flag. One mob that wants me here, one that doesn't!" Jenny turned to watch them more closely; with nothing to do but circle, with stick and rudder locked for the moment, Bambi had a free hand to squeeze Jenny's arm. Jenny covered it with her other hand and twisted in the cockpit to hunch over toward Bambi.

Well, damn, I guess someone has to be the comforter.

At last the police lines seemed to be holding, the cross-and-eagle and fish-sign wielders were driven from the field, and the American flags began to cluster around the entrance to the terminal. A heliograph winked from the tower, indicating permission to land.

Not sure how long this relative safety was going to last, Bambi came in as swiftly as safety permitted. When she rolled to a stop in front of the terminal crowd, two uniforms with a lot of braid, one of them a woman, came striding up and delivered a very ostentatious salute.

Helping Jenny down from the plane, Bambi asked, "Are you going to be okay?"

"Probably not, but I'm going to do the right things, I hope," Jenny said, under her breath.

The two uniforms came nearer; the man, a tall African-American with a shaved head, said, "Mrs. Grayson, I don't know if you remember me—"

"Of course I do, Colonel Steen, and it's good to have you here. I'm guessing you're on my side?"

"Yours, the late General's, the Constitution's, and America's, ma'am. This is Colonel Jardin, once upon a time she was a public affairs specialist."

Jardin said, "I'm afraid we need you to give a speech that will result in some calm focus on our side; we have about equal problems with people wanting to go home and give up, and wanting to throw bricks. You don't happen to know Monroe Motivated Sequence by any—"

"Speech competitions all through high school, speech minor in college, I'm your girl. Feed me the steps and I'll make it happen." Jenny's smile was genuine, but Bambi wondered if anyone else noticed how tired she looked dragging herself upright.

"Good. I think we can stall them five more minutes but then we'll have to put you up on the rostrum, ready or not."

Sudden yelling from the crowd, apparently about nothing, seemed to confirm that.

Jenny turned back to Bambi. "I know you have places to be, and I'm guessing Colonel Steen can make the arrangements for you to get fuel and so on?"

Steen nodded. "Happy to. I don't think I've seen you since I performed your wedding."

"That was a happier time," Bambi agreed, "but maybe just as busy. Yeah, I should try to be in Paducah tonight, and I've got a couple hours' work to do on the ground here."

"We'll get you squared away," Steen said confidently.

Bambi gave Jenny a last firm hug. "You need asylum, ever, you know Pueblo and all of California will open their doors, lady."

As she followed the ground crew, which was using a mule to tow the Stearman backwards into a hangar, she could hear Jenny's unamplified but powerful voice beginning to speak over the crowd, and the hush-and-shush of a crowd trying to make each other listen. Bambi was a little surprised at how affectionately she thought, *Good luck, sister.*

. . .

Jenny felt like when she turned her back on Bambi, she had truly lost her last friend, but she didn't look back, squared her shoulders, and marched forward. *Just like when Mama dropped me off at preschool and when Daddy dropped me off at Sarah Lawrence. Keep moving forward, try to play well with others.*

Beside her, Jardin was murmuring, "The whole city is crazy, ma'am, that's not an exaggeration, it's just the way things are. Your carriage is coming, but it was delayed a few minutes so we could provide it with a cavalry escort. When it takes you back to your house you'll have more of an escort, because the carriage with you in it is a much better target. Your house has been under guard since early April; I don't know if the general ever told you."

"He just muttered something about damn silliness. Is all this really necessary?"

"Oh, it's necessary. Pay attention to your guards, ma'am. They'll ask you to stay away from windows, not answer doors, and if you hear something moving and you don't know what it is, head for the nearest guard, don't go look yourself. And I'm afraid they're right. Sorry to say there's some fire damage to your garden, one whole row of rosebushes got burned when a firebomb bounced off your house."

"I can see them being mad at me, but what did the roses ever do to them?" She did her best to make her smile genuine; it must have worked because Jardin looked relieved. *She was probably wondering how I'd take all this.*

Jardin added, "Also you've got a couple windows boarded up where someone shot them out, and we're sending someone by the post office to pick up your mail and bring it in, because your mailbox has been set on fire a few times. Basically most of the attacks have been cowardly vandalism. But with you home, that house will attract worse things than cowardly vandals."

"I will listen to my guards. Remember my husband was murdered while I was in the bathroom just three days ago."

Colonel Jardin winced; Jenny sourly thought, *Older military women sure are surprised when younger civilian women fail to be shrieking little mice, I guess. Well, I hope she's suitably impressed, and she'll start being blunt with me. I never had much patience for kindly ambiguity, and now I have none.*

Jardin seemed to catch on. "All right. I'll just lay it out straight. We're trying to turn rioting in the city into a real revolution that will make the National Constitutional Continuity Board abdicate and ideally leave the city. The Army could probably do it ourselves but some of us would fight on their side, and we don't want to fight each other, and besides once you start letting the military take power in coups, you never get them out of the business. So we need a popular uprising, after which we restore order, recognize the Provi government, and get things back on track for beating the tribes and electing a real government under the real Constitution in November."

"I've been around the Army enough, even in not much more than a year, to understand that oath is serious," Jenny said. "So you're the PR person officially and I'm guessing unofficially you're the minister for propaganda? Tell me what you need me to do and I'll do it as well as I can."

Jardin's smile had broadened. "This is pleasantly easy, now that I know I can just tell you. You need to play the grieving widow card pretty big—"

"For sympathy, or more waving the bloody shirt?"

"Sympathy, for the moment. General Grayson was the closest thing the Army had to an actual hero, and the major thing we need you to tell them is that if he could only be here to lead them, he'd back the rebels and oppose the reverends."

"He would. All right, I'm badly stressed out but I'll manage, and if I cry on the rostrum I guess it'll just enhance the effect. So, since you wanted a Monroe Motivated speech, that's the Attention Step, then the Need Step is—"

"The rebels have been saying they just want their country back, they want to be Americans again, so I thought—"

"Great. I can run with that, and Jeff would've been all for it. No shading of the truth necessary. So then, Satisfaction Step, we're going to take it back, Vision Step, taking it back is what America's all about, so Action Step, so let's take it back."

"Perfect, ma'am. The one little side note is there's a faction in the mobs that I think of as anarchic looters, and some people that are sorta Reds and just troublemakers, and we don't want to give them too much encourage-ment, but we also don't want to discourage them because frankly they're better fighters and more determined than a lot of the middle of the road types. So you need to signal that we're behind the radicals enough to keep them fighting, but we want to hand power over to the moderates."

"And how do I do that?"

"Well, I was thinking some work-ins about the Constitution, maybe something that implies that Daybreak was foreign or unAmerican, remind them how many end-of-the-world fundamentalists were in the original Daybreak movement back before. Stress that the minute the government surrenders we want real law and order, that we're not taking over to create mob rule, we want order under the Constitution."

"I hope you're not surprised, Colonel, that I am totally down with that program."

Jardin smiled. "I'm glad you're here, ma'am."

In its way it really wasn't different from speech contests in high school and college; really, just like extemp except she didn't get fifteen minutes alone in the quiet to make notes. Afterward, she only remembered the outline that she and Jardin had sketched, and a few phrases here and there, but every pause for breath drew wild cheers, and she couldn't have been doing too bad a job since Jardin was grinning at her when she came down from the rostrum.

Then they guided her out through the old air terminal to the street, and Jardin helped her into her carriage between two guards, and sat down facing her. "If you can give me just a little more energy for a few more minutes, please stand up and wave, and try to look confident and happy; we're going through mostly rebel neighborhoods and there'll be a lot of people out to cheer for you. Mind you, we might need to pull you back into your seat if trouble starts, so please pardon that in advance."

This wasn't so different from having been part of the court for Miss Clarke County, really. Except that when she was third runner up, there were other girls waving, and soldiers were not randomly jumping into the crowd to push people to the sidewalk, chase people down, or tear crosses out of people's hands.

"We're getting kind of loose in how we interpret free speech and free-dom of religion, aren't we?" she asked Jardin.

"We're leaving cardboard signs and cloth banners alone, mostly. But wooden crosses have been used as clubs. Cardboard-box crosses have been used to conceal knives and pistols, so that's different. Mind you I don't like the PR of having soldiers knock people down to tear their crosses apart, but we're finding enough weapons in them that we have to keep doing it."

"What do all the signs about 'Don't Just Appoint, Anoint' mean?"

"The reverends are caught between the way most people read the Con-stitution and the way their crazy followers read Revelations, ma'am. Some of the real dedicated crazies over on their side want the reverends to anoint a king of America, like Saul or David was anointed the king of Israel. And start building ships and building up the army to go fight at Armageddon. *And* mass-execute a whole lot of gays and unmarried non-virgins and known atheists, and make Catholics and Jews swear an oath of allegiance to the Bible. And after that there's the crazy stuff."

Jenny shuddered. "Daddy used to struggle against those people."

"Well, you know, we can tell he still doesn't like them much, ma'am, but he can't afford to throw them out, either."

"Like our radicals?"

"Just like." Jardin's flat expression invited no more conversation.

At last they reached the house, and it wasn't until Jardin was walking her up the front steps that she thought, *Oh, god, it's really Jeff's house, not mine, and it's crawling with his stuff in every closet and corner, how am I going to bear up in front of everyone?*

She didn't. Maelene and Luther were just inside the door, hugging her and saying how sorry they were and how worried they'd been. She just let go and cried.

As her cook and maid steered her upstairs, Jardin followed. "I'm an experienced mother and old enough to be yours. Make this easy on us, and just let us all take care of you. The next meeting of the Board, which you're going to crash, isn't till early tomorrow morning, and then you have a rally afterward. I'll be by to prep you for that meeting, right after breakfast—"

"*Over* breakfast," Luther said firmly. "Mrs. Grayson hates to eat alone and she's fine after that first sip of coffee. We'll set that up after we get Mrs. Grayson settled in."

"Over breakfast, then. Meanwhile, rest, sleep, recover, find whatever strength you have left because we're going to ask you for all of it."

After a short, blessedly hot bath, she curled up in the huge bed she used to share with Jeff, and just let the tears flow and the sobs come. There was still full daylight through the curtains when she fell asleep, and then she knew nothing till just before dawn, when Maelene woke her with coffee on a tray and the offer of another bath if she wanted it. She finished the pot of coffee in the tub, dried and dressed quickly, and was seated at the breakfast table when Jardin arrived. "How are you feeling this morning?" the colonel asked.

"A million years old, but ready for the next million. Let's eat."

ABOUT THE SAME TIME. PADUCAH, KENTUCKY.
4:30 PM CENTRAL TIME. FRIDAY, MAY 8, 2026.

The heliograph and the flaggers directed Bambi to land on a long straight stretch of Park Avenue where they'd knocked down power poles and wires.

The city was filling up rapidly. Paducah was on what was left of two transcontinental rail routes, and troops from the Temper and Provi states and the semi-independent states between were converging. When she went in to report to General Phat, she found he was trying to sort out the most complicated organizational chart she'd ever seen. "We have two national armies, ten state militias that aren't affiliated with either army, and troops from maybe a dozen government entities that didn't exist back before, all piling in," Phat said. "We have Unionist Texan companies and battalions that voted to leave the Texas Army and come here to fight for the USA, and Christian States of America separatists who just want to beat the tribals before they go home and start their own country, and a certain number of only slightly crazy hillbillies, rednecks, bikers, brawlers, bored teenagers, thugs, and goons who just want to get in on a fight against Daybreak because they like Daybreak even less than they like authority, and we're in process of parceling them out to units that will take them and getting them something resembling minimal training."

"I have a private letter, eyes only and no record, for you from Jenny Grayson."

He accepted it. "Thanks for delivering this."

"Heather and James wouldn't like it, so don't mention it to them."

"Heather and James are safe back in Pueblo. Or as safe as anyone can be, considering things like poor old Arnie Yang and Allie Sok Banh both were attacked by Daybreak right there in the city. And they don't like anything they don't control, because they are intelligence staff, and intelligence staff has been like that since some guy in Sumer was trying to stamp out unauthorized cuneiform." Phat opened the letter, and read. "She wrote this—"

"Just this morning, she wanted me to apologize for the last couple pages being so shaky, she literally wrote them on the fly—I should know, I was flying us."

He read, folded the letter, nodded. "What do you think of her? Your completely indiscreet unpolished opinion, I mean."

"You're the second RRC person to ask in the last couple of days. She's young, or she was, but she's getting older fast. Funny to say that about someone who's only a year younger than I am, but you know, back before, people had some choices about how mature to be, and now we don't, and she's at least willing to be more mature than she was a while ago. She's much brighter than her public image would make you think. She's had a lot of godawful shocks and she seems to be willing to learn from them.

"I think after her involvement in Cameron Nguyen-Peters's murder, we all thought of her as Barbie Macbeth with a side order of Too Much Jesus, and maybe that's what she started out as, but she learned from what happened. Or maybe she picked up some more rational ideas from her psycho husband. But however she did it, she's not putting so much priority on pleasing her idiot religious maniac father, or climbing the Temper power ladder, or collecting cheers from the crowd. I don't know what's really important to her, now, and maybe she doesn't either, but she's gotten over a lot of her dumber and more destructive ideas."

"That's my impression too." Phat seemed to be replaying something mentally, nodding as he did. "Chris Manckiewicz says he's impressed with her, but you know, Chris really does think all the time about how he is writing 'the first draft of history' and he thinks we're all going to be giants and legends in the next generation, so he's kind of, um—"

"Easily led into hero-worship," Bambi finished. "And a little in love with nearly all his subjects, and it's probably pretty easy for a straight male to be a little in love with this one. I know. Well, the next generation really does need heroes, and Jenny isn't any worse basis for a hero than any of the rest of us."

Phat nodded, having decided, and smoothed out the letter so Bambi could see it too. "I wanted to hear your opinion before I told you why. She's offering to slam the door shut behind Lord Robert and his horde; she can send a good-sized force north that would make it impossible for them to retreat if we beat them here. And a big smashing victory would probably cement me for the presidential election."

"What's she want in exchange?"

"Me to be her bad guy. In 2034, which is when my second term would be ending, she'll be old enough to run for president. By that time she needs the First National Church broken, or at least squashed back into being the very eccentric Post Raptural Church that seemed like a joke when it started, so she won't have it running a candidate on her right. And she can't be seen to be the one who suppressed it. It's actually not a bad deal; I'll have to tackle the Church early on, anyway, and it wouldn't hurt to have their main defender quietly cooperating with me." He tapped the letter in his hand. "If I'm going to be President of the Restored Republic, I will have to deal with worse than a realistic politician that killed an old friend of mine, won't I? And it's impossible to know what the specifics of the deal will involve, so we'd basically have to trust each other to keep our word."

Bambi nodded. "That's what you wanted to talk about?"

"Yes, I suppose so."

"Well, I'll say to you what I'd say to her if she asked me. Better to make a deal with a reasonable devil while you can, than with a crazy devil when you have to. But worst of all is to let yourself forget, even for one second, that it's a devil. Everybody's accepting a lot. Someday someone will find something they can't accept, and then we're all screwed."

FOURTEEN:
THE MAKING OF A DUCHESS

"We bow our heads around here, when we talk to God," an old man in a ministerial robe said to Jenny.

She ignored him, keeping her head upright and her eyes open. Her father was down front, repeating, "We just want to begin with a little prayer here to kind of unify things, so if you'd all bow your heads . . ."

"Bow your head for God," the old man said again.

Jenny turned to him. "God is not asking me to, you are. And because people like you presume to speak for God, I don't feel safe closing my eyes and looking down, because I can't trust you. I will talk to God my way; you can do what you like."

She must have spoken louder than she intended, because she saw her father look up at her, see who was standing next to her, and give a tiny but stern shake of his head. The old minister moved sideways as if he had received an electric shock, and walked down the aisle to join the extremist caucus that sat just right of the aisle. Reverend Whilmire's lip twitched slightly, as if the incident had amused him, but all he said was, "Let us pray."

It was a rambling, complicated prayer that verged on being a full-fledged lesson, with many citations in the form of "As you clearly told us in the verse of your word found in the book of . . ." Jenny smiled to herself. Most of the time when she was growing up, her father had complained about that format for prayers, "as if God hadn't read the Bible very well and needed footnotes, or like he was the Holy Tax Auditor and you were trying to argue the rules with him." Apparently Reverend Whilmire had come to the realization that whatever God might like, his followers wanted this.

When the prayer wound down through the last complex footnote and faded out in a burst of HOLYS, ETERNALS, DIVINES, and THEE-THOU-THY-THINES, the Reverend Whilmire announced, "I would now like to present my own daughter, Jenny Whilmire Grayson, who has recently returned from the expedition into the Lost Quarter, for her full report on the tragic situation there."

Jenny walked down the aisle wondering how many of those billowing black robes concealed pistols. Probably they wouldn't do anything that overt. At least not right in front of Daddy. Probably.

She couldn't help noting, when she glanced toward the too-small population of uniforms on the other side of the room, that their holsters were empty. *Funny nobody ever mentioned such a useful rule in political science class: in a revolutionary situation, the side of the legislature that has to check weapons at the door is losing.*

This was only supposed to be a report and a discussion, but she wasn't sure how soon that might change. She had heard distant shooting on her way here. It seemed as if in every block, some building had a cross, a fish, a star-stripe pattern, or "1789!" painted on its burned and blackened walls. Jardin had told her, unofficially, that there were anywhere from five to ten politics-connected deaths in Athens per day. A few officers had declined to be part of the Army delegation on the Board because they were afraid of being helplessly disarmed and surrounded by so many National Church people.

She did her best to tell the story absolutely straight, not minimizing the disaster, but also pointing out that the advantages were still mostly with the United States. "In short, there is little hope of destroying tribal power in the Lost Quarter, particularly the Castle Earthstone version, at least not for a year or two, unless they very badly overextend or make other big mistakes, and so far Lord Robert has not been making many mistakes. There is a fairly high chance of another defeat at Pale Bluff, and both symbolically and logistically, that's much worse. The land routes west are looted and burned out, and the tribes depend on looting to survive, so they'll almost certainly go down the Wabash and the Ohio for a drive into the middle of the country, probably a mass raid of opportunity, and because Kentucky, Tennessee, Missouri, and Arkansas are lined up with the Temporary National Government, that will hit our particular government and people very hard. They can hurt us, very badly, and we need to fight them wherever we can, but they still take many more deaths than we do in every encounter, and in the long run they don't do anything to rebuild their strength."

"Till now."

"Yes, Colonel Streen, you're right. Till now. Lord Robert's heresy is in some ways more threatening, because he's *not* trying to exterminate the human race, so he takes some care of his forces. But in other ways, honestly, he's a plain old conquering tyrant, and he's not very well armed, as long as no one supplies him, and there's nobody behind him—he doesn't have an assistant or a lieutenant worth talking about. When he does make a mistake he won't have much to recover with; he has an army and a territory that he has to keep together, so there's something for our armed forces to fight; and anyway, he might be killed in battle or the RRC might arrange something, and that will be the end of that menace. So for the moment Lord Robert's True Daybreak might get farther and win more battles than, what would you call it? Daybreak 1.0? but you have to keep in mind he's much more vulnerable too. His castle can be taken and torn down, his army can be defeated and broken instead of just scattering into the woods to fight again, they have crops we can burn and kids they'll cut a deal to save."

One of the reverends growled, "No deals with the Antichrist."

"I think it would be better to just knock him flat if we can, rather than cut a deal with him—but I don't think he's the Antichrist, either. And if we can't beat him right this minute, better to get a deal and then thrash him later. That's what I think." She looked around the room and saw some heads nodding, some arms folded, on both sides of the political divide.

"I'm going to take a moment to mention I'm proud of my daughter," Reverend Whilmire said. *Thanks, Daddy, that felt like a pat on the head.* "I suggest we take a few minutes' break to caucus and consider our options."

In a large, comfortable room that had probably once been some athletic official's office, he said, "I am proud of you, you know, and I do admire you. Your role is unBiblical but you are playing it so well."

"My role is what it needs to be," she said, "and I believe I already made it clear that I'm no longer giving you a vote about it."

"You did. Since you won't take my advice, though, I thought you might be willing to take my offer. The First National Church has adherents in places other than the Christian States of America, and we must never forget that the eventual goal is to have all the old states rejoin under a fully Christianized Constitution. We needed the first President under the Restored Republic to be someone who would work toward that goal, and we still do. And if the arrangements are coming unraveled, then we need the right first president for the CSA even more urgently. And so, even though you and I have some very deep disagreements theologically, it seems to me that with what you have shown you can do—"

"Daddy, are you suggesting you want to run me for president? Has it occurred to you that it's eight years till I'm eligible under the Constitution?"

"The Constitution was made to serve America, not vice versa. The country needs a popular, effective Christian president—"

"And a woman president? Wouldn't that be an unBiblical role?"

"It would. But these things can be changed over time—"

"Not if we're in Tribulation, Daddy. Less than six years left to go before Jesus shuts the whole show down, if you've been telling people the truth."

Whilmire gaped at her; his face was slack, but blood was rushing into it. "You are *mocking* me!"

"You don't believe it yourself, do you? You know in your heart that you are going to have to come up with some reason, when it gets to be seven years from Daybreak day, why that wasn't the Rapture, and it didn't start the Tribulation."

"My faith in the Bible is deep, complete, and not the issue here. You will not speak to your father that way."

"Or are you just hoping it will work out? You *want* it to have been the Tribulation, you don't *want* to be wrong, but at the same time you're afraid you might be, even if you won't admit it, so you keep making plans for what to do if the world doesn't end like you expect, because—"

He shouted; no words, just a cry as if he'd been punched in the stomach, and stormed out.

THAT EVENING. PADUCAH, KENTUCKY. 5 PM CENTRAL TIME. SATURDAY, MAY 9, 2026.

"But you *have* seen him," General Phat said, mildly, looking up from the maps spread out on his desk. "Twice since you've been here, and we've tried to make sure that happens. You just saw him this afternoon when he came to pick up the volley guns. The blackout will last till midnight tomorrow, at longest, and then you can fly over to Pale Bluff. I'm sorry that we've needed you and your plane so badly, or if it's made you feel like my chauffeur."

Bambi nodded at the apology. "Look, I know you've only asked me to fly these missions because they were absolutely necessary, and I know I saw Quattro a couple hours ago. But there's nothing left on our slate for tomorrow morning and blackout doesn't start till noon, and there's more than enough daylight for me to make Pale Bluff easily if I go right now, and the plane's fueled up and ready. And yes, I just plain want to be with my husband tonight, and I'm not technically under your command, I'm an RRC op helping you out, and for that matter, that's *my* airplane."

Since arriving here on Friday, she had ferried General Phat to half a dozen locations where he had applied some good old-fashioned shaking and desk-pounding to get troops and materiel flowing toward Pale Bluff. She had watched him push the people of Green Bay, New State of Superior, to load a whole supply and troop train and get it rolling in less than a day, persuade a militia regiment from Kentucky into moving a week early, and bring together another locomotive and string of boxcars in the ruins of St. Louis.

If Lord Robert's horde didn't hit till Tuesday evening or Wednesday morning, as expected, the reinforcements and supplies would reach Pale Bluff first, and they would have a good chance to break Lord Robert's horde before it got any farther. Till then, it was a race, and decades of leading troops had taught Phat that nothing caused motion like a demanding superior arriving in person. So they had flown, and flown, and flown again, the general scribbling fresh orders on his pad in the Stearman's front cockpit, then jumping out the moment they were on the ground, running off to cajole or bellow, whichever seemed to work, coming back almost as soon as Bambi had the Stearman refueled and checked out for takeoff again.

Quattro's last couple of days had been similar. After refitting the Gooney as a gunship/bomber, he had begun flying out children and the disabled from Pale Bluff, and flying in specialty weapons and crews from wherever they could be rounded up, together with experienced officers. With some coordinating and risky overuse of radio, it had been contrived that Quattro and Bambi had been on the ground in the same place for about forty minutes yesterday and twenty minutes today, spending most of the time clinging to each other.

"I know I'm being kind of ridiculous," Bambi said. "And we're not quite newlyweds, and sometimes we spend weeks apart, but . . . maybe it was just the way he reacted when he thought you were going to abandon Pale Bluff, the way he was when he decided to come out here, he just seemed like he'd made up his mind to die here—"

"I think I can understand your feelings." Phat rested his hands flat on his desk and said, "And if you were going to apologize for Quattro's impulsive actions—"

"I wasn't."

"Well, I was about to say you shouldn't. He made us try, and it wasn't till we started trying that we saw it might be possible to win. We need about three days of luck, and then maybe we can pin Lord Robert's horde between a fortified Pale Bluff and a rebuilt Army of the Wabash and send him back to hell where he belongs."

Bambi said, "But here's what's worrying me, and *nobody seems to be answering me.* We know that at Lafayette, Lord Robert pulled out a sizable force and let them sleep on the rafts most of the way, then had them run to the battlefield in a long burst and surprise us by getting there early. His forces started landing at St. Francisville this morning. I mean, Quattro flew over and shot up their advance guard, but he said the river was solid rafts and canoes for miles upstream. We had to call back the snag-cutting operation that was supposed to help block them because it was already too late.

"Nobody answers me when I ask, so what's to stop Lord Robert from just doing it again? What if an advance guard of tribals run all the way and hit Pale Bluff before we're ready?"

"It's thirty-seven miles from St. Francisville, which is the nearest point." General Phat stretched his thumb and index fingertips across the map, not quite reaching all the way between the towns. "That's a marathon and a half, Bambi, they're not going to run all that way and then assault the walls—"

"All right, so they'd have to do something more complicated." She set her thumb on St. Francisville and her index finger a comfortable distance to the west. "They *could*, that's the point. Maybe one team runs halfway, carrying supplies, and sets up a camp for the main force that were quick-marching empty-handed behind them." She closed her thumb up to her index finger. "Then the main force walks in, eats, gets a night's sleep, eats again, and . . ." She rotated her hand and brought her thumb down easily on Pale Bluff. "Tomorrow afternoon. It would still be way before we're ready—and in the middle of the blackout, so our planes will be on the ground and our radios turned off.

"I mean, maybe I'm crazy, but then again Lord Robert is crazy. Being crazy is his major strength. If he can pull something like that off, they might hit Pale Bluff tomorrow afternoon, and if my husband is there for that, I want to be there with him."

"That was what I thought you might be feeling," General Phat said. "It's really very natural and human, isn't it?" He walked to the office door and opened it slightly. "Mister Lyle, would you come in here, please, as we discussed?" Then he looked Bambi squarely in the eye, with complete sincerity. "I am so sorry for this."

The moment was so odd that she froze. Before she realized, two men had come through the door, and one was behind her. She started to struggle only as he grabbed her arms, but they knew what they were doing and she was handcuffed quickly.

General Phat sighed. "We are rapidly losing aircraft and pilots. Right now the most advanced working airplane on the continent is being risked in an exposed forward position, but I can't do anything about that. But I can't let the situation be worse. I can't let you take your plane into Pale Bluff until things are less dangerous, Bambi. I thought you'd understand but obviously you don't."

"Don't plan on having me or my plane ever again," Bambi said.

"It's a chance I'll have to take. I can't lose you—or the plane—right now. You're under arrest till the EMP or till blackout ends, whichever comes first. At that time I'll try to square it with you. But for the moment, I'm sure you've been through enough arrests from the other side to know that there's nothing personal and these men don't want to hurt you."

ABOUT 11 HOURS LATER. PALE BLUFF, WABASH. 4:15 AM CENTRAL TIME. SUNDAY, MAY 10, 2026.

Quattro Larsen had been awake since the rain had stopped, about half an hour ago, unable to sleep longer because he was so on edge. He always slept badly without Bambi. He had been hoping she'd make it back before blackout, but meanwhile, well, blackout wasn't till noon, and the last rain-clouds now billowed down beyond the eastern horizon, with a wind rising from the west. Pre-dawn twilight seemed brighter than usual, perhaps because there had been so little light the last few nights, perhaps due to the almost-half moon well up in the sky.

It was light, he was awake and dressed, and he really wanted to know what the hell was going on over east. He stuck his head into the ground crew quarters and said, softly, "Cup of coffee in it for anyone wants to be door gunner for me."

Caleb made it to the door first by carrying his shoes rather than trying to put them on, and only vaguely stuffing his shirt into his pants. Quattro felt a slight pang at having lured the guy with coffee, but on the other hand, he didn't seem to be complaining.

"Take a sec and put your shoes on, Caleb, the job is yours. Nice clear day, maybe a little windy."

"I can't sleep anyway. It's getting near, isn't it, sir?"

"We're going to fly out and find out how near. I'm hoping they're still sorting things out at St. Francisville, and if they are, we'll just take a quick pass around and remind them that real Daybreakers are not supposed to like Mister Gun. At least not Mister Gun in the Gooney. And maybe lay some bombs where they'll make people nervous and slow them down. If we find them on the way here, it's the same program but more urgent, and we get back here as fast as we can."

He'd been sleeping in the DC-3, partly as a guard, partly for a quick takeoff if he had to, mostly because it was home, and so his little oil stove, percolator, and coffee stash were there. As they huddled around the hot pot for a few minutes till the coffee was ready, he gave Caleb a lightning review on how the Gatling worked, how to clear it, and most importantly, "now, you leave that locked down, 'cause I'll aim it with the plane and we don't want you shooting holes in the plane or yourself on your first mission. You keep your seat belt on and your feet on the braces. Crank when I holler crank, stop when I holler stop, and yell 'Jam!' when it does, which it will. Then wait for me to yell that we're level and clear before you try to unjam it. We are going out with a crew of two, and we are coming back with a crew of two, and if you fall out that door, I'm a pretty awesome pilot, but swinging around and catching you might be more than I want to try, 'kay? All right, now about the bombs—"

As he poured the coffee, Quattro explained the basic mechanics of lightly screwing together the three glass jars that formed the shape of the bomb: the big piece with fins, filled with turpentine, the nose piece filled with strong acid, and the little sealed vessel that went into the nose tip, with a blob of mercury in it. "Never tighten down hard, always remember it's thin glass meant to break. Put them in the ready rack with the fins facing you. If one of them starts to sputter just toss it out the door. You hand load them one at a time into the bomb rack, tail toward you, so they roll down and come out pointed nose first. Never, never-ever, *don't* load another bomb till the first one clears, and if you have to push a stuck one through, holler so I know, and wait till I take the plane up high and level it off, because you'll have to kind of hang partway out the door and poke it with the mop handle that's on the bracket there. The one rule about that is *poke the fins, not the nose.*"

Caleb's eyes widened. "Uh, yeah."

"I know it's obvious but you'd be surprised how many obvious things people get wrong. And with bombs I don't like surprises."

Caleb clearly enjoyed the coffee, taking it with enough sugar and powdered milk to make it something of a meal in its own right, but he also seemed at least as eager as Quattro to get into the air. *Probably the same damn silly romantic streak I've got. He's gonna be able to tell people he was the door gunner for the Duke of California, I guess, and if there was any place much left to dine out, he'd be dining out on that. Next to that, what's a hot cup of aristocratic privilege?* "Now, let's make sure you know how to strap in, since I won't be able to help you with it when it's time to rock and roll. But till I need a gunner, you might as well ride front seat. It's mostly a reconnaissance flight, and two sets of eyes will see more."

The takeoff was smooth, and they gained altitude in a wide swing to the west, staying high in hopes of seeing before they were seen. Quattro angled a little north to pick up the Little Wabash River, following it for a few miles till turning east along the bullet-straight county roads.

Mornings and evenings were good times to see detail, but the immense swarming camp that suddenly appeared below them would have been impossible to miss.

"Holy crap," Caleb breathed.

"So right, dude. And we're only—I'm gonna set it to circle and see if I can read a mile marker through the binocs—"

"No need, I'm from around here, man, that's where County 13 takes a bend and becomes County 9. They're only sixteen and a half miles from Pale Bluff. And look at all that smoke rising; they're cooking already this morning."

"Probably fixing a meal for the guys that are supposed to run in and kill us," Quattro agreed. "All right, I'm going to circle once to get my bearings and see if I can figure out where the leaders are sleeping. You might as well go back and get ready on the bombs."

They had circled twice when Caleb screwed the last fuse into the last nose, lowered the bomb rack out the door, and announced, "All ready!"

"All right, going in, put the first one on the bomb rack and don't let him roll till I yell 'now!'"

It was not a steep dive by any means, but it felt strange and Caleb clung to the locked-down bomb rack until, as the plane leveled off, zooming low over the tribal camp, Quattro shouted, "Now!"

Caleb let the first one roll; it was about as long as his torso, holding three gallons of turpentine besides its fuse. He turned, hugged the other, set it on the bomb rack, looked down to make sure it was clear, and saw the flash of the first bomb bursting below. He kept hugging, lifting, and letting them roll, as fast as he could, and shouted "fifteen!" as the last one went.

"Hold on!" Quattro put it into a climb; through the open door, Caleb could see that there were fires blazing up from a couple of tents, people running around, and arrows and rocks flying ineffectively into the air.

The plane leveled off as they drew away and higher. "Strap in."

Caleb did, checked the Gatling, and waited to turn the crank. This time the enemy knew they were coming, and scattered before the stream of bullets that Quattro walked down one long aisle of tents and up another; twice, Caleb cleared jams, but for a Newberry Gatling, this thing really hadn't worked badly at all. As they climbed up for another reconnaissance circle, Quattro said, "Well, that was pretty much just spite. They know we saw them and a few of them are hurt or dead, and some more had a bad scare. It won't slow them up even five minutes, but at least they know we don't like them."

. . .

During the ten minutes or so it took to return to the airfield, Quattro dictated and Caleb scribbled. "The second I brake the props, run and wake up the ground crew and tell them to get out here; won't need any more fuel but if I can get some reloading I might be able to get in a few more bomb-and-shoot runs before we're in blackout. But don't wait around for an answer; just wake'em up, get'em moving, and then run to HQ with that note. Tell them it's extremely urgent, and from me, and that your orders are to only put it in the hands of Colonel Birdsall."

They had been in the air such a short time that the linen tires had not begun their usual deflation; the plane touched down almost as well as it would have on the old rubber. Quattro taxied around to the arsenal end of the hangar, killed the engine, and yanked the prop brake. The props had barely thudded to a stop when Caleb jumped out and ran across the gravel toward ground crew quarters.

Quattro had shoved the ramp against the door and was rolling another load of bombs up when the ground crew rushed in to take over and begin loading; that gave him a moment to check his watch. Not quite 6 a.m. yet; it had already been a busy morning. Someone handed him a sandwich and a mug of chicory; he gulped it down without tasting while the crew ran through the checklist. By that time Asanté Collins, his regular gunner/bombardier, had scrambled there from the barracks, and they were ready to go again. "We'll get that turnaround down to five minutes next time," the chief assured him.

"Seventeen minutes from just waking up to ready to go isn't too shabby as it is," Quattro said, "but yeah, they'll be running toward us for about four hours to come, and that's nearly all before blackout, so we can fly against them all that time."

Collins nodded. "Is it going to do much good? Bunch of guys running through a field, I can spray but I don't know that I'll get many hits."

"Yeah, and it's way too wet to get a prairie fire going in front of them, too, at least this morning. Mostly we just do what we can and hope to slow them down a little, but most of the effect will probably just be to scare them and make them lie down for a minute or two while we're right over-head. I wish we could do more but I don't see how."

"Yeah, well, I think you're right. At least we help them understand that they are not wanted, and it's always possible we'll hit a leader or something, if they have leaders now. I'm ready when you are, Your Dukeliness."

Quattro laughed and switched hats back to his flying helmet. The two of them ran the checklist one more time, and took off.

. . .

When they heard the plane coming in, the tribals running at the front of the group scattered into the ditches beside the road and lay down; Quattro circled to strafe and bomb along the ditches. "Too wet to get a grass fire going," Asanté shouted.

"You still got some ammo left?"

"About ten-fifteen percent reserve—"

"When I say use it, do it."

As soon as Asanté was strapped in again, Quattro climbed steeply up and away, as if departing, and said, "Hold on tight, I'm going to come in out of the sun, fast and low, once I loop around."

This worked somewhat better; Quattro flew virtually as if doing a touch-and-go parallel to the road, keeping his speed up but flying only about ten feet off the abandoned, grassy field. The road was raised a couple of feet, just enough for Asanté to be able to rake it chest high, and because the running tribals had not been ordered to take cover, and were bunched up like the main pack in a marathon, many more bullets hit bodies; when Quattro circled around one final time, they could see that there were dozens of people lying on the road.

But even as Quattro pointed the nose homeward, Asanté pointed out, "They're just stepping right over their dead and wounded and coming right on," and Quattro noted that they had been almost two miles closer than their night camp.

When they landed again, Pale Bluff was awake. Troops were moving through the streets and out into the orchards, toward their positions along and behind the outer walls. The reserves were mustering in the town park by the Civil War memorial. Civilians carried bags and boxes to their support stations. "They might not win but they won't be unprepared," Quattro said quietly.

"Ready now," the ground chief said. "Four twenty-two. And we topped up your fuel and lye. We'll get it under four next time."

This time they flew very low and crossed the T on the enemy column, shooting up the avant garde (but most of them made it safely into the ditch), raking back along the road until they were out of ammunition, then bombing their way back up to the head.

This attack had no more effect than the previous one. The advancing Daybreakers had already flung the corpses into the ditch and were back at a run. Quattro made a low pass at full throttle, scaring them back into the ditch with the roar, but Asanté, looking back through the main door, saw them standing up as soon as the plane had passed.

As they descended toward the airfield, Quattro noted that the brush windrows on the east-side roads were growing quickly, and that damming the drainage ditches and opening the irrigation gates upstream was rapidly flooding the cornfields. "There'll be some pretty effective sniping for the last few hundred yards," he said.

"Has to be a lot, to make them care," Asanté said. "Tell you two things right here, Your Dukeliness; one, I'm scared, more than I've ever been, and two, I'm glad my family's not here with me."

They flew sorties for the rest of the morning, and each time the distance to the oncoming Daybreakers was shorter. "Do you think we're accomplishing anything?" Quattro asked.

"Man, worrying about stuff like that is a Ducal issue. Me, I work the gun, I load the bombs, and I figure I don't like these guys and I don't want them to think I do, and this definitely makes sure I get that across to them." Asanté sighed. "Getting tired?"

"Yeah. You must be exhausted."

"I can keep going as long as I have to."

"Yeah. Well, up for another?"

This time, the Daybreakers were not even over the horizon, and since there was no other air traffic, Quattro just whipped the plane around in a steeply banked turn, dove to almost ground level, and headed straight up the road at full throttle. He had guessed right; the tribal horde was now between overflowing ditches, and some of them hesitated at the brink of the water for an instant too long; Asanté's gun cut them down.

As they pulled up from the shooting run, over the thundering engines, Asanté shouted, "Quattro, I got an idea!"

"Good, 'cause I haven't had one in a while!"

"All those guys further back with backpacks, gunpowder maybe?"

"Or just food or loot."

Asanté climbed carefully forward and leaned in close so Quattro could hear him. "What if we bomb a bunch of big-pack-people between ditches? I mean, fly in a tight circle and keep dropping the bombs there? If it's gunpowder they either burn or take it into the water. If it's anything else, no big diff."

"Worth a try. Let each one roll when I shout *release!*; if we're going to try to put fifteen bombs on one small target, we'll have to make fifteen passes, and we probably have to stay under a thousand feet to have any hope of hitting something we're aiming at. I'm going to sort of cloverleaf or figure-eight it so we don't become too good a target. Be ready in five; I'll go looking for a backpack group."

Quattro flew in a sort of meandering S along the two-mile long column of Daybreakers. *Man, another place where we were stupid, way back, Arnie Yang was telling us to make poison gas. If I could have laid about a ton of that down on their camp and kept hosing them with it all morning, these guys would be about whipped by now. Sometimes it pisses Bambi or Heather off that James talks about how dumb it was to kill him, but James is damn well right. Or at least we should have listened to his advice. There's—ah-hah.* Below him, a couple hundred tribals were flinging themselves along the road, heavy packs reaching from their beltlines to a foot over their heads. Behind them about twice their number trotted; probably they spelled each other to keep moving at the same pace as the rest of the horde. Maybe those packs held the mattresses for Lord Robert's sacred orgies, maybe looted jars of peanut butter, but this was worth a shot. "'Santé, how we doing?"

"Ready when you are."

"All right, here we go." He put the DC-3 into a shallow dive across the pack-bearers, and trying to visualize how long it took a bomb to drop, shouted "release" when he thought it should work.

This first shot went way over, landing and bursting into flames on the other side of the ditch without doing more than startling the runners, but to judge by the reaction, they had reason to fear flame; they bunched and huddled. Quattro threw the Gooney into a tight turn, almost standing on its wing, came in at another angle, and shouted "release!"

Undershot this time, but not by much; the bomb splashed into the ditch. Around again, and now they were clearly bunching up, trying to find some way to get away from the plane. He aimed, he visualized, he let things be, and said, "Release!"

This one burst among the packs, and the panic was immediate. Whatever was in them was flammable, if not explosive, and fire blazed up from the road below. Two more bombs created a panic and an apparent riot.

"Let's try two more of those backpack bunches," Quattro shouted. They flew farther down the line, and the results were identical; whether that was fuel, ammunition, sapper's supplies, or whatever, the stuff in the square white backpacks was obviously a bad thing in a fire. As they turned away from the last bomb, Quattro felt some grim satisfaction; he wished he had learned earlier, but now he finally knew how to hurt them from the air.

Something thumped and Asanté shouted "Incoming!"

"Hold on!" Quattro threw the DC-3 hard to the left, righted it, and opened the throttle into as much climb as the old plane had with far less engine power than it was designed for. To his right, he saw broad-headed spears passing, trailing long pieces of wire; same gadget they'd killed Nancy Teirson with. He heard two clanking thuds from the rear. "Did those penetrate?"

"Nope!" Asanté took the seat next to him. "Sounded like someone throwing a brick against a garage door, but nothing came in."

At first he thought they'd gotten clean away, but then he noticed that the rudder wasn't responding. "Probably there's a spear jammed in the rudder, or maybe they cut a control line. No big one, I can land this without it. But we'll have to get the ground crew right on it and we might not get it fixed before we have to shut down for blackout."

"Damn. You and me could end up mere ground-pounders."

"You know it, dude." Quattro glanced sideways at his gunner, who was grinning at him; he grinned back. "Actually that scared the piss out of me, you know."

"Yeah. Well, they didn't get us."

On touchdown the loud bang-thump made them both jump, and the tail wheel felt draggy. Sure enough, when they climbed out, they found a spear butt wedged in the rudder, and the tail tire was a torn cloth bag around the wheel. "Thirty minutes," the ground chief said. "Go get yourselves something to eat. Might be a chance for one more mission before blackout starts, or we might have to start grounding and shutdown as soon as it's finished, but either way, we can do it, you've trained us more than well enough, and having you tired and impatient and pissed off and worried about your goddam baby here is not going to help a bit. Now go eat, breathe, maybe get a dump, we have work to do here."

"You know," Quattro said to Asanté as they gulped down bland, bean-laden chili that ordinarily he'd have thought a disgrace, "that guy was fixing lawnmowers and snowblowers three years ago. Now he's as high tech as it gets."

Asanté nodded. "It ain't a very nice world anymore but it makes more sense." He tore off a chunk of bread from the loaf between them, dipped it in the almost-chili, and gobbled hungrily from it. "At least I know how everything works. And I haven't had to look for work. How's that Duke job working out?"

"Better than I wanted it to," Quattro admitted. Huddled over the little table in the corner of the improvised hangar, which had been a boarded-up church before its steeple was commandeered for a tower, they watched crew scurrying in and out, and let the food warm and hearten them. Part of his mind feared that he would look like the idle aristocrat eating while others did urgent work, but everyone here knew how they had spent their morning.

It was a quarter of twelve, almost an hour later, when the chief said, "You'd be good to go if we didn't have to ground it right this minute, for blackout. We've got—"

A clatter of gunfire from the east.

They all turned.

Smoke was rising high into the sky from the blazing brush windrows that were supposed to bar the roads and force the enemy into the flooded fields; the gunfire grew in intensity, and half a dozen donkeys and mules towing Gatlings and volley guns appeared on the far end of the airfield, headed for the noise.

. . .

The road east ended in fire, and on each side it was surrounded by water. The soldiers on the low earthen wall were out of range of the tribals' weapons, so a great deal of their time was spent merely watching closely. A group of a hundred or so tribals would pop out from behind the burning windrow and splash into the muddy, ruined cornfields, trying to charge at the wall; the soldiers would shoot them down. Another group would emerge; sometimes a group from each side of the windrow; sometimes as many as four groups at once.

The Gatlings and the volley guns arrived, and then the reserve troops who waited behind the wall, plus snipers who climbed into the apple trees, and every few minutes there would be another massacre in the muddy field, until it was a wide scattering of corpses on mud.

Messages went back and forth to Colonel Birdsall for an hour.

No, no trace had been seen of the one-shot muskets that had done so much damage at Lafayette.

No, where guards still patrolled the walls facing the unflooded land, there was no sign of a flanking maneuver.

No, it was not possible to see anything beyond the burning brush; 150 yards of dry deadwood, piled four yards high, was too big a fire to see what lay beyond it.

Yes, everyone was staying ready.

Through binoculars and spyglasses, some of the officers on the wall were able to observe that at the far end of the fire, there was occasional movement. Their best guess was that the tribals there were slowly dragging or knocking the burning brush into the overflowing ditches, perhaps advancing into the fire by throwing buckets of water ahead. It might take an hour or two for them to clear the fire; then they would have to come straight up the road, and the heavy weapons were already trained on it and waiting.

Birdsall himself came out to that stretch of wall. "We haven't seen five percent of their force," he said. "But from the steeples and the trees, we can see for miles all around. The nearest place they could hide a force that big would be on the other side of the bluff itself, three miles away, and at least on the map, I don't see how they'd get there." His officers all nodded. "This Lord Robert is smart; possibly much smarter than I am. There's some reason he would keep launching these futile attacks, but it doesn't seem like a diversion for a flanking attack, because I don't see any way he can get at the flanks. And as for—"

Shouts from the watchers on the wall and in the trees.

When everyone looked, they saw that tribals had become visible, through the flames and smoke, beyond the burning windrow. So big and hot a fire could not have lasted in any case, but it was clear now that Daybreakers had simply attacked it with shovels, buckets, and sticks, putting it out, shoving burning matter to the side, and splashing water to cool the road. Snipers took shots at some of the clearing crew, but it was clear that in a few minutes, the road would be open again.

Birdsall looked around at his officers again. "What did this Lord Robert character want us to focus on instead of—"

Drums began to boom, and from each side of the dwindling fire, many hundreds of tribals swarmed across the field of corpses, led as always by spirit sticks, in long, thin lines. Gunfire rattled and banged from the wall and the trees, and the defenses were shrouded in their own black smoke; the Gatlings and volley guns swept the field, adding to the smoke and noise.

There were so many of the oncoming tribals that a few lucky ones almost reached the wall before two and three soldiers in a group would shoot them down.

Birdsall tried to see through the smoke; then he realized there was no longer a plume above the burning windrow, that the Daybreakers had at last cleared the road, and though he didn't know what was coming, he suddenly knew what they had to do. "Reload!" he shouted. "All weapons! Now! *Reload now!*"

A dark shape moved through the blue-black smoke of that immense volley, on the road, and a few soldiers shot at it; it was big, perhaps the size of an old-style two-car garage, and rested on enormous spoked wheels, something from some strange museum piece. The shots screamed off it in a shower of sparks; it was armored with pieces of sheet metal on it every which way, several thicknesses of them—there must be fifty or more people pushing it—

Birdsall realized, "It's a bomb! Shoot, shoot, we can't let them push it here!"

The troops who had reloaded shot at whatever they could see or find; as the juggernaut rolled in toward them, with the pushers now actually running, some pushers went down clutching a shattered knee or ankle, or fell out of the pack where a lucky shot had found a way through the armor.

Behind the juggernaut came a sort of huge metal turtle; men running with corrugated metal sheets held out to the sides or over their heads, and something in between and under. Birdsall shouted for someone to take some shots at whatever that was, as well, but in the din of gunfire he couldn't be heard, and most of the troops who could fire were concentrating on the onrushing bomb.

As it rolled up to the thick log gate that closed the road into town, Birdsall screamed, "Down! Take cover!" Most of the soldiers did; the explosion that knocked the log gate flat killed very few of them. They were deafened and stunned, but on their feet. There had been a carnage, but it was of the Daybreakers pushing the wheeled bomb; their remains stained the road red.

"Reload and fire on that next target!" Birdsall shouted, again, but he could not hear his own voice; when he touched his ear, he found blood running down. The metal turtle came on; when shots felled one shield carrier, someone else within grabbed the shield and closed the hole.

Birdsall shouted to them to shoot low, to try to get under the shielding metal, and he shot there himself, but the defenders had simply been overwhelmed, first by the suicide rush, then by the bomb cart, and now with this. Many were fumbling to reload, some were trying to clear jams, and most were deaf from the blast and blind from the smoke. So the turtle was almost at the gate when the metal sheets were thrown aside, and from beneath it, almost a hundred tribals rushed—each clutching a Newberry submachine gun.

Objectively the Daybreaker submachine-gunners were poor fighters. They wasted ammunition, often not even aiming. Some of them were blinded, maimed, killed as guns blew up in their hands. But they kept coming, kept shoving in fresh drums of ammunition until the guns blew up, and kept attacking every living soldier they could find around the gate.

Automatic fire at such close range, in such volume, swept Birdsall's forces away from the gates, drove the crews away from their heavy weapons, and opened the gap for a critical few minutes, as ten thousand Daybreakers, spirit sticks, hatchets, clubs, torches, and spears raised high and screaming for Mother Gaia, poured into the orchards and toward the town. Birdsall's thoughts, dying among others on the wall, were first that he didn't think a messenger could get to town with a warning before the tribals did, then that anyway he had no messengers, and finally that his tummy really hurt and he wanted to go home now.

. . .

When the first tribals with spears appeared at the other end of the field, Quattro, Asanté, and the ground crew had already pulled off the grounding wires and reconnected everything on the Gooney. "I still wish," the chief began.

"They'll burn it and us with it on the ground here," Quattro said. "And we don't know that the moon gun shot was even aimed anywhere near us. The last few have been over Pueblo, and the jolt from that might damage a radio, but it won't shut off my ignition. And we only need to fly about forty minutes to reach Paducah and safety. So die for sure here, or try to make it out on the Gooney. Now departing from all gates, dude."

The ground crew piled in, the chief going last, and strapped down on the benches. Asanté took his place at the gun. Quattro revved up; the sound of the plane apparently attracted more tribals, for suddenly they were running out onto the end of the runway. He gave the engine full throttle and roared toward them, lifting off just in time to clear them by scant feet, and climbing as quickly as the Gooney could manage.

The brilliant flash of light gave him just a moment to realize that the EMP, this time, was right overhead. The spark for the engines stopped, and they coughed on fuel-air mix they could not ignite, the propellers slowing, not even finishing a complete turn. Wires on the plane reached far above their kindling points, but most did not have time to burst into flame; the men in the back were lashed by shocks but the signals from the neurons just under their skin never reached their brains.

In the small airspace in one of the almost-full fuel tanks, a spark touched off an explosion just big enough to rupture the tank and mix the fuel thoroughly into the air in the heated, sparking interior of the plane; there was a moment of terrible light and pain, and then nothing for those within. Outside, in the burning town strewn with bodies, the cheers and drumming grew louder and louder.

2 HOURS LATER. PADUCAH, KENTUCKY. 3:30 PM CENTRAL TIME. SUNDAY, MAY 10, 2026.

He was the sort of guy that Lyndon Phat had always disliked on sight, and always forced himself to be nice to. Somehow, even through the food shortages and the disappearance of most mechanical work-savers in the past year and a half, this guy Davey Prinche had managed to remain pudgy and out of shape; there was something subtly dirty and messy about every aspect of him, from his grimy T-shirt to his crude coat-hanger glasses, and from the dirty dishes scattered among the tools on his workbench to the grime under his fingernails.

But he had invented an EMP detector and direction finder that worked even for a close-in hit like this one, and if listening to him brag about how clever he had been was part of the price of having it, well, so be it. He was nattering away right now. "The big trick was realizing that these old-style recording thermometers were mechanical and wouldn't react to the EMP. So as long as all the loops are identical, the ones that got the hottest are the ones where the plane of the loop was closest to parallel to the wave front coming out of the EMP, and by doing a linear interpolation between the hottest and second hottest pair of loops on each side of the circle, and stretching that string between the points, we can come up with a more exact direction. So, yeah, it was right over Pale Bluff, at least if the topo maps from back before were accurate."

Phat thanked him and didn't wince while shaking his hand. He raced down the stairs, a couple of aides chattering after him. On the street outside he told them, "Be polite, and she won't be, but have Bambi meet me at the airfield. I'm taking the pedicab."

He told his pedicabbie, "Airfield, right away."

Ground crew had cleared the Stearman to fly by the time that Bambi rode up on horseback. "This was their quickest way to get me here," she said, dismounting and handing the reins to a slightly bewildered lieutenant, who managed to persuade the horse to go with him off the field, but it looked like the deal might unravel at any moment. "Are you going to give me my plane back?"

"You must have felt that EMP even in the shelter—"

"Even in jail," she said. "We'll stick to right names for things."

"In jail, then. I am sorry I had to put you there. But the EMP was directly over Pale Bluff, and we have not been able to raise them on the radio. We need to take a look right away, and I'm going to ask you to fly me over—"

"Get in."

She talked to the ground crew chief for less than a minute, until another ground crew member came running up with her flying helmet, scarf, and jacket. "Thanks for taking care of these," she said. She looked around at the ground crew. "Remember you can always come to California, if anything gets shitty out here, 'kay?"

She hopped up on the wooden step and into the plane so quickly that Phat couldn't think of anything to say; he just got into the front, passenger cockpit. Ground crew wheeled up the magneto cart, connected it to her coil, and cranked it to charge the capacitors.

"Chocks out?"

"Chocks out."

"Charge?"

"At charge."

"Coupez!"

They unhooked the magneto cart and rolled it away; Bambi engaged the prop clutch. "Coupez," the ground chief confirmed, walking around to the prop, and grasping one tip.

"Contact!"

He spun the prop hard and stepped back; with bang and a couple of pops, the engine fired and caught. Bambi disengaged the clutch for a moment to let it rev up to speed; these cold starts with a deliberately dead battery, after an EMP, were always touchy affairs, but the short flight to Pale Bluff should be enough to recharge.

She engaged the prop and taxied around slowly; the engine was still running fine, so she opened the throttle and headed down the runway, into the air, and out over the broad green Ohio River, across into Illinois, and on to the northeast.

80 MINUTES LATER. PALE BLUFF. 5:50 PM CENTRAL TIME. SUNDAY, MAY 10, 2026.

Thirty miles away, they could see the columns of dense black smoke. Bambi circled above the town, taking a look from all angles; the Daybreakers had managed to get the orchards burning despite the damp (the smell like frying oil meant that perhaps they had used fuel from the airfield). Bodies by the hundred lay in the streets and along the walls. Some of the tribals were still in the town, carrying armfuls of whatever had caught their fancy, or dancing in lines behind spirit sticks and drums.

She swooped lower, and then Phat saw what she had seen: the Gooney Express lying on its back, the rear part of the fuselage bent as if with giant pliers, at the end of the runway. A lower pass revealed a great, gaping hole on the bent side; black char covered the old yellow-and-black checkered markings.

She brought the Stearman around and he started to lean back to confer with her, but she shoved his head out of her way, and landed the plane, threading between bodies on the runway as she brought it around and taxied back to the Gooney. By the bigger plane, she locked the clutch down so that the propeller was disengaged and whuffed to a halt. Leaving the engine running, she jumped out and ran to the Gooney.

Phat could not think what to do; they had seen tribals in the town, they couldn't afford to be caught here on the ground, was she out of her mind with grief?

She knelt beside the open door of the overturned, burnt plane, peered inside, and began to keen and wail. Tentatively, Phat climbed out of the Stearman and approached her, trying to think how to tell her that they had to go, afraid to say he was sorry, afraid to sound wrong in any way.

When he was close enough to see the texture of her leather flying jacket, Bambi stood, turned, sighed, and drew a pistol from her jacket. "You are not getting back on my plane," she said. "Move that way"—she pointed toward the orchard—"or I will shoot."

He stood without speaking or moving, realizing what this must mean, until she fired a shot into the dirt to his right. He flinched away, and she said, "You know I'm a better shot than that. Next one is into your center. Run."

He had been stout, back before, and he was in worse shape now, but he turned and ran, an undignified, pumping, fast waddle, for the trees. Before he reached them, behind him, he heard Bambi shout, "I told you it was my airplane!"

The propeller engaged in a deep buzzing roar. When he turned around he saw the Stearman racing down the runway and taking off.

General Lyndon Phat stood and stared at it. From here she could reach St. Louis, Columbia, or Iowa City, easily, and be refueled without question. It would be hours before they were overdue in Paducah. He had a pistol under his jacket, and a reserve knife strapped to his thigh, and nothing else.

The drumming grew louder and closer. He turned around to see a flock of tribal shamans walking toward him, with hundreds of armed men behind them. Reckoning that with four shots in the revolver, he didn't want to take a chance on the last one being a misfire, he took a firm shoulder-width stance, shook out his shoulders (still stiff from the flight that had ended only minutes ago), relaxed, steadied, and shot two of the men carrying spirit sticks. As the rest began to run toward him, he put the still-hot muzzle into his mouth, ignoring the burning because it was just for a moment, pushed far back and up, and pulled the trigger.

. . .

Bambi Castro Larsen, Duchess of California, did not look back, or even think again about the vile little man. He was in the past. *This is my airplane,* she thought. *They'll refuel me on my say-so at Columbia, and again in Hays. Once I'm at Hays, I'll have to decide whether to avoid Heather and fly on to Vernal, or face up to things and fly down to Pueblo. Heather better not expect me to turn myself in, but I feel like I owe her a confession, and an apology for the things that didn't work out. And if she ever needs it, I'll never turn her away from Castle Larsen.*

But maybe not. She might try to arrest me or hold me for having gotten rid of General Shithead, instead of thanking me that he didn't end up as our president. And nobody's making me that helpless again. Nobody. I have my airplane and my Castle, and I'm going to keep them. I've already lost my Duke and my country.

3 HOURS LATER. COLUMBIA, MISSOURI. 9 PM CENTRAL TIME. SUNDAY, MAY 10, 2026.

There wasn't much of twilight left as Bambi came in to the field, but unlike so many of the places she flew the Stearman into and out of, Columbia had been a real airport, back before, though a small one, and there was so much room on a jetliner runway that the Stearman could practically have landed crossways. She taxied up to the hangar, shut down, and climbed out of the plane.

"Always a pleasure to have you here, ma'am," the ground chief said. Bambi couldn't quite remember her name, and it took her another moment to think, *Right, I'm in Columbia, en route to Pueblo.*

"Good to be down for the night," Bambi said. "I'm pretty well exhausted. Can I just ask you to fit my plane out, and if there's a carriage to the hotel—"

"We'll have you there right away. You look pretty well worn-out, ma'am."

She had to be awakened when the carriage came by, almost an hour later. The hotel was just an old religious-retreat facility near the airport, but the staff knew how she liked things, so when she staggered into the only room with a private bath, it was all set up, with the tub already filled with hot water and towel-covered board covering it. There was bread, meat, and cheese on the sideboard. She made up three sandwiches, stripped, ate while she soaked, toweled off, and fell asleep on top of the covers without setting an alarm.

FIFTEEN: THE LAST PRESIDENT

THE NEXT DAY. PUEBLO. 10 AM MOUNTAIN TIME. MONDAY, MAY 11, 2026.

James wished they had met at his home; Heather's office was comfortable enough, and the logbooks and records were there, but it would have felt good to be cooking. Here, he had nothing to do. A review of the facts would have been useless.

All three of them were miserably aware that there had been an EMP over Pueblo, just after Carol May's last fragmentary radio message, in clear, that the tribal horde was inside the walls. About an hour later, Phat had sent the cryptic message from Paducah that he was going to take a look himself with Bambi Castro, and nothing had been heard since. The Army of the Wabash had only reached Terre Haute yesterday, finding everything destroyed, and would not have air reconnaissance that could reach Pale Bluff until Sally Osterhaus reached them in her Piper Cub later this week.

It was what they had known last night, what they had known this morning, what they had known while they pretended to eat breakfast.

So they sat and waited. Leslie was restlessly patting her dog; Wonder had picked up on her nervousness and was whining and nervously licking her. Heather was fussing over Leo much more than usual, and he wasn't happy about it. *The Good Soldier* lay neglected in James's lap.

Something caught the corner of his eye out the window. "Patrick's coming, and he's running hard."

Heather moved Leo into his crib, opened the door, and called down to the guards to wave Patrick through. She shoved a wad of meal tickets into the boy's hand. "Sorry, guy, urgent and secret, no socializing this time. Take a rest someplace where you can hear us yell from the window."

Patrick looked—*stunned?* James thought. *No, scared. Because he's never seen us so scared before, and we're the people he depends on to keep the world working. Man, I wish I had someone I could depend on like he depends on us.*

The moment the door closed, Heather ripped the envelope open, pulling out an inner envelope on which Ruth Odawa had written *I suggest highest possible security.*

Heather sighed, sat, opened it, read, looked again, and said, "She wasn't kidding. It's from Bambi. Here's the short version: as far as she could determine, everyone in Pale Bluff was killed, though there may still be some survivors hiding out. The city is a total loss. Quattro died on takeoff, and the Gooney Express was totally destroyed. Here's a strange sentence: 'You may assume Lyndon Phat is also dead.' She's in Columbia, Missouri— or she was, she's in the air now, she'll refuel at Hays and then come here— and she says, full report then. And one last detail: she won't come here to my office, or anywhere in the city. We have to meet her at the airport."

"What the hell could that mean?"

"We'll probably find that out at the airport," Heather said. "She's estimating she'll come in about four p.m."

"Wow," Leslie said quietly. "A week ago we thought we were winning the war, worried about getting Phat elected if Grayson ran well or Weisbrod was a spoiler . . . now, there's no Phat, no Grayson, no Graham Weisbrod . . . no Quattro . . ." Her voice cracked. "Sorry, the rest were people I'd worked with and respected, but Quattro was like, like—"

"Everybody's hero. I feel like crying myself. And there's no Pale Bluff," James said quietly. "We've lost the living presence of almost anything we could build a myth out of, to put the country back together. God, I'll miss Pale Bluff the most. Every issue of the *Post-Times*, you had this little town struggling bravely on, making the new America. I mean, I knew how Arnie Yang was playing those sentimental cards, he showed me before he was turned, and I've been doing it myself for months, now, too, and . . . that story's over, in the worst possible way. Including that when the Army of the Wabash finally gets there, there will be a thousand real horror stories, and within a year ten thousand made-up ones, about the death of that town. You know, neither Leslie nor I ever even visited it before it was gone. And the symbolic value . . ."

Heather stared into space. "And Allie Sok Banh is in a hospital bed and it'll be months before she's up and around, and of course Bambi is going to be some kind of psychological wreck, she was my favorite employee back before, and she was so happy with Quattro, it was like he changed her whole life. . . ." She got up and walked over to her string-and-card chart, which was lying on the table, and raked through it with her fingers, tearing everything out, flinging it over her shoulder. "There is not going to be a Restored Republic, or a United States," she said. "Everyone is out of action, most are dead, we've lost every useable resource. Texas will secede today. White Fang says that the Commandant is probably never going to make an official declaration, but he's got at least twenty people in jail on suspicion of 'spying for the United States,' so whether we admit it or not, we've already lost Manbrookstat too. Red Dog reports that Jenny Whilmire Grayson doesn't have the votes and might have to flee here for political asylum. No options left. We've lost. We've just plain lost."

Very quietly, James said, "I have two arrows left in the quiver, actually. One you'll hate and one that you will never forgive me for."

Tears were trickling from her eyes, and she said, "Well, let's start with the one you think I will hate. You know me, James. You know if someone tells me there's a chance, I have to know what it is."

"Graham Weisbrod was technically, correctly, the legitimate President of the United States. Everyone who knows the law admits that now."

"Now that he's dead and they don't have to put up with him," Leslie said, bitterly.

"True but irrelevant; the relevance is that everyone agrees he should have been President, and therefore he was, in retrospect. Clear as a bell, actually, a sitting cabinet official appointed by the last elected president and confirmed by a fully legitimate Acting President. The TNG was all the result of a series of mistakes: if Cameron Nguyen-Peters hadn't been so full of doubt, if Norm McIntyre had found some guts, or if Lyndon Phat had thought things through, there'd never have been a Temporary National Government." James sighed. "The trouble was that Graham was highly partisan and, forgive me, Heather, but kind of a rude jerk, and even people who liked him didn't like Allie, and President Weisbrod would really have meant President Allie in all but name. But now that everyone is dead, if we have a legitimate successor to Weisbrod, *that's* the President of the United States."

"Doesn't that mean the whole Provi government is?"

He shook his head. "No. Graham Weisbrod was a legitimate President of the US but setting up the Provisional Constitutional Government exceeded his authority by astronomical distances. He was a president who violated the Constitution, but he was legitimately the President; the PCG was never legitimately the government. Now, there's a provision in the Succession Act that an acting or an emergency appointment to the cabinet is in the line of succession, same as one confirmed by the Senate. So anyone Graham appointed to his cabinet—"

"Doesn't that make Allie Sok Banh next in line? They've got her in an induced coma, and she may not be fully conscious for another few days. And you were right in the first place, even her closest friends don't want her to be the president. So the next one is . . . Treasury?"

"I was getting to that. Yeah. Bindel wouldn't make a bad choice, either, but he's naturalized, born in India. But their Secretary of the Armed Forces—which is what Graham renamed the Secretary of Defense—is Norm McIntyre."

"But Norm is a wreck, you say so yourself. Even if he takes the job—"

"He probably won't," James said. "Blue Heeler reports that he's despondent, not even in Olympia right now, he's outside the city, pretty much just hiding. But technically speaking, he's the Acting President. He could appoint a Vice President and resign. Then we have a president with at least a fig leaf of legitimacy and some shreds of authority. Then if a new Congress was elected—this year is an election year on the old calendar—they could validate the whole thing. Retroactively we'd be back under the old

Constitution with a mess to straighten out, but technically it would be legit."

"Well, I wouldn't have wanted Norm before, to tell the truth, and if he's hiding in a cabin in the woods, I guess he'd better keep hiding. But what good would it do to have a President with no government?"

James said, "This is the part you'll *really* hate. Then the President calls a summit meeting of state governors and everyone else controlling former American territory—even Lord Robert—and demands that they plan for a national election. Kharif, that guy the PCG just appointed. Jenny Whilmire Grayson if she can get in. Bambi. Governor Faaj down in Texas. All of those would probably go for it. Others, we'd have to campaign over the leadership's heads, stir up trouble for them with their own people, because we know most Americans *do* want to put the Constitution and the Republic back together, even if it's just out of pure sentiment. Get all the little governments and alliances to play as much as we can. Elect the Congress, we already have a President, start setting up, pretend that the last couple of years didn't happen."

"So whoever we made the president that way would have to serve out the rest of the term?"

"For stability and legitimacy, yeah. So it can't be just a figurehead. It has to be somebody who can actually run a government putting the country back on its feet, and play by the rules, and while we're at it, if we don't want guerrilla uprisings, it'll have to be someone that most people in the country have heard of and trust. Someone who already has contacts everywhere and that people think of as wielding some power in her own right."

Heather O'Grainne stared at him; she had seen it. "You are working your way around to saying that it has to be me."

"I told you you'd hate it."

"That's why you're my main advisor, you're so good at predicting."

"Then you know I've already thought through the rest of the list of possibles and I'm not suggesting this just to be mean or because I want my boss to move up in the world, or anything of the sort. Is there anyone else *you'd* pick?"

"Doesn't mean I want to do it. Wouldn't it make more sense to just let the Republic quietly fade out, and give up? I can find something useful to do somewhere, so can everyone else, and, well, we tried to keep our oaths, kept them as long as we could, but there's no more America."

"You could do that." He looked down at his hands. "I hate to bring this up but there's another kind of trouble we might head off if you were willing to be President for a day or two. If we don't do this now, when Allie Sok Banh recovers, she's much too smart and ambitious not to realize that she is the President."

"Ouch. That would tear the country apart."

"If we do this now, your appointment would supersede her position. And while we're at it, it also shuts off half a dozen other minor people, various deputy undersecretaries and so forth, who might be able to contend that since they were legitimately the acting secretary of something or other, they are now legitimately the president. If you read your Shakespeare or you know the Wars of the Roses, you know that there is only one good number of legitimate successors, and that's one. Any more than that is an invitation to civil war, and we've been close to that a few times already, in fact you could pretty much say the Lost Quarter Campaign was a civil war—just one we lost. So one clear succession would be good to establish even if you decide you don't want to do anything more than that."

"And it would have to be now, wouldn't it? Who knows how long till Allie recovers and tries to take power? Much as I love the lady, personally, I don't want to see if she can make a bigger mess than Jefferson Davis did."

"So . . ." Leslie said, "has James talked you into this?"

Heather sighed. "I might have known you were in on it."

"And Wonder. And he agreed with us too."

"Well, then, I guess it's unanimous, and it does make sense. Set up a voice encryption, and let's get hold of Norm McIntyre and see if he'll go along with it. He probably will, because he has enough sense to be terrified of the idea of being stuck as president. And promise me that I'll be the president for the shortest possible time that works."

2 HOURS LATER. PUEBLO. 1:00 PM MOUNTAIN TIME. MONDAY, MAY 11, 2026.

"We haven't been using the voice encryptor much," Heather observed. "They seemed kind of surprised that we wanted to. A few months ago they pretty much had staff on it all the time."

James sighed. "A few months ago, we were actively conspiring with Cameron Nguyen-Peters, Graham Weisbrod, Allie Sok Banh, Bambi Castro, and half a dozen other people that were important in various places around the country. Now we get our reports from the few spies we still have in place and there's nobody working on our side in most of the other capitals on the continent. The gadgets still work but nobody wants to talk."

The operator was going through the complicated process of encrypting a request to the Olympia voice encryption room, sending it by Morse, and getting back an acknowledgment that included a time check so that they could synchronize the big wooden cams that controlled the encryption and decryption process, and in between stints at the headset, jumping up to make sure that the recently-disused machine was back in shape: camshaft turning freely, locking screws snugly in place, contacts clean and free of crusty white nanospawn, and the handbuilt jelly-jar vacuum tubes warm and ready to go. After one more trip around the machinery, she looked up at them and said, "All right, we'll start running in seven minutes."

"Hey," James said, smiling, "I didn't recognize you with your head down over the machinery, Melissa. How are things for the new Watch Captain?"

"Considering I'd never been a school crossing guard before, and now I've got the Graveyard Company, I don't think I'm doing too badly," she said. "Still a little surprised to be promoted, but at least the job is easier than it was, now that the general's got his wall built." She hesitated a moment and then said, "The rumor is all through the crypto section here. Is it true? Is General Phat dead?"

"It's true," James said. "Public announcement is probably tomorrow morning."

Melissa was wiping her eyes. "Who's going to be president, then?"

"We're working on that right now," Heather said.

"It's just, the general was such a down-to-earth guy. He walked to work, you know? We guarded him a lot, my squad and me. He knew our names, and he asked us to show up at City Council to put the pressure on to get us the city wall built, and . . . well, he was just good for the place. I know we'd've been losing him to Springfield, anyway, but I'm sorry to see him go. They say he was killed at Pale Bluff?"

"Probably. We don't know all the details. Can you encourage your co-workers not to say too much till it's official?"

"I can try. Most of 'em are even bigger blabbermouths than me." She looked at her carefully restored old railroad watch, and said, "Ninety seconds."

Norm McIntyre sounded old and tired even through the wails and clicks of the encryptor. "So Shorty Phat is gone, and so is Jeff Grayson. I always thought I was lucky to be managing people who were better at their jobs than I was." He coughed as if fighting for air.

"General Phat spoke highly of you," Heather said, only lying slightly.

"I was a good administrator. I could get stuff to them when they asked. They were the fighters, and a general should fight." He sighed. "You heard that they're going to purge Graham's cabinet while Allie's out of action? Our little Congress up here was a lapdog till now, but they see a chance to get rid of everyone who did anything at the national level, and make the Congress of the PCG something more like the Tacoma Sanitation District Board, which is where most of these guys should be. And I guess I'll probably just let them, there just doesn't seem to be any point in it any more." No mistaking the whine in his voice; this was a man who wanted things to be over.

James and Heather looked at each other, and Heather said, "General, there's a fact that you may or may not be aware of, and something we need you to do for the country because of it. The fact is, you are the President of the United States. James, if you'll explain—"

Understanding did not make McIntyre any happier. He pointed out that he had had a chance to put matters right, right after the superbombs, and had not taken the chance. "Heather, if you really need me to, I'm willing to be the last President, like the last guy in a game of hot potato who gets caught holding it, that's fine. Kerensky, Pu Yi, and the Kaiser all found something to do with their time, and nobody bothered them because they clearly weren't going to do anything. But you're decades younger than I am, and the type that does things. Nobody'll leave you alone. Are you sure you wouldn't rather leave the whole mess in my hands?"

Heather sat very quietly for a long time before she said, "No, actually, I'm not sure. But I think I would rather have tried than not."

They made the arrangements quickly; as far as they knew, the verbal appointment was enough, but they had him arrange for an encrypted Morse transmission, and he promised to handwrite a letter with the same text, dated today, and send that along as well, as soon as there was a train or plane headed for Pueblo.

ABOUT THE SAME TIME. RUINS OF PALE BLUFF. 3:00 PM CENTRAL TIME. MONDAY, MAY 11, 2026.

"It's a good thing you're not worried about sanitation," Bernstein said, gesturing at the corpse of General Phat, which lay on its back, stripped naked, with flies crawling in a dense black wad like a shower cap covering the missing top of the general's head.

"Oh, I am worried about sanitation. Worried as can be. I want to make sure it's bad, so bad that this little tight-ass all-American pull-together-and-bring-back-the-old-world town, this little boil on God's ass, ain't coming back, ever. Reminds me too much of where I came from, you know? Places like this are the seeds of that whole plaztatic thing, and even if I'm not a dirty hippie asshole like *some* Daybreak people"—he looked pointedly at Glad Ocean, but she had her eyes closed and was humming, hands folded in the prayer position in front of her—"I don't want that old world back either. That's why we had to make sure the orchards burned, and before we go we'll get every house going good, that's why we've been stuffing bodies down the wells, and leaving them out arranged to upset their dumbass soldiers when they get here."

"Did Nathanson tell you about their old Town Hall? Rows and rows of heads on the tables in their meeting hall, bodies in a pile leaned up against the door, and then they climbed out the window to leave it that way. First soldier to open that door, avalanche of bodies without heads, and when they get through that, all the heads are facing the door."

"Nice work."

Glad Ocean opened her eyes and nodded enthusiastically. The slim, older woman was a senior shaman. Her eight-foot spirit stick was encrusted with so many decorations that she had a slave carry it for her most of the time. She was supposed to be Robert's liaison to the Daybreaker leadership, to the tribes who had come with him, and to the moon gun, which she insisted on calling the Guardian on the Moon and referring to as "he." "Absolutely right," she said. "We can't let the plaztatic world have places to grow back. I'm so glad you're being thorough here, Lord Robert."

He nodded slightly, just a slight dip of the head, which, as usual, she took for agreement. Even though Glad Ocean was old and scrawny, nothing like the hot chick that Daybreak had sent him to play with before, he thought about that one every time Glad Ocean favored him with her smug little tight-ass morally-correct smile. *You have something in common with Pale Bluff,* he thought at her. *You are completely in my power. The only difference is, Pale Bluff has already found out what that means. But I'm still looking forward to you finding out.*

He turned back to Nathanson and Bernstein and said, "Don't call anyone away from the party right now. I know they're still finding stuff and still finding dumbshits who are trying to hide or sneak away, and they'll want to have time to play with all the new toys and pull out all the good parts before they burn it all. But around sundown, we're having a little bit of . . . oh, I guess you'd call it a bonfire here tonight." He pointed down at the corpse at his feet. "Tar the general here the way we did Ecco's body last year, and nail it to a nice tall post. We'll start with a little ceremony raising it up. You realized this was the last guy that really might have been the president? They are *so fucked.*"

ABOUT THE SAME TIME. PUEBLO. 2:15 PM MOUNTAIN TIME. MONDAY, MAY 11, 2026.

"Wish we'd had a Federal judge living here, at least," Heather said. "But James assures me that Calvin Coolidge took the oath from a Vermont notary public, and it counted. Let's get this done."

Michelle Trevor had been a Colorado Court of Appeals judge back before; her term had not expired, but the court hadn't met since Daybreak day. Nowadays she worked in the general labor pool (usually cooking in the town mess hall), moonlighted as a waitress at Dell's Brew, and taught history in the night school. Patrick had managed to locate her within fifteen minutes of James's thinking of her, and she'd come over to the Old Pueblo Courthouse as soon as she had finished cubing a large elk steak and washed her hands. She seemed to be mildly amused. "Are you sure you don't want me to make you the Pope, crown you queen of France, and marry you to somebody, as long as I already came over here?"

"Oh, I guess President is enough for one day," Heather said. "You're the history teacher. What do we need to make this legal?"

"Three witnesses is a good number," she said. "It's better if they're public officials. That's covered with James, Leslie, and Dr. Odawa. There's no rule against a witness being a minor, so Patrick and Ntale, you count too, and Leo might, though he'd have a heck of a time giving testimony. Wonder, I'm afraid this country does not extend full civil rights to dogs yet."

Wonder wagged his tail slightly. "He's not big on irony," Leslie said.

"Oh, well. Anyway, the text of the oath is prescribed in the Constitution, which I have here. The Bible is traditional, not required, but I think it's a good idea given the politics of the southeastern part of the country. As for my authority, as you said, I'm at least a couple jumps up from a notary public. Coolidge retook the oath from the Chief Justice, on the sly, when he got back to Washington, just in case there was any question, but there never was. I guess you could do the same if you're ever around a Federal judge. And that, my friends, should cover all the issues. Shall we get back to swearing in the President?"

"Sure."

Heather followed the instructions and said the words. Afterward, she said, "You know, that's probably the first all-hugging inauguration."

"I shook your hand," James pointed out.

"History is always open to revision," Judge Michelle said. "Give him a good hug before we go, Heather. And I do have to go; I have an afternoon shift at Dell's and papers to grade."

30 MINUTES LATER. AUSTIN, TEXAS. 4:15 PM CENTRAL TIME. MONDAY, MAY 11, 2026.

Big cumulus clouds piled across the deep blue Texas sky, and Governor Faaj Tong-George read faster than he would have liked, afraid that there might be rain before the end of the ceremony. When he read fast, he could sound too much Kennedy School, where he had been a professor, and not enough Brownsville, where he had grown up, and that could be very bad for re-election.

Yet though his words were coming out softer and faster than he intended, the crowd was still cheering wildly at each point. When he began his paragraph about the pride every Texan felt in the TexICs and pain of their irreparable loss, the cheering became so heated that he had to start that part again. Without microphones or loudspeakers to quiet the crowd, he finally had to ask them to keep it down so he could finish. At last, he went on:

> . . . yet the loss of so many of our most valued citizens of the Texas Independent Cavalry might have been a sacrifice we would willingly have made for the larger nation, and even now we must remember and honor that they died in the hope of saving the United States of America. But remembrance and honor are a debt to the past, and the graver and more serious debt is the one we owe to our children. We cannot ignore that the states, agencies, and powers seeking a Restored Republic, however noble their cause, however unrelenting and brave their efforts, have suffered a series of grievous defeats from which they cannot be expected to recover.

We cannot now, or in any reasonably near future, responsibly place our trust in a power so broken and so defective, when our country and our children's lives depend upon it. Having therefore concluded that our security is best entrusted to our own hands, with affection for our former brethren of the United States, with renewed effort against our shared enemies, but without reservation, condition, or any offer, explicit or implicit, of reconciliation, we hereby declare that the Union between the State of Texas and the United States of America is dissolved, and of a right ought to be, and we resume our full and equal place among the nations of mankind.

He still wasn't sure how much the crowd heard, or cared whether they heard, over the rising roar of their own cheering.

At the visible end of the speech, they gave up all restraint and cheered madly for what the words did, whether or not they knew what they said.

He put his speech text carefully into its leatherbound folder. His aides were to take it to a frame shop immediately, and within a few days it would hang next to the first Texas Declaration of Independence, in the Capitol building behind him. *Funny. Weird. Hunh. There'll never be a recording of this; kids in school won't complain that they can't understand my old-fashioned accent or make fun of my weird olden-days clothing.*

Governor Faaj nodded at the honor guard, which hauled down the Temper Cross and Eagle and the Provi nineteen-star double-circle Stars and Stripes from the two flanking poles where they had been flying. As soon as they were down, the Lone Star flags went up, and the cheering became deafening.

Faaj felt an ocean of sadness surge within him when he nodded again, and the crew pulled down the old fifty-star flag from the high center pole. *Not quite 250 years. Missed by less than two months.*

Something of that feeling must have been there in the crowd. There had been cries of "Shame!" from some demonstrators, and another bunch had been singing "Ding Dong the Witch Is Dead" and still another group was bellowing a Carlene Redbone hit from a few years ago, "Don't Let That Door Hit Your Ass," and here and there people were trying to start up "The Star-Spangled Banner" and "The Eyes of Texas" but being drowned out by their neighbors. One very old man in the front row, tears streaming down his face, was trying to sing "You're a Grand Old Flag" but couldn't seem to recall it past the first couple of lines, and kept starting over and over.

In different parts of the crowd, people were enthusiastically waving the Stars and Bars, the rattlesnake, the pine tree, and one lone Jolly Roger.

But when the old flag had descended a couple of feet, the crowd plunged into a hush, like the moment when a casket is lowered into the grave, and you could hear the creaking of the pulleys as it came down. In the rising wind of the coming storm, it snapped and rippled as if it were trying, one more time, to get back into another fight.

The honor guard of US Army Rangers at the base of the pole were openly weeping as they folded the flag. This flag would be framed and displayed in the Texas Capitol, between the two Declarations.

Then the Texas Rangers stepped forward and briskly ran up the Lone Star, and the applause was so much like thunder that many of the crowd didn't realize that the storm was coming in, till gusts of silvery rain fell on them in sheets, and they fled through the gardens surrounding the Capitol.

Faaj had already handed off the folder, and the aides were gathering up the folding chairs, suddenly emptied of dignitaries. No one was paying much attention to the governor, so he looked around once more before going in. The old man was still standing there, still trying to sing, and Faaj walked down the steps to stand next to him. He had learned "You're a Grand Old Flag" for a President's Day concert in eleventh grade, and he put his arm around the old guy, and sang it all the way through. That seemed to break the spell, and the old man went off sniveling, wiping his face uselessly in the rain.

I was singing it for him, but I wonder if he was singing it for the Stars and Stripes or for the Lone Star? I guess in the long history of the universe that question probably won't matter.

"Governor Faaj, aren't you going to come inside?"

"Son, my people are Hmong and my first job was on a fishing boat. This ain't rain, this is a sprinkle." Lightning cracked nearby with a deafening boom. "Coming right along, though."

At the top of the steps he paused and looked. All the flags on all the staffs were now so soaked that you couldn't really see what they were.

ABOUT THE SAME TIME. PUEBLO. 3:45 PM MOUNTAIN TIME. MONDAY, MAY 11, 2026.

They were at the airfield early because "Let's face it, we want to know what's going on," Leslie said. "We'd've been no use anyway, sitting around at the office, right?"

"Well, we could have pretended to work, but that's probably your point," James said.

"I think Leo was just relieved to be dropped off at the sitter's," Heather said. "He's sort of sensitive to my moods lately and I was making him nervous." She touched her shoulder holster. "Also I think that I feel weird to him because I'm always extra careful whenever I'm carrying."

James said, "Why are you? We have guards around and no reason to think Bambi is dangerous."

"No, but Bambi thinks something is," Heather said. "Why is she insisting on meeting at the airport? All I can think of is that either she's got urgent information that she can't trust to encryption, or she has reason to fear being attacked in town. Either way means something bad going on that we have no idea about."

"Is there any possibility that it's us? That she's decided *we're* the enemy, somehow?"

"James, based on what we know right now *anything* is possible. Bambi worked for me for three years back before, and I like to think there's a lot of friendship and respect. But she just lost a husband and we don't know the circumstances except it happened in battle, and something killed General Phat and all we know is that she's apparently the only witness, and we've had traitors in the ranks before, as both of you would know. So I'm just thinking that till I know what's going on, I'd rather have my gun close by and my baby far away. And besides—there she is." They looked to where Heather pointed to the tiny buzzing dot in the sky.

The Stearman made a slight whump on landing, the greased linen tires having deflated during the long flight from Hays, Kansas. The plane taxied around in a broad circle to stop about ten yards in front of them.

Bambi shut the engine off, braked the prop, climbed out, and walked toward them. Leslie said, very softly, "Her hand is by her holster."

"I know," Heather murmured. "I'm keeping my hand away from mine."

Bambi walked as if she had counted and measured the steps between her plane and her colleagues, and was putting each foot carefully on its mark, like an unconfident movie actor or as if she were crossing a river on not-quite remembered stepping-stones. She had not taken off her flying helmet, but her goggles were pushed up onto her forehead; despite the warm afternoon, she left her jacket zipped. And, as Leslie had noticed, her right hand was resting by the grip of the pistol strapped to her thigh, almost as if she expected a gunfight.

Quietly, Heather said, "You can just tell us what happened, Bambi. We haven't heard anything from anyone else."

She nodded. "Lyndon Phat decided that my plane and I should stay in Paducah because he needed us and wanted to keep us. He arrested me and locked me up. He didn't let me fly to Pale Bluff, where my husband was fighting for his life, kept me locked up while bad news was pouring in over the radio and barely bothered to tell me about it afterward. Then ten minutes after the EMP, he ordered me to fly him to Pale Bluff for a reconnaissance. I saw Quattro's burned body in the wreckage; all the ground crew died with him too. I think maybe they tried to fly out just as the EMP hit, or maybe they were shot down and the plane flipped. I don't know. It was too badly burned. So . . . I walked back to my plane, and I pointed a gun at General Lyndon Phat, and made him get out of *my* airplane. I left him there on the runway with tribals starting to run up on him. I'm pretty sure he's dead by now but I'm hoping Lord Robert got to take a personal interest and treated him like Steve Ecco."

The hideous silence stretched as if it might go on forever.

James didn't see any point in bringing up any arguments that she should not have done it; it was done, with nothing to change. He didn't see a reason to blame her; either she would blame herself, or not. He didn't fear the gun at her hip; she clearly had control of herself. He just wished someone would think of something to say.

When it seemed painfully clear that no one else was going to break the silence, James said, "Is there any chance anyone survived, or there might be anybody holding out there?"

Bambi shook her head, and now tears were flowing. "Not a chance. We circled. No fighting. Bodies everywhere. If anyone was still alive they were hiding in a cellar or something, and the tribals were lighting fires everywhere."

Leslie said, "I am so sorry about Quattro. He was special to all of us but he was your husband and you'd loved him a long time."

"Even before I knew I did," Bambi said softly. Her hand moved decisively down away from her holster. "What now?"

Heather asked, "Are we the only people who know? Because if we are, then I think we're the only people who decide. There's nobody I have to report it to, now, and there never will be."

Bambi's shoulders began to shake, and Heather said, "I don't want any accidents, so, is it okay if I come over there and hold you? You know, old friend to old friend, not—"

Bambi raised her hands away from her weapon, and the two women embraced.

Heather looked at James and Leslie over her friend's shoulder. "Uh, guys."

Taking their cue, they went into the office.

After a long time, Heather and Bambi joined them. Bambi sat quietly, looking at her boots. Heather said, "Well, to begin with, Bambi knows I'm now the President. So really, this is the President and her closest advisors dealing with a difficult situation. I guess . . . Bambi, can you tell them about how you feel about the Duchy of California? The same way you told me?"

Bambi said, "I can try. It's hard to say this. Look, my father . . . the whole time I was raised with his libertarian Ayn Rand right-wing thing going on, and hating it, because, well, Daddy always thought somehow or other that everything that happened around all that money and all those people working, he thought he did it. Like, all by himself, you know? Ten years after Obama said 'You didn't build that' he was still in hysterics about it because he couldn't stand the idea that the people who drew a paycheck from him had anything to do with the work that got done.

"So you know, you want to piss off your parents, or anyway at least I wanted to piss off mine. In eighth grade, I showed him a copy of 'Questions from a Worker Who Reads' and he tried to get my English teacher fired, and I went to the School Board meeting to testify against him. He had a whole career track laid out for me at Castro Enterprises and I never showed up to do anything he wanted me to, instead I went to a public university and volunteered for all kinds of unpaid do-gooding and ended up as a Federal agent. I don't think you can imagine how angry that made him, that I was working for the tax-and-spenders and revenuers and gun-grabbers, even if I was carrying a gun myself.

"But he was proud of me too, in his weird way. And he kept telling me to take care of things, make sure guys like Donald, his favorite chauffeur, were taken care of. And then later . . . Quattro was one of the few other people in the world who understood me, I think. You know he was raised all his life to figure that someday the government would be all gone, and it would just be crazy looters in the street and red barbarians in the State-house, and . . . but he'd loved me, forever, really, I guess, since we were kids, and since putting the United States back together was what mattered to me, and my oath, and being part of society, and being in it for something bigger than myself, and all that"—her hands sawed the air—"it's important and I can't seem to keep it all in order, but you get the idea. Since I wanted my United States put back together, Quattro wanted me to have that.

"But he always wanted to go home and take care of the duchy—his duchy, as far as he was concerned. He joked about it and made fun of it and wore those silly hats, but he thought about California as ours. Ours to take care of, ours to protect and guide . . . it was all personal to Quattro Larsen, and, well, I think he was right. Or if he wasn't right then, he sure is now. We need to look after our own.

"I had a lot of time flying to think. I know that the general saw a pilot and a plane and said, vital resource, have to have that for the country. Well, I say, fuck that. My airplane. Me. My duchy. I will take better care of them *and besides they are mine.* So I left him there to take care of his own shit, with the tribals, and I sure hope they took care of it for him.

"I still love you all and you can come for asylum any time." She made a strange choking noise, and then smiled strangely. "After all, Daddy always said California was one big asylum. Or a visit or because you'd just like to say hi. But the years I put into the United States of America . . . and the husband I lost for the cause . . . none of that was worth shit, and I wish I had everything back. From now on, I take care of my duchy. And Heather, I wish you'd just resign as President, come out to California, I'll give you a fief somewhere where you can have your dad with you and raise Leo and make your part of the world decent. Because I think you're going to end up losing everything else, and there still won't be any United States, and even if there was, it would never be what you imagine. It never even *was*, you know?"

Heather said, "Bambi, I'm so close to agreeing with you."

"Come down to Castle Castro at San Diego. Stay with me for a long while. Get reacquainted with your father and let him get to know his grandson. Seriously, think about it. You could get Leo, climb into the front cockpit, and be gone with me today. You have your oath, but there's no country to keep it to."

Heather thought for a long while. At last she said, "James, maybe it is just because of the compliment you paid me earlier, about how I don't give up and so on. But I can't help thinking, before we all part company, you said there was one more thing we might try before we give up forever. And you said it was something I might not forgive you for."

"Actually I don't think anyone will forgive me for it. Anyone on our side, I mean. And it really . . . it isn't something we can do. I don't think it will even lead to anything we can do. But it's one last place we could look for a suggestion, or an idea, or some pathway or approach. And chances are there will be nothing in it."

"You're a hell of a salesman," Leslie said flatly, and they all began to laugh, even James. "Seriously, dude, do you want us all to think about this, or is this something you're trying to scare us away from before we even hear it?"

"Some of both." James looked back at each of them, drew a deep breath, and said it. "I kept Arnie Yang alive. He's Interrogation Subject 162. I switched in a different prisoner when he had that seizure on the way to his hanging, and we hooded him. He wasn't very happy when he woke up from his seizure and found us still prying at the Daybreak in his head. About half the time he warns us about how dangerous it is, and the other half he sounds perfectly reasonable and helpful—sometimes because he's actually providing insights and helping us, and sometimes because Daybreak has taken him back over and he's trying to trick us into doing something against our interests. The problem the interrogation team and I have is sorting out which is which, at any given time. But he's alive, and we've been using him all along."

Heather was staring at him, slowly shaking her head. "So your little digs at me about getting carried away and executing him and how much that was senseless, you were just . . . getting me ready for when you pulled him out of your hat?"

"I'm afraid so."

She shrugged. "He was one of my closest friends for a long time. A day hasn't gone by that I haven't missed him. I think I might even be glad to see him alive. You'd better take me to him. Bambi, would you like to join us for this?"

"Arn and I used to be regulars at the departmental happy hour, back before," Bambi reminded her. "I guess it's going to be old home week. Keep our guns or check them at the door?"

"We've never allowed weapons near him," James said. "Well, let me send out some runners." He thought for a moment. "We'll need to get the interrogation team together to meet us there; that's just safety. Then a carriage for us, I guess, we have him in the super-secure wing of Facility 1 and that's about a mile and a half, unless you want to walk."

"How about two carriages?" Leslie said. "One for you guys to do old home week in, one for James and I to talk. Because, frankly, we need to talk."

"I think the budget can stand that," Heather said. "Considering there's about to be no government of the United States, and we run on its credit."

James nodded and headed for the messenger's bench at the other end of the building.

"Besides," Heather said, "I might as well spend it now before it goes away."

Bambi smiled. "Spoken like a true bureaucrat. You really think you're going to lose your budget?"

"Oh, hell, yeah. One big funding source is going to disappear when the Tempers turn into the Christian States of America. Who knows how long the PCG will want to keep funding us, especially once Allie wakes up and finds out I prevented her from being President?"

Bambi snorted. "Jeez. Our old office politics are now running the continent. Well, look, hon, I'm a duchess. You were a pretty good bureaucrat, and I bet you'll make a pretty good vassal. And one advantage of being a duchess is, le budget, *c'est moi.*"

. . .

"Well," James said, closing the carriage door, "You said you wanted to talk."

"Yeah." She reached out and grasped his wrist. "James, I—shit. I don't have any idea what I feel. I mean, he almost killed me."

"He did. For what it's worth, he's gone after me or one of the others with his bare hands, or silverware he stole, or a piece of broken plate or a garotte he tore out of his underwear. More times than I can count. About a third of the time he's plain old, gentle, nerdy, numbers-and-graphs-loving Arnie. Another third, he's a treacherous evil snake of a liar, but very persuasive, and he sounds just like he does when he's himself. And the last third . . . well, no predicting, but he's tried to kill us, sometimes by biting out our carotids, sometimes by sounding as reasonable and mellow as a stoned kindergarten teacher. And he jumps from one to the other and there's no warning."

"Yeah. But . . . okay, whether you feel good about it or not, this is about me." She sighed, and played with Wonder's ears; he panted and looked up at James.

"Yeah," James said, "I knew it was going to be."

"*Why* did you save Arnie Yang's life? I mean, James, just this once, I'll admit I know how you feel about me, that you haven't changed, you're still forcing yourself to be the best friend I could ever wish for, but that's not what you want—"

He sat up stiffly, looked out the window, and kept his voice very flat. "You're right, we don't talk about all that."

"But—"

"You wanted me to let him be hanged, as revenge for what he almost did to you? Don't think I didn't consider that. I would honest to god have *enjoyed* hearing that cable snap his neck. Because he tried to frame you, because he betrayed Ecco, because he fooled me, because he smiled right into the faces of people who thought he was their friend and were trying to be good friends to him. Ten million reasons I would have liked to see him dangling dead.

"But I did it all, anyway, instead. I arranged with MaryBeth to handle the switch, and got the note from Allie that we could be sure would trigger a Daybreak seizure. Then when he had the attack, MaryBeth and I took him to the infirmary. We only needed a couple of minutes because we had a prisoner we hadn't logged. Deb and Larry Mensche knew a guy about Arnie's size and coloration, who had been a Daybreaker, and killed his own family while he was under it, and didn't want to live. They were waiting with him in the infirmary, and they had already dosed him up on barbiturates and got him all weepy and sleepy and hooded him, and that's the man we took back out to ride in the wagon to his hanging.

"Meanwhile Jason and Beth took Arnie Yang to the high security section we had just set up in Facility 1; there are about a dozen high-level deeply infected Daybreakers in there at any given time, and the roster tends to change pretty fast because what we do to interrogate them, um, uses them up."

"Kills them?"

"If they don't find a way to kill themselves, or die of a related accident, or turn into gaping, drooling mannequins." He rubbed his face. "It's one hell of a job for an ex-librarian to take on, but there was no one else for it."

"Did it have to be done?"

"Yeah, I still think so. If we'd won, anyway, I think it would have been justified. Anyway, it was the fake Arnie that went back out on the gurney, up the steps, and down the drop. Nobody saw his face till MaryBeth and I took his hood off, and you know, with the weights on his feet and using aircraft cable on such a long drop, we had turned his face into one big swollen bruise, with a big black tongue sticking out and red eyeballs bulging like Ping-Pong balls. No one who had been friends with Arnie was going to look closely. We let them have one glimpse, then MaryBeth signed the death certificate, I fed fake-Arnie head down into the incinerator—supposedly to prevent his grave becoming a pilgrimage site—and we made it work. That's how we did it, and no, at the time, I didn't tell you about it. You'd just been released from death row yourself and you were drinking and partying like all of a sudden there *was* a tomorrow."

"When I've been scared, I like a lot of sex. And I'd never been so scared before."

"I know. I understood that, Leslie. We've been friends a long time."

"Yeah. I try to keep you from hearing too much about it, or seeing me when I'm that way."

"I appreciate it. Anyway, the point is, I didn't hang Arnie, and I decided not to hang Arnie, but it had nothing to do with you. Not that I wasn't angry enough, just that it made no sense, if I was trying to do my job running an intelligence service. I certainly didn't save Arnie because I loved him, or forgave him, or wanted to spend time in his company. So I'm sorry but for once in my stupid, infatuated, never-learn life, this *wasn't* about you."

Leslie leaned forward, looking at him with an expression he couldn't read, astonishment, maybe, even shock. "James, James—shit, I'm handling this so badly, I was trying to be careful not to hurt you. I just wanted to say . . . James, you didn't have to keep it secret from me, you don't need my forgiveness because there's nothing to forgive, *I understand*, James."

She reached over and clutched his arm; he looked at her hand as if it had magically appeared there. "James," she said again. "What I wanted to tell you was . . . of *course* you had to keep him alive, of *course* you had to have him for interrogation, because you are running an intelligence organization, with very fucking likely the fate of civilization at stake, and he's the richest possible source of intelligence about the enemy you could have, the senior analyst from our own side infected by Daybreak.

"*Naturally* he was telling you that you had to hang him; it was the same thing as the suicide pills any spy carries. Executing him looked like the stupidest piece of melodrama in the world, just a show for the mob in the street because our big dumb sloppy public still hasn't recovered from being raised on movies and comic books and they had this fixation that they needed to see 'justice' done. Justice? Emotional satisfaction because it makes a tidy story. Nothing to do with what works or what matters. Just melodramatic 'justice,' one more way people made themselves stupid, so stupid they couldn't keep civilization going when the first bunch of dipshits came along and wanted to take it down. And I just wanted to apologize to you."

"You? You apologize to me? For *what*?"

"I really thought you were that dumb. I thought you were so infatuated that you felt like you had to be loyal when it didn't make any sense, and I thought . . . well, it was something I felt for a long time. Maybe ever since we became friends, ever since you got that crush." She was looking down, now, embarrassed herself. "I had the impression that you thought I was a little bit dumb, myself, I mean, nice and articulate and all, but not really capable of thinking and deciding like a mature person, and your life was built around pleasing me even though you thought I was silly and dumb. Like, patronizing self-sacrifice, you know? Doing what you thought I wanted because you didn't think I was smart enough to see what was right. So when you hanged Arnie Yang, or staged the hanging, anyway, I thought you did it for me because you thought I was stupid enough to want it and demand it."

The carriage rolled another couple of blocks before James ventured to say, "And now you're thinking . . . or feeling . . . differently?"

"You used the staged execution to convince Daybreak we didn't have that intel source," she said. "Didn't you?"

"Yes, actually. At least that got some mileage out of that silly piece of theatre."

"Well, I think that bit was brilliant, and pretty damned cool, and I'm proud of you." The hand moved from his arm to caress his cheek; startled, he looked straight into her eyes, as he rarely dared to do for fear of revealing his feelings.

She smiled and winked. "Maybe we should have some long talks, later. Meanwhile, let's go see if we can get anything more out of that little asshole."

. . .

James had invited the whole "senior interrogation team," which meant Jason, Beth, and Izzy. It was rare that they all worked together, so they knew something was up even before he showed up with Leslie, Bambi, and Heather. "So today's the day we come clean?" Jason asked. He was grinning like a child at Christmas.

"It just might be the end of everything," James said. "Or the beginning." He looked around the group. "Now, everyone be ready. And if you're carrying any concealed weapons as a backup, now is the time to leave them behind. He's got literally inhuman abilities to detect them and he can move faster than you'd believe—I don't know if that's Daybreak, insanity, or that he spent so many years in martial arts. If you have a knife on you somewhere, he'll take it from you and use it on all of us before you know it."

"No shit," Beth said. "I used to carry a little blackjack for just in case. Arnie was talking reasonable as could be this one time, just like the small talk before we started, and holy fuck, Jason slapped my blackjack out of Arnie's hand and put him into a half-nelson strangle, or I'd've been dead, and the first I knew that my blackjack wasn't in my coat pocket was when I saw it flying across the room."

Heather and Bambi exchanged glances; Bambi pulled out a steel spring whip from somewhere, and Heather a short set of nunchaku.

"You can pick'em up on your way out," James said, locking them into the box by the front door.

When James slid the door panel open, he stood well back, then looked through carefully. Arnie Yang sat on a single-piece poured concrete bench, big enough to be his bed as well as his seat, at the center of the floor in a windowless room. "Coming in, Arnie. Big group."

"Good, it's been lonely."

When Arnie saw all of them, he said, "Something has happened since we talked last. Did Pale Bluff fall?"

"Yes," James said.

"I had thought that sometime soon, there would be a bigger group to see me. It makes me happy to see you again, Heather, Bambi. Leslie, you probably won't believe me, or accept it ever, but I really want to say I'm sorry about everything."

"Actually I do believe you," Leslie said. "That you want to say that, and even that you mean it. You know I'll probably never accept it?"

"I know. I just wanted you to know I offered my apology, sincerely." He paused a long time. "So Pale Bluff has been destroyed. I was rather thinking you would have brought along General Phat."

"He died in Pale Bluff," James said, very quietly. "And nobody is here to gape at you. We want to ask your advice, just as I have regularly asked it. Could you say one of the phrases, please, while we watch you?"

"'Daybreak is a mind virus,'" Arnie recited. "'Daybreak exists only for its own purpose. Daybreak's purpose is to degrade and destroy the human race, everyone I love, and me. Daybreak is entirely evil. The world must be rid of Daybreak so that it can resume the development of technological civilization, whose benefits are the birthright of the whole human race.' Hey, no seizure, today *is* a special day."

"Or Daybreak doesn't want you to have that clear period like you get after a seizure," Beth said. "You know it could be either, and we don't know any more than you do if it's got you right now. But you're right all the same, it's a good sign."

"Well, then," James said. "Here's the situation. Pale Bluff is burned, orchards and all, and will probably never be rebuilt. The Army of the Wabash is so far behind Lord Robert's horde that there's really no likelihood that they'll ever catch them; they just can't move as fast and there's still more than a hundred miles. They can loot their way down the south bank of the Ohio and arrive at Paducah in better shape than they are now. Then they can bypass Paducah or overwhelm it, and that's the last thing between them and the really good looting on the other side of the Mississippi. So if you were right that this is basically one last giant suicide raid to try to crash what's left of civilization on this continent, well, we've probably lost our last chance to stop them before the blizzards start on the Great Plains next fall, and it's only May.

"Every competent person we could have elected president was killed in the last week."

"Have you thought about Quattro—" Arnie saw it in Bambi's face, and said, "Oh, god, no, I'm so sorry."

"You may trust me, no one with the charisma, ability, and national reputation we need is left. Nobody. We played a little fast and loose with the succession rules, so Heather is now the President, officially, but as far as any of us can think, we don't see any way to turn that to our advantage.

So the current plan is that we're going to give up here. Heather is going to join Bambi in the Duchy of California, the rest of us will fold up shop, and the middle of the country will do whatever it can in the face of the Great Raid. Maybe their death rate will be higher, sooner, and their raid will be less effective, than they are thinking, and they'll empty out the Lost Quarter enough so that Manbrookstat or the Christian States of America—"

"Wait, has that been declared?"

"Going to be any minute. You'll never believe it, but Jenny Whilmire Grayson is the biggest asset the Army has in trying to stop it. But she's not enough, and it's too late. They will formally declare the CSA within two weeks, according to our source. Anyway, maybe Manbrookstat, the CSA, or whatever the Provis organize will be able to reconquer the Lost Quarter, if the tribes pay too high a price this summer or stay out on the plains too long and get caught in the winter too far from home. But the dream of the Restored Republic is finished."

"I've decided to resign as soon as I'm at Castle Castro," Heather said. "And there's no line of succession left after me. In a couple of days, I will have officially been the last President, of the United States that is no more."

Arnie howled like a coyote with its balls in a trap, arched his back farther than any of them might have imagined possible, and tried to backflip toward the bench. Jason lunged forward, knocked him sideways, and tackled him to the floor. Beth and Ysabel joined in holding him down.

The seizure ran "longer than most, and more violent than anything we've seen this year," as Beth noted.

When it was over, Arnie Yang seemed more unfocused and blurry too. They thought they would just put him onto his bench with his blankets and go, but then he spoke very softly. "That was a bad one. I think that was because Daybreak is giving up on me, trying to scramble my messages as it goes, I'm no longer useful it doesn't want to leave me around as a record of what it did." He was crying. "I think it will try to get me confused enough to have an accident or get me someplace where I just die. James, I'm sorry. I'm really sorry."

"It's all right, Arnie, but tell me what you are sorry for. I'll forgive you."

Normally a seizure didn't come this quickly after a previous seizure, but this one tried; Arnie again arched and kicked, but subsided very quickly. "The whole thing. The whole thing. Daybreak gets gets gets stronger from people fighting it, and we got you to fight a whole war. . . ."

James seemed to sit back as if he'd been kicked.

Arnie babbled a little longer, then fell asleep. They covered him and left.

In the conference room, James said, "I know what he meant."

Heather nodded. "Does it matter anymore?"

"We should all know, if only for the history books. Look, the big camps along the Ohio were on the brink of starvation if they didn't start moving; we went in and attacked them and created our big scary army to motivate them. What if we'd just built up defenses for a rapid response, then sat down and traded with them? Kidnapped shamans, recruited defectors, sent over agents to sow doubt and confusion, let the camps collapse? Arnie steered us toward making it a war in the first place—one where Grayson would have to win eleven battles back-to-back.

"So then they retreated. We could have just said, the danger's over for the summer, because it was. They couldn't have come back to mount a raid across the whole territory. What they could do, though, was rally all the tribes against an invading army—and we sent them one. Not only that, they put themselves under Lord Robert's command; now he's surrounded by an army of loyal Daybreakers, who might reconvert him or his followers.

"And then . . . well, this one wasn't through Arnie, but isn't it interesting how Quattro suddenly pushed us all into defending Pale Bluff, which couldn't be done, instead of evacuating it, which could? Where do you suppose a guy who had been fighting Daybreak for a couple years got that idea?" He looked down at the table, and then looked up again. "You see it? I absolutely blew it. I am the biggest idiot in the world. Daybreak knew that we would give it a war, and the war would be how it would unify the Lost Quarter around a plan that has now totally defeated us. Heather, I know the RRC probably won't last another two weeks, but I would like it on the record that I resigned on grounds of manifest incompetence."

"Only if we agree that I did too," she said quietly. "It's been a terrible day full of terrible news. I want us to all gather at James's house, for one of those quiet evenings of food and being together, and then maybe tomorrow we will tackle Arnie again. But I'm very afraid you're right, James. In fact I wouldn't be surprised if Daybreak has only finally let us realize just to make its triumph more complete."

"And to demoralize us," Leslie said, very quietly. "I was just thinking how much I feel like giving up, and then I realized Daybreak wants me to think that. So we are going to hang on for a day longer, and if that doesn't make a difference, maybe another. Meanwhile, tonight, there's food at James's, if he'll cook."

He sighed and spread his hands. "I'm not going to give up the only thing in the world that feels right. All right, let's all give it one more day, after the best meal I can make you."

SIXTEEN:
AND THE LORD SET A MARK UPON CAIN,
LEST ANY FINDING HIM SHOULD
SLAY HIM

**ABOUT THE SAME TIME. MANBROOKSTAT. 6:15 PM
EASTERN TIME. MONDAY, MAY 11, 2026.**

Back before, Jamayu Rollings thought, *when this place was Brooklyn, we were all worried about how the police come late if they come at all, or however that old song my dad used to like went, and holding marches to try to get some decent protection, and I was so glad to move out to the other end of Long Island and know the cops would come if I needed them.*

Well, welcome to Manbrookstat, where the police come about a day too soon.

He looked up to see that Deanna was looking at him, not moving. Shouts from downstairs at the front door were rising up toward them. He thought, *Stop reminiscing, old fart, and save your family's ass.*

"By the drill," Rollings said. He unclipped the antenna wire from where it connected to an inconspicuous bolt in the wall that happened to go through to a west-facing wire loop on the back of an old billboard. He detached the ground wire clip from the old radiator. He dropped both connector wires onto the radio, and removed the C-clamp that held it to the coffee service table. Then he lifted out the removable section of the old heating duct, creating a two-foot across hole, into which he dropped the whole radio. He put the section back, set an account book on the table where the radio had been, and opened it to yesterday's entries.

When he glanced sideways, Deanna had the correspondence and the one-time pads in a single heap, and was lifting the rug to expose the slot in the floor. She slid the papers into it and let the rug fall back into place; the papers were now between two plaster walls on the floor below.

The Special Assistants coming up the stairs might have heard the radio falling into the bend of the duct in the cellar, of course, though they had long ago stuffed it with old rags to muffle the impact. Perhaps if they found the slot in the floor, they might get ambitious enough to tear the wall apart. For the moment, though, the incriminating evidence was gone.

Just outside the door, a Special Assistant was telling Rollings's clerk that they didn't give a damn for the company rules. *They must be trying to keep it a* quiet *arrest.*

Rollings risked striking a match, reaching out the window, and lighting the fuse that ran up an old rainspout and through a length of pipe to a firepot on the roof peak. The firepot was visible from *Ferengi*, currently moored in the harbor, and from the family home—if the fuse burned all the way to it, if it ignited, if anyone was looking. But it was nice to have one more thing to do. He dropped the match, pushed the window closed, rested his finger on an entry about a roll of chicken wire—the knob turned.

Rollings loudly said, "I told you no interruptions ever—"

"We are not your clerk!" the Special Assistant said, entering.

He turned around. "I can see that." *Oh, spirits of Lando and Sisko be with me.*

The Special Assistant lunged forward and struck him in the face; Rollings glared at the man with all the dignity he could muster. "If you are taking me to the Commandant, I am sure you were supposed to deliver me unharmed."

"They didn't say," the man said. The four Special Assistants bound Rollings and Deanna, and shoved them roughly through the door. They didn't go out of their way to push or trip them down the stairs but they didn't seem to be worrying that that might happen, either.

Four guys, Jamayu thought. *Well, crap, I hope you're smart enough not to try anything, Geordie. Wish I hadn't sent the distress signal at all.* His older son was impulsive and brave to exactly the kind of fault Rollings was afraid he might be about to exhibit.

As they turned onto a broader street, Rollings saw that it was worse than he had thought; dozens of prominent citizens and their families were being marched through the town, and the Commandant's supporters and hangers-on had brought the city crowd out onto the sidewalks to jeer and point. *I thought the secret police had come for us, but this is feeling more like we're going to the guillotine. Well, probably they won't be looking for the radio or the code pads, then; this looks like a roundup of people that don't like the Commandant, not like me getting caught spying.*

Deanna pressed against him, and at first he thought she was huddling in fear, but though her wrists were tied behind her, she managed to elbow-bump him in Morse:

G WAVED 2D FLR WNDW HE IS LOOSE

He bumped back:

STAY LOOSE UR SELF

As they walked and more prominent citizens joined the group, the Special Assistants prodded the prisoners much closer together, and it was easier for Rollings and his daughter to signal each other. The Special Assistants and their militia backup seemed to be herding them together mostly to open up a separating space between them and the yelling, cheering crowd on the sidewalk.

Other prisoners were shouted at and sometimes struck if they tried to speak, so Rollings and Deanna kept communication discreet, brief, and necessary.

After a while, glancing back, he noticed that the crowds from the sidewalk were following them, and bump-signaled Deanna. She replied,

WE R PART OF EVENT I GUESS

but then neither of them had any more to say.

The Special Assistants marched their prisoners over the Brooklyn Bridge; in places where the pavement was crumbling there were sometimes frightening holes through which they could see water far below, but no one seemed to be trying to push them in. From there, they walked south toward the area near the former Battery Park where the Commandant had established his headquarters.

In all, it was only about two miles, but many of the prisoners were elderly and people don't walk fast with their hands tied behind their backs. It was almost dark as they were herded, with the rest of Manbrookstat's elite, into an open-air pen in front of the gas-lit rostrum. All around them, the city mob was restless, happy one moment and angry the next, apparently unsure whether they had been summoned to a purge or a festival.

Finally the Commandant stepped into the pool of warm gaslight on the rostrum. "My friends," he said, "my dear friends, let me first make an announcement that will sadden some of you. Just a few days ago, the Army of the Wabash was defeated at Tippecanoe, in what used to be the state of Indiana, and beaten so badly that they were unable to come to the defense of Pale Bluff, that charming little town some of you may have read about in foreign newspapers. On Sunday, Pale Bluff itself was lost, and my agents tell me the fires are still burning there. The former United States no longer has a viable transcontinental connection, and Lord Robert's Domain has become a secure nation with defensible frontiers." There were so many lies in that single sentence that Rollings felt as if he might explode; dozens of routes remained open and the Domain was no bigger than it had been. *But,* he realized, *most of these guys don't know that.*

"I have therefore come to a painful decision, one I had been forming for some time. The United States of America is not united anymore, many of its states have ceased to exist and are being replaced by other states and nations, and all that is left is an American continent in which we must carve out our own destiny. I am therefore proclaiming that the Commandancy of Manbrookstat is now and will remain a sovereign nation, with its northern boundary at the St. Lawrence and the Great Lakes, its southern boundary at the James, Greenbrier, New, Kanawha, and Ohio Rivers, details to be worked out with the Christian States of America which is now forming.

"Our western border will be fixed in negotiations with the Domain, which we have the honor to be the first nation to recognize and to accept in trade negotiations.

"The Commandancy of Manbrookstat intends to join the Atlantic

League as a founding member; at this moment it appears that other founders will be the Galway Republic, the Grand Duchy of Halifax, the Kingdom of the Azores, Trinidad/Tobago, Dominica, Argentina, Puerto Rico,
and a number of states now being organized around port cities in the former Brazil, Iceland, Norway, Morocco, Portugal, and Ireland.

"Finally, I realize that many of you had hoped there would someday be
a United States again. I myself, as a cadet, took an oath to uphold and
defend it. But however bereaved we may be, however deep our grief, however much we wish it were not so, the fact is that there is no United States
anymore, and the dreams of reviving it are idle fantasies, and can only be
dangerous delusional dreams in years to come.

"Now, I have every faith that the common people understand this. The
common people, after all, are *born* practical, and besides, they are well
aware that the old arrangements were not really in their favor; many of
them can look forward to prospering much more in our newer, fairer
world than they ever did under the old United States regime. And since
the common people understand it, and gain by it, it is only a victory for
democracy that we listen to them and pursue the independent and free
Commandancy of Manbrookstat according to their wishes."

Rollings tried to keep his face impassive as the mob surrounding their
pen cheered and whooped. Apparently some of the people nearer the barriers were less good at hiding their feelings, for the crowd was jeering and
throwing things at some of them, and the militia slowly, reluctantly, half-
heartedly was trying to make them stop.

When the uproar had quieted, the Commandant went on. "Now, my
friends and fellow citizens, you also see before you the business, educa-
tional, and political leadership of our Commandancy. These are of course
people who did very well, back before.

"And then they continued to do well as the world moved, at first,
toward re-establishing the old regime, and putting the United States of
America back together.

"But as we have noted, there is no possibility now of a Restored Republic. Any hope for a Restored Republic, now, would be an aggressive plot to
preserve wealth and privilege, or to gain more of it unfairly.

"So we can very fairly look at these citizens and ask, 'Can we trust them? Will they work toward the new, democratic Commandancy, and for the common good?' And, to be blunt, I am sure some of them won't, but fellow citizens and good friends, let me point out to you that I have worked with many of these people, and know them, and like them, and that I am equally sure that most of them will make a full commitment to the success of the new Commandancy, and it would be the very height of injustice to treat them with suspicion or to vent anger from any bygone unfairness on these hardworking, upstanding people who have made our city a much better place to live.

"Therefore, we're going to do the following, and I really do think it is all we will ever need to do. We're going to ask each family, or as many of its members as were in the city this evening, to come forward, onto the rostrum here, and swear an oath of allegiance to Manbrookstat, to the Commandancy, to the citizens of the Commandancy, and of course to me personally as well since I am serving you as your Commandant. Then once they have given their oaths, our militia or our Special Assistants will escort them peaceably back to their homes, and they will peaceably go about their normal business tomorrow, under the fair and democratic laws of the Commandancy, just as they did under the laws of the old United States. We have a number of them to get through tonight, so I'll ask you to hold your applause till the end."

The first family pulled out of the crowded pen and pushed into the light, not roughly but firmly, were the Theards; Rollings knew them slightly, as the owners and operators of a large fish market. Henri Theard seemed very relieved to see his wife, three daughters, and elderly mother, and they all repeated their new oath of allegiance with calm acceptance.

After a smattering of clapping, the Commandant reminded everyone to hold applause till the end. The Theards were escorted from the stage and out into the night.

That set the pattern until the Commandant called up the Steigers. Joseph Steiger had several adult grandchildren and ran the city's compost industry, which was rapidly turning large parts of Staten Island into truck gardens. In the business community, he was an outspoken public critic of the Commandant, and fifty-star flags flew from every building in his operation. It was clear that the family was being pushed more than helped onto the platform, and that it wasn't easy to find places for all of them to stand.

"And now the Steiger family will take the oath. Please repeat after—"

Old Joe Steiger bellowed, "Like hell we will. This bullshit is treason, blatant treason, and—"

Doubtless, the Commandant had planned it.

The Special Assistant behind Joseph Steiger whipped out a heavy, short piece of pipe and brought it down on Steiger's head in one savage motion. Steiger fell to his knees, moaning, and the Special Assistant struck again, knocking him to his face, kicked him in the ribs, and brought the pipe down on his head so hard that the thud was audible where Rollings stood.

The crowd was silent for a moment, and then someone laughed, and then many of them did. *Maybe that first guy that laughed was a plant,* Rollings thought. *But everyone that laughed after him, they weren't all plants. The mob's with the Commandant.*

The Commandant said, "Now we will continue with the oath. Mrs. Sharon Steiger, if you will lead—"

Joe Steiger's wife (or was she already his widow?) screamed a few words of denunciation before the same Special Assistant, with the same pipe, knocked her down. The way she twitched on the little stage looked more like a spasm than a struggle. The mob was still laughing, but with a nervous, hysteric edge.

The Commandant sighed with just a hint of impatience. "Since the oldest members of the family won't lead, let's try a younger one. Tory Steiger, please step forward."

The girl was tiny, maybe ten years old and small for her age, and trembling. The Special Assistant stood behind her, not even concealing the length of pipe, and the Commandant said, very gently, "Sweetie, you just need to say the words."

Tory's mother said, "Do what the Commandant says, honey, it will be all right."

"Yes, exactly," the Commandant said. "And the rest of your family will speak along with you."

They did, mumbling, and it was conspicuous that when the Steiger family left the stage (except for the oldest generation, who were carried down the steps and dumped into a cart), there were numerous armed men around them, and they went into the dark in a different direction.

At last the Commandant called for the Rollings family. Deanna had already bumped, WE SAY IT to him and he'd bumped back HELL YES. As they were led up the steps, Rollings's wife, Matilda, and their other daughter Uhura, joined them.

It was easier than he thought it would be; he said it loudly, clearly, and firmly, just as, when drug addicts had robbed his dental practice, he had always spoken politely and clearly so that they would have no cause to harm him. It was over in no time and he didn't even feel like he had to shower or brush his teeth afterward. *I suppose if you truly understand that an oath given under duress is meaningless, then it just doesn't matter much. Thanks for Ethics 202, Professor Blaine.*

Their two militia guards (it looked like the Commandant was using militia for the more cooperative, less suspect people) had walked them back over the Brooklyn Bridge, and they were a few blocks from the house, when a voice said, "Is that the Rollings family?"

"Yeah."

The man who stepped out of the shadow and into the lantern light wore a long coat and a black scarf around his face, and held up a Special Assistant's badge. "The Commandant wants this asshole's sloop searched *tonight*, and we want him and his family there while we do it, so they can help—and so we can remind them they want to help. Sounds like there's a lot of stuff on there that has never been recorded for tax purposes, a lot of small valuable pocket stuff."

The militia men, probably thinking there would be a chance to fill their pockets, were immediately, happily willing to comply. So was Rollings, but he made sure it didn't show. Deanna bumped against him.

G?

He bumped back

HE

and contrived to rub against Matilda, who bumped

DUH IM HIS MTHR

Rollings was nervous and scared that his son's deception might be exposed, but soon he reflected that had Geordie been a completely different person, he might have been *good* at Special Assisting. Within two blocks, by dint of overbearing nitpicking, Geordie had the militiamen discouraged and trudging along aimlessly as they made their way to the Brooklyn wharfs. As he pretended to rough up his family, he cut his father's bonds and slipped a knife into his hands; after another block he quietly said, "Now," and they heard a startled, soft cry of pain behind them. Rollings sprang forward and slid the knife into their front guard's throat, two quick stabs that silenced him and left him dying on the sidewalk. *Two years ago I'd've puked; but between pirates, muggers, wreckers, and that guy I think was probably an assassin, it's kind of a technical business, like taking out a badly fractured wisdom tooth.*

When Rollings looked back, the one that Geordie had knifed was lying still. "All right," Geordie said. "Let me douse that lantern out, Pops, and you all stick close to me. Should be enough moonlight to make it to *Ferengi* without needing to show a light."

As they climbed the gangplank, Rollings muttered, "I would've thought they'd have had a guard on this ship."

"They did, Pops. Where'd'ya think I got the outfit and the badge?"

Ferengi had been deliberately kept fully stocked for a long voyage, and the Commandant's men hadn't disturbed anything. The land breeze and the tide were in their favor, and Geordie knew the harbor well; when the moon rose, just before midnight, they were well clear.

"Man, one thing I won't miss, it's that broken Statue of Liberty," Matilda said. "Broke my heart every time I came over to Manhattan. Did you hear that Commandant's got convicts out there in chains every day, cutting up the fallen-off arm-and-torch, so he can sell it for scrap? Besides being crass, and a fascist dictator, he has no sense of irony." She drew a deep breath. "Love the smell of the air, and I don't mean just the salt water. What time is it?"

Rollings said, "Moonrise was going to be just before midnight, and there's not even a glow on the horizon yet. So it's not late. I don't think we should chance a light till we're further out to sea and we're running before a good stiff breeze."

"Well, we're all safe for the moment. Sorry we lost the business, Jamayu, but that's the world nowadays."

Rollings laughed. "Heck, 'Tildie, if I start worrying about the past I'll soon be sorry that I'll probably never do another root canal. We got the fam, we got *Ferengi*, we got skills and our health."

"Yeah, that's a cargo of blessings, isn't it? Well, then, has anybody thought about where we're going, yet?"

"There's nothing north, Europe's too far away and a bigger mess than here, that leaves south," Rollings said. "We could probably live okay in the Christian States, but we've got the range to go farther. If we can trust Whorf's last letter, St. Croix sounds like a decent place to do a little trading, shipping, and salvaging. What do you all think?"

"I think whether we're going to Savannah, St. Croix, or Rio, we sail exactly the same for the next week," Geordie said, "and come dawn, I'm going to want someone to relieve me at the helm, which means somebody ought to get some sleep, right now, and we have a week to talk all this out."

"Nothing to argue with there," Rollings said.

"I'll stay up for this watch with you," Uhura said. "We can figure out rotation later. Pops, Mom, you've had a day and I think you ought to go sleep."

In the skipper's cabin, as they settled into their familiar, beloved bunk, Rollings asked his wife, "How come we've got such great kids?"

"Proper culling," she said. "You just never heard the splashes when I'd toss the dumb, mean, ugly ones over the side."

It was an old joke, shared as comfortably as the bunk itself, and with half a thought more about how lucky he was, he fell asleep.

ABOUT THE SAME TIME. RUINS OF PALE BLUFF. ABOUT 9:30 PM CENTRAL TIME. MONDAY, MAY 11, 2026.

"Now, heave, heave, *heave!*" Nathanson shouted, and the old phone pole moved forward and under the trip bar. "Trip her!"

The other crew hauled on their lines, dragging the trip bar down and pushing the tall pole's tip down into the hole.

"And *heave!*"

The pole seated in its hole, slid a little in and down, and rose as the main line hauled it upward. With a thump, it slid into place, and while the guy lines still held it, the crew dumped rocks and dirt around the base; in a minute or so, it was secure enough to stand for years.

Nathanson turned and waved to the men standing by the big bonfire, who hurled in shovels and buckets full of ripped-up books from the town library and school. The fire roared up in a great burst of blazing pages, wiping the stars from the sky and sending orange light dancing up the pole to where General Phat's body was attached by many wrappings of old electric wire.

The drums boomed out a quick, infectious rhythm, and the crowd cheered and sang. Others ran forward to help throw all the paper into the bonfire, making it blaze higher and prettier still, and a huge circle of dancers wove around the immense fire until it burned down, and at the urging of the leaders, they sat down to listen to Lord Robert.

He stood on the high platform with the fire lighting him from the side, and began, "As you all know, True Daybreak and traditional Daybreak have joined forces, and we have made the country from the Wabash and the Ohio to the Lakes all ours. The enemy army is now only trying to find their way out, trying to run away while they still can. They are shattered. I proclaim that this is now the Domain of Lord Robert!"

When another long burst of drumming and dancing had subsided, and he was growing impatient, Robert continued, "Now, there was a condition attached to this. Traditional Daybreak has said to us, via Glad Ocean here"—he actually embraced the old bony bitch, and smelled her unwashed body as he did, to make his point, and she beamed up at him—"that it would send tens of thousands of fighters, and it has. It pledged to make this victory possible, and it has. And now . . . traditional Daybreak says, their price for their help has been, now throw it all away. Let us not have what we have fought for."

The crowd moaned, some with the onset of Daybreak seizures, some old-school Daybreakers booing him, and many of his own True Daybreak people excited and getting ready.

His arm slipped from an embrace of the woman to a forearm wrapped around her throat, and he began to squeeze. "Glad Ocean here, Glad Ocean is the teacher of the *Daybreak that does not work*, the *spoiled and ruined Daybreak that will rob you all—*" Robert was squeezing her neck and she was beginning to struggle desperately. "And I say, that is a bargain we don't need to keep. We needed this victory, and so did Daybreak, and now we are done with each other!"

The crowd was milling; fights were breaking out, some people were trying to flee, others suffering seizures.

"The old Daybreak of your old tribes demanded that if you came here to fight by our sides, I would then lead you on a huge fucking raid from here all the way across the plains, to break and shatter plaztatic civilization wherever we find it—and then die!

"You all know that Daybreak tells you to kill as many people as you can and then die yourself! They want us to clean out the plaztatic assholes, scrape them off the world, and then lie down and die on top of them and free the planet. *Never* have kids, *never* raise a family, live out your life as a slave or a soldier, die for Daybreak! Die for Mother Earth because . . . because it's a *lie!*"

He nodded at Bernstein and Nathanson. Bernstein went to grab Glad Ocean's master, super-duper extra powerful spirit stick from the slave carrying it; when the slave resisted, Nathanson felled him with a hatchet chop to the face. Bernstein wrenched the spirit stick away and hurled it high into the air like a javelin, so that it came down in the very center of the bonfire. "Daybreak is broken!" he shouted. "Long live True Daybreak!"

Robert was screaming his message over the uproar, not worrying because his own side knew it and was shouting something similar as they fought back and forth with their tribal allies. "True Daybreak says—live in the beautiful world you have made! True Daybreak says—fish in those streams when they run clean again! True Daybreak says—sit by a warm fire and *enjoy* your freedom! No slaves! Keep your babies and raise them! Clean Earth and real freedom!"

Glad Ocean had been a small woman before, and though she'd probably toned her muscles in the last year, much of it had been a year of slow starvation and struggle to stay warm and not die of flu or a cold. He had worked his forearm down into the crease of her neck, with his wrist biting into her carotid, and now he lifted her up onto her tiptoes and shook her like an old towel, letting her have just enough air not to pass out yet.

"That is what True Daybreak says. I say, I want True Daybreak! True Daybreak and I want peace! No more war! No more deaths! No slaves, everyone equal! Families to raise and corn to grow, living the good life on the good clean planet, because we fought for it and it is ours and we deserve it! I want you to join True Daybreak, join me, join us tomorrow when we return to Castle Earthstone. All you tribes who have fought and bled beside us: come and live with us too. The Domain is big and wide and open, it's the best hunting ground, the best place to raise corn and make whiskey, the best place to make babies and raise kids, to fight and fuck and love and dance and live the life a natural man was meant to live—"

There had been a swelling noise in the huge crowd; Robert had been waiting for it. For weeks, ever since the tribal forces had come together at Castle Earthstone, his True Daybreak believers had been moving among the tribes, befriending where they could, not so much arguing as just presenting the idea over and over, pointing to the beauty of the Earth and asking, "Now that it is ours, why do you want to leave it so soon?"

His followers had been trained in the techniques for caring for people after a seizure, and for helping the victim to break free of Daybreak after a seizure. Slowly, a seizure at a time, the Castle Earthstone people had been pushing their newfound tribal friends through the process. Bernstein had guessed that they had about sixty percent of the tribal allies ready to convert; Robert figured that Bernstein had never quite recovered from being an accountant back before, and he figured that sixty percent was a SWAG for "more than half," but good enough.

"Stand up and declare for True Daybreak!" he shouted. "Come with us! You can marry, have children, a family! You can grow the good food and work in the good Earth! You don't have to die a dirty death out on the plains just because a few fucked up people made a mess of the Earth back before! The plaztatic world is dead, blessings be to Daybreak, and long live the Domain!"

Thousands of his True Daybreak people from Castle Earthstone, and tens of thousands of recent converts, leapt to their feet and shouted that real Daybreak was at hand. The remaining traditional Daybreakers shrieked, assaulted people near them, reached for weapons, but the preparations had been thorough; most of the True Daybreakers had brought a knife, a club, or a garotte, and most of the old tribals were unarmed, as they usually were for celebrations and ceremonies. Besides, another large part of the traditional Daybreak followers had been partly converted or were conflicted, and many thousands who might have fought for Daybreak instead fell into seizures. At Robert's orders, his forces left the seizure cases alone for the moment; many would emerge ready to convert, and at the moment they were no more than a minor hazard underfoot.

In less than an hour, an army of 30,000 mixed tribals and Castle Earthstone True Daybreakers had become an army of 24,000 Castle Earthstone True Daybreakers. The bodies from the fighting lay in the streets, but since what was left of the town would burn tomorrow, they could just lie there, with the soldiers and the townspeople, something else to remind plaztatic America never to insult free people and despoil free Gaia again.

When the crowd had re-gathered at the fire, Robert had been amusing himself by tormenting Glad Ocean with his knife, and when he told her she was a sacrifice and ordered her to walk into the fire, to all appearances she did it willingly. A shout of joy went up as she fell forward into the coals.

"More fuel, do you think?" Bernstein asked, as it burned lower around the charred corpse.

"Naw. Let's hope they get some sleep before they start walking back. Tomorrow's going to be a long day, and then we've got a good month of walking to do, without the river doing most of the work this time. Meanwhile, though, life's pretty sweet."

He rose and stretched. "I think they were going to fix a special supper for us, and have some nice clean girls waiting, back at our main tent. Speaking of rewards we've earned, let's go get ours."

3 HOURS LATER. A MOWER SHED, IN THE ORCHARDS OUTSIDE THE FORMER PALE BLUFF. 12:30 AM CENTRAL TIME. TUESDAY, MAY 12, 2026.

Pauline Kloster slipped into the corrugated iron shed without making a sound; only the brief dark moments as her body blocked the moonlight through the crevices revealed she was there. Then Carol May Kloster felt the warmth of her niece's shoulder next to her own, and a soft exhalation into her ear. "Aunt Carol May, they're gonna party all night, sleep it off, and then start walking home. They're going back to Castle Earthstone and taking all these tribals with them. How are the little guys doing?"

"So far nobody that wakes up yelling, thank the lord. How's it look like the party is going?"

"Right now? Just getting started. They've still got some prisoners they're gonna do stuff to. I kinda hurried to get back so I wouldn't have to see none-a-that. Aunt Carol May, I want to help them but I don't see how I can."

Carol May put her arms around Pauline and whispered, "No, you can't, honey. Most of us would love to be more help, but sometimes we just can't. We've got five little kids to try to sneak out with, and they're gonna wake up scared and hungry and mad at us, 'specially when we have to say they can't see Mama right now, and we can't go find their teddy. It was just dumb luck we found them at the airport; probably Quattro was supposed to fly them but no one told him."

"I was so upset when I saw him already taking off, I mean he didn't know we were coming but we tried so hard to get there and missed him by just that much. Then . . . right when I thought how can we be so close and still miss it . . . that was terrible, wasn't it?"

Carol May hugged her niece closer. "Yes, it was, try not to think about it, relax."

"It looked like the whole inside just filled up, all at once, with white-hot fire. Why'd his plane blow up?"

"EMP, I'm pretty sure. Poor guy, I really liked him, and his wife is such a sweetheart, and they were only married less than a year ago. At least he couldn't have suffered much."

They sat in the dark and listened to the whooping, the shrieking, the occasional cries of pain and hoots of laughter, and the never-stopping drums. No one seemed to be coming back into the orchards, probably because there was no loot here, most of the trees were already burned, and nobody felt any need for privacy while copulating.

The noise went on while Carol May observed the moon moving a handsbreadth-at-arm's-length across the sky, crossing one crack and then another; she watched that one more time, then spoke as softly as she could. "Pauline, honey, you still awake?"

"Yeah. Can't sleep. I keep hoping they've killed the people they were playing with, but then I hear another scream."

Carol May shuddered. "How's the leg?"

"Not bad. Tired, and it gets sore when it's tired, but it's got some miles in it. Were you thinking of going now?"

"It's going to take these tribals most of the night to fall down and go to sleep, I'm afraid, and then all day tomorrow before they're even half-way started walking back to Castle Earthstone. So if we wait till tomorrow, and let it get light, we'll have to stay under cover for most of the day and keep our little friends quiet. It was bad enough doing that all day today, and we had the help of all the noise from town, and the fires in the burning orchards, to help hide us. Tomorrow anyone who's half curious or hears a funny sound is going to be able to walk right up to the shed and in through the door, and we won't be able to fool them into thinking the place is already torched by burning a little junk right by the door."

"Makes sense. Packs are still loaded, right?"

"Yep. I grabbed a pilot emergency radio kit at the airport, and that's in my pack—"

"One of those radio in a jar things?"

"Yeah."

"Man, Aunt Carol May, all I thought to bring was that applesauce and apple butter we've been eating," Pauline said. "I didn't even think where there might be anything useful."

"Pauline, sweetheart, you can't get more useful than food. Especially the kind where kids'll eat it, and you got enough to get us a couple days down the road. And I'm glad it's all applesauce and apple butter, because, honey, you know it's the last thing that's going to taste like home, ever. Aw, don't cry on me, Pauline, please don't cry or I'll start. Come on, we need to wake these kids up quietly and be on our way."

4 HOURS LATER. PUEBLO. 8:30 AM MOUNTAIN TIME. TUESDAY, MAY 12, 2026.

"Who's the most excellent boy in the whole stinking world?" Heather asked Leo, who was making noises that indicated he knew. She hugged him close and thought, *And I do mean stinking. Well, at least Dad'll get to know his grandson, and there are worse places to live than San Diego, and . . . man, we are so beaten.*

The knock at the door was soft. "Ms. O'Grainne? Got an emergency message from Incoming Crypto."

She opened the door to find Ntale standing there. "Patrick sent me 'cause it was further to Mister Hendrix's house. And Melissa at Crypto told us both to run, run, run, she said it just like that, three times, she said you'd want this news right away."

Heather handed Ntale a pile of meal coupons and said, "Hang around till I read it, just in case I need to send a message with you."

She set Leo down with a final little tap of her finger on his nose, which made his eyes cross in a way that always made her laugh. She grinned at the silly boy, then got the letter opener from her desk, slipped it under the envelope flap, and drew a deep breath against the coming bad news. The horde was already on its way down the Ohio, perhaps an advance party had already attacked Paducah? The Army of the Wabash ambushed and cut off again? Another declaration of independence somewhere? The tribes that had been moving around in the Tennessee Valley and the Ouachitas had broken out again?

Whatever it is, we'll get through it, she thought. *Strange that I'm still the President, this morning, so I guess getting through whatever it is, is my job.*

Then she opened it, and saw that it was from Carol May, who was alive and transmitting from a barn fifteen miles northwest of Pale Bluff, and expected to make it into Wayne City late today. She teared up; *Carol May, alive!*

She had to wipe her eyes before she read the even better news. When she did, she handed Ntale a fistful of meal tickets, and said, "If James hasn't started cooking breakfast, make him start. If he needs groceries, get his order and take it to the commissary, put it on the RRC tab. And then you and Patrick go get Leslie, and the Duchess from wherever she's staying, and Jason and Beth, and Izzy Underhill, okay? We need to meet, which means you and Patrick get us all into James's house, quick as you can."

Ntale grinned. "Let me *show* you how quick that is. I've been getting my growth this year and Patrick's not the only fast one in the family anymore."

2 HOURS LATER. PUEBLO. 10:30 AM MOUNTAIN TIME. TUESDAY, MAY 12, 2026.

"Well, the attendants are saying he only started to move about an hour ago. He's had time to pee and they gave him a little breakfast, and they're saying he's kind of drifting around, which is pretty usual the morning after a severe seizure." James looked up and down the conference table. "So we're agreed on the basic strategy, right? Shock him with the news and see what happens. Maybe we can get him loose enough from Daybreak to clue us in to something else. Now, any other thoughts?"

There were none. When they filed into the little room, Arnie barely looked up from where he sat on the bed, leaning forward, arms folded as if he were a small boy with a stomachache.

James said, "The horde led by Lord Robert of Castle Earthstone has converted, en masse, to the version of Daybreak that he calls True Daybreak, which preaches that the clean, natural Earth is here for human beings to enjoy, and instead of driving forward in a great raid against the plaztatic world, they are going home to plant crops, raise children, and repopulate the Earth."

"Liar."

"All true. Every word of it. Daybreak is betrayed. The Lost Quarter is in the hand of heretics, or whatever your stupid bush-hippie movement calls them."

Arnie shuddered and wiped his eyes. "I can't feel Daybreak," he said. "It's not reacting. It's just me, left here, now that it's done with me."

"Then why won't you believe me?"

"I don't know." He wiped his eyes again.

"Do you remember what we talked about yesterday? Do you remember telling me how Daybreak tricked us into playing its game, and losing the war?"

"Like it was a hundred years ago." He rocked back and forth. "Daybreak . . . it's in trouble. Or not, maybe it's just finished what it came for. This True Daybreak, is, is, is, not yet, no, no seizure this time. True Daybreak or not, it doesn't matter. This plaztatic world will rise no higher, this world will not . . . your species, this species, my species, doesn't matter, the world will be wild and safe, no danger to anyone." He looked up at them with a vacant stare. "James? What have I been talking about?"

"Nice fake, Arnie."

"I can't remember what we're talking about."

"Do you remember that True Daybreak is taking over the Lost Quarter, and Lord Robert has betrayed you?"

"No, I . . . maybe, you just told me, didn't you?"

"Can you feel Daybreak inside you? It almost gave you a seizure. You said you couldn't feel it."

"It lies a lot. I lie a lot. I'm sorry. Can I sleep now?"

Back in the Facility 1 conference room, James said, "Well. I think that Daybreak definitely wants us to believe that Lord Robert's heresy is not something Daybreak approves of and it's not the next move in Daybreak's development. We're being set up to believe that it's his own particular invention, and what he has re-invented is barbarian tyranny. That's pretty awful if you consider all his subjects were ordinary Americans or Canadians, regular people with regular jobs, two years ago. But if you consider that he's just a plain old barbarian conqueror, not too different from Attila or Chaka Zulu or one of the Khans, and civilization has five thousand years of practice in how to deal with those, well, yeah. We couldn't live with the tribes, but we can live with the Domain. They'll come to us to trade, maybe not this week or this year, but soon, and they'll want all those nice toys and a warm house in the winter and out of season food, and in a hundred years they'll be absorbed. That's the story it's telling us."

"But you don't believe it's true?" Bambi asked.

"Not really. It looks like classic Daybreak, the lies are just wrappers for more lies."

Jason nodded. "That's the way I see it too, James. Yeah, I buy that civilization can absorb some of Daybreak, but that doesn't mean the end of Daybreak; it means Daybreak is going to be all through civilization. Everywhere, all the time, as the new world grows up, Daybreak will be there whispering that machines are wicked, knowledge is poison, and people were meant to be big hairless monkeys huddling in the bushes and dying before they're forty. That was around before, but look at Castle Earthstone. Me and the other scouts didn't see a city that's going to grow and advance and change. It was a hunting cabin, a place for guys to play out their big man in the woods fantasies. If it turns into a real castle, it's still going to be a backward, primitive, progress-and-people-hating kind of place. Kids that grow up there are gonna grow up with the idea that dirty, smelly, overworked, and sick is virtuous, and that enjoying life and comfort and having the tools and leisure to explore a long way is degenerate and wicked. Lord Robert hasn't defeated it; he's just driven it underground, and it'll trickle up all around his Domain, and keep it stuck in the mud forever."

"But he's not burning down the civilized world," James pointed out.

"True."

Beth said, "I have the strangest idea."

Heather smiled, trying to look as encouraging as she could, because Beth was often nervous around people who had a lot of schooling, big vocabularies, or impressive titles. "Well, share."

The young woman looked down nervously. "So if Daybreak is trouble for, like, regular civilized people, and Lord Robert is trying to set up a regular civilized Domain, but it's all made up of ex-Daybreakers or heretic Daybreakers or whatever they are . . . what if we gave him a shot of the original Daybreak to cope with? Something to keep him more backward, and focused on his own troubles?"

James clapped his hands. "I get it. Fighting Daybreak with Daybreak. And it gives us something to do with poor old Arnie. I'd been afraid that someday we'd have to decide he was too dangerous to keep, or all used up, and kill him. And since the research here is over . . . yeah, why not? Either we release him or we murder him, and the world has had enough murders."

THE NEXT DAY. IN THE ADRIATIC SEA, ON BOARD
***DISCOVERY.* 9:00 AM CENTRAL EUROPEAN TIME.**
WEDNESDAY, MAY 13, 2026.

Captain Halleck thanked the watch that would still have been in their bunks, and said, "This is simplicity itself. I think we've all been staying up with the radio reports from home, and we know that things are in a very bad way indeed back there. Well, not surprisingly, the government in Athens, which created this mission and owns this ship, has sent us orders that we are to abandon our research and return to Savannah, there to be outfitted as a warship. They do not want us to bring back or report on our research; the ship's company will be disbanded and members returned to their homes 'as expeditiously as possible.' I suspect but cannot prove that this precipitate decision is in reaction to some of our biologists having done some field studies, back in Florida, in which the word 'evolution' found its way into the titles.

"Now, there are two possible ways we can react to this. We can dutifully sail back to Savannah, protesting over the radio the whole way if we like, and when we get there, they'll toss our research notes and samples into the bay and convert us to a warship. Or we can go somewhere else and place ourselves under their protection, and avoid going to ports in—now this is truly weird—the CSA. For one awful moment I thought someone had revived the Confederacy, but actually that's the Christian States of America.

"Coincidentally, I happened to be talking by radio to Captain Highbotham in Christiansted, a place some of you may remember."

Laughter and applause swept the deck.

"I thought we might take a vote."

The vote was overwhelmingly for Christiansted. Only two very duty-conscious sailors, and two scholars who thought it would be more convenient to get off the ship in Savannah, voted the other way.

As Whorf returned to his station, Halleck stopped him and said, "I thought you might like to know that I have a relay, via James Hendrix at Pueblo and Captain Highbotham, addressed to you." He handed him a sheet of paper, and said, "I assume this is some code I'm not familiar with."

Whorf looked and grinned. "It's my family code, sir, we all use it in the family business—which has just relocated to Christiansted. This is great!"

"You're telling me," Ihor said; he had been standing there quietly listening. "Now there's someone I can bother for a job."

9 HOURS LATER. PUEBLO. 9:00 AM MOUNTAIN TIME. WEDNESDAY, MAY 13, 2026.

"We've put enough food in your pack so that if you're careful, you should be able to walk all the way to the Wabash from Wayne City, where the train will drop you off. If you cross any bridge along it, a patrol will challenge you. And then you cooperate, and they take you to Castle Earthstone, and you can decide what to do from there."

Arnie Yang nodded. "Thank you. And if I ever come back out of the Lost Quarter, wanting to talk, what will you do?"

"Talk to you. Mostly about the Lost Quarter and what's going on there," Heather said. "We're not exiling you for your ideas, Arnie—especially since they are not really your ideas and you don't hold them voluntarily. It's just that, while you're infected with them, it's better to have you keeping company with the other infected people, than out here."

Arnie looked for a moment as if he might speak, then shrugged and hugged all of them before he boarded the train.

The next stop was Outgoing Crypto, where Heather told them, "All right, special request. Broadcast in clear."

"You mean not coded, so anyone can read it?"

"Yes, that's exactly what I mean. I know it's not really crypto if it's not enciphered, but you folks have the biggest and best radio in this part of the country, and I need to make sure everyone reads this." It was a short note explaining her claim to be President of the United States, resigning the office without a successor, and therefore declaring the end of the United States.

"Really," she said, as they rode in the carriage to the airfield, "it's almost more of a relief. Now that I'm not the President, I'm not a target, or not much of one, anyway. And it will be nice, if Bambi really does make me a baroness—"

"I'm thinking at least a countess."

"Well, whatever. I guess I should be happy it's not waitress or steward-ess. Anyway, running a feudal fief seems like a much more reasonable job in the new world. And it'll be a decent place for Leo to grow up, if I have any say about it, and we can bring my father out to live with us, free baby-sitting with bonding on the side. Certainly better than the old job here." She sighed. "Even though I'll miss everyone."

A few minutes later, James and Leslie watched the Stearman, carrying Heather and Leo in the front cockpit with Bambi behind, bound off the runway and head west.

"This place was home for both of us, back before," James observed. "And there's still some library work to do, getting those pamphlets and brochures out to people who need them but don't have them already. So we'll eat, eh?"

"If you cook, we'll eat well." She slipped her arm into his. "It's funny, just when I start to see how big you grew in that job, you go and lose it. And I guess after you fail at restoring America, there's not very many jobs that could ever have the same appeal."

James sighed. "Just when I get a job that impresses you, I find I'm more into the job than into impressing you."

"That's perfectly okay. Can we take this very slowly? Long walks, com-plicated conversations, that kind of thing? There's just so much we don't know yet."

"Actually we don't even know what country we're going to be in yet. Slow is fine."

SEVENTEEN:
EVERY NEW BEGINNING COMES FROM SOME OTHER BEGINNING'S END

Dave and Arlene Carlucci, and Terry Bolton, all began by trying to tell Bambi how sorry they were about Quattro, and how much they had liked him. It was little consolation that they were simply telling the truth, but some stern glares and aggressive subject-changing from Heather shut them up gently, and after that, the luxury of really good food in abundance made them nearly as quiet as the Carluccis' teenagers, Paley and Acey.

It was a long time before they got down to business, too, because none of them had met Leo before, and "proper baby-admiring takes time," as Terry pointed out. He seemed to be visibly brightening with each minute spent on the broad terrace, overlooking the sea, where Bambi preferred to entertain whenever the weather was favorable.

Finally, though, Pat O'Grainne took Leo down to the other end of the terrace to play, and it was time for adult business.

"Just to begin with," Heather said, "you guys should know how grateful I am."

"How grateful *we* are," Bambi said. "And I can't imagine what you're going through and won't pretend to understand; you all were career FBI with decades of experience, and now . . . there's not only no job, there's no Federal Bureau of Investigation, there's not even a Federal. So we wanted to make you a special offer, in two parts.

"One, Heather has graciously agreed to be the Countess of Laguna Beach, and we'll start construction of Castle O'Grainne or Castle Laguna or whatever she decides to call it this summer, and probably she'll move in next summer, because the weathermen say that was our last really cold winter after the disaster; most of the soot is out of the air now, so we won't have snow next year, and only a normal volume of rain.

"Heather will need all of your skills—not just Dave and Terry's guns, but your experience with small-scale firefights, and Arlene's nursing experience. Any of you can have a job there, and the job will start well before the castle is built, since you'll be putting together a team. Carlucci, that also means that any of your local deputies that are interested will be first in line with Heather—or with me.

"Two may be more interesting, or less. I need a freehold to anchor your end of the coast; that's a very vulnerable area in my county, and therefore in my duchy, right now. So you guys could freehold together, set up two small freeholds, or one could freehold and the other could hire him. Any combination you like."

Carlucci said, "Could I just . . . man." He was wiping his eyes. "Bambi, I'm sorry, but I just feel like I lost the argument with your father, and him on the other side of the grave. I mean . . . no more America, you know? And I was a pretty rah-rah go-America U!S!A! kind of person— embarrassed my kids with super-patriot names and all"—he saw their glares—"which I won't explain right now, but anyway, it's a lot to give up. And you both know, we've been through a lot together, it might take me some days to make up my mind."

Terry Bolton sat back and said, "You know, I guess I feel differently. If I could get the whole, old, back-before world back in one big swoop, sure, I'd do that in a heartbeat. But in this new world . . . well, I don't know about being a freeholder. But, uh, if you need a chief of arms, Heather—is it okay to call you Heather?"

"I'll insist. Especially if you work for me. And I like 'Chief of Arms.'

Can I ask, since you seem to be baby-experienced, to judge by how you get along with Leo, what you'll need for quarters?"

"Space for me and three kids, girl ten, boy eight, and boy six."

"Caucasians, with any identifying tattoos or scars?" Heather was smiling.

"Yeah, well, we all get that way after a decade or two of filling out reports, don't we? My online dating profile had things presented pretty much the way they would be on a handbill in the post office. Anyway, I'm a single dad, now. My wife divorced me and she and her new husband were honeymooning in Hawaii on Daybreak day. Haven't heard from her since, not even in the first days when the hams were still up and operating. But if there'd be room for a little family at Castle O'Grainne? Even if the older boy is sort of ADD and aspy?"

"There would be. Start looking for guys you'd like to have serve under you, Terry." Heather gazed at Carlucci thoughtfully. "Dave, I know you a little better, and just to point this out: you'd make a good freeholder."

"That's what worries me," Carlucci said. He nodded at his son. "Paley already tells me my politics are medieval."

THE NEXT DAY. RUINS OF PALE BLUFF. 3:00 PM CENTRAL TIME. SATURDAY, MAY 16, 2026.

When Larry Mensche and Dave McWaine met up again after combing through the town in opposite spirals, they still had not found Freddie Pranger. Pale Bluff had been his home town; he'd known who lived in most houses, climbed most of the apple trees in the orchards, and recognized most of the names in the town cemetery. The Army officers had asked him to identify bodies but he'd darted into the town and vanished as soon as they'd arrived.

Larry and Dave finally found him by giving up; he was saying goodbye to Roger Jackson, who was hobbling on crutches, but whose leg seemed to be healing straight, at least so far. "Just wanted to make sure I said bye-bye to all my old scout buddies before I took off for good," Freddie said. "I'll do their body identification, though it makes me sick, but then I'm resigned and off on my own."

"What will you do, then?" Larry asked.

"Well," Freddie said. "You, uh, ever hear of a guy named John Johnson? That's kind of how I feel about those Castle Earthstone assholes. Haven't quite figured out what my trademark is going to be, but I'll have one soon enough."

Larry considered for a moment. "Yeah, I guess I have. Going to make a career of that?"

"Well, Johnson didn't. He did lots of things afterward, mined and ranched and was a lawman. So maybe not forever. Maybe just till I catch up with Lord Robert and give him my personal payback, after paying back some of his men. But for right now, that's the project that I'll be undertaking. So I'm out of the army, out of the scouts, and off to take care of that."

He very solemnly shook hands with each of them, slung up his gear, and walked off to the chief of scouting to tender his resignation.

Roger Jackson said, "Okay, so who is John Johnson, and I'm betting his trademark wasn't on baby shampoo?"

"Well, he was a mountain man who had a real big vendetta against the Crow, which is why one of his nicknames was 'The Crow Killer.' And as for his trademark, they called him 'Liver-Eating Johnson.'" Mensche looked around at the many carts hauling bodies and the soldiers with clipboards compiling lists, and said, "Mind you, looking at this town, if I were from here like Freddie is, I'd be seeing his point of view very clearly."

2 WEEKS LATER. PULLMAN, WASHINGTON. 6:15 PM PACIFIC TIME. SATURDAY, MAY 30, 2026.

No one recognized Neville Jawarah on the walk from the railroad station; maybe they hadn't seen much of this uniform before they all went east, maybe they didn't want to see anyone in this uniform because so many had not come back, maybe it didn't occur to them that Neville might be inside this uniform. Didn't matter, he didn't want to talk in the street. There was one place he wanted to be.

When he came through the door, his mother virtually pinned him to the wall with her hug, hanging onto him and crying. "I don't even know how to ask how it was," she said, rubbing her face with her apron. "We heard such horrible, horrible things."

"They were mostly true," Neville said.

"Did you see any bad things?"

"More than I'm going to tell you about."

"And . . . did you do anything . . . ah—"

"I survived and I did everything they asked. That was a lot."

"And . . . Jimmy?"

"He didn't make it, Maj'. Something big and sharp got him in the face, I wasn't there when it happened, but I saw him laid out afterward, there were long rows of bodies, I never . . . aw, shit."

Neville hung on to his mother and cried until she pried him off and gave him a bowl of soup and some warm bread. That night, he looked up at the old dog-eared *Lord of the Rings* on his bookshelf, thought *Well, I'm home*, and felt the tears begin to flow just before he fell asleep.

5 WEEKS LATER. CHRISTIANSTED. 10:15 AM ATLANTIC TIME, SATURDAY, JULY 4, 2026.

When James Hendrix, Leslie Antonowicz, and her dog Wonder stepped down from the pontoon of Bret Duquesne's seaplane and into the row-taxi, it was a little awkward for James, natural as breathing for Leslie, and time for a joyful jump and bark for Wonder. Wonder wedged himself between them, so they held hands around him as they approached the beautiful little town under its deep blue sky.

"Pretty place," James said. "Going to have to brush up on those fresh-seafood skills."

"Looks like there's space to get some exercise," Leslie added, practically.

On the pier, he met the local dignitaries, each of whom had to tell him how much they had always appreciated the Jamesgrams, and shook his way through a forest of hands before meeting the two people he most wanted to talk to.

The first of these was Tarantina Highbotham, who seemed more sol-idly muscled than he had imagined, but even more alert and quick. She gave him a lightning-fast rundown of the arrangements she had made; he would have a week to settle into his new quarters and go over the paperwork before the summer term started at the new academy. There was already an abundance of students sixteen and younger; he would be adding and developing courses for older students, up at least through a bachelor's degree. They'd have an extension service that would publish newer and better pamphlets than Pueblo had had available, and eventually occupational journals as well.

He'd never met Highbotham in person before, but they seemed to get along very well, and by the end of the conversation, she was cheerfully explaining, "You get knowledge into them, I'll keep the pirates away from them, and we'll have ourselves a civilized Caribbean again before you know it. The rest of the world can go through a Dark Age if it wants to; we're doing a Dim Decade, max. Now, this handsome young man is Whorf Rollings—don't look so surprised, Whorf, you are handsome, and it's the privilege of a lady old enough to be your grandma to discuss it in front of you. Whorf was the person who wrote to you, and brought it to my attention that there was good reason to bring you here and employ you. Then after you freshen up a little in your quarters, he'll be taking you, and you too, Ms. Antonowicz, to hear two gentlemen with a remarkable story."

Their rooms, on a second floor of the old country club, were pleasant and spacious, and someone had set out fresh fruit on the table. "Headmastering is definitely looking better than librarianing did," James said, between bites of orange.

"I'll miss skiing but I have a feeling the swimming and sailing will make up for it." They each took turns washing in the basin, and then, since Whorf hadn't knocked yet, they sat down in the wicker chairs facing the big French doors onto the balcony, and looked at the view over the town toward the sea.

"Well, we could definitely have done worse for a place to live," James said.

When they opened to a discreet tap at the door, Whorf was waiting for them with a slim young red-blond man about his own age, and an older, burly black man with thick dreads. "This is my buddy, Ihor Reshetnyk. He was along on *Discovery* too, and saved my ass several times. He's coming along because I trust his judgment. And this is my father, Jamayu Rollings, who is skipper of the good ship *Ferengi* where Ihor is second mate. Dad is coming along because if he didn't get to he'd curl up and die."

They walked the half mile or so down into town to the little house; the three men pointed out many more things than James and Leslie could possibly remember, ranging from the bar with the cheapest beer to the spot where a pirate treasure had been uncovered two hundred years before. Everyone seemed a little nervous.

The two men living in the small brick house were an Iranian robotics engineer, Rezakhani, and a Chinese software engineer, Tang. When everyone was seated and had been served tea, Rezakhani said, "Now, I don't know how much Mister Whorf Rollings shared with you in his letter."

"The main thing he did was to explain that the two of you had worked on the Iranian-Chinese industrial expedition to the moon—that test-bed project to see if you could manufacture anything worthwhile there—and that you had some insight into the moon gun. Other than that, everything you say will probably surprise us."

"Oh, it will do that," Tang said.

Rezakhani said, "Let me launch directly into the parts that were never released to news media; you can ask about anything that's unfamiliar as we go, but I'll assume you know anything that was widely covered.

"All right, then. So as you probably know, what we sent to the moon was actually not a fleet of construction robots so much as they were a demonstration set of mobile rock-sorters with some little drills and saws for cutting bigger samples. Well, shortly after they landed and we activated them, all the little mining units stopped acknowledging control signals from Earth and crawled away—eighty kilometers to the Northwest, right to where the moon gun is, at least if Captain Highbotham and her excellent observatory team are right. But the mining robots could not have built it, any more than a flatworm can play the guitar.

"Well, our bosses were hardly going to come out and admit that anything of this sort had happened. Instead they covered it up and kept monitoring the site from the lunar orbiters. In mid-2023—about eighteen months before Daybreak—the mining robots were seen by a Chinese lunar orbiter to be fleeing the area where they had been working, putting themselves on the far slopes of a number of ridges from an immense flare that appeared on August 1, 2023, with a full moon at midnight right over the Pacific—the time when there would be the fewest observers, with the least ability to see what was happening. The US Naval Observatory reported a possible meteor impact; at that time, only the Chinese orbiter was working, and the government of China was not sharing any information. But Mister Tang eventually became privy to what they had seen: on the next orbit, a large object, something the size of a good-sized warehouse—which I am quite sure was your moon gun, it was the right size, shape, and everything—was standing where the flare had appeared.

"Over the next few days, it disgorged rovers ranging in size from about a shoebox to a small car, and the mining robots came back over the ridges and began to work with the newly arrived rovers."

Tang took up the story. "We watched it for more than a year afterward. Before the ground link failed irretrievably due to the EMP from the superbomb at Shanghai, the aliens had constructed a strange sort of glass pyramid almost 30 meters tall. We did not know but we were watching them build the re-entry vehicle for their first shot, the one that silenced KP-1 and destroyed so much technology."

"But who are 'they'?" James asked.

Rezakhani nodded eagerly. "Well, as you might guess, we were curious about that. No one on Earth had that kind of technology—they had to be from another star system. If you take the generally accepted date that the British radar experiments in 1936 were the first radio to reach outside Earth with a signal that was at least possibly detectible, and if whoever it was took a while to locate us and get ready, and they were advanced enough to build such machines, it did not seem incredible that they might have dispatched ships as long as fifty years ago. And remember, back before, the Priestley satellite had found a dozen planets in habitable zones with free oxygen in their atmospheres."

"More than that, I thought," Leslie said. "I was a nerdy pop-science fan, I thought it was like a hundred?"

Tang nodded. "It was. But the Priestly actually reached out to 180 light years. And with planet types, it depends on the cube of the distance; if you double the distance, you get eight times as many planets of a given type.

Anyway, out to fifty light years, there were twelve candidate planets to be the home world of the device we now know as the moon gun. At the time, we thought it was some sort of an extraterrestrial exploration mission, though we were very puzzled by how it had taken over our mining robots, and we were going to mount a secret expedition to investigate the Fecunditatis site in 2025. And then Daybreak hit."

James asked, "How could they send a mission that must have taken decades to get here, and know we would build supply robots for them, apparently exactly what they needed?"

Tang nodded. "That was where I came in; my specialty is automated reverse-engineering, which is why, if you could still look through the files where Lake Washington is now, you'd find me on several lists of people not to be let into the United States, ever, and high priority for recruiting for defection. Also why they bombarded me with English lessons from an early age.

"Here's what I realized—not that everyone agreed with me, but as the sole survivor, I get to be right, eh? As long as you thought of them hijacking our system, it made no sense. The robots were not even designed till 2016; if they somehow dispatched a mission at light speed the instant they could possibly have heard of the robots, they'd still have to be almost on top of us—closer than Alpha Centauri, which is not one of the systems with a habitable world. So the mining robots weren't compatible because they hijacked them; they were compatible because they designed them."

"But *you* designed them—"

"Three engineers did. And when we investigated those engineers, we discovered something else that made little sense to us . . . we discovered Daybreak. We were tracking it too, like your Heather O'Grainne and her OFTA, back before. We only got so far with it, for the same reasons you didn't get very far—Daybreak day arrived too soon, and we lost our capabilities before we had all the pieces of the puzzle. But in the five months we were looking into it, we established that it went far, far back—all the way to before 2000."

"Arnie Yang always thought it was at least that old," James said.

"He was right. What a loss that we don't have him here, but, well, life is long, perhaps someday we will be able to pick his brains about this. Anyway, when we arrested the three main design engineers, two suicided right away. The third claimed that Daybreak had simply begun sending them these marvelous designs, magnificent leaps in coding, all sorts of useful advances, always calling itself the 'anonymous friend' or the 'friend of good computing' and asking them, if they liked the software, to pass it off as their own. Once we knew what to look for, we found a dozen other researchers who had all had experimental proposals that seemed to sail right through the review process, and whose work looked like once-in-a-lucky-century breakthroughs. You see? It was the way that it not only won us over but made us dependent on it. Our rapid progress of the last few decades, every time Daybreak could plant an algorithm or a pattern, made us easier and easier to read, made our networks easier for them to penetrate, gave Daybreak more hooks to attach to—"

"Daybreak grew in our Internet," Leslie said, "but the seed it grew from was . . . extraterrestrial? It was planted here?"

"It was friendly soil," James said. "I keep going back to what Arnie Yang said about it, that he thought Daybreak had grown from human self-hatred, from the way that so many people were unhappy, back before, with things about ordinary modern life, whether it was the way the Third World got screwed, or how ugly all the parking lots were, or how bad they felt for the animals being crowded out, or the way that media got in everywhere and undercut their religion. But he always wondered how it managed to cross over from the people who hated tech to the people who lived to make tech. Now, I guess we know."

Tang nodded. "I think we know a lot more. I'm guessing this is the root of the Fermi Paradox."

Jamayu Rollings coughed and said, "Some of us may not be nerdy enough to know what that is."

"Sorry to admit I'm one of them," James said.

"You had company," Ihor added. "Mister Rezakhani had to explain it to me."

Leslie said, "The Fermi Paradox was in one of the more recent NASA documentaries we had for the schools, back before. The physicist Fermi pointed out that there were probably a lot of habitable worlds—and it turns out he underestimated by a lot—and no reason to suppose intelligent life wouldn't grow on all of them given enough time, there were billions of years of time available, times billions of livable planets, and technological progress is so rapid once it starts that on the geological time scale, basically all intelligent species should be leaping from the caves to the stars. So why hadn't dozens or hundreds or thousands of intelligent species in our own galaxy made the leap and come to visit us? As he put it, where was everybody?

"Well, that only became more mysterious in 2021 when the Priestly Space Telescope started finding all those planets with free oxygen in the atmosphere and in the habitable zone; just from what you could find close by, they were estimating that the galaxy contained maybe seven billion planets with life, and even if intelligence and technology were both incredibly rare, there still should have been thousands of species that could have visited us by now. So we were back to Fermi's question, where was everyone? And I'm starting to see what Mister Tang is getting at."

He nodded. "Suppose Daybreak is not an Earth problem, but a galactic one. Perhaps it started on one world, somewhere, once, but by now, it may have existed for billions of years.

"Suppose there is Daybreak throughout the galaxy, with listening posts everywhere, and probably industrial plants attached to asteroids or perhaps small airless moons, places where civilizations would not notice if they looked. And they wouldn't be looking for very long, because Daybreak would find them and collapse their civilization while they were still just struggling off the planet. Maybe Daybreak was once a weapon, or it might have been created by a civilization that was much more environmentally conscious than ours, or maybe all life in the galaxy really is one and Daybreak evolved, somehow, as the way that life protects itself against the disaster of intelligent technological species. So when Daybreak notices a civilization that has risen as far as radio . . . it knows there will soon be networked computers. . . ."

"And it gets into covert contact, finds its way in like a hacker breaking into a secure system, and shuts it down," Whorf said, quietly.

Ihor cleared his throat. "Chinese and Americans are clever, and can even be devious, but they have mostly been happy nations with big successes. Now, nations like Ukraine and Iran, because we have lived by our wits, and done what we had to, or we would not be here, we understand more about treachery.

"Doctor Rezakhani and I were jamming about this too. Maybe Daybreak is just like Galactic Greenpeace and shuts down high-tech civilizations. But what if it is a softening-up weapon and in another hundred years the alien invasion ships will show up to hand out blankets and beads and herd us onto reservations, while they turn this planet into a resort. Or maybe they plan to harvest all the protein on the surface, and they didn't want us crapping all that protein up with chemicals. Whatever it is, we know three things about Daybreak: one, it's bigger than we thought, maybe bigger than we can imagine. Two, it's not our friend. *And three,* we've already lost almost everything we had to fight it with."

James nodded. "And all this is assuming it has anything we would understand as a purpose at all. Maybe it has something instead of purpose; you know, a colony of ants doesn't do things for reasons and an oak tree doesn't grow from ambition."

"But whatever it was," Jamayu Rollings said, "it has just kicked our butt, and it is fairly likely that sometime not far in the future it will come back to do it again. So we should either get ready to be kicked some more, or get ready to kick back."

"And *voila,*" Rezakhani, "we present these ideas to the headmaster of a school, and the former leader of a spy organization—"

"And the complete dupe who was fooled by Daybreak itself, and lost the war with it in his home country," James said. "And though I suppose I am more experienced, I don't feel one bit smarter."

"Well," Leslie said, "We are who we have to work with."

. . .

Afterward, as they took their first-ever walk on a beach, agreeing that they would try to do this daily if they could, James said, "I suppose the program is obvious. Start steering the governments of the world toward re-unions and mergers, and give them as much truth as they can handle. Rebuild tech to get around the nanospawn and biote barriers. Produce a bunch of smart young people who will have the brains, training, and energy to do that; maybe we can get Patrick and Ntale down here, it'd be a better place for them than Pueblo. Keep going till whatever zapped us with Daybreak shows up, if it ever does, and then do whatever we can to take our own destiny back."

Leslie took his hand and leaned against him. When they had walked a little way in a closer embrace than he'd ever felt from her before, he said, "Are we ready to, um, take things to the next level?"

"You already have," she said. "And I love that we have something to defend."

ACKNOWLEDGMENTS AND A POSSIBLY NEEDED ALIBI FOR THE COPY EDITOR

First of all, I want to begin by saying that Luann Reed-Siegel has done an absolutely brilliant job in copyediting a very difficult manuscript.

The difficulty of the manuscript is only partly a matter of its sloppy author; a problem throughout this series so far has been how to mix the more conventional Chicago style with the peculiar style variously called Federal, Federal Security, and Defense/Security that is used within the American federal government. Because public servants in the United States are required to be extremely mindful of the requirements of the Constitution (which I hope most of you will see has a great deal to do with the story and how things unfold), it has long been customary in Federal documents to capitalize nouns when they refer to Federal and Constitutional functions (as I just did there) and not when they refer to other matters, in effect supplying tiny warnings to public officials when they are in areas where they may have important legal responsibilities.

Thus the President is the Commander in Chief of the Armed Forces and the Vice President presides over the Senate, but the president and vice president sometimes order a pizza in and spend the evening watching the Three Stooges (who, curiously, have no Federal function).

Similarly, the United States has an army and a navy but the Constitution governs the relationship between the rest of the government and the

Army and Navy. This can result in apparently inconsistent, yet correct, capitalization on the same page or within a single sentence, and I just wanted it clearly stated that Luann Reed-Siegel has in fact done an excellent job with it, and that since I reviewed and approved it, any errors remaining are entirely my fault.